AWAKENING

The Commune's Curse: Book 1

LUCY A. McLAREN

sfwp.com

Library of Congress Cataloging-in-Publication Data

Names: McLaren, Lucy A., author.
Title: Awakening / Lucy A. McLaren.
Description: Santa Fe, NM : SFWP, [2022] | Series: The Commune's curse ;
    book 1 | Audience: Ages 15+. | Audience: Grades 10-12. | Summary: In a
    kingdom controlled by the authoritarian Commune, eighteen-year-old
    Evelyn Folksman, herself in hiding and haunted by a traumatic past,
    reluctantly helps siblings Raif and Rose Huntsman evade the Commune's
    agents and seek shelter with rebels.
Identifiers: LCCN 2021043665 (print) | LCCN 2021043666 (ebook) |
    ISBN 9781951631178 (trade paperback) | ISBN 9781951631185 (ebook)
Subjects: CYAC: Ability—Fiction. | Brothers and sisters—Fiction. |
    Fantasy. | LCGFT: Novels. | Fantasy fiction.
Classification: LCC PZ7.1.M457 Ch 2022 (print) | LCC PZ7.1.M457 (ebook) |
    DDC [Fic]—dc23
LC record available at https://lccn.loc.gov/2021043665
LC ebook record available at https://lccn.loc.gov/2021043666

Published by SFWP
369 Montezuma Ave. #350
Santa Fe, NM 87501
www.sfwp.com

The Kingdom of Septima

The Isles of Soree

Scree Tundra

Thallies' Sisters

Thallies Island

Alpinside Mountains

Thallion Strait

Cold Stream

Laetius Range

Alpin

Hession

Laetius Forest

Hession Heights Range

Laetius

Laetius Lagoon

Mountain Tribes

Alpin Bay

Mountain Tribes

The Abandoned Isles

Hession's End

Scale Desert

Barren Mountains

Scale Range

Veritas

Ancient City of Scale (Ruins)

Thistleton

Crystal Mountains

Boat

Oak Inn (Ruins)

Lake of Scale

Tunnel

Haven Forest

Old Oak Woods

Haven's Cove

Tavern

Castleton

Nook Pass

Little Haven

Monarch's Ocean

Lake of Kings

Monarch's Garden

Nook Town

Nook Flow

Haven's End

Taskan Forest

Torrant Estate

Taskan

Magister's Mile

Amble Hills

The Commune's Compound

Crag's Edge Lake

Wolf Cove

Ambleside

Cragside

The Crags

Taskan Bay

The Great Ocean
↓

Noman Islands
↓

For Ross—

from the bottom of my heart, thank you.

Contents

Prologue

Samalah

Within the white walls of the temple of the Goddess Veritarra, on the shores of the Noman Islands, the holy woman knelt and prayed. She was alone, the sun had long since set, and the scent of flowers sweetened the air. Beside her, a small bowl of firestones flickered with a warm orange glow.

She might have stayed there until morning, adrift in the depths of her own mind, had she not been distracted by the sound of footsteps at her back.

"*Samalah*. Here you are." A woman leant down, placing a gentle hand on the holy woman's elbow and easing her upwards.

"Tiah," *Samalah* whispered, straightening the lengths of her white robe. "You did not need to come for me."

"I think I did," Tiah said, giving a mock frown. She led *Samalah* to a white stone bench and encouraged her to sit. "You pray too long. Veritarra will understand you need sleep."

Samalah smiled. "And what of your sleep, su'laha? You have a young boy to raise."

"It is that young boy who woke me," Tiah said, laughing gently. "Jonasaiah has his father's fire." Her face grew serious as she glanced towards the ceiling. "I am only grateful that, by Veritarra's blessing, he did not inherit more of his father's ... traits."

The holy woman turned her face away. "Mm."

"What is wrong, *Samalah*? Have you learned something of the Curse? Of my son?"

Samalah met Tiah's dark eyes. Seeing concern there, she waved a hand. "Oh, it is not your son I worry for. He is protected, thanks to our beloved Goddess. It is just …"

Tiah took the seat beside her and clasped the holy woman's hands. *Samalah* smiled to feel their warmth and softness against her own cracked and tired skin. "What have you seen?"

Samalah sighed. Tiah was perceptive; she would make a wonderful *Samalah* herself, when the time came. "It is the Curse," she confirmed. As she spoke, her eyes drifted to the tapestry on the wall ahead of them. It depicted the rising of the God Ezzarah and Goddess Veritarra—the battles that ensued, the destruction caused by a greedy, callous God. "It will soon cause us all great sorrow."

Tiah gasped. "Great sorrow?" She followed *Samalah's* gaze, jaw clenched. She shook her head sharply as though fervour alone would take back the holy woman's words. "But Ezzarah has remained silent all these years. For generations, those born with His curse have been abandoned, left to exist without His rule." She shifted on the bench. "Fighting among themselves with the powers He afflicted upon them, too distracted by petty squabbles to pose a threat to those of us who follow the guidance of our beloved Veritarra."

Samalah patted Tiah's arm. "I am afraid we have become complacent. We believed that Veritarra's protection would be enough." She placed a hand over her heart. "We wanted to believe that Ezzarah could no longer hold power over us if we welcomed those cursed by Him into Veritarra's arms. Taught them restraint. But that does not make it so. The peace has been tenuous for some time, has it not? We have taken great risks to ensure our children's futures against the Curse. The Goddess could not promise that Her Gift would be absorbed by all …" She didn't speak aloud of the children lost in the womb because of their mother's consumption of Veritarra's Gift. It was a risk, many believed, that had to be taken to keep their community safe, and *Samalah* prayed daily for those who'd been taken into the Goddess's arms too soon.

Tiah leant forward, eyes full of pain as though she knew *Samalah's* thoughts exactly. "Could those in Septima not aid us? The Commune, isn't it? They were granted our aid some eighty years ago, during their own fight against those born with the Curse. Our people were even granted homes there after—"

"No." *Samalah* spoke the word more harshly than intended. She let out a long, slow exhale. "Veritarra has shared with me a sense of growing unrest in Septima. I feel it in my heart. I fear our people will be forced away from the kingdom before long, despite the agreement made after their war all those years ago."

"How can that be so, when *our* help was what allowed the powers to be contained and brought under control? Without us they would have …" Tiah scowled. "They do not fear the powers as they should."

"Some there choose to view the powers as a gift. As long as those holding them are trained and kept under the Commune's control, they believe all will be well." *Samalah* lifted her face, feeling a gentle breeze drift by. "This third Grand Magister cannot be trusted, su'laha. Those before him were simple men, seeking to rebuild a kingdom ravaged by war. But this one … He *craves* the powers above all else. I hear rumours from those based in Septima of increasingly drastic measures to hunt down those who possess them."

"Then he is a servant of Ezzarah, unwitting or otherwise," Tiah muttered. "And he cannot help us."

Samalah nodded. "We are alone in this. Whatever lies ahead, we must find our own way. We must protect our people against whatever Ezzarah inflicts upon us."

Tiah's eyes shone with sadness. "My husband has long been haunted by the link he bears to Ezzarah. By the powers within. He has told me before of the … temptations they present. We saw no other option when I was with child. The risk of consuming Veritarra's Gift weighed far less heavy than the thought of our babe being born with those accursed abilities. Of being so conflicted within, like his father before him."

"Su'laha, all of those touched by Ezzarah in such a way have fought hard to keep their powers inside, to forget the terrible purpose Ezzarah had intended for them, and to follow the ways of our beloved Veritarra. For those of us untouched by Ezzarah's Curse, we cannot know how it truly tests them to fight against themselves."

"I fear we may be about to find out. Your words have awoken something I have long tried to push away, but in my heart I know the tension has been building for too long." Tiah's dark eyes reflected the light of the firestones dancing like flames. "This news will cause a stir." She peered up at the tapestry. "What did Veritarra show you, *Samalah*? When will this sorrow—this test—be upon us?"

"Ah, if only I had the answer to that. Veritarra, too, can be unclear in what She shows me. For that is the way of those who watch over us, is it not?" *Samalah* stood, smiling sadly. "The seed is planted; a fate long decided will come to pass. There is no avoiding it. The flower shall grow, su'laha, but when and how I cannot say." She held out her hand. "Now, I am tired. When morning comes, we will speak of this with our people. We must decide what this means for us. How we can prepare. Together, we can see it through."

Tiah kissed her thumb, pressed it to her forehead, and raised it to the ceiling. "I hope so, *Samalah*," she said.

Together they made their way from the temple of their beloved Goddess Veritarra and into the black shroud of the night.

Prologue

Eirik

The boy was afraid.

He wasn't sure how long he'd been kept in this dark place. The days had passed by in a blur of endless errands—cleaning, cooking, serving faceless robed men and women who occupied the compound that housed his prison. The guards encouraged whispers of horrific punishments for any who tried escaping, and he'd long since given up hope. Each night, as he watched the stars rise through the solitary narrow window high on the grey stone walls of his cell, the guards would come and bolt the doors, one by one.

When he closed his eyes, he dreamt of home. There had been decadence, feasts, servants. His parents, often absent on affairs of state, kept their distance even when home, believing too much attachment to be unhealthy for their children. But he remembered loving his brother, Ythan, dearly; his heart ached at memories of their time playing with swords in the garden or going on mock wolf hunts in Taskan Forest. For his last birthday—his ninth—his brother had gifted him his very own bow. *"Now you can join the hunts for real, little brother."* The boy turned his mind away from the thought, the pain almost too much to bear. The bow had been left behind, along with all but the clothes on his back, the day he'd been taken from his home.

He sighed and retrieved a shard of glass from beneath his threadbare cushion, wiping away stray pieces of hay and moving to scrape his initials on the wall of his cell.

E.T.

He pressed harder with the shard of glass, scraping and scraping, even as it bit into his hand. He pushed through the pain, entering a trance-like state, going over and over those two letters as the blood ran down his fingers and dripped to the floor.

He'd learned quickly not to make friends with any of the other children in this place. Eventually, they would be taken away. He told himself he'd be safe if he behaved, kept his head down, did as he was commanded, obediently returned to his cell when his work was done. Deep down he knew it wouldn't matter. His time would come like all the others.

Then, one day they came for him.

He was hauled from his bed before sunrise.

"Where are you taking me?" he croaked, but there was no response from the hooded guards who dragged him forward even as he tried to dig his heels in. "Please." He bit his lip to hold back the tears that would betray him. The guards were silent.

The mansion, previously forbidden to him, loomed in the centre of the courtyard; its walls black as the night, its windows like dark, emotionless eyes. As he was shoved inside, a cold dread clamped across his chest. The hallway was lavishly decorated, much as his home had been, but that gave him no comfort. Though he'd lost count of the passing months since his imprisonment, the sudden recollection of his father's study, similarly panelled with dark wood, was enough to send his heart racing. He gulped in air with panicked breaths, finding it thick and difficult to inhale—a stark contrast to the cool night breeze. There was a sickly-sweet incense that seemed to be covering a deeper, more malicious smell. He imagined, suddenly and against his will, something hidden, slowly dying, and rotting away; the rich perfumes smothering the truth.

Portraits of stern-faced men in red robes hung throughout the hallway. The boy's eyes never left them. His jaw began to tremor. Each portrait was steely-gazed, each man sure of his power and control, his ability to command, to be obeyed. Beneath each, shining plaques read: 'His Benevolence, Grand Magister of the Commune'.

Grand Magister. Something in his memory stirred, a niggling sense that he should know something more about that title, about why he was here.

They reached a door, the boy walking now with a numb resignation to whatever awaited him. The door creaked open, he was forced inside.

"Kneel before the Grand Magister," one of the guards said. The boy's legs shook as he lowered himself to the wooden floor. *Grand Magister. This is it.*

With his head bowed, he scrunched his eyes shut. He was in his father's study, head down as his father paced in front of him, hands clasped behind his back. *"The Grand Magister's work is necessary for the kingdom, to ensure there are no future wars or uprisings. I'd never thought to see one of my own children so ... afflicted."* He'd given his son a look of pure, unadulterated disdain. *"A disappointment to the last moment, boy."* He shook his head. *"This is the way it must be."* His father turned away, dismissing him with a wave of the hand. The boy had not seen him again.

And now, here I am.

He opened his eyes, finally daring to look up.

The Grand Magister sat between four hooded individuals, his red robes striking compared to the uniform blacks and greys of those around him. His chair was carved wood, polished to a dark sheen and raised on a dais so that he appeared unnaturally tall. Like the men in the paintings, his eyes were hard and unfeeling, his mouth downturned, his very presence emanating authority. The boy met the man's stare, a shiver running down his spine. He tugged at the ragged sleeves of his stained white shirt—the last of his once fine clothing—and pulled at the scrap of cloth tied loosely round his hand as a makeshift bandage.

The door opened behind him and he turned to see a scruffy, brown dog being led into the room. The animal's claws scrabbled across the floor, fighting against the rope around its neck. The boy wanted to go to it, to clutch it tightly to his chest and shield it from harm, but he remained rooted to the spot, watching and waiting.

"Show us the extent of your powers," the Grand Magister said. His voice sent a jolt through the boy, the words unexpected yet all too enticing. His powers, the abilities he'd known of since he was very young, that he'd kept hidden inside for as long as he could remember. *Could this be a trick?*

His breath quickened as he recalled the only time he'd dared to use them. The kitchen cat; he'd been delighted to see the unsuspecting feline obey his every command. The beating from his father had been severe.

"A curse, the Nomarrans call it. And here we are, my own son. You are not worthy of the name you were born into. This is why the Commune must take …" His father's nostrils flared, eyes burning with disgust. *"You will not use those abominable powers in my household again."*

But he wasn't in his family home anymore. Not long after the speech in his father's study and the abrupt dismissal, the early morning carriage had come and silent, black-robed men dragged him from his home. *He spurned me even before he knew of my powers. I was never good enough.* The boy's lip curled into a sneer. *Father never cared.* He stood with his back straightened, pushing his chin forward as he met the Grand Magister's eyes. This could be his chance to prove himself. To prove his strengths, not failures.

Or it could be a trap.

He chewed his lip, torn inside. He felt an immense weight pressing down on his shoulders, a sudden realisation that what he decided in this moment would somehow determine the rest of his life. *What will become of me if I do this? If I refuse … ?* He peered at the guards, begging for aid, an answer, a hint, *anything*, but their faces were, as always, impassive beneath their black hoods. *It doesn't matter. This is my chance. I can become what Father never thought I could.*

He faced forward once more and found the Grand Magister's iron gaze unwavering, lips pursed into a hard line. This time, however, there was an air of interest. *I can be worth something to someone at last.* Convinced by the thought, the boy gave a brief nod and approached the dog. *I just need to show him.*

The animal cowered, tail tucked between its legs and body hunched. It was filthy, half-starved, and pitiful. He fiddled with his shirt sleeves, wishing he could cover the cuts and bruises mottling his pale skin, hoping he didn't appear to the Grand Magister as pathetic as this creature did to him. The boy reached for the dog, hand hovering above it. The fear radiating from its ragged form was palpable. *It knows.* He drew his hand back, trying to steady himself. The dog sensed his hesitation; taking advantage of the boy's uncertainty, it growled and snapped at him, teeth bared. The boy jerked back, thudding onto the floor. *You idiot.* His cheeks flushed and he glanced up at the Grand Magister, finding neither sympathy nor reassurance—only that constant, unflinching stare.

In the silence, one of the figures sitting beside the Grand Magister stood and approached him. The rest of the room still, their footsteps echoed. They leant down and offered a hand. The boy thought he saw a woman's face beneath the dark hood, a gentle smile and sad eyes. He thought of his brother then—a time when he'd fallen amongst the jutting roots of Taskan Forest, when Ythan picked him up and dusted him off. *"I'm here, little brother."*

You're not here now.

He shook his head, waving away the offer of help. When the woman retreated, he stood and brushed himself off, running the back of his hand across his nose.

"Proceed. Now." The Grand Magister's tone was sharp, displeasure evident.

The boy closed his eyes and took a deep breath. He thought back to his cell a final time, wishing he could run back and hide. The metal bars were rusted, the floors cold, the bed damp and unwelcoming, yet it was the only place that was his. He thought of the dark stone of the wall, scraped and scraped to reveal the lighter grey beneath: *E. T.*

I can do this. The boy lifted his head, clenched his fists, and stalked towards the quivering dog, careful to avoid a puddle of urine which reflected the flickering candelabra light above their heads. He moved slowly, footsteps light and breathing even. *It mustn't know my true thoughts.* He thought of the kindness of the hooded woman; he sought to emulate it, focusing on reassuring the dog. *I won't hurt you. You are safe.*

As he got closer, the animal's violent shaking stopped. It blinked up at him, sadness flooding from its deep brown eyes—a plea for mercy. He placed a cautious hand on its neck and a fleeting smile flickered across his lips despite himself. "There," he whispered. "There, girl." He *pushed* outwards with his mind. Seconds later, it was there—the connection building between them.

For a moment, panic pulled him back; the image of his father's rage-filled face at the forefront of his mind. He lifted his hand and studied it as though expecting some tangible evidence of the "curse" his father had spoken of. No; only pink flesh, calloused, bruised and broken. The dog whimpered, licking his fingers with her rough tongue.

He curled his fingers inwards, felt the trembling strength of his own anger. *I am more capable than you believed I was, Father. I am no foolish child.* Pushing aside the memories, he clasped the dog again. Their connection was immediate this time. His mind linked with hers and he felt a rush of immense excitement and intrigue. *A companion, all my own. Look at me now, Father.*

He was swept up in the moment before he could stop himself. His heart thrummed; his powers couldn't be as evil as his father predicted. This dog could be his, body and mind. He could control her every movement and action if he wished. In turn, she would be by his side. He could confide in her, converse as people do—she would know his every thought. He would never be alone again.

She could abandon me too, just like everyone else. The moment the thought entered his mind, the dog yelped and slumped to the floor. The boy frowned and loosened his grasp. He knelt to examine her, saw the shallowness of her strained breaths, felt her mind retreat from his.

She's dying. He held up his palm. *Did I do this?* It had been outside his conscious mind. There was no sadness around the realisation; simply an understanding that it was true.

She got too close, had been overwhelmed. Though he knew he'd allowed her to, he couldn't stop the flood of hatred that poured forth then. *How dare she?* He pressed his hand down on her back, allowing his powers to take hold once more. "You can't leave me," he whispered harshly, shaking her delicate body. At the edges of his awareness, he knew his face was contorted with an unspoken fury— cracked lips pulled tight across his teeth, eyes burning into the collapsed dog, caring nothing for her growing weakness. He imagined he looked like his father.

See how worthy I am now. See my power.

"Stop." The Grand Magister's voice shattered his concentration. He blinked as he focused once more on the room around him, powers instantly receding.

Yet he couldn't forget the feeling of control that had flowed through him. To have the life of another within his grasp. It was intoxicating. He spared a final look at the dog. She twitched as the last tendrils of her life drifted away and then was still.

Worthless mutt.

Turning towards the Grand Magister, he sensed a ripple of approval at his display.

And so he began to understand.

To understand why he was here. Why his family had betrayed him, leaving him to be treated as nothing more than a peasant despite the noble blood that flowed through his veins.

The Grand Magister nodded, bringing his hands together in a single silent clap, and the boy knew: this was only the beginning of his training.

24 Years Later

1

Evelyn

Sweep. Scrub. Stir the stew.

Evelyn leant the broom against the kitchen wall and wiped a loose strand of hair from her forehead. The sounds of the tavern's common room were muffled through the closed door but she knew well the scene playing out— patrons were enjoying a dish of fresh stew or steaming apple pie, washed down by some honeyed ale or spiced wine. The tavern keeper's wife, affectionately known as Fat Bessie, would be laughing and joking, refilling tankards with a deft hand and a twinkle in her eye.

Focused as she was on her tasks, Evelyn barely registered the snatches of conversation filtering through the open serving hatch.

" ... Grand Magister is increasing his reach. He has to, I've heard, else—"

Sweep.

" ... damned foolish to be caught, in my opinion. They've only got themselves to blame."

Scrub.

"By His Benevolence, the harvest will yield a plentiful—"

Stir the stew.

"Children with powers must be brought under control. They are a threat to us all, our forefathers witnessed that first-hand. What else are we to do?"

Evelyn froze mid-stir, the words tugging at a distant memory in the recesses of her mind, one she hardly dared acknowledge.

Suddenly, the tavern's front door creaked open—audible even over the chatter of voices and the gentle tones of a bard's singing. Evelyn dropped the wooden spoon into the vat of stew, splattering the back of her hand with searing gravy.

"Shit," she muttered, wiping the scalding liquid away on her already stained apron.

It was only then she noticed the silence that had swept across the tavern. The conversations had ceased, the bard no longer strummed his lute, even the fire seemed to crackle less fiercely. The change in the atmosphere was so abrupt that Evelyn found herself drawn towards the kitchen hatch.

"No children and certainly no grubby mutts," Fat Bessie snapped, usual merriment gone. At first Evelyn couldn't see who she was speaking to. She stretched on her tiptoes and strained her neck and—

Her stomach lurched.

Two years ago, Evelyn had left Little Haven, the sheltered village she'd called home for sixteen years. She tried her hardest not to think of the place— afraid to admit what caused her to flee, the secrets she kept. She swallowed back a cry of fear as the memories attempted to force their way back in, moving her attention to the children.

They were brother and sister, she recalled—Raif and Rose. The last time she'd seen them they were playing with the other children, carefree and content; a stark contrast to now. Raif had grown, so much so that Evelyn wondered if she could even consider him a child any longer. He stood much taller than his sister, with the gangly limbs and awkward posture of a boy growing into manhood. Even so, in that bustling tavern common room, they both seemed pitifully small—or perhaps it was simply the way they shrunk away from Fat Bessie's words. Their eyes were large within their gaunt faces, clothes ragged and filthy. At their feet, a black spaniel let out a low growl.

Raif placed himself in front of Rose, jaw clenched and eyes blazing with defiance, yet feverish with desperation. Even with the bow and arrows strapped to his back, his appearance was all too unthreatening—but still the air was heavy with an unspoken tension, as if every adult in the room was afraid of the two starving children. Some averted their eyes, looking at anything else. A brown-skinned old man close to the kitchen door became intrigued by the woodgrain of his table. A couple near the door regarded each other with wide, unblinking eyes, lips pinched tight within pale faces, the woman clutching tightly to the hand of her own young child, not dissimilar in age to Rose. Fat Bessie stood with arms crossed over her ample chest, face creased. Evelyn was hit by a wave of indignation. After all, she had been in the same position herself, afraid and alone, not so long ago—Bessie helped her then; what had changed?

Someone has to do something.

But then another thought, sharp as a knife, *What if they know why I left?*

"Please," Raif croaked. "We have nowhere else to go. My sister, she needs food. Our home, it was … Little Haven was attacked, everyone's gone—"

Attacked.

Evelyn's blood rushed in her ears as she backed away from the hatch, trying to clear her racing mind. *Everyone's gone.* That meant *he* could be—

No, she daren't even allow herself such a thought.

She wrung her hands together. Perhaps she should help these children. They wouldn't know what happened to her in Little Haven. They couldn't have known they would find her here. *It could be my fate.* Her heart hammered a fierce drumbeat at the idea.

What if… She closed her eyes and forced her breathing to slow, feeling the rise and fall of her stomach beneath her hand.

I might be overreacting. Would they even recognise me?

Before Evelyn could calm her cluttered thoughts and make a decision, she heard Fat Bessie bustling the children towards the tavern door. She hurried back to the hatch in time to see Raif and Rose shuffling out without argument, though their dog let out a rebuking bark.

None of the patrons intervened—the atmosphere remaining strained until the door slammed shut on the young travellers.

"By the Powers, you don't think *they* were involved, do you? Can they be so close already?" said the brown-skinned old man, voice low and trembling.

"The Commune … it would seem the Grand Magister's hunts have reached us at last," answered another man. "Do you think those children might have," he peered around, hand half-covering his mouth, *"powers?"*

"It's as I said earlier. There's been gossip for a time now—they've spread their searches. He doesn't just want the babes of nobles anymore," said an old woman matter-of-factly. "P'raps it's true. Little Haven—is that one of the villages in Haven Forest? D'you think …" She trailed off, scratching her chin before giving a decisive nod as though compelled by the evidence before her. "Well, I think we know now. We all need to keep an eye, watch out for each other. The Commune has started seeking out children from—"

"You're all fools," came an accented voice from a hooded man tucked away on a corner table by the fire. "You turn away helpless children on the word of a paranoid old man." He removed his hood, revealing a bald head, wrinkled black skin, dark brown eyes full of judgement.

The old woman he'd interrupted cleared her throat irritably. "What would a Nomarran know of such things?" she said, crossing her arms. "You shouldn't even be—"

"Hush," Fat Bessie said, moving towards the Nomarran man. She glared around at all who had spoken. "Powers above, that's enough. *All* are welcome here, but there're times when caution must take priority. We don't want the Commune's soldiers coming down on us." She laid a hand on the Nomarran's shoulder and gave it a gentle squeeze. The man's anger seemed to melt away as he met Bessie's gaze for a moment, some unspoken message passing between them.

"Now," Bessie clapped her hands, "who's for more pie?"

The change was palpable. The mood lifted as though everyone had simply been awaiting permission to return to normal. Conversations thawed and reawakened, the room warming in an instant.

Evelyn picked up her broom and began sweeping again, mind whirring.

The Commune.

Powers.

Such things were always spoken of with wariness. When Evelyn first arrived at the tavern, Fat Bessie made sure she knew of the threat the Commune posed, obviously surprised at Evelyn's lack of knowledge on the matter. Little Haven was sheltered in more ways than one, she'd quickly learned.

"To those who have powers and use them without the Grand Magister's knowledge, away from the watchful eye of the Commune, the threat is greatest of all. If caught,

they face severe punishment." Though the woman hadn't directly asked her, Evelyn had seen the understanding on Bessie's face from the moment they met.

"*You can stay here, girl. But know that I can't protect you if you should reveal any such powers.*" A fixed stare with those hazel eyes, full of warmth despite the words spoken. "*But this is your home now and I'm sure you can keep them* … " Bessie cleared her throat, patted Evelyn's knee. "*Well, that's enough on the matter now, isn't it? You'll be safe here, girl. I've always wanted a daughter of my own.*"

And little else had been said about it these past two years. Foolishly, Evelyn had allowed herself to believe things could continue that way forever.

Idiot. You thought you could escape the past? Well here it is. It's finally come for you.

"Evelyn." Fat Bessie flitted into the kitchen, layered skirts flapping about her, apron, as always, impossibly white and crisp. She shut the door, peeking through the serving hatch. Her usually ruddy cheeks were pale as milk; that might have been what scared Evelyn most of all—she'd never seen Bessie in such a state.

"Be a good girl and go after those children. Bring them back here, feed and water them. Don't let anyone see you."

"But Bessie, I—"

"Go now, Evelyn, before they get away and into more trouble. Powers above, girl, the one time you defy me." Bessie fixed her with a hard stare and Evelyn knew there was no arguing. She propped the broom against the wall and hurried from the tavern's rear door, palms clammy despite the light drizzle of rain and sting of the cold autumnal air against her face. Her hands clenched closed and open as she tried to convince herself. *They won't remember, it's fine. It's fine, it's fine.* She inhaled the damp scent of moist soil as she darted through the vegetable garden.

Past the chicken coop and round the stables, Evelyn made for the road running along the front of the tavern. The children hadn't gotten far. She moved towards them, all the while glancing about to ensure no one else was in view.

They won't recognise me. They won't recognise me. Please, please, please. It was almost a prayer, though Evelyn cared little for praying and believed in it even less—she trusted only in herself; life was simpler that way.

"Wait," she said, voice quiet. They didn't hear her—maybe that was what she wanted. But then she recalled Bessie's face, so drained of colour, so full of concern. Evelyn bit her lip, rubbing a hand across her forehead—she couldn't let her own selfishness take hold, not now. She scanned back over her shoulder and seeing the road was still empty of travellers, raised her voice and called, "Wait!"

This time the children stopped walking but didn't turn, instead tensing as though ready to flee. When they did face Evelyn, Raif placed himself in front of Rose, eyes narrowed as his hand floated to touch the tip of the bow at his back. Evelyn saw in that movement how afraid he was; though he was taller than most his age and his hair had been cut into the shorter style of the village men, his face still held some of the softness of youth and there was an uncertainty in the way he held himself. He was a boy, yet one desperate to protect his sister, who stood no higher than his waist, peering out at Evelyn with bright blue eyes that glimmered even in the dim light of the autumn afternoon.

She held her hands out to try and ease his fear. "It's okay," she said. "Come with me. We can help." They remained where they stood. Up close, Evelyn saw the state of their clothes. The bottom of Rose's skirt was torn and muddied while Raif's tunic and cloak appeared in a similar state of disrepair. "Please," she said.

Raif's brow creased, grey eyes darkening as he stood strong and faced her; a flicker of the man he would become. "That woman," he said. "She seemed … angry."

Evelyn nodded. "I'm sorry. Bessie—the woman who … Well, she can explain." She took a step closer to them. "It's okay. I promise." In that moment, an icy wind blew past them, lifting Raif's cloak and causing Rose to visibly shiver.

Raif's hand dropped from his bow at last. He glanced down at his sister, mouth pinched with indecision, momentary confidence seemingly gone with the passing breeze. The dog stood at their side observing Evelyn with dark eyes, tail twitching.

"We have food and water. You can warm yourselves by the fire." At those words, the boy's defiance disappeared and he gave a curt nod. Evelyn ensured they remained unseen as she led the two siblings back to the kitchen.

"Sit down. You must be hungry," she said, pointing them towards some wooden chairs. She avoided their eyes, fearful of the recognition that could alight their faces at any moment. The scent of sweet apples and cinnamon filled the kitchen as Evelyn sliced a freshly baked pie, dishing it into some bowls before handing it to the children. She retrieved a cleaning rag and dipped it into a pail of water, seeing in the brightness of the kitchen fire the mud that mottled the children's pale skin. As she handed the cloth to Raif, Bessie appeared.

"Oh, you poor things," she said, leaning down to them. "Don't eat that too fast, you're like to make yourselves sick." She hovered over Rose, taking in the young girl's clothing. "Such a little thing, you must be frozen to the bone. Wait, wait a moment. Let me …" Bessie retreated upstairs, the rest of her words unspoken.

There was a drawn-out silence while the siblings took small bites. They seemed as eager as Evelyn not to make much eye contact and for that, at least, she was grateful.

Perhaps the past can stay the past, she thought, checking on the stew. *It's for the best.* When she was finished stirring, Evelyn filled two cups with water. As she handed Raif his cup, their fingers touched and their eyes locked.

And there it was, a twitch of his eyebrows, a flicker of realisation. He frowned, pushing back the dark blonde hair hanging over his forehead. "Are you—"

No.

At the same moment, Fat Bessie returned with bundles of fresh clothes. "There. Those should keep you warm enough." She held a long skirt up to Rose. "Hmm, might be a bit big. So young to be out alone, you can't've seen more'n four summers, girl."

"She's six," Raif said through a mouthful of pie. "And she's not alone. She's got me."

"That's true, boy, and I meant no offense." Bessie chuckled. "Well, no matter, there's room for growth. It's sure to be warmer'n what you have on now." She set the clothes down at Raif and Rose's feet.

"Thank you," Raif said.

"Nothing fancy, I'm afraid. Plain clothes, well made." Bessie exhaled, brushing her apron clear of non-existent dust. "I'm sorry about what happened.

It's just, well, there are certain expectations to- I mean, I have to make sure I- It would be *dangerous* to—" She shook her head, puffing air through her lips. "I'm sorry, that's all I can say. But enough o' that. It's not your concern. You can stay here tonight; there's plenty to eat and beds to spare. Oh, and I'm Bessie. This is Evelyn. My husband, Dick, he's travelling back from Castleton. Should be with us by tonight, if all's well."

The boy raised an eyebrow at Evelyn, suspicions evidently confirmed. To her relief, he didn't acknowledge it. "I'm Raif," he said. "This is my sister, Rose. And Rose's dog, Dog."

Bessie clasped her hands together and gave a warm smile. "Big age gap between you, eh?"

Raif nodded. "Our parents, they, uh … lost a child between us."

"I see, boy." Bessie gave him a sympathetic pat on the back, turning to Rose. "Is he a good big brother?" She beamed at Rose and the young girl gave a tiny smile before hiding her face beneath a curtain of blonde curls, saying nothing.

Raif shuffled towards his sister, placing his arm around her shoulders—an instinctive and protective gesture that caused a stir of jealousy in Evelyn. "Rose hasn't spoken much since, um, our village was …" He bit his lip as though to stop it from trembling.

"Ah, I'm sorry." Bessie's mouth pinched into a hard line. "Little Haven, was it?"

Raif gave a curt nod, eyes downturned.

"Mm, I know the place. I've never ventured into Haven Forest meself, though Dick has sold his fair share of wares about the area." Bessie knelt down to examine Rose, brushing the hair from the young girl's round face and turning it from side to side. Apparently satisfied there was nothing to be concerned with, she stood and dusted herself off again. "He always spoke fondly of the villages in the forest." She gave a wistful smile. "I'll do what I can to help you. You 'ave my word. Was it—"

"What does a man need to do to get some bloody service in this place?" The irritated voice filtered into the kitchen, interrupting Bessie's question. Fear flashed across the woman's face as she flitted towards the hatch, attempting to conceal the view of the children. But it was too late; the man had already noted Raif and Rose, a curious smirk on his face. Without a word, Bessie moved into the common room, placed a hand on the back of the man's fine red woollen cloak and steered him away.

"Follow me, good man," she said. "I haven't seen your face afore, which means you can't've tried my speciality sweet beer. How about a tankard? On the house, o' course." Evelyn watched as the man was led towards the bar, apparently appeased by the promise of free alcohol.

Raif cleared his throat. "Evelyn. I know you, don't I?"

Shit.

Evelyn stood with her back to him, shoulders hunched.

"You're from Little Haven, aren't you?" he said. His footsteps drew near. "Evelyn Folks—"

"Yes," she snapped. She had no wish to hear the family name assigned to her as a babe. The one reserved for the unwanted, unclaimed.

'Family' name. A cruel jest. She composed herself for a moment before turning to find Raif far closer than expected. She edged back, running her sweat-moistened palms down her apron.

"Yes, I remember," he said. Apparently unperturbed by her abrupt tone, his face creased into a grin. "You used to help Mother with the cows."

"Oh," Evelyn said, feeling a twinge of embarrassment as she recalled a blonde-haired woman with kind eyes and an easy laugh. "I'd forgotten all about that."

But the mention of his mother had cast a shadow upon Raif's face once more and he bowed his head, returning to sit next to his sister without another word.

Evelyn dragged a stool to sit in front of them. "I'm sorry about ..." She shook her head, knowing words could bring little comfort. "Can I ask what happened?"

Raif chewed on his lip. Beside him, Rose watched Evelyn with wide blue eyes. Finally, he said, "There were soldiers. There was a lot of smoke and fire, it was hard to see. They came at night when—"

Before he could say any more, Fat Bessie marched back into the kitchen. "You two," she said, preparing a tray of food and drink before herding the children from their seats. "Bring those clothes and follow me. You can stay upstairs until I know what to do. It's too risky down here. Too many prying eyes. Come on now." Evelyn stared at their retreating backs, Fat Bessie's voice brooking no argument. "Girl, go and serve in the tavern."

Evelyn reluctantly shuffled through the kitchen door and picked up a jug of beer. She wove around the tables, forcing herself to reflect the merriment of the patrons, to laugh and join in their conversations, all the while trying not to think about Little Haven or what the attack might mean. She would need to speak to Raif later, to learn all she could.

What was it the old woman had said? *"He doesn't just want the babes of nobles anymore."*

What could it mean? But a part of her already knew. *The Commune is closing in. I'm not safe here anymore.*

As she served and cleaned up after those coming and going in the common room, Evelyn spotted the keen-eyed man who had spied the children through the serving hatch. He sat alone in the corner, head leaning on his hands. She approached him, offering more beer.

"Hmm?" He blinked up at her, disturbed from his thoughts. "Oh, beer. No, girl. I should really be on my way if …" He trailed off and stood, securing the scarlet cloak at his neck and scurrying towards the door without a backward glance. Evelyn watched him go. He'd said nothing to worry her, yet even so …

But there were customers to serve and chores to be done and she soon forgot all about the man's curious behaviour, the odd sense of unease he'd stirred in her mind becoming no more than a muted whisper.

When the tavern had emptied and the cleaning was completed, Evelyn lay in her bed, trying to push away the flood of memories returning to her in the quiet of the night. Thoughts of Little Haven, of her life there before she left, of the day when everything changed. When she'd been shown her true worth. *Lack of worth, more like.*

She tossed and turned in her bed. There'd been no chance to speak to Raif and Rose again, but she had to find out what happened. What had become of the villagers? The Elders?

Arthur?

He deserves to be hurt. He deserves to be punished. Images flashed across her mind almost too fast to grasp onto: blonde hair, a confident grin turning into a sneer, his hand upon her arm, around her neck, the red of blood upon—

No! She fought against herself, crushing her face into her pillow and letting out a silenced scream. She stayed that way until her heartbeat calmed and her breathing slowed.

You'll never amount to anything.

The words Arthur snarled at her retained their cruelty, their ability to wound, even after two years. The children's arrival had brought them back, the link to Little Haven all too tangible. The sudden recall of those words made her weak and dizzy, helpless, just as when they were first spoken to her.

Well, almost.

What had come afterwards … She refused to go there, forced her mind to blank it out.

You'll never amount to anything.

A wrench in her gut told her what she already knew: those words were true. He was right. He'd known. She shook her head, trying to scatter the shards of memory threatening to slot together once more.

But something good had come of what had happened, hadn't it? She'd found Bessie, who was soft and gentle when others had only chosen to turn her away when she needed them the most.

"You'll be safe here, girl. I've always wanted a daughter of my own."

But Arthur's words were louder still, smothering the kindness of Bessie's.

She must have fallen asleep, and in her dreams Arthur's face floated before her eyes—deep blue eyes, golden-blonde hair, smirking lips. She cried out but her screams meant nothing. He laughed in her face, thinking himself in full control; he didn't know what was coming for him. She hadn't, either.

"Wake up."

Evelyn was dragged from her nightmare by Bessie, who shook her by the arm, holding a lantern to her face. Evelyn squinted, lifting her hand to cover her eyes.

"Wake up, girl." Bessie glanced over her shoulder. "Get dressed. Gather what you need, be quick. I'll be back." Instantly alerted by Bessie's abrupt tone, Evelyn jolted up. Before she could speak, the woman was gone. She stood and tugged on her trousers and tunic—plain brown and beige, just like the clothes Bessie gave Raif and Rose—before securing a leather belt at her waist. Once she'd completed her outfit with woollen socks and brown boots, she went to the wooden chest in the corner of her room and retrieved her battered sword, a rare gift she'd received from the village smith in Little Haven. The weapon had seen better days, even before it had been stored away for two years—but something told her it might be useful.

Finally, she retrieved her green wool cloak—the only link to her parents, the very one she'd been wrapped in as a baby, left on the outskirts of Little Haven. It might have been a vivid shade of emerald once, though it had faded with the years. She shook it out and tied it at her neck, knowing she would wear it always, even as it reminded her that whoever her parents were, they'd chosen to abandon her. No explanation, no hope of finding them, of knowing who she was. And yet the cloak was a part of her.

By the time she was ready, Bessie had returned with the children and their dog. The woman was dressed for travel, Evelyn noted, walking boots peeking out from beneath her ample skirts and a thick woollen cloak tied about her neck. Raif and Rose were dressed similarly, wearing the outfits Bessie had supplied—the boy with clean tunic and linen trousers tucked into his own worn boots, the girl with an ankle-length, long-sleeved linen dress, and both with a thick brown cloak secured at their necks.

"Come," Bessie said. "Follow me. And stay quiet."

Evelyn glanced at Raif who shrugged, evidently understanding as little as she did. Together, they followed Bessie to the top of the staircase where the woman held up a hand to stop them. As they stood, voices drifted up from the tavern. "Keep quiet," Bessie whispered, waving them on once more. They snuck down the stairs, pausing whenever there was an audible creak. From the common room, Evelyn heard the occasional broken sentence.

" … you understand, my friend."

"When we receive such a report, we have no choice but to investigate."

"Of course. Another round, good men?" Something was said in response, the words too muffled to make out, and a round of too-forced laughter followed.

Once in the kitchen, Evelyn noticed the dim glow of lamplight gleaming through the hatch from the common room. The conversation was clearer now and she listened intently, curious as to who these late-night visitors could be.

" … doing our duty, as I'm sure you're aware."

"We were told they'd been seen here."

"Of course, soldier. And I'll be glad to let you search the premises. I am nothing if not a loyal servant of His Benevolence. But first, how about some of my wife's famed apple pie? You must be weary after your long journey." It was Bessie's husband, Dick, confident and sure, ever the adept peddler.

Bessie bundled a folded knapsack into Evelyn's arms. "This way," she mouthed.

The woman led them out into the icy night air and towards the stable, their path lit only by her lantern. She unbolted the door and nodded them inside.

"Saddle Bert, girl." Bessie waved to the lone horse in the nearest stall. "That's it, quick now. Boy, keep an eye on the tavern door."

"It's hard to see, there's only one torch," Raif whispered, peering through the cracked-open stable door. "Oh. There's a wagon. Two men, I think."

"Two inside. A wagon, that's good. No riders," Fat Bessie said. "My husband is outnumbered but he should be able to keep them entertained while I get you as far as I can. We need to make for Castleton. There're people who can help. Least, last I heard, that's where they were."

"People?" Evelyn asked. "What people?"

At the same time, Raif muttered, "Red cloaks." Dog snuffled at the door, growling. The boy gasped, hand flying to his mouth. "They're the same as the men who attacked—"

"I thought as much, boy, but there's no time to explain," Bessie said, hurrying towards Evelyn. "Put the supplies in Bert's saddle." Evelyn did as she was told, strangely calmed by the clear instructions. "The three of you can ride the horse. If only there was another I could ride." Bessie pursed her lips. "Naught to be done about it."

My powers. The thought was a hard jab within Evelyn's mind, sudden and sharp. She'd barely allowed herself to acknowledge them these past two years— dare she do so now? Before she could convince herself otherwise, she pulled Bessie to one side, tilting her head close and speaking in a whisper.

"I could use … you know. I could help." *I could try, at least, though I'm not sure I'd know how.*

But Bessie's head was shaking even before she'd finished speaking. "No, girl. Keep 'em hidden, just like I told you afore. It's best that way." She squeezed Evelyn's arm. "Come on, we must—"

Suddenly, a shout sounded from the direction of the tavern. Bessie froze, eyes widening. "Quickly now, on the horse. We have to be away."

As they made their way round the back of the stables, Bessie's gaze kept drifting towards the tavern.

Dick is alone.

Evelyn looked between Raif and Rose, already on Bert's back, and Bessie, the woman who'd given her a home for two years. In that moment, she made a decision.

"Bessie," she said. "I'll take them to safety. Castleton, did you say? Dick's told me how to get there enough times. Stay here, go to your husband." She spoke with more confidence than she felt, hoping it was enough to convince Bessie.

"Oh, don't be silly, girl. I couldn't leave you—"

Raised voices flared up, clearly outside the tavern now.

"There isn't time to argue," Evelyn said. "If the three of us ride we can escape far quicker. I'll go north to the abandoned hunting cabin where I forage for mushrooms. We can rest there for the night."

Fat Bessie swallowed, eyes shining in the lantern light. "The soldiers aren't local. They won't know the hidden paths." She reached for her belt, untying her coin purse and handing it over. "Take this."

Evelyn felt the weight of coins in her hand. In Little Haven, they'd traded goods with passing pedlars, any coin was handled by the Elders; money had never been common and, consequently, when she'd run, Evelyn had not a copper to her name.

When Bessie granted her a place to stay, she'd offered a handful of coppers every now and then. "Treat yourself, girl. You've worked hard," she'd say, but Evelyn would refuse. What use did she have for money?

Yet now, it was all too clear she'd need it if they had any hope of escape. They were going to a city—they would need to pay for a room, food, drink. She shook her head, suddenly unsure of herself—of the offer she'd made just a moment ago. "I can't take that," she said. "I know how much you need—"

"Nonsense. Take it," Bessie insisted, folding her hands over Evelyn's, enveloping the leather purse within. She nodded towards the saddlebags, leaning her head close. "And I've packed some rags for your monthlies, 'case you're caught unawares."

Evelyn looked down at their clasped hands, lip beginning to tremble. She bit down on it, determined to be strong even if her legs were threatening to collapse beneath her. A thought occurred to her and she asked it before she could stop herself. "Did you pack any ..." She glanced over her shoulder to ensure the children weren't listening, "wine?"

Bessie shook her head. "You'll need a clear head for this, girl." She reached over to pat Evelyn's hand, her skin calloused but warm. "Besides, I've told you afore that stuff does more harm'n good. You don't need it, much as you might think you do."

Evelyn couldn't meet Bessie's eyes; she simply nodded, gut sinking. She couldn't quite agree with the woman's faith in her.

"You can do this, girl," Bessie said. "I know you can. Be careful. In the morning, make for Castleton. Search for a man called Mak. A group called Veritas. Dick and I, we've been in touch with 'em over the years. Tried to do right by the children who ... Well, we did what we could. I should've told you about 'em before ..." She let out a weary exhale, cutting off her own words. "I s'pose I just didn't want you to leave me for them. And now our time has run out it seems. Anyway, they can help—jus' be wary of who you ask. *They* have eyes everywhere."

Evelyn gave a brusque nod, afraid to speak for the emotion bubbling up in her throat.

"Go, go now," Fat Bessie said. "I'll distract 'em best I can."

"Bessie, I ... I'll see you again, won't I?"

The woman looked at her then, a smile softening the concern on her round face. "'Course you will, girl. I'll want to hear all about your trip. I'll bake an apple pie special for the occasion." Their eyes met, the lie hanging between them.

"I'll look forward to it." Evelyn forced a grin through the pressure building in her chest.

"Go. Make me proud." Their gazes were locked for a moment longer before the woman suddenly threw her arms around Evelyn, pulling her tight into her chest. Evelyn stiffened for a moment, though quickly allowed herself to soften into Bessie, trying to silence the voice in her mind that told her this might be the last time she'd feel such a comforting touch.

The embrace lasted for a few heartbeats—then, as quickly as she'd reached for Evelyn, Bessie pulled away, squeezed Evelyn's shoulders, and smiled. "On-ward, now," she said, drawing herself up and marching towards the tavern.

"Evelyn?" Atop the horse, Raif's hand was hovering over his bow.

"Unless you're sure of your skill with that, leave it," Evelyn said. "It will only draw more attention to us."

"It stays," Raif replied curtly, though his hand dropped to his side.

Evelyn gazed into the darkness. All four soldiers were standing outside the tavern alongside Dick. Bessie shone her lantern across their faces. "It's already near cold as winter," she declared loudly. "Had to check on my horse, y'see. Prone to catch a chill this time o' year given his old age. Anyway, I heard some commotion. Surely nothing that can't be solved by a spot more ale by the fire?"

Evelyn climbed onto Bert's back in front of Raif and Rose, giving the horse a gentle pat. The old beast was strong and sure-footed. She trusted he would take them to safety. If she was careful, they could walk slowly, blend into the darkness and get away without being seen. She gave Bert a gentle tap with her heels. She hoped the men would be tempted by Bessie's offer, appeased by the promise of comfort and warmth.

"What's that? Over by the stables."

"No, there's nothing out there, I can assure you. I—"

"You'll be quiet woman, or lose your tongue."

Without a backward glance, Evelyn kicked Bert into a run, Dog close at heel.

"Stop, by order of the Commune!"

"They're just children, please!"

"Stop! In the name of His Ben—"

"Evelyn, keep going, girl! Don't look back!"

Evelyn kept her eyes forwards, head low, elbows locked, reins deathly tight in her fists. There was an awful, gut-wrenching howl, and Bessie didn't yell again, but Evelyn didn't look back. Even when the tears blurred her vision and it was all she wanted to do, she didn't look back.

She spurred the horse northwards, away from the soldiers. Away from the tavern. Away from the woman who'd saved her.

She didn't look back.

2

Hector

Hector was relieving himself on a tree near the outskirts of camp when the clattering of hoofbeats reached his ears. "Who is it, Cara?" he called to his companion, keeping watch nearby. As she darted away, Hector pulled up his trousers.

Messengers. Scouts returning.

Cara twirled in between his legs as she delivered her findings, white fur nearly blending in with the snow-scattered ground. "Scouts?" Hector tugged on the end of his moustache. "Come on, we should find out what news they've brought." His companion let out a purr, butted his leg gently with her head, and trotted off ahead.

They made their way towards the large hut sitting at the centre of the Veritas camp from which a curl of smoke drifted up towards the dense grey clouds above. He rubbed his arms, anticipating the heat of the fire pit within. As he did so, his skin tingled. "Mm," he said, sniffing the moisture-heavy air. "Storm's coming." He scanned the Crystal Mountains that stretched across the horizon, imagining he could almost hear a deep, anticipatory rumbling in their peaks.

By the time they arrived at the hut, the scouts had already been herded in to see Avanna. Hector nodded at the two guardsmen—the bearded Tavin and the young Bo, cheeks reddened by the cold mountain air—and pushed his way through the furs hanging over the doorway. Inside, the heat was almost unbearable. He shrugged off his grey fur cloak, unbuttoned his jerkin, and made for the seating area where the two scouts were relaying their message to

Avanna and her brother, Mak. He sat beside them, Cara nestling into his lap, and listened.

" … heard it wherever we went. Villages have been ransacked, people taken or killed," said young Griff, cheeks flushed and eyes shining with exhaustion.

"It's as the lad says," said the other scout, a relative newcomer named Arturo whose grey hair hung loose from its horsetail. Though Hector hadn't spoken to him much since his arrival, it was evident he had experienced much harsdship at the hands of the Commune—his brown skin marred with scars, dark eyes full of barely repressed rage. "We ventured into one of the villages on the outskirts of Haven Forest, found it abandoned. Huts burned down, people gone. Three dead by sword, left to rot where they fell. Signs of horses trampling the ground, of scuffles between men. It can only be *them*."

"That's not all, is it, Arturo?" Griff said, looking to his older companion with fear in his eyes.

"What is it? What else did you discover?" Avanna asked, the strain in her voice all too evident.

Arturo exhaled. "There's a decree. The Nomarrans, they're being driven out of the cities by order of the Commune. The Grand Magister's madness is truly growing, to treat those who were once seen as allies like—"

"Nomarrans?" Avanna's lips pinched tight. "Are they … Have they been able to find safety? You know you could have brought anyone seeking sanctuary here."

Arturo nodded, mouth downturned. "I'm afraid we were too late for that. Those who were not rounded up by the Commune have fled. Where to, no one appeared to know."

"Rounded up?" Mak gasped. "How could they? Surely the soldiers know of the history between our people. Of the aid they granted during the—"

"Hush, brother."

Hector saw in Avanna's drawn expression the same apprehension that was burrowing into his gut.

"Thank you for bringing this news to us, Griff, Arturo. We've long wondered at the Grand Magister's increasing brutality. We suspected his paranoia was mounting, and now this?" Avanna shook her head. "It seems to me the whispers were true. The bastard's powers are fading and he's doing everything he can to keep control. He expels the Nomarrans he fears will turn against him. He hunts the children of commoners, for it's clear the noble offspring no longer satisfy his … *needs*."

"When will it end?" Mak asked, incredulous. "Those ignorant nobles … Not to mention our foolish bloody King!" His lip curled into a snarl. "Don't they see what that *bastard* is doing? Amassing the power for himself, dividing it how he sees fit. Even, if the grossest gossip is true, merging his mind with the most powerful individuals so he can retain his own strength."

Griff gasped but Arturo simply gave a resigned nod. "I fear it has always been so," he said. "True, the children taken are often trained to be soldiers, guards, workers for the noble families. But what happens to those with the strongest powers?" His eyes lingered on Hector before sweeping back to Avanna. "Yes, they are rare, but there must have been some over the years, out of all the hundreds handed over. What does the Grand Magister do with them? What choice does he have but to take what is theirs for his own? Wouldn't they be a threat to him if he didn't? Just as he shuns the Nomarrans now—an imagined threat he seeks to crush. I fear the worst is yet to come." He paused, looking at everyone as his words sunk in. "I think we all know the truth of it. We have been too scared to admit it until now."

Hector ran a hand across Cara's back, taking comfort from her presence. The thought was a dreadful one, but Arturo was right. The Grand Magister had grown more and more reckless as the years passed—even the heinous act spoken of was no longer a surprise.

Hector glanced towards Avanna; his friend's eyes were downcast, hand covering her mouth. Of late, her once-full face had grown lean and hard, her expression guarded, her lips creased downwards with ever-deepening worry lines. He wondered what she wasn't telling them. If he was so inclined, he might have used his powers to sense her thoughts and feelings. As it was, he could only guess at what she was thinking. Despite their years together, she'd always kept certain concerns to herself, believing as their leader she had to carry the weight of such burdens alone.

"It hardly bears thinking about," Mak muttered. "Those poor children."

"Whole villages, gone," Arturo said, voice cracking. "It is as it was when I was a lad, when the last Grand Magister died. With the changeover came a stricter implementation of the rules. Noble families were searched, their homes ransacked. I was heir to an estate to the north of Castleton. My parents sent me away before I was found. I never saw them again. Those nobles whose loyalty to the Commune had begun to slacken … Well, the young Quilliam Nubira Antellopie, third of his name, meant to show that the Commune was *never* to be questioned. The punishments were severe. And now …" Arturo hesitated, eyes burning, hands clenching in his lap. "And now, he is pushing his need for control further still."

Mak abruptly stood. "We won't let it continue, my friend. I'll set off for Taskan at once. We'll see if we can—"

"No, brother," Avanna said, holding her hand out. "I need you here with me. Besides, what can we do? Our identities are too well known. It's too much of a risk."

We could go. Cara sat up in Hector's lap, yellow eyes unblinking. He stroked her head, nodding. If they could save one person, adult or child, it would be worth it. "I'll go with Mak," he said. "We can't forget what Veritas was formed to do—why we're hunted by the Commune in the first place. I, for one, wear the badge of 'traitor' with honour."

"Hector's right," Mak said, convictions renewed with Hector's support. "I know it's dangerous, Avanna, but think of what we used to do—the raids on the Commune's wagons, the joy when we brought back just one or two children who would have otherwise been imprisoned in that wretched compound. Most of the people here wouldn't be part of our camp if we hadn't—"

"Enough," Avanna said, rubbing her temples. She looked to Griff and Arturo. "Your scouting missions are complete. Send out two in your stead and get some rest."

The two men bowed their heads and left. In the ensuing silence, Hector shared a glance with Mak. In recent months, Avanna's moods had darkenened, her caution increased. The group had remained confined to their camp in the Crystal Mountains, doing as little as possible to put themselves in danger of discovery. Before, they had kept a constant presence in Castleton, staying alert to any news about the Commune's actions with brief scouting surveys. If he was honest with himself, Hector had grown increasingly restless.

This is the chance to stretch our reach once more.

"I know, my love," Hector muttered to Cara.

"What was that?" Avanna scowled. "Speak up if you mean to say something."

Hector drew himself up, meeting her fierce gaze. "I think we should go," he said. "We haven't helped anyone in a long time. Who knows how many people have sought us out in Castleton only to find we've taken to hiding ourselves away. It's not right. It's not what we set out to do, all those years ago."

Avanna crossed her arms. "Hector, you know full well—"

"You don't need to say it. I know you did what you thought was best for us. But now, it's time we made our mark again. Why else are we sending scouts out, seeking information about the Grand Magister and his men, if not to take action once more?"

"I agree," Mak said, taking a rare stand against his sister. Hector gave him a grateful nod.

Avanna inhaled sharply, fingers drumming her knee. The final decision would lie with her, as it always did—but with both her brother and Hector speaking up in favour of the plan, she could hardly allow her own reluctance to take precedence. "Very well," she said.

"Thank you, sister, we won't—"

Avanna held her hand up. "You will go to Castleton," she said. "From there, learn what you can about the raids on the villages in Haven Forest. Be cautious. Keep your eyes open. And then, only if you deem the risk to be … *manageable*, may you head to Taskan."

Hector flitted his eyes to Mak and, seeing the man open his mouth to argue, said, "Good idea. As you say, it wouldn't serve us to be foolhardy now."

Mak's lips smacked shut. He combed his long hair back from his face. "Yes, I suppose so."

Avanna stood. "We'll make preparations. You'll leave within the hour, before that storm hits." She moved to speak to her serving girl, dictating a list of supplies they'd need for their journey.

"Hector." Mak approached, leaning his head close. He glanced about conspiratorially, checking his sister was still occupied before continuing. "Up for a little bet?"

Hector stroked his moustache, mouth twitching into a smile. "Go on …"

"First of us to gain a lead in Castleton—ten silver pieces."

"May I remind you that this is serious." Avanna appeared at their backs, brow creased.

"Oh, yes, of course," Mak said, bowing his head. "It's just a bit of fun to—"

"What's fun about people being imprisoned, Mak? Tortured? Murdered?" Avanna shook her head. "Like bloody children." She pushed past them.

Hector waited until she was out of earshot before tapping Mak's shoulder. "Make it twenty pieces. It's been a while."

"Done." His friend grinned. "I'm going to enjoy this. Back out there again after all these months. We'll show those bastards what we're made of." He clapped Hector on the back before rushing ahead to join his sister.

Hector patted Cara's head before securing his cloak at his neck once more and following them both from the hut.

A new mission at last.

He smiled towards his companion. They'd been sheltered for too long.

It was time to fight once more.

3

Commander Sulemon

Commander Sulemon hesitated as he approached Lord Torrant's door. His hand sat on the leather pouch at his waist—a small trinket to the unknowing eye, but for those who knew beyond the disconnect between the cracking, aged material and the Commander's otherwise pristine uniform, a symbol of solemn reminders. A reminder of the destruction ravaged through the Noman Islands—the Commander's home—by a traitorous group of his own people cursed with powers when he was just a child. Over twenty years had passed, yet the pain and rage burned on within his heart, fueling his resolve to stay in Septima, working for the Commune and bringing those with powers under control. A reminder of honor, of duty.

"Veritarra protect me," he whispered, releasing the pouch and tilting an ear towards the door. Though he knew from the sound of voices and laughter inside there were guests being entertained, his pride willed him to make his report without delay. Lord Torrant would expect no less.

Commander Sulemon inhaled deeply, drew his hand into a fist, and knocked twice on the dark oak. Inside the room, the conversation ceased. He imagined all eyes watching Lord Torrant, waiting for a reaction to the disturbance. Despite his trepidation, he twisted the door handle and pushed it open, beating his fist twice against his chest before dropping it to his side.

"Commander Sulemon," Lord Torrant said from his seat at the head of the dining table. He was joined by a man and woman, resplendent in their fine dress, the remnants of a vast feast scattered on the table before them.

"My Lord," the Commander said, bowing his head. "I am sorry to interrupt, but I have your report regarding the raids on—"

"Let's not bore my guests with such talk."

Lord Torrant smiled at the woman, apparently sharing in some private joke. The Commander tried to ignore the shard of envy it drove into his gut. "Of course, my Lord," he said. "I can return at a more appropriate time." He swerved back towards the door, red cloak snapping behind him.

"Commander Sulemon," Lord Torrant said, stopping him mid-step. The sound of a chair scraping on floorboards was followed by light footsteps. The Commander jerked at the touch of an elegantly jewelled hand on his arm. The great ruby ring upon Lord Torrant's middle finger—a sign of his loyal service to the Grand Magister—glimmered in the light of the candelabra beside them. "You must be tired. Surely you can join us for a glass of wine?"

"No, my Lord, I don't think—"

Lord Torrant's pale blue eyes pinned him to the spot, lips curled into an all too familiar smile, a pulsing heat flowing from his hand. "You're allowed to relax, aren't you?"

The Commander swallowed, nodding briskly. "Of course, Lord Torrant." *Just one glass. That won't do any harm.*

"Excellent. Come, Lord Ambleside here brought a bottle of his family's own vintage." Lord Torrant withdrew his touch and returned to his seat.

"Oh, Lord Torrant, surely not. Something plainer must do for a simple soldier. And a Nomarran at that." It was the woman who spoke, voice filled with indignation. Commander Sulemon clenched the back of his chair, fixing her with a glare. *Simple soldier. Nomarran.* As though his life could be summed up so plainly. But the woman was raising an eyebrow at Lord Torrant without so much as a glance towards him, full of arrogance at her own assumed superiority. The Commander daren't speak and disrupt whatever good will was being sought here, so he stood and waited.

"Now, now, Lady Cragside," Lord Torrant said, teeth flashing into a grin beneath his close-cropped black beard. "This is no simple soldier, as you so delicately put it. Commander Sulemon is my most trusted man. I would lay my life in his hands." He shared a glance with the Commander, a bolt of electricity passing between them, an unspoken link binding them together. The connection was shattered all too soon by the light tinkling of Lady Cragside's laughter. Commander Sulemon suppressed a shudder as he took his seat and helped himself to a glass of wine, knuckles tightening around it to conceal his trembling.

"Well, if you say so, my dear Lord Torrant," the woman said, finally turning to study the Commander with emerald green eyes, perfectly complimented by the matching jewels at her throat and the creamy gold bodice of her gown. She was attractive, it could not be denied—if you were a man who appreciated such things.

Lord Torrant was not such a man.

"Hmm," Lady Cragside said, smirking between Lord Torrant and the Commander, evidently believing them both to be beholden to her beauty. Commander Sulemon coughed back a laugh, trying to catch Lord Torrant's eye to share in mockery at her ignorance.

Lord Torrant gave him an almost imperceptible smirk before giving Lady Cragside the reassuring smile one might give a slow-minded child. Taking it for encouragement, she tapped a finger to her full pink lips as she turned towards the Commander. "Hmm, perhaps it would be interesting to speak to one of your ... *birth*. I'd thought the Grand Magister had put restrictions on the entry of Nomarran immigrants into Septima of late."

"He has." Lord Torrant steepled his long fingers. "Commander Sulemon has been with me for some years. He came to Septima before the borders were restricted."

Lady Cragside nodded with interest, eyes roving over the Commander as though he were a specimen on display. "Truly, quite remarkable, Lord Torrant. Such black skin, such dark eyes. Well muscled, too. Look at those shoulders." Her eyes glinted. "I know women who would pay well for his *services*. Especially now that it is harder to find a Nomarran in any decent society. The Grand Magister's decree has seen to that."

Decree? Commander Sulemon snapped his gaze to Lord Torrant, the question forming on his tongue. But before he could ask, the woman let out a throaty chuckle and said, "A well-chosen bodyguard, my Lord. You have done well."

Bodyguard. Services. He bristled. *How dare she speak of me like some prized possession?* If only she knew the true extent of his relationship with the man she believed under her thrall. If only she could see the constant, torturous memories that swirled inside his head.

Blind bitch.

His thoughts were disturbed by the harsh sound of Lord Torrant's laughter, eyes dancing with merriment. It was a cruel laugh, the Commander knew, one containing a sneering disdain—but the woman was too besotted to notice. "You make an astute observation, Lady Cragside," he said. "I've done well, indeed. The Commander here has been in Septima long enough to understand our ways. Besides, he knows the importance of bringing those with powers under control—his own home was brought to ruin not so long ago by a small group of Nomarrans wielding them. *Ezzarah's Cursed*, they called them. A small rebellion, no more, yet it was enough for him to see what needed to be done. Is that not so, Commander?"

The Commander bowed his head, unable in that moment to verbalise the horrors commited by the traitorous Nomarrans, his own father included, who possessed those accursed powers—the very powers he despised, yet now found his own existence, own merit, in Septima, inextricably linked with. "My Lord," he said curtly.

Lord Torrant waved his hand in the air dismissively. "In Septima, those with powers are simply children in need of proper direction. Nevertheless, this man is my closest advisor and trusted companion. Aren't you?" Those ice-blue eyes flitted towards him—a look that said, *How little she knows.*

"Yes, my Lord," he said. "And I will stay by your side." *Unlike this stupid wench.*

Lord Torrant spluttered on the wine he was sipping as though reading the Commander's mind. He mopped his mouth with a napkin and said, "That's right. Though I can assure you, my Commander is not available for … hire. He is a man of honour and duty."

Lady Cragside laughed in return. "Oh, I wouldn't dream of taking him away from you, my Lord. We want you kept safe now, don't we? No doubt that's why he remains in your service." As she spoke, her eyes explored Lord Torrant's face with a hunger the Commander knew only too well. He couldn't blame her; the man's pitch-black hair shone in the firelight, his beard freshly trimmed and oiled, his burgundy waistcoat and breeches well fitted against his lithe form. Yes, Lord Torrant commanded any room he entered and set many a heart to racing.

As Lord Torrant and Lady Cragside became embroiled in mindless chatter, Commander Sulemon clenched his jaw and stared into the deep red liquid in his wine glass. *I cannot think of him in that way anymore. He has made himself clear.*

Overwhelmed by his own thoughts, he gulped the wine down and felt the flush of heat course down his throat. He was half-tempted to leave, reluctant to see the shared glances, near-touches and smiles between Lord Torrant and this despicable woman.

Yet he knew he would stay. He had to, lest his own imagination create a scene far worse than that he was witnessing. He removed his red cloak and hung it over the chair behind him, awkwardly fumbling in an attempt to distract from the blatant flirtations taking place before him.

To his credit, Lord Ambleside must have noticed the Commander's discomfort. He shuffled down the table, giving Commander Sulemon a genuine smile before handing him the almost-empty bottle of vintage burgundy. He slammed it down a little too violently, having consumed more than his fair share judging by the ample wine stains decorating his cream silk shirt. "Some more to drink, uh, Com- Commander ... Sulemon, was it?"

"Thank you, my Lord," Commander Sulemon said, emptying the bottle into his glass and taking another generous gulp. *What harm will a little more do? I may as well enjoy myself, just like* he *is.*

"Nomarran, eh?" Lord Ambleside's bloodshot eyes widened. "Never met one before. An interesting people, though. You'll forgive my cousin's bluntness, I hope." He flashed a wine-stained grin. "My father told me all about the assistance you, your—" He interrupted himself with a hiccough before slurping a great mouthful of wine. "Your people gave in the Seven-Year War. A hundred years and more ago, yet we still remember what you did for us." He gave a lopsided grin. "What was it, Vegi ... Veriga ..."

"Veritarra's Gift," the Commander said, brushing a finger over the pouch at his belt.

"Yes!" Lord Ambleside's face lit up. "Vetirarra's Gift! Such a simple thing, yet it turned the tide and put those *foolish rebels* down once and for all, didn't it? Brilliant. Who'd have thought it, eh? Help, such needed help, coming from a scattering of islands so far away."

Commander Sulemon barely contained a scoff. He was in no mood to deal with such ignorance, no matter how well-intentioned. "A scattering of islands? A *simple thing?*" He snorted, curtly shaking his head. *These people have no idea the power of what they praise so casually.* "My Lord, you know nothing of the sacrifices of my people. Veritarra's Gift was a blessing from a beloved Goddess, a sacred secret, and it was what won the war, was it not? It was given to Septima, the only hope you had of defence against the powers. Without it, all of *your* home would have been lost. Do not speak lightly of that about which you clearly understand so little. Do not—" The Commander let out a long exhale, releasing the fistful of table cloth he hadn't been aware he'd grasped. Lord Ambleside, despite his inebriated state, was watching him with wide-eyed fear. He had to be careful; these nobles were shallow, fickle people, and Lord Torrant was working hard to ensure their loyalty to the Commune.

He glanced up towards Lord Torrant, still conversing with the despicable Lady Cragside. Now was not the time to let his rage take hold—he'd held it in for so long, ever since the traitors had caused ruin in his home. It was second-nature to him now, after all these years, to swallow it back down.

The Commander looked to Lord Ambleside, holding his wine glass up. "Forgive me, my Lord," he said. "It has been a trying day."

Lord Ambleside let out a strained laugh. "Think nothing of it." He cleared his throat, mouth flapping open and closed for a moment before saying, "Did I hear you mention raids, S-S-Sulemon?" He waved his arm around as he spoke, dragging his sleeve through a pot of congealing gravy left over from dinner.

The Commander met Lord Ambleside's surprisingly steadfast gaze. "You did, my Lord," he said, plucking at the long sleeves of his black undertunic, self-conscious of such close scrutiny.

"I see." Lord Ambleside held his own glass up, slopping some more of its contents over his shirt. "On the villages on the western coast of Septima, I presume? Lord, uh, Lord Torrant here has filled me in on the Commune's work." He gave a conspiratorial wink, the Commander's earlier vitriol evidently forgotten. "I believe it is of the utmost importance for our beloved kingdom!" Commander Sulemon flinched as spit flew from the man's lips.

"Yes, my Lord." He wiped a fleck from his cheek. Noting from the corner of his eye that the nobleman's drunken ranting had drawn Lord Torrant's attention away from the woman, he said, "Please, go on."

Lord Ambleside beamed. "Well, I'm no expert, Commander. But from what, er, from how I see it—" He hiccoughed again, running a hand over his mouth before continuing. "You see, we can't allow the common folk, especially those born with such powers, to be running around with the freedom to use them however they wish! What could they do? Your people helped us win the Seven-Year War, yes but what risk remains?" He grabbed the Commander's forearm. "That it has been allowed for so long already, well ab- ab- abominable! Who can say what is in the minds of commoners? This Grand Magister, may His Benevolence bless us, is doing what his father and grandfather were too afraid to do before him. And I—" He stood, lifting his glass. "I, for one, am in full support."

"Hear hear, Lord Ambleside," Lord Torrant said, raising his own wine glass. "You are a true man of the Commune."

"Oh, th- thank you, my Lord," Lord Ambleside said, blushing a shade of red to match his family's burgundy vintage. "We saw what these powers did in *those* islands when left unregulated, only 23 years ago. After one hundred years of peace in our land, Commune be praised, we don't want another war here at *any* cost. Whatever it takes." He drained his drink and slumped back into his chair.

Lord Torrant frowned, running a hand along his jaw. "A much appreciated sentiment. And, now that I think on it, Commander, it may be best I hear your report sooner rather than later. Lord Ambleside here has filled me with renewed purpose."

Commander Sulemon's heart raced as Lord Torrant's gaze locked with his own.

Lady Cragside gasped. "Really, Lord Torrant? And I thought I was to have the joy of your company all evening," she said, leaning across the table, cleavage on full display. Her hand brushed his arm as she fluttered her eyelashes.

The slightest flicker of disgust passed over Lord Torrant's face, quickly replaced by a strained smile. "It would be my pleasure, my Lady, to entertain you until the dawn," he said. "Unfortunately, my duties call this evening."

"Come, cousin," Lord Ambleside said, pushing himself backwards on his chair. "We've taken up quite enough of Lord Torrant's time. A lovely evening, my Lord. Wonderful." He braced himself on the table and heaved himself up.

"Oh, cousin …" Lady Cragside pouted out her lower lip. "Must we?"

"Now, Imelda," Lord Ambleside said, moving to retrieve her from the other side of the table, remarkably sure-footed despite his inebriation. "Lord Torrant is an important man—wi- with important business to attend to!"

Lady Cragside huffed, crossing her arms as her cousin tugged her upwards.

"Thank you, Lord Ambleside," Lord Torrant said, leading the two towards the door.

"And remember, Lord Torrant, if our family can be of any assistance in hunting down these, these *peasants*, you have my word it will be so. As you say, it is extremely dangerous for them to be roaming the kingdom without the watchful guidance of the Grand Magister. May his powers bless us all." He let out a long belch as though to underline his point.

Lord Torrant patted his back. "Indeed, Lord Ambleside. Your willingness to assist the Commune shall be duly noted. The Grand Magister will hear of your most gracious offer."

Lord Ambleside's face lit up. "Oh, aha! Thank you, Lord Torrant, thank you."

"Goodbye, Lord Torrant," Lady Cragside said, elbowing her cousin out of the way so she could be centre of attention once more, embroidered skirts taking up the entire doorway. "We'll be in Castleton for another day, at the King's Tavern in the southeast quarter, should you wish—"

Commander Sulemon could listen to the woman's incessant chatter no longer. He emptied his glass and stood, walking to the fireplace and rubbing his hands together.

"You have my word, my Lady," Lord Torrant interjected. "I will send for you just as soon as I can. Goodnight." The sound of a light kiss was followed by the door closing. The Commander had to physically stop himself from smashing his fist against the wall.

"Thank the blessed powers they're gone," Lord Torrant muttered, reaching to undo the tied collar of his ruffled white shirt.

"Lord Torrant," the Commander stepped forward, fist held at his chest. "If I had known you were entertaining that *particular* company, I would never have—"

Lord Torrant rolled his eyes. "Oh, stop, Jonah. It is a necessity as you well know. Part of my work for the Commune, nothing more."

There was a pause before Commander Sulemon dared to speak his greatest fear. When he finally built up the nerve, his voice was a hoarse whisper. "Will you go to her?"

Lord Torrant moved to the table and picked up his wine, taking a sip before responding. "I must maintain a relationship with her. The Commune's progress relies upon the support of such noble families. Lady Cragside requires flattery, nothing more."

"Nothing more?"

Lord Torrant exhaled. "Nothing more, Commander. You know I would never ..." He wrinkled his nose. "The thought alone is enough to make me nauseous. The woman requires flirtations and gifts. That is as far as I will go."

The Commander remained unconvinced, the snaking envy in his gut trying to uncover any lie in the words. He bit his tongue hard, afraid of what he would say if he allowed himself to speak. *I have had too much wine.* He took long, slow breaths—a futile attempt to push back the thick fog encompassing his mind. "My Lord Torrant, I- I didn't mean to imply—"

"Of course not," Lord Torrant said quietly, stepping closer. "Think nothing of it."

The Commander shook his head. "You heard how she spoke of me. Of my people. How can you entertain such a vile—"

"Hush, Jonah." Lord Torrant moved closer, the coarse black hair at the top of his chest all too visible. "What do the ignorant views of such a woman matter? It is her money and support I need, nothing more. You know that what I do is for the Commune. For the Grand Magister. For the kingdom."

"Yes, but what of—"

"She means nothing to me." He reached a hand up to touch the Commander's cheek—his touch warm and soft and all too tormenting. Thirteen years together, yet for seven of those his love had been denied.

"One day, Jonah."

Only vague words, fleeting touches, unprompted promises whispered to keep some tiny spark of hope alive within him. He knew what every one sounded like by now. Always more of the same, always just enough to keep him close.

"One day we can be together again."

Does he think one touch will be enough to draw me back? The Commander clenched his jaw, kept his gaze steady, did not lean back, did not return the touch. Yet he also did not move away.

Lord Torrant closed the space between them. "There are things you can never understand, Jonah."

At those words, Commander Sulemon turned away, though he still felt the heat of Lord Torrant's presence behind him—heard the sound of breathing, fast and shallow. He balled his hands at his sides and closed his eyes, sure that the sound of his pounding heart must be filling the entire room.

"Would you like the report now, my Lord?" he croaked.

Lord Torrant emitted a weary sigh. "No, Commander. It can wait until the morning."

Before Commander Sulemon could respond, Lord Torrant moved away. His footsteps receded to the door at the rear of the room. It was closed with a firm click. Lord Torrant had never responded well when his baiting was ignored.

Alone, he remained in front of the hearth. Despite its blazing heat, there was a chill at his back, in his gut, in his heart. It was only when Lord Torrant had gone that he remembered the woman's words.

"*… it is harder to find a Nomarran in any decent society. The Grand Magister's decree has seen to that.*"

What damned decree? And what did it mean for him? He pinched the bridge of his nose. *Lord Torrant didn't want me to ask. He was distracting me.*

There will be another time, he told himself, even as he pushed the realisation to the back of his mind.

Weak-kneed and light-headed, he ran a finger along the top of Lord Torrant's wine glass, standing over the still-warm cushion of his seat, inhaling the lingering aroma of his floral beard oil, scented with a spice from the Commander's homeland. Despite himself, despite his resolve, he relished at the scent. *He holds onto what we had, just as I do … We'll be together again someday. Then everything I do for the Commune—everything I have done—won't be in vain.*

"Fool," he muttered. Eventually, he regained himself enough to retrieve his cloak and leave.

As soon as he stepped outside, the Commander knew where his feet were taking him. As he neared the door of the establishment, he could hear the sound of drunken patrons within. He spat on the ground in an attempt to rid his mouth of the taste of wine, ashamed that he should be considered the same as such men, even knowing it was his own drunkenness that drove him here—his own impulses unleashed.

"Veritarra, forgive me," he muttered.

Of course, there were other places he could have gone—those in the Noble Quarter of the city were more suited to his station; their settings grander, prices all the higher. Yet, regardless of his thirteen years by Lord Torrant's side, the Commander was uncomfortable in the midst of such finery. He was a man of humble beginnings and his tastes remained so. Besides, in the finer establishments, there was too much risk he would be recognised by some noble bastard seeking to prove his loyalty to Lord Torrant. *If word got back to him …* but no, that didn't bear thinking about.

And yet, even with that fear, he couldn't stop himself. The wine had sparked something within him, something he kept pushed down in his mind most days. Seeing Lord Torrant with that woman, though—the flirtations, no matter how false … *False wanting can feel true, to the right ears.* He was furious with himself for allowing the envy to maintain such a hold over him. In that moment, he needed release—he couldn't focus on anything else, especially when he thought of the way that *wench* had stared at Lord Torrant, the hunger in her eyes …

The jealousy jabbed at him once more—incessant, taunting, telling him again and again, *What did you expect?* He worried if he didn't do something to shut it out, he might be driven mad.

He would deal with the guilt, the shame, the self-loathing in the morning. There would be time enough to scorn himself when the sun rose on another day.

Commander Sulemon moved to a side alley and headed for the back entrance. The door was lit by a single lamp filtered through red glass. He ensured he was alone before knocking hard, impatient to be inside. Though the streets were nearly deserted, there was always a risk that some starving peasant or drunken lout would see his red cloak and think to pick a fight.

To his relief, the door was soon opened by a keen-eyed woman in a faded purple gown, corset so tight her breasts were pushed almost to her throat. "Ah, Commander, welcome, welcome," she said, red lipstick seeping into the wrinkles around her mouth as she smiled.

"Madam Rhom," Commander Sulemon said, edging in behind her, clamping his mouth shut so as not to choke on the heavy incense in the air.

"It's been some time since I last saw you." She curtsied. "I've kept your room ready these past weeks." She closed the door, trapping him in that suffocating hallway. It was dim, flickering candles ensconced on walls and scattered on tables, bright pink cushions and red curtains doing their best to brighten what was otherwise a drab interior. "The usual, Commander?"

Irritated by the woman's assuming tone, Commander Sulemon grunted. "It would seem you already know my answer."

"Very good," Madam Rhom said, unperturbed by his sharpness. She led him up the threadbare-carpeted stairway. The room he frequented was hidden away from the noise and stench of the rest of the establishment; the Commander had made it clear on his first visit that he would not put up with disturbances of any kind and paid the price accordingly.

"Made the room up fresh meself this morning, Commander." Madam Rhom flashed a brown-toothed grin. "It seems me old bones had a sense you'd be joining us." She unlocked and opened a familiar black door, leading him into the finest room available. "You know, I have plenty of options—others who might serve you just as well. Perhaps you might like a change—"

"The usual, Madam Rhom." Commander Sulemon glared. *Why does she challenge me when she knows what I will say?*

The woman smiled, dark eyes gleaming. "I'll send for Cole," she said, leaving the room in a flurry of thick skirts.

The Commander massaged his pounding head as the door was pulled shut. *What am I doing?* Even as he asked himself the question, he knew he would stay. He removed his cloak and loosened the leather straps that secured his single piece of armour. Though his men were wont to wear cuirass and vambraces and greaves, he'd never liked the cumbersome feel of such things. Lord Torrant had especially commissioned an iron breastplate to sit across his chest, beautifully decorated with a golden royal crest. He shrugged himself free of it and rolled his aching neck and shoulders before placing it carefully on a chair, for a moment watching the flames from the fireplace reflect upon its polished surface. With a sigh, he turned to take in the room. The four-poster bed had crisp white sheets and woollen blankets. Commander Sulemon averted his gaze, almost embarrassed at the knowledge of what would take place upon it.

There is no shame in clearing my mind. In forgetting all that has been … stirred this evening. He almost believed his own lie as he reached for the bottle of wine on the bedside table. He poured a glass and drank it down, unable to afford himself the clarity of sobriety just yet. Although some distant part of his mind protested—knowing the regret that awaited him in the morning—he shook it away.

There is no harm in a night away from my duties.

He poured more wine and sat on the bed, glass in hand, waiting.

It wasn't long before there was a gentle knock at the door and the young man called Cole peered his head round. As always, the Commander's heart lurched at the similarities.

"Come in," he said gruffly.

"I'm at your disposal, Commander Sulemon." The young man knelt down in front of the closed door—as he had done on so many visits before—and waited.

Commander Sulemon watched him for a moment, enjoying the power he held. He finished his wine and slammed the glass down. He stalked round the bed and squatted low, grasping Cole's chin with his fingers, turning his face one way and then the other. The same shining black hair, the same pale blue eyes, the slightest hint of dark stubble upon his chin. True, his jaw was not so well defined, his skin not so perfect, his manner not so confidently arrogant.

So like him, and without those accursed powers—

He shoved Cole's face away, halting the thought before it could fully form. If he allowed it clarity, he might finally crack. He would not breathe life to the truth about the man he loved—the similarity Lord Torrant held to his own father, who had caused such pain and destruction. He gritted his teeth, recalling Lord Torrant's promises that he only used *them* for the good of the people, everything done purely in service of the Commune, he took no pleasure in the pain caused by—

No. I will not do this to myself tonight.

The Commander stood and turned away from the young man. "Get up," he said. "Take your clothes off."

Cole did as he was told, diligently removing his ruffled white shirt and form-fitting black trousers. Beneath, he revealed smooth white skin, a lean, well-muscled body, fine black hair running from chest to stomach.

Commander Sulemon's breath quickened. It was almost cruel how alike they were. He closed his eyes, seeing clearly that first night with *him*, so long ago.

No, do not think of it. The Commander steadied himself against the bedframe, suddenly dizzy. Cole rushed over, hands soft and gentle. "Please, Commander," he said. "Let me."

He focused on the caress of the young man's lips against him, the sweet scratch of stubble over his chest as his tunic was pushed upwards. He sighed as he allowed himself to relax into the touch. This was all he needed—was that so wrong? Just some blessed relief from the hunger that consumed him, day and night. Cole caressed his cheek, a playful smile on his lips. He smelled clean, lightly scented with sweet floral perfume.

He grasped Cole's wrist, leaning down so their faces almost touched. *I am allowed this,* he told himself. *To feel something other than longing, shame, heartache, rage.*

"Get on the bed."

Cole seemed to understand the transfer of power in that moment. He traced a line down Commander Sulemon's chest, beckoning him down.

The Commander willingly obliged.

4

Raif

Raif was lurking somewhere in the clouded landscape between sleep and wakefulness, head lolling from side to side, when the horse was drawn to an abrupt halt.

"We're here," Evelyn said, jolting him awake. He rubbed his eyes, blinking towards a ramshackle cabin nestled amidst thick, imposing trees, some of which appeared to be close to breaching its roof with their twisted branches.

Evelyn clambered down from the horse. "Wait. I'll check inside."

She crept ahead to the cabin, visible only by the light of the overhead moon illuminating her auburn hair. Raif watched as she pushed the door open, disappearing inside.

"Are you okay?" he whispered to his sister, squeezing her with the arm clutched round her tiny waist, feeling the hard outline of her ribs against his hand. Rose remained silent in front of him, head moving in the slightest of nods. "We'll be able to get some proper sleep. You and Dog can curl up nice and warm. That'll be better than sleeping outside, won't it?" Another brief nod.

Evelyn emerged. "Come on," she said. "It's a bit of a mess but it'll do. Can't risk a fire though, might burn the whole place down." She gave him a tight smile. "You two go inside and sleep. I'll see to Bert."

Raif climbed from the horse's back and held his arms up to help Rose down.

"Here," Evelyn said, handing him a thick blanket. "Bessie packed well." She averted her gaze as she spoke the woman's name.

"Thank you," he said, lacking the energy to provide any words of comfort to ease her evident pain—his own was too fresh. Evelyn gave another fleeting smile before turning to the horse, rubbing his nose and whispering soft words.

Inside the cabin, a single window—ringed by the jagged remains of smashed glass—allowed stray beams of moonlight into the single room. There were stacks of broken wood that might have once been chairs and a table, a long cold brick fireplace filled with dust and twigs and blackened logs, and what seemed like an entire tree's worth of dead leaves scattered all across the filthy floor. While Dog snuffled around the debris, Raif carefully removed the bow and arrows from his back. *Father's bow and arrows,* he reminded himself, handling them with all the care and gentleness he could muster. He propped them by the door, within arm's reach. He then used his boot to clear the floor, unrolling the blanket Evelyn gave him, looking from it to Rose with a raised eyebrow.

"Hmm, yes," he said, measuring it up against her. "I think I could wrap this round you a whole ten times! You'll be like a cosy little bug. Come here." He lunged at his sister but she darted away from his reach, letting out a high pitched giggle. Dog was by her side, panting and wagging his tail. Raif frowned in mock concern. "Don't you want to be warm?" He leapt for her again, blanket outstretched.

"No, Raif!" she cried, jumping aside once more, long skirts whipping around her tiny frame.

He froze, heart pounding as a lump engulfed his throat. They were the first words she'd spoken since finding Dog after the attack—and even that had only been a brief respite from her silence. He knelt down and held out his arms. "Come here," he said. "Promise I won't wrap you up."

Rose seemed to sense his sudden change in mood as she moved forward and nestled into his chest.

"Everything's going to be okay," he whispered, stroking her hair. "We have Evelyn to help us."

Rose pulled her head back and met his gaze, blue eyes bright and gleaming even in the darkness of the cabin. Raif nudged her chin with his finger and got to his feet.

"Let's get some sleep." He laid out the blanket and encouraged her towards it. "Go on." Rose obeyed, lying down and beckoning for Dog to join her.

They curled up together and both closed their eyes, the picture of innocence. "Goodnight," he said. And though she didn't say another word, Raif couldn't help but smile. She'd spoken. That had to be a good sign, didn't it? He tried hard to believe it. *We're going to be okay.*

Even without—

There was that lump again; a hard ball he tried—and failed—to swallow away.

Raif peered out of the window to distract himself. Evelyn was standing beside Bert and staring up at the sky, face cast in shadow. *Some luck at last. What would we have done if we hadn't found her?* His gut knotted at the thought. He felt the urge to go to Evelyn then—to ask her about Little Haven, to speak to someone else who knew about their home and what it had once been, anything to drive away his last memories of it, but something held him back. Perhaps the knowledge that his questions were likely to be met with questions in turn. He ran a hand through his hair, already growing out from the short cut his mother had been so excited to give him—*"You're almost a man now, Raif. You'll be responsible for going out hunting with your father, keeping your family safe."* She had still ruffled his hair afterwards though, just like when he was young, and he'd gently pushed her aside with an embarrassed groan.

As if to drive the bittersweet memory away, images of that last horrific night in Little Haven flashed into his mind. *No. Not now. Please.* If he was to even begin properly thinking about the attack, to try and make sense of what happened, he needed rest. As if on cue, he let out a jaw-cracking yawn, vision blurring. *Sleep,* he thought. *Worry about everything else in the morning.*

He dropped to his knees, crawling in beside Rose and pulling his cloak and the blanket around them both.

Despite the agony in his heart, he was asleep almost as soon as he laid his head down.

It wasn't long before his sleeping mind took him back to that terrible night once more.

The smoke was thick and billowing, the fire burning bright as it consumed the Elders' hut. The flames licked high, colouring the sky so the whole world seemed ablaze. Raif clutched his sister in his arms as he backed further into the shadows beside their hut, pressing her head against his shoulder so she didn't see what was happening.

"Keep your head down," he said to her, though he couldn't be sure she could hear his words over the furious shouts, terrified cries, crackling flames. "Oh, please, where are they ..."

He squinted against the choking grey cloud, trying to see their mother and father amongst the chaos of other villagers, of armoured men on horseback with red cloaks streaming behind them, their swords poised for attack. The soldiers appeared to be herding the villagers like cows, directing them to stand in a line. But they hadn't seen Raif and Rose yet—it had to remain that way, Raif knew, even as he desperately searched for their parents.

They should have been together; would have been, if Father hadn't forced the two of them beneath the bed as they were awoken from their sleep by shouts from the forest.

"In the name of the Grand Magister, you are commanded to submit!"

"Stay here, keep quiet. I'll come back for you," Father said.

But he didn't come back, and soon Raif's fear overtook his obedience, especially as the smoke began to creep beneath the door of their hut. "Come on, Rose," he'd said, picking up his sister and sneaking from their hut. He could already picture Father's disappointed face, Mother's shaking head and crossed arms. But at least they would all be together. Everything would be fine once they were together.

Yet the illusion was shattered in an instant as Raif looked out on the terrified faces of the other villagers. He realised then—had a terrible, gut-wrenching surety—that nothing would ever be fine again. He couldn't help, couldn't stop this. He remained where he was for a moment, wished there was someone to tell him what to do. But then a cool breeze gusted through the village and, with the brief lifting of smoke, his mind cleared.

Rose. He still held her clutched against him, so small and light for her age—like a tiny, delicate bird. Their eyes locked in that moment and, though the distant flames cast a shadow across her young face, he saw clearly his own fear reflected back at him. He squeezed her tightly. He would get her away from here, then he would come back for Mother and Father.

Before he could change his mind, Raif darted into the treeline of Haven Forest behind their hut. He knew the track well, even in the darkness of night—he and Rose had played there often when he was younger. Of late, Father had been taking him on daily hunts. "You're fourteen, son," he'd said. "You must learn how to provide for your family."

Raif almost choked as he recalled the words; he had to be the man his father expected him to be. He had to keep his sister safe.

He guided Rose into the base of a great, ancient oak tree some distance from the village—her favourite place to hide—and stood to gulp in some fresh air, legs quivering. He wanted to scream, to get in beside Rose and squeeze his eyes shut and wait for this nightmare to pass.

Just a few minutes to rest, he told himself. *Then I'll go back.* He nestled down beside the tree, reaching his hand in to hold Rose's and laying his head on the ground.

Father.

Oh, Father. I'm sorry.

Raif groaned, bolting upright, sweat dampening the fresh tunic Bessie had given him. He'd somehow entangled himself in a mess of cloak and blanket, tugging both away from his sister as he thrashed in his sleep. He freed himself, leaning over to check on Rose. To his relief she slept soundly, breathing slow and deep. Raif stood, tucking the blanket back around his sister before stretching his arms over his head. No sense in trying to sleep again; not when his mind would only continue to taunt him with those dreadful memories.

Outside, the sky was beginning to lighten, streaks of pink and orange spreading out like stains of blood. He glimpsed around the cabin, expecting to find Evelyn asleep in her own corner, but she was nowhere to be seen. *Perhaps she's risen already.* Dog lifted his head and let out a gentle whine.

"Stay there, boy," Raif whispered. "Look after Rose."

Outside, the air was refreshing against his sweat-moistened skin. He lifted his face to the sky and allowed it to wash over him, to blow away the sadness and guilt his nightmare had once more dragged to the surface.

"Can't sleep?" Evelyn emerged from the shadows beside the cabin, startling him back to the present.

Raif puffed air through his lips. "I, um, had a bad dream." He looked down at her; this close, he could see the smudges of purple beneath her amber coloured eyes, the freckles dotted across her nose and cheeks. "What about you?"

Evelyn shrugged, flicking the worn green cloak at her back with the movement. "I wanted to make sure we weren't found," she said. "I didn't want anything to happen to you two. I promised Bessie." She jutted out her jaw, daring him to question her.

Raif dropped his gaze, scuffing his boot against the ground. "Thank you," he said. "For everything. I should have asked you about keeping watch. I was just … it's just, since the attack, I've been keeping Rose safe. Haven't slept well. Didn't want to, really. I was so tired." He gulped, aware he was rambling. "Sorry."

"Don't worry," she said. "I needed some time to think anyway." Her gaze lingered on his face for a moment before she continued. "Do you want to tell me about it? The attack?"

Raif pushed his hair back from his face, chewing his lip. *I'll have to speak about it eventually.* "Okay," he said. "But first I need to …" He shuffled on the spot, holding his hands over his lower stomach to indicate the urgency of his full bladder.

"Oh," Evelyn said. "Of course. I'll be behind the cabin when you're done."

Once he'd relieved himself, Raif joined her in what appeared to be a well-used camping site. There were large, worn logs positioned for sitting alongside a round pit ringed with fist-sized rocks.

"Found some dry kindling," Evelyn said, indicating a pile of bark, dry leaves, twigs and branches beside her. Raif watched as she began building up the fire; starting with bark and dry leaves, jamming a thick branch into the ground and leaning the other twigs and branches around it.

"Seems like you've done this before," he commented, admiring her deft movements.

Evelyn let out a brief laugh. "You could say that. I used to come here to collect mushrooms for Bessie," she said. "I'd sometimes stay for the night. It was good to get away. Have some space to myself, when things at the tavern got a bit …" She glanced up at him, cheeks flushing. "Sorry, you don't want to hear about that." She retrieved a small loop of metal and chunk of flint from a pouch at her waist.

She leant forward, striking the metal against the flint, sparks flying. As the dried leaves and bark caught, the flame took hold. It was small at first, growing rapidly to consume the skeletal outline of the kindling. He turned away, unable to look upon it without thinking of Little Haven.

Evelyn placed the metal and flint back in her belt pouch before standing to brush the dried leaves and mud from the knees of her brown trousers. "So, what happened to Little Haven? I mean, if you feel okay telling me about it. You don't have to speak about it if you're not—"

"No," he said sharply. "It's fine, I just need a moment to …" He trailed off, trying to gather his scattered thoughts.

"I'll get us something to eat and drink." Evelyn moved towards the horse tied up nearby. As she rifled through his saddlebags, Raif closed his eyes.

I can't talk about Father.

Not yet.

"You said the village was attacked," Evelyn said, handing him a chunk of bread and a wrinkled apple. "That everyone was gone."

"Mm," Raif said. He placed the food on his lap and held his hands over the fire, grateful for its heat despite the memories it stirred within him. "Well, I, uh … I don't know why we were attacked or who the men were."

"But you recognised those men at the tavern?" Evelyn asked, eyes ablaze. "Their red cloaks?"

"Y-yes, I think so."

Evelyn nodded her head, chewing on her bread as her eyes grew distant. "The Commune," she muttered.

Raif's heart skipped a beat—the very name his father had said before he'd … He narrowed his eyes at Evelyn. "What was that?"

"The Commune soldiers." Evelyn's eyes locked with his own. "That's who they were."

He frowned. "What do you know about them?"

"Why? Have you heard of them?" She raised her eyebrows. "I only learned about them once I left the village. Bessie told me about them. They hunt down children with powers."

"Powers?" Raif shook his head. "I don't know anything about that. What do you mean powers?"

"For now, all you need to know is that we have to avoid the Commune at all costs. We have to be careful. I'm going to help you both as much as I can, but we need to stay alert." Evelyn prodded at the fire with a stick, embers drifting into the early morning air. "And if you can tell me all you know about the attack, that might help."

Raif took a deep breath to steel himself. "It started with shouting. It was late, we'd all been asleep. Father told us to hide." He told Evelyn about everything up to the moment he'd chosen to rest beside the oak tree. His leg fidgeted as he admitted his delay in returning to the village, ashamed at his own cowardice. "I should have gone back sooner, I know that now. I was just so …" He banged his fist against the log on which he sat.

"Raif," Evelyn said softly. "You can't blame yourself for what happened."

He glanced up, wanting to believe her words. *She doesn't know about Father,* he reminded himself. *She doesn't know everything.*

"Did you hear me?" she said, moving to sit beside him. "It's not your fault. You can't control what other people do." Her eyes clouded, dulling her fiery gaze for the briefest of moments. She stood, marching back and forth. "Those bastards need to pay for what they've done to you and Rose." She paused, turning back to face him. "Did anyone else survive?"

"I … I don't know." Raif pulled off a piece of crumbly bread and placed it in his mouth, chewing slowly, tasting nothing.

"Please," Evelyn said. "There were people there who … Well, it would be good to know. It was my home once."

He placed his food back on his lap. "When I woke up, I went back to the village. I don't know how much time had passed, but it was getting light." *Stupid, stupid, too late.* He ran a hand across his face, imagining she would somehow be able to read his thoughts, sense his burning guilt.

"What did you find?" she asked, sitting beside him again. It was oddly comforting to have her so close. Here was someone he could speak to more openly than he could his sister, who he had to shield from the truth of what had happened. She was too young to know.

"Everyone was gone. Taken, I think. There were no, uh, bodies—that I could see, anyway. Except ..." *Father.* His throat became strangely constricted. "I- I found, um ..."

Evelyn made to place a hand on his knee but drew it back at the last second, instead picking up the end of her cloak and twisting it between her hands. She exhaled. "I'm sorry," she said. "This must be hard for you."

Just say it.

"I found Tomas." The words came out quickly, bursting forth like a loosed arrow, as if that would somehow make them less real.

"Tomas?" Evelyn's brow furrowed. "I remember him. Dark hair, broad shoulders. Gave me my sword." She touched the scabbard on her belt. "What happened?"

"Shot in the back," he said. "Three arrows." Raif flushed hot. Father always said you had to look your prey in the eye when you killed it. You had to be willing to do that. "He promised to teach me with the practice swords soon, now that I'd started hunting with ..."

"Poor man," Evelyn said. "Must've tried to fight back." She pulled her cloak tighter between her hands, knuckles paling. "And everyone else was gone? Your parents? The Elders? *Everyone?*"

Raif stiffened. "Um, y-yes." Evelyn nodded, lips pursed, and held out the waterskin for him. He took it and gulped down the icy liquid, hoping that doing so might wash away the thoughts of his father.

"They took everyone," he said, staring into the fire, hoping she wouldn't detect the tremble in his voice, the truth he concealed. "Our parents, they might still be alive." *Mother, at least. She has to be. I couldn't cope if ...* He clenched his fists. "They have them. We have to get them back, Evelyn. Well, *I* have to. For Rose."

She met his gaze and, to his relief, didn't show the slightest hint of amusement or disbelief. "I'll help you," she said. "I wonder where they've been taken." She stared blindly into the distance, as lacking in answers as he was.

Raif suddenly felt very small and helpless. "I don't know." He let out a long and weary sigh. "What do you think it means, all this?"

Evelyn shook her head, releasing the ends of her cloak. "I don't know, Raif. I'm sorry. I wish I did."

He hadn't believed she would have an answer to that, not really—but he had hoped.

"But we'll do what we can to find out." Evelyn squared her jaw. "Bessie told us where to go. Castleton—to find this man called Mak, this Veritas group. I trust Bessie with my life. She won't have sent us there without reason."

"Okay." Raif allowed the ghost of a smile to flicker across his lips, flooded with a sense of absurd gratitude at having the decision-making removed from his shoulders.

They sat in silence for a time. Raif finished his bread and apple, feeling lighter, somehow, for having spoken to Evelyn. But a weight still remained over him for the words unspoken. He swallowed down the last of his apple and threw the core aside. At that moment, he heard the sounds of movement inside the hut. He glanced at Evelyn. "That's Rose," he said. "Do you mind checking she's okay? I need a moment to ..."

"Oh." Evelyn frowned. "Of course." Raif hurried away from the campfire and into the surrounding trees, aware of her watching him with concern in her eyes.

Once he'd lost sight of the fire, Raif leant against the thick, moss-covered trunk of a tree, breath coming in desperate, gulping gasps. He hadn't cried since that night, not properly. He hadn't been able to; he'd told himself he must stay strong for Rose. He'd promised his father.

"Father," he whispered, lower lip quivering. He slumped to the ground. "I'm sorry." He curled in on himself, resting his head down as the tears began to flow. With his guard dropped, the memories once more flooded his mind, forcing their way into his waking thoughts as they had his dreams the night before.

Beside the oak tree, Raif sat up with a start. How long had he been asleep? No time to dwell on it.

"Stay here," he said to Rose. "I'll be back soon."

He ran back in the direction of Little Haven, driven by a terrible, heart-clenching panic. In the early morning sun, the drifting smoke soon came into view. The forest was filled with it, the stench catching in his throat and stinging his eyes. In the eerie stillness, he stumbled past the tree line and into the village.

He came across Tomas's body first, face down in the dirt, the tails of three arrows protruding from his back. He couldn't look for long, alarm and terror already threatening to send him fleeing back into Haven Forest. He had to keep his head until he'd found Mother and Father. Then they could go back to Rose together.

"I'll find them," he whispered. "Please, please."

He made for their hut, hope rapidly floundering.

Too late, I'm too late.

Raif touched a hand to the door, letting it creak open as dread tightened his stomach. He held his breath as his eyes adjusted to the dimness inside.

There was a trail of blood, leading back to …

"Father," he croaked.

He was leaning against the wooden bed pallet. His face, once alight with kindness, lined with laughter, was drawn and ashen. His tunic was stained red, hands covering his stomach in a futile attempt to stem the flow of blood. Raif collapsed to the floor and crawled to him, choking back tears.

As he drew closer, he saw his father's chest fluttering with shallow breaths.

Still alive.

"Father?" Raif rushed forward, touching a hand to his father's cheek; it was cool to the touch. His grey eyes fluttered open, unfocused gaze finding Raif.

"Ra- Raif. Son."

Raif placed a hand upon his father's. "It's me. I've got Rose. We're both safe." Tears flowed down his cheeks. He wasn't sure if his father heard what he said.

"Protect Rose," he wheezed. "She- she has … They want her … Promise me."

"I promise, Father. I promise."

"The Commune. Everyone's been taken … Run, Raif. Run." He squeezed his eyes shut, groaning, struggling for breath. "Everyone taken. Run."

"The Commune? Who are they? Where is Mother?" But his father's eyes drifted to look somewhere behind Raif. With a final exhale, his head slumped.

"No, no, no. Father, please, no." Raif's body was wracked with sobs. He rested his head against his father's shoulder, wishing with all his might that this was a nightmare from which he would soon wake.

He remained frozen that way for a time, minutes feeling like hours as the tears fell, dampening his father's bloodied tunic.

Eventually, he dragged himself away. He had to stop crying, had to be strong. He must return to Rose and protect her like he'd promised.

Run.

Rose couldn't know about this until the time was right. She was only six— too young to be burdened with such knowledge. They might yet find their mother. There was still a chance of that.

There had to be.

There was no sense in lingering here any longer—no further answers to be found.

The Commune. Who were they? Why had they done this? He shook his head, too numbed by shock to even begin to comprehend the questions.

He stood and began gathering what he could from the hut. He strapped his father's hunting bow and arrows across his back, picked up a scrap of cloth in which to wrap the last of their bread. The village store had been destroyed with the Elders' hut, there would be no other food to salvage. He picked up a water skin to fill from a nearby stream.

Before he left, he dragged Tomas' body into the hut, laying the blacksmith inside the door. Though it left him weak, shaking with exhaustion, and drenched with sweat, he couldn't have done otherwise. He wouldn't leave Tomas and his father to be torn apart by scavengers.

Raif retrieved an unlit torch before giving his father one final glance. "Goodbye," he said, pushing through the door one last time. He lit the torch on the still-smouldering remains of the Elders' hut. As though floating through a dream, he moved back to his hut and held the flames to the door, waiting for them to catch. He felt nothing as they climbed upwards with surprising speed. Perhaps the entire village would burn; perhaps that was for the best.

His father was gone. His home was gone. Little Haven was no more. He would go back to Rose, and they would run.

5

Evelyn

Evelyn watched Raif disappear into the trees, fighting the urge to call him back, to say something—anything—that might help alleviate the pain he was trying so hard to hide. *I know what it is to suffer in silence,* she wanted to say. *I know what you're going through.* But, of course, she didn't. While the attack on Little Haven had left a near-tangible mark upon him, Evelyn lived with an empty void in her heart. She had long since cut herself off from Little Haven and everyone in it—there'd been no choice if she was to continue on without being driven mad by the pain.

As if on cue, a craving for wine snaked into her mind, restlessness and agitation its constant companion. She scrunched her face, furious at her own weakness. *Need to stop thinking of myself.* She stretched her arms above her head, trying her best to drive away the invasive desire for alcohol. *Focus. Perhaps I can help Raif deal with what he's been through. Perhaps it'll help me to feel less—*

Evelyn startled at the sound of rustling behind her. Rose peeked round the corner of the cabin, smiling shyly, her dog urinating against the base of a nearby tree.

"Morning," Evelyn said. "Would you like something to eat?"

Rose nodded, blonde curls bobbing.

"Come and get warm by the fire." Evelyn retrieved some more bread and an apple from Bert's saddlebag, hoping Raif wouldn't be too long. "So ..." she said, handing over the food as she took a seat. She rubbed a hand across her tunic. "Um, Bessie baked the bread."

The young girl ate without a word. Evelyn watched her, seeing how small she was beneath a mass of faded brown fabric. She smiled and shook her head. Trust Bessie to put her in a heavy-skirted dress that dragged on the muddy ground, drowning the poor girl in layers of material. Evelyn decided she'd have her in trousers as soon as possible. Far more practical—though Bessie had never agreed.

"So, um …" *I wonder how much she knows about the attack. Best not mention it.* Evelyn glanced around, desperate to find some inspiration in their surroundings. *Bessie would have known what to say.* Her eyes settled on the black dog sitting close by, his focus glued to the bread Rose was chewing. Evelyn cleared her throat. "Have you, have you had him for long?"

Rose shook her head. The dog let out an excited bark as he was given some bread, licking the crumbs from the young girl's hand.

"Oh, okay." Evelyn sat back on the log, kicking her legs outwards. *Come on, idiot, say something.* "What's, er, what's his name?"

"Dog," Rose said. Her voice was so soft it was almost drowned out by the sounds of the forest around them.

"Dog?"

Rose nodded, brow furrowed as though waiting for Evelyn to question her beloved pet's name.

"Well I don't suppose I'll forget that."

Suddenly, the young girl's head snapped in the direction her brother had walked. "Raif," she said.

"Oh, he had to go and—"

"He's sad." Rose met Evelyn's gaze with a seriousness belying her youth.

Evelyn shivered, hair along her arms standing on end. "Yes, I think he might be," she said wondering what had caused the odd sensation. Before she had time to think on it, Raif emerged from the trees, eyes bloodshot and cheeks mottled red.

Rose darted towards him, nearly knocking him to the ground in her eagerness to hug him. His eyes lit up, a lop-sided smile brightening his face. "It's okay," he said, chuckling. Evelyn averted her eyes, uncomfortable with the jealousy rising within her. She'd never had a family, not really. Not until she met Bessie, and now she was—

Gone.

The wave of grief was sudden, knocking the wind from her in an instant. She leant her head down, pressing the heels of her palms into her eyes—*don't cry, don't cry*—as the sound of Bessie's gut-wrenching shriek echoed through her mind.

I can't do this. I'm not good enough.

Bessie's round face appeared in her mind, hazel eyes gleaming. *"You can do it, Evelyn. I know you can."*

"Evelyn?"

A hand touched her shoulder and she flinched. She looked up to find Raif, hand held awkwardly in front of him as though he'd been scalded. "Sorry," he mumbled. "I just wanted to make sure you were—"

"I'm fine," Evelyn said. She stood, straightening her cloak and tunic. "We should go. It'll take a while to reach Castleton."

Raif nodded—though the glimmer of hurt remained in his bloodshot eyes. "Okay, I'll get everything from the cabin." He moved away, followed closely by Rose and Dog.

Evelyn smothered the campfire and untied Bert. *Idiot. You can't keep them at a distance forever.* They needed her, didn't they? She'd just decided to help Raif bear his pain, hadn't she? She took a long, slow exhale, misting the cool morning air with her breath. Bessie believed she could help them. That had to be enough.

An hour or so into their walk eastward, she found herself studying the bow and arrows strapped to Raif's back.

"They're good quality," she said. "Will be helpful."

"Hmm?" Raif peered over his shoulder, hand drifting to touch the bow. "They were my father's. He started teaching me before he, uh … before the attack. I'm not very good though." He gave an apologetic smile, as though she'd expected him to be an expert hunter.

"That's okay. I know a bit about using them. I was taught by …" She stopped herself, afraid the name might lead Raif to finally realise the reason for her flight from Little Haven. Hoping her hesitation had gone unnoticed, she said, "I can teach you, if you like."

A flash of pain passed over Raif's face, quickly blinked away. He bowed his head, running a hand through his hair. "I, uh … Yes, yes please. That'd be good." He smiled at her and she smiled back and, for that moment at least, it seemed everything might be okay.

Evelyn set a swift pace that day, intent to put as much distance between them and the tavern as possible—as though doing so might somehow relieve the grief that washed over her again and again.

Along their way, they passed other travellers—farmers, merchants, peddlers, beggars, men and women old and young. Each seemed eager to avoid meeting Evelyn's suspicious glare. She recalled a conversation with Bessie once, as they'd shared some hot chicken pie and a glass of sweet wine. "*It's those who meet your eye you must be most worried about,*" she'd said. "*For you'll soon find they're the ones with the least to lose.*" Of course, that had been about negotiating with travelling merchants who brought their wares into the tavern, but she supposed the sentiment remained the same and took comfort from the hurried steps and downcast faces of those whose paths they crossed, even if a niggling sense of unease gave the occasional sharp prod at the back of her mind.

At one point, they passed a small group of Nomarrans, eyes down and huddled together as though they daren't separate even by a few feet. Evelyn thought back to the Nomarran man in the tavern, to the look that had passed between him and Bessie. Had he known what Bessie planned to do? The danger she risked by helping Raif and Rose?

Why didn't he help?

But something told her there was a much bigger game being played, one for which she could scarcely guess the rules.

Evelyn watched the Nomarrans disappear behind them, stomach knotting ever tighter.

As they walked, she did what she could to quell her rising anxiety, trying to make herself, Raif, and Rose as insignificant as possible. She kept their pace steady, not passing others too quickly, not lingering anywhere too long, taking turns on the horse to make as much progress in their journey as possible. *Don't make eye contact, don't look back, appear comfortable on your own feet.*

On one occasion, Raif and Rose stopped to gawp at the wares of a travelling pedlar. Such a man would have been a celebrated visitor in Little Haven, so she could hardly blame them. But when Evelyn realised what was happening, she marched over to hurry them on, glaring towards the grubby-clothed old man who blinked back at her with what she could only assume to be mock innocence. Even when she saw the half-full wineskin he had on offer, she pulled Raif and Rose away, resisting her own selfish urges.

He'd take them if he could, she told herself. *We can't trust anyone.*

"Don't do that again," she whispered to them both.

I hope you were right about me, Bessie.

As the sun began to set, they crossed a cobblestoned bridge over the rushing waters of the Crystal River and before long, they found themselves approaching a dense wooded area.

Glad at the promise of shelter from the rising wind, Evelyn drew Bert to a halt. She studied the tree line and surrounding road to ensure they weren't being followed. "In here," she called to Raif and Rose, walking ahead with Dog. "We can rest."

"What is this place?" Raif asked, pulling Rose closer to his side.

The trees were close-set, branches entangled above their heads, underbrush thick and untrodden beneath their feet. It could only be one place. "The Old Oak Woods," she said. "Bessie told me stories of it. Few people dare to venture past the border." She raised a playful eyebrow, hoping to lighten the mood. "I was told it's haunted."

Raif's eyes widened. "Haunted?" He rubbed his arms. "It feels—"

"Strange, I know. Perhaps there's something to those tales. But at least that means we won't be disturbed. Not by people, at least." She grinned, hoping he'd understand the jest.

Instead, he clutched Rose's hand tightly and muttered, "I s'pose so," as he glanced into the shadow-filled forest around them.

Evelyn chuckled. "Don't worry. I'll do my best to keep the phantoms away." She drew her sword and focused her gaze ahead. "Come on. I'm sure we'll find somewhere clear enough to camp."

She used her sword to clear a path as best she could. Even so, their progress was slow, clothes snagging on thorny bushes, feet catching on jutting roots. On the odd occasion, Bert refused to go a certain direction so they had to divert their path. *Ghosts aren't real,* Evelyn told herself as prickles ran down her back. *Don't be so foolish.* Still, she kept her eyes fixed on the path ahead, afraid of what she might find staring back at her if she dared look round.

Finally, sweaty, scratched, and shaking, Evelyn emerged into a great circular clearing amongst the ancient trees. "At last," she said, smiling back at Raif and Rose. "Here, didn't I say? Somewhere to camp." She spread her arms wide. "Plenty of room." She peered round, trying to ignore how peculiar the area was; a perfect circle, as though carved out for some long-forgotten ritual.

Too weary to allow superstition to overcome reason, she clapped her hands. "Raif," she said, "find some firewood. Rose, fill these up from that stream we just passed." She handed over the waterskins before tying Bert's reins to a sturdy, low-hanging tree branch. "Good boy," she whispered to the old horse, stroking his chestnut brown nose. "You'll keep watch over us, won't you?" He let out a gentle whicker.

When they were all sitting cross-legged around a small campfire, Evelyn unfolded the knapsack Bessie had packed and retrieved more bread, hard cheese, and salted pork. She felt a pang of longing for some sweet wine; just a little to ease her racing mind and aching body.

"I remember when you left Little Haven," Raif said, brushing the crumbs from the front of his tunic.

Evelyn's stomach lurched. She swallowed the bread she was chewing. Here it was. She couldn't avoid it forever. *Say as little as possible. Don't raise his suspicions.* "I- I had no choice."

"You were missed. Our mother was always fond of you, wasn't she, Rose?" The young girl didn't respond, too busy teasing Dog with her dinner to pay attention to their conversation.

Evelyn grunted. "I doubt that," she snapped. *No one in that place cared I was gone.*

Least of all—

"She spoke about you," Raif insisted, brow furrowing. "After you were gone. She tried to have the Elders send someone out looking for you. She was worried. That's how I knew we could trust you."

Evelyn saw the sincerity in his eyes and regretted her harsh tone, though she had to hold back a scoff of disbelief. *No one has ever worried about me. Why would they?* But she also knew that Raif wasn't responsible for what had happened.

Agitated, she stood and paced around, casting her eyes across the canopy of the woods. In the growing darkness, individual trees were barely discernible, as though forming a vast, impenetrable wall around them.

"I ..." She clenched her jaw. Her instincts to stay quiet silenced her desire to explain. *He'll never understand.* "Get some sleep. We'll rise early, make as much progress as we can tomorrow."

Raif frowned. "I'm sorry, I didn't mean to upset you." He turned his back on her, settling Rose down on the ground and lying beside her, blanket draped across them both.

Evelyn rolled her eyes. He didn't know what she'd been through—why she was how she was. He might trust her but that didn't guarantee she could trust him.

I could run. They don't need me, not really. But she stayed, rooted to the spot as she watched the gentle rise and fall of their backs. *A promise.* It was all she had to link her back to Bessie. The only person who'd believed in her—who believed she *was* good enough. She had to see it through, no matter what.

She sat and watched the fire burning, knees drawn up to her chest and head resting on her knees. The flames were hypnotic, their heat washing over her, scorching away the memories of everything that had happened.

I'll keep my promise, Bessie. It was the last thought in her mind as she drifted into a deep sleep.

Evelyn shivered, sure that something was wrong even before she had fully woken.

"Shit." She sat up, taking in the burnt-out embers of the untended fire and the lightness of the sky. *Raif and Rose.* She crawled over to them. *Asleep.* She sighed with relief, surprised at the tension that lifted from her shoulders once she knew they were safe.

She stood and stretched, recalling that Bessie had packed some of her apple pie. She'd been saving it. They'd share it for breakfast, discuss what they might find in Castleton. With a night of sleep, she felt far better focused, more positive than she had since they'd left the tavern. *Things will be okay.*

She took a step towards Bert and froze.

Two men were sitting at the far side of the clearing.

"Awake at last," called one, skinny and hard-faced. "Slept well, I hope."

Evelyn darted to Raif and Rose, squatting down to shake them. Meanwhile, the men stood. The skinny man walked with slow, calculated movements, while the other man, tall and barrel-chested, loped behind with a broad grin on his face.

Shit, shit, shit.

"Ow. Evelyn, what are you—"

"Up," she said.

Raif saw the men, mouth dropping open. "Rose, quick," he said, dragging his half-conscious sister away.

"Get behind the horse," Evelyn said. She made sure they obeyed before turning towards the men. As they drew closer, she backed towards Bert, stopping when she felt his heat at her back. Dog was at her feet, hackles raised, ears pinned back. He let out a deep growl as the men came to a stop in front of them.

The skinny man's eyes flitted across them all, pink tongue flicking over thin lips. "Well, what do we have 'ere?"

"We're leaving now," Evelyn said, glad, at least, that she was able to keep the tremble from her voice. "Let us be on our way and we'll cause no trouble."

The skinny man smirked. "Won't cause any trouble, she says." He elbowed the large man beside him, eyes glinting with cruel amusement. "I should think not. But, y'see, children shouldn't be travellin' alone in these parts. Dangerous, innit, Chet?"

Chet nodded, snorting with glee. "Dangerous," he repeated. "Dangerous, Rommy."

"So," Rommy continued, "seems to me you three might be in need of our 'elp. Wouldn't want to leave you out 'ere all alone, what with so much danger lurking about." He smiled, lips peeling back over teeth brown with rot. Evelyn moved her hand to the hilt of her sword; his eyes followed.

"I'm not a child," she said. "I'm the, the protector of these two. I'm taking them to their parents in Castleton." She puffed out her chest, meeting his gaze. For a brief moment, the man must have seen something in her face to make him pause.

Good, she thought. *Perhaps he senses it inside me.*

The darkness, the powers I used to—

"Evelyn," Raif whispered, peering round from behind Bert. "Are you okay?"

"Raif, don't—"

"Everything's fine, *Raif,*" Rommy said, regaining himself. "Chet." The larger man snapped to attention.

"Yes, Rommy?"

"You can't stop us from travelling," Raif said, standing side-by-side with Evelyn. "It's like she said, we're going to our parents. We have every right to—"

"I think you'll find, *boy,* we are simply doing our job. By the Grand Magister's behest, we hunt down stray children. No parents 'ere to protect you. You're *ours.*" His eyes lingered on Evelyn, willing her to argue. "Bet you thought you was safe in these woods, eh? The locals stay away, it's true. Bloody fools believe the tales of ghosts, phantoms, and ghoulies." He barked a laugh, spitting at her feet. "But we ain't local, are we, Chet?"

The large man guffawed. "No, we ain't."

Evelyn swallowed. She had the option to use her powers, didn't she? She'd done it before, what was to stop her now? But she knew the answer to that: Raif and Rose. *What will they think of me?* It had been two years since she'd last called upon them. Did she even know how to do it again?

"I can see you're beginning to understand the situation." Rommy moved closer, stinking breath washing over Evelyn's face. "We 'aven't eaten in a while. Times are 'ard, ain't they, Chet? We think it'd be real nice of you to share what food you 'ave strapped to that horse o' yours."

"Don't take another step forward," Evelyn said, drawing her battered sword. "We'll be on our way."

The men's laughter echoed across the clearing. "Powers above, Chet, we've got ourselves a fuckin' fighter 'ere. Watch out."

While the large man chuckled with genuine amusement, Rommy's laugh didn't reach his eyes. His dark, greedy gaze remained focused on Evelyn's face.

She'd seen that look before; she knew what it meant. Her stomach tightened, bile rising in her throat.

"I'd leave that, boy, if you know what's best for you." Rommy clicked his fingers at Raif, who was trying to retrieve his bow from Bert's saddlebags.

Damn it, Raif. Stop trying to be brave. She glared at him, signalling for him to move back to Rose before jerking her sword towards the skinny man. "I mean it. Get back," she said, pointing the blade at Rommy's bony chest. He sneered, unperturbed by her poised weapon. She watched in horror as he grabbed the blade with a skeletal hand, pushing it down with surprising strength. There was no pain in his eyes, even as blood leaked between his fingers.

He's mad.

I've no choice. Evelyn braced herself, trying to recall how she had summoned the immense strength two years ago.

Suddenly, Chet lurched forward, alarmingly fast for a man of his size. He grabbed Raif by the arm, dragging him away from Rose.

"No, Raif!" the young girl screeched, trying to follow. Dog growled and snapped at Chet's feet.

"Stay back, Rose!" Evelyn cried. She turned to Chet. "Please, don't hurt him."

Raif kicked and punched, trying in vain to free himself. It was useless; he was no match for the man's height and strength. Chet's arms were pinned across Raif's chest, holding him in place with remarkable ease. The large man moved away, gripping his prize. Meanwhile, Rommy's hand was still wrapped around the blade of Evelyn's sword, blood now running down his arm and dripping onto the crisp leaves at their feet.

"We know just what to do with children such as you. Oh, yes. We'll 'ave a fine reward for the three o' you, I'm sure. The Grand Magister is sure to be pleased. But first, you and I're goin' to 'ave a little *fun*. A little somethin' to put you in your place." He stepped forward, close enough to see the tiny, broken veins on his face, the yellow tinge in his eyes.

"Don't fight," he said. "It'll be over faster that way." Quick as a flash of lightning, Rommy released his grip on her sword and clamped his bloodied hand around her neck.

Behind him, Raif squirmed and groaned in Chet's arms. The large man grinned with delight. "Rommy, can I—"

"Go on," Rommy said over his shoulder. "Be quick about it." He turned back to Evelyn. "Now, for my own *reward*." The warmth of his blood ran down her neck, seeping into her tunic. She sucked in desperate breaths, flailing her sword arm in an attempt to strike him. *I won't let this happen. Not again.*

She swiped the sword again but it was useless. She grew weaker by the moment. *No.* She gritted her teeth. *Come on, please. Please.*

Her powers didn't respond. *Stupid, useless, pathetic.*

In her desperation, she allowed her mind to go back to that moment two years ago when they'd been unleashed. She even saw a flash of *his* face for a moment.

Nothing.

Arthur.

Fury burned in her heart to recall what he'd done. She hoped it would be enough. Reaching, *pushing*, her whole body was tensed, her mind focused entirely on her powers, yet still nothing happened.

There was no flare of certainty in her gut, no unstoppable force building within her.

No, no, just when I need you.

Shit.

They've gone.

Hair came loose from her braid as she struggled. She clenched her eyes closed, desperate to push away both the memories of her past and the reality of what was happening.

No, no, no.

Her strength began to drain as Rommy's grip tightened around her throat. The sword dropped from her grasp, its clatter muffled by the dried leaves underfoot. Raif had been dragged away, some part of her mind noted. There were shouts somewhere in the distance, echoing through the trees. A loud slap sounded.

Silence.

Bony hands groped at her tunic. *No, please, no.*

The thought was a whisper in the recesses of her mind now and growing fainter. *Not again, please.*

Her teeth chattered, so loud she thought they might shatter. "Please," she croaked. *Not again.*

As though able to read her thoughts, Rommy chuckled above her, rancid breath choking her. "Just let it happen. You know what's best."

No!

But the fear became all-consuming—she could no longer move, resigned to her fate.

It was best not to resist, to let it end, to retreat inside herself.

As her mind obliged and began to close itself away, she was distantly aware of the sound of fabric ripping. She lost consciousness for a moment then awoke to find herself slumped on the ground. Rommy's mouth was hot and moist on her neck as he pinned her down.

She noted with eerie clarity that a piece of broken branch was stabbing into her right shoulder blade—she focused on that. Her vision blurred, eyes filled with tears, throat rasped. She let out a quiet sob, the smell of stale sweat almost suffocating. She scrunched her face, trying not to gag.

"The Grand Magister's wisdom hasn't led us astray," Rommy hissed in her ear. "We'll be rich men, thanks to you."

She stared blankly up at him, his words no longer holding any meaning. He moved to undo his trousers, releasing his grip from her shoulders.

She was no longer pinned down.

Now was her chance.

A surge of anger fired up within her.

Evelyn pushed herself upwards with shaking arms, groping around for the sword.

"You little brat. I tell you when you can get up, d'you hear?" Rommy punched her, an explosion of pain across her cheek. The thud reverberated through her head, ears ringing, vision dimming.

It's too late.

As the darkness took hold, a high-pitched scream pierced the air.

Rose!

Rommy lurched backwards, dragged away from Evelyn by—

"Chet? What are you— No, Chet, no!"

There were screams of pain, sickening thuds, the smell of fresh blood filled the air.

Evelyn collapsed into the embrace of darkness.

6th Day of Solstice
13th Year of King Cosmo Septimus
33rd Year of Grand Magister Quilliam Nubira Antellopie III

For the eyes of His Benevolence
Grand Magister Quilliam Nubira Antellopie III

Grand Magister,

I am writing to inform you I have settled into my post in Castleton, as per your instructions. Needless to say, the nobles have been more than accommodating in welcoming a loyal servant of the Commune, and word has quickly spread since the day of our arrival here. They understand the necessity of your work; the chaos that would be allowed to spread should your control and wisdom not prevail.

In the city's Lower District, it was as you predicted. You will not be surprised to hear that traitors to the Commune have already been located; peasants and beggars who scorned our arrival, tore down our posters, spat at our comrades and loyal servants. You have my word that such treachery has been dealt with in the name of your benevolent justice. After several public executions, the bodies of the disloyal rot upon the walls of the city as a warning to all who would dare to defy your power.

We will continue to patrol the city, spreading your wisdom and upholding the Commune's law.

I shall await your further orders.

Your ever loyal and faithful soldier,

E.T.

6

Raif

Raif squinted his eyes against the bright, grey sky above as he regained consciousness, a moan escaping his lips.

Where am I?

Rose!

He jerked upright, head pounding. He looked around; still in the woods, but no sign of his sister or Evelyn or Dog, the horse or—

"The men." His head dropped back down to the earth, heart pounding.

Don't panic.

But his body disobeyed, vision blurring as he took short, sharp breaths. He scrunched his eyes shut, trying to calm himself. The right side of his face throbbed. He touched a tentative finger to it, wincing at the tenderness. There was no blood, at least. He dragged himself into a sitting position, straightening his cloak beneath him and leaning his back against a tree.

Okay, okay. You're okay.

Rose. Evelyn.

What happened? Where are they? Those men, they wanted to . . . Raif shuddered, wrapping his arms around himself, noticing his tunic was torn at the armpit. The trees swayed around him, the breeze whispering through their half-bare branches. A terrible sense of foreboding settled in his gut.

With sickening clarity, Raif recalled the great, barrel-chested man's grip around him, tight as a vice. The stench of stale sweat, the sound of the man's ragged, excited breaths in his ear.

Unable to hold it back, Raif bent over and vomited, tears streaming from his eyes.

He took a moment to gather himself, spitting in an attempt to clear the foul taste from his mouth.

Have to move. Find Rose.

Raif took a deep breath and stood. He scanned the area, trying to be vigilant even as his head remained heavy, his thoughts slow.

"Rose? Evelyn?" he called out, voice cracking.

Silence.

There was a track through the leaves. He followed it, wiping a hand across his running nose, flinching as he touched his bruised lip.

"Rose?"

No response.

"Evelyn?"

Nothing.

He kept moving forward with dogged determination. A rustling sound alerted him to movement ahead. Something—*someone*—was coming.

"No, no," he whispered. He fell to the floor, curling into himself, holding his hands over his head. The blood rushed in his ears, heart hammering a drumbeat of pure fear.

"Watch how the rabbit freezes, son. It knows of the danger it's in. It should run, save itself—but its own nature fights against it."

The rustling drew nearer.

No, no.

He trembled, awaiting the inevitable.

Heavy panting.

A rough tongue licked his hand.

Raif lifted his head. "Dog? Oh!" He pulled the animal into a rough hug, letting out a relieved cry. "Where's Rose? Do you know the way back?"

Dog barked, tail wagging. Raif nodded. "Let's go."

The black spaniel darted back the way he'd come, Raif close behind. It wasn't long before they arrived. The fire was cold, the horse still tied up, the blanket he and Rose had slept in strewn across the ground. The air was full of tension, the silence a near-tangible presence that pressed down on him.

Something nagged at him from the corner of his eye. He was afraid to turn and see what—

"Raif!" Evelyn called. Sheltered from sight behind the horse, she was huddled against a tree with Rose in her lap, both wrapped tightly within her green cloak.

Raif stumbled forward, dropping beside Evelyn and his sister. "Are you hurt?"

Evelyn shook her head, freckles stark against her pale skin. "We're okay," she said. She had a red welt on her cheek, her lips were white, eyes glazed. Rose was curled against her chest, blonde curls covering her face, dress and cloak twisted round her fragile body.

"Rose?" He leant down, pushing her hair aside.

"Raif," she whispered, reaching for him. He held his arms out and pulled her in.

"What happened?" he asked. Evelyn avoided his gaze. "Evelyn?"

Her head snapped towards him. She exhaled a shuddering breath. "Those men," she said. "Rose stopped them."

Raif scowled. "What do you mean?" His sister buried her head in his chest.

"I- I'm sorry, Raif," Evelyn whispered. "*I* should have been able to. I tried, I really did. I haven't used them in—" She let out an exasperated choking sound. "I didn't mean for her to- to do that. I didn't know she had them."

"What? Evelyn you tried what? Didn't know Rose had … ?"

Evelyn nodded her head across the clearing. "Over there," she said.

Raif placed his sister gently on the ground, turning to where she pointed. He had the absurd urge to laugh. This wasn't right, was it? How could this be real? But the laughter caught in his throat, stifled by terror. He moved forward, hoping—wishing—his eyes were deceiving him.

The men were still here. But they wouldn't hurt anyone else, ever again. He struggled to comprehend the scene, peering back at Evelyn over his shoulder, at his sister beside her.

Rose … did this?

He moved as close as he dared to examine the bodies. The skinny man— Rommy, had it been?—was a mess of blood and crushed bone, his face beaten beyond recognition. The large man—*stale sweat, heavy breathing*—lay next to him, knife still clutched in his outstretched hand, throat a ragged, gaping wound. And blood.

So much blood.

Raif held a hand over his nose as the smell hit him in a sudden wave; the deep, metallic scent intermingled with the acrid stench of urine and faeces— the overwhelming odour of death. He had never seen such a sight, never experienced it in such a visceral sense. Not even when his father had brought a deer back from the hunt and showed Raif how to drain, skin, and butcher it. He swallowed back his nausea as he turned his back on the bodies.

"No," he muttered, moving towards his sister as though through thick honey—limbs slow and awkward. "Evelyn, how?"

Please, after everything that's happened. This can't be real.

He knelt in front of Rose, holding a hand to her cheek. She met his gaze— she was still his sister, blue eyes full of innocence. *She can't have done this.* His mouth dropped open, then snapped shut again as he tried to align everything he knew. "H-how, how can you …" He dared to peer over his shoulder, towards the dead men. "You said Rose stopped them?" A mistake; it had to be. He'd misunderstood. "Did she distract them somehow?"

"I'm sorry," Evelyn said. She closed her eyes and laid her head back against the tree. "I should've known. Maybe I could've sensed it in her if I'd allowed mine to …" She let out a gentle groan. "Bessie was wrong." She let out a bitter laugh. Raif stood, agitation forcing him to move, not really comprehending Evelyn's words.

"But how could Rose possibly have done … *that?*" He waved his arm behind him, unable to look again.

"Protect Rose … They want her."

"She saved us, Raif," Evelyn said finally. Her amber eyes were bloodshot, hands fumbling at the edge of her cloak. "With her powers."

"Powers?" Raif gulped. "But didn't you say the Commune, they hunt those with …"

Evelyn nodded, lips pinching together. "This means we're in more danger than we thought."

Raif didn't know what to say. How could his sister have *powers? What does it even mean?* He knelt and held out his arms, allowing his sister to move into them once more. "Everything's fine," he whispered in her ear. He placed a gentle kiss on her head. This was Rose, his tiny, kind, gentle sister. Evelyn was confused, she had to be. And yet, even as he tried to convince himself, he couldn't ignore the sadness in Evelyn's eyes, her voice so full of apology and regret. He knew the truth then. Like a great, crushing storm, Raif felt the omen over their heads, waiting to unleash its full force.

This could change everything.

It already has.

"Come on," Evelyn said, pulling his attention back. "We need to leave."

Raif stood. "Yes, we do." He brushed the leaves from his trousers, straightened Rose's cloak and dress, and squeezed her shoulder. "Ready to go?"

She nodded briskly. Was her face paler than usual, or was he only imagining it in the dreary grey light of that late autumn morning?

As Evelyn eased herself up, Raif noticed the red hand marks round her neck and blood stains on her tunic.

"I thought you said you weren't hurt." He frowned, reaching out a hand to help her.

"I'm fine," she snapped, shunning his touch. "We have to move. We can find somewhere to talk away from here."

He withdrew his hand, raising an eyebrow. *She's in shock.*

In silence, they gathered themselves. Evelyn lifted Rose onto Bert while Raif scanned the area one final time. Before walking away, he looked back at the dead men. It was then he noticed a corner of white sticking out of the skinny man's threadbare trousers. Raif needed something, anything, to tell him why this had happened. He held his breath against the souring smells and marched towards them, leaning to pull the paper free.

The scroll was printed with the face of a young man, golden curls tumbling about his forehead, a red-jewelled crown on his head. He focused on the words beneath the face but they jumbled together as he tried to make sense of them. He thought about putting it back, too embarrassed to admit his difficulty reading—yet he couldn't shift the need for some clue, some logic, a reason that might explain this awful scene. He swallowed his pride.

"Evelyn," he called. "What's this?"

Her brow creased as she took the scroll from his hand. "It's a King's decree," she said, eyes flitting over the words. "He, um … It says he supports the Commune. He commands that any children with powers be taken to the Grand Magister. There's a reward." She scrunched it up, throwing it towards the bodies. "Bastards just wanted to make a quick penny from us."

Children with powers.

"No." Raif gasped. "Evelyn. Rose, she—"

"I know. But I'm going to do everything I can to protect her, okay? I made a promise to Bessie. And I promise you." She narrowed her eyes, defiance and pride intermingling in her gaze.

"O-okay," Raif said.

She leant down to retrieve her sword from the ground, wrinkling her nose as she attempted to remove the congealed blood from it using some leaves from the ground. Once it was as clean as possible, Evelyn sheathed it and gathered Bert's reins. "Come on."

She led them away from the clearing, away from the bodies of the men whose lives Rose had somehow ended.

Evelyn remained quiet on the journey towards Castleton.

As they walked, Raif tried desperately to block out the images of those two men, his father's words, the nagging feeling that everything was connected. He watched his sister as she ran ahead of them, long skirts streaming behind her as she played chase and catch with Dog, who clutched a large tree branch in his mouth. Raif couldn't merge the horrific way the men had died—the blood, *so much blood*, the violence and anger—with his younger sister, so sweet and kind and full of love.

He needed answers.

He sped up, falling in line beside Evelyn. Her hand tightened around Bert's reins, her shoulders tensed. She must have been waiting for this moment, perhaps hoping he'd choose not to question her. But he had to—this was his sister.

"Evelyn, please tell me," he said. "What happened?"

For a moment, she didn't respond. He thought she might ignore the question altogether, and tried to come up with ways to coax it from her. To make her trust him.

Children with powers.

"Protect Rose … They want her."

Over and over, those words whirred through his head. He was desperate for answers, yet also terrified of what Evelyn may know. Rose seemed so … well, *Rose.* Unaffected by what they'd left behind, what she'd apparently done. She was normal, happy, even—as much as she could be in their current situation. He watched her darting about the road ahead, running back and forth with Dog at her feet, not a care in the world.

"I know it will be difficult to hear," Evelyn said. "Believe me, Raif, it was hard to witness."

"What? What did you see?" Raif asked, heart suddenly pounding.

"He was on top of me, the skinny one." She swiped the back of her hand across her mouth. "Another moment and he would have … I tried to stop him, to use my …" She swallowed. "I tried to fight back. He hit me, I blacked out for a moment. And then I heard Rose scream. The skinny man was pulled away. He was shouting at his- his- the other one. Chet, the one who …" She met his eye, lips pursed. He nodded for her to continue. "They were … I don't know. It happened fast. But Rose saved me. She saved us both."

Raif screwed up his face, trying his hardest to recall his own memories. Blind panic, sheer terror. The large man crushing him. The more he'd struggled, the tighter he was squeezed. Eventually, he must have tired of Raif's struggles, slapping him across the face with a massive hand. That was the last he remembered. He ran a hand through his hair, eager to forget those images. "If Rose saved us, I need to know how."

Just then, a shrill giggle pierced the air as Rose dodged one of Dog's jumps. Raif's stomach flipped; it was a sound that should've made him happy but, just then, it hurt.

Evelyn glanced at him with a sad smile, an awkward condolence for the words she spoke next. "Rose, she was standing beside Bert. But her face, it was—" She shrugged, slapping her hands at her side. "I don't know. Different, somehow. She was staring at the men. Chet, the big one, was hitting the other one. Beating him to the ground. Kept going, even when the cries stopped. A part of me was glad." She inhaled sharply. "Perhaps that's wrong of me."

"No, I- I understand," Raif said, chewing his lip. "They- they wanted to hurt us, didn't they? Whatever happened to them, it meant we were saved." *Whatever Rose did to them.*

Evelyn met his gaze, mouth downturned. It was clear they both wanted to believe those words. "I shouted at Rose. She didn't seem to hear. I managed to stand up. Chet was pinning his friend down. He kept punching, beating, over and over again. I don't think I'll ever forget that sound."

Raif wished he had something to say, to offer Evelyn.

"He was dead—Rommy. Stopped moving. I realised we had to go before Chet saw us. I grabbed Rose, shook her by the shoulders. It broke her, uh, her concentration, I think. She looked at me, her face was back to normal. I asked her what she was doing. She didn't answer me. The large man stood up, I pushed Rose behind me. Told him to stay back but he was just staring at his hands—all the blood. He started crying—sobbing like a wounded animal, a terrified child. I told Rose we had to run, I tried to grab her hand." Evelyn's voice tightened. Raif remained silent, needing to know more.

"Rose wouldn't come with me," she said finally, composure regained. "She took my hand, looked up at me, and I was calm. The panic melted away. It was as though I was floating, watching the scene, unable to do anything to stop it. Rose focused on Chet, got *that* look again. His face dropped, mouth fell open. He didn't make a sound. He walked back towards the body of his- of Rommy. And then ..." She halted, pulling Bert to a stop and turning her gaze to the sky.

"Evelyn," Raif said. "What is it?"

"He reached for the knife in his friend's belt. Lifted it to his own neck. Drew it across his throat. Didn't make a sound as ..." The colour drained from her face and she rubbed her eyes.

"It's okay," Raif said, trying to believe himself.

Rose, what did you do?

She and Dog had stopped playing. Rose was investigating a small copse of blackberry bushes by the side of the rode. At her feet, Dog's tail wagged furiously as he waited for whatever treat she might scavenge for him.

Evelyn reached into Bert's saddlebag and retrieved a waterskin. She drank deeply and ran a hand across her chin. She laid a hand on the horse's nose before continuing. "Nothing else to say really. It was a blur until you came back. I don't know how long I was sitting there with Rose." She pulled her cloak tight around her arms. "I'm sorry."

"You don't need to apologise," Raif said. "What do you think it means?" He wasn't sure what he wanted from Evelyn. Reassurance, maybe. Some kind of comfort, though he couldn't see what could possibly provide any just then.

"What do you know of powers? Of the Commune?" Evelyn said, walking on once more.

The sudden change of subject took Raif by surprise.

The Commune.

"I …" He shrugged. *Still too soon to mention Father.* "Nothing other than what you've told me."

Evelyn turned her face away from him. "Bessie taught me about the Commune. They never told us about them in Little Haven, did they?" She snorted. "They never told us anything. They kept the truth from us." She glanced at Raif, face full of hatred. "Sorry, that doesn't matter now. Anyway, it was the first I'd heard about them. Bessie warned me. Told me what they wanted."

"And what *do* they want?" Raif asked, all the while hearing his father's last words echoing through his mind, over and over again. *"Protect Rose … They want her."*

"Like I said before, children with powers. Children like Rose."

"Children like Rose," Raif repeated. A flare of indignation coursed through him. "But Rose has never shown any sign of …" He scowled. "Well, not before today."

"I can't see any other explanation, Raif. She has these powers they're searching for."

All he wanted was reassurance. He supposed Evelyn was trying to provide that, in her way. He was getting his answers; they simply weren't ones he was ready for. Had Father known? Had Mother? Had they both chosen to keep their daughter's apparent powers a secret? Was he the only one who hadn't seen it in Rose? Did anyone else, others in Little Haven—

Evelyn cleared her throat. "Do you think it's justified?"

"Justified?" He raised an eyebrow. "What do you mean?"

"What happened to those men. When they- they were going to hurt us anyway." Her voice cracked as she spoke. "Do you think they deserved it?"

Were things that simple? He saw the pleading in Evelyn's eyes and knew how he had to answer. "I suppose so," he said, though his mind fought against the idea. He chewed on his lip. No matter what those men had done, or intended to do, did they deserve such gruesome deaths? And what would that make his sister? That she had caused such ... *brutality.* "I know one thing for sure. Whatever happened this morning, it can't happen again. Maybe Rose did save us. But what does that mean for her?"

Evelyn's expression was guarded. "I don't know."

Without thinking, he reached out and grasped her arm, disregarding the flicker of dismay that passed across her features at his touch. "We can't tell anyone about this. Not until we know more. I don't want anything to happen to Rose. Promise me, Evelyn. We have to keep her secret."

Evelyn pulled her arm free, rubbing where he'd held her with irritation. But when she looked at him, she must have seen his desperation. Her face softened and she gave a curt nod. "Of course," she said. "I swore to protect you, didn't I? I promise." She studied the sky where the sun was already reaching its midpoint. "We need to keep going. Put more distant between us and ..."

Raif nodded vehemently. "Yes, we do."

They walked on, following in the wake of Rose and Dog.

That evening as they huddled around a modest campfire in the burnt-out husk of an old building, Raif tried to turn the talk to happier times. With his sister and Dog already soundly asleep, he was desperate to focus on anything but that morning. "Do you remember the autumn harvest feasts?" he asked, salivating as he recalled the fresh chicken and mushroom pies, the honey-roasted vegetables, his mother's fresh-baked bread.

Evelyn's gaze remained steadfast on the flickering campfire. "Of course," she said, the corners of her mouth twitching into a smile. The dark bruise and shadows playing on her face made her look much older than her years.

"What about the annual hunt?" Raif pressed. "Father let me join them for the last one, though I wasn't able to catch anything." His heart clenched in his chest. He turned to Evelyn, determined to distract himself from the memory. "Did you say you were taught to shoot?"

Evelyn blanched. "Yes, I was, although …" She shifted where she sat, eyes remaining fixed on the fire.

Raif picked up a stick, idly passing it between his hands. "Why did you leave Little Haven?"

She pulled her knees up to her chest. "There was, um … Something happened," she said quietly. "I had to leave."

Despite her hesitation, Raif suddenly had to know whether his suspicions were correct. "Was it because of Arthur?" He thought of the blonde-haired, blue-eyed boy, only four years his senior, who the village girls all swooned over. "The Elder's son? I remember he had an accident, didn't he? On a hunt."

The change in Evelyn was immediate. She squared her shoulders, face lifting towards him. "Arthur?"

He shrank back, shocked to have caused such a response. *So stupid. I've said too much when all she's done is help us.* "I'm sorry, I didn't mean to—"

"All you need to know is we were lied to in Little Haven. Or, at least, the truth was kept from us." The flames played upon her face, her features shifting. "Arthur showed me how little I was valued, that's all."

Rose stirred beside them. Raif moved closer to Evelyn. To speak such words about their home, he could hardly imagine what must've happened to her. He sat beside her, jabbing his stick into the ground. *What about today? What about the secrets our parents kept?* He watched his sister as she slept, unease nestling in his gut.

"I didn't mean to upset you by mentioning, um … by asking about Little Haven."

Evelyn shook her head, dropping her gaze once more. "I had to leave," she said, resting her chin against her knees. "That's all you need to know."

Raif knew it wasn't his place to push anymore. Evelyn had helped them when no one else would, that was what mattered. Even so, part of him couldn't help but feel annoyed. *More secrets. More hidden truths.*

And aren't I keeping a secret of my own? The guilt burrowed into him. *Who am I really protecting by hiding it?* A chill ran down his spine, the answer flashing into his mind. *If I'd gone back home sooner, I could have saved him.*

He glanced at Rose, at Evelyn. *Perhaps I should tell them about Father. About my failure. About what he said, before he …* His lip began to tremble as he let out a long, shaking breath.

"Are you okay?" Evelyn asked, lifting her head.

Raif forced a smile. "Just tired, I think."

Evelyn studied him across the fire, amber eyes boring into him. He felt as though she was trying to read his thoughts. Finally, she said, "It's been a long day. Get some sleep. I'll take first watch."

Raif could scarcely bring himself to argue, his head pounding and limbs stiff. He laid next to his sister, pulling the blanket over himself and nuzzling close for warmth. He was exhausted, desperate for sleep, but his mind was tormented.

Is my sister a killer?

Who are the Commune?

Protect Rose.

What is Evelyn hiding?

Why didn't Mother and Father tell us about Rose's powers?

How can I save my sister?

Should I tell the truth about Father?

Run. Danger.

His father's face was the last image in his mind before sleep finally dragged him into its dark embrace.

7

Evelyn

After five long days of travel, Evelyn's entire body ached. She kept putting one foot in front of the other, driven only by the promise she'd made, the belief Bessie held in her—though that belief faded with each passing day as Evelyn's growing exhaustion and ever-present self-loathing become more and more overwhelming.

On the third day, they'd passed a merchant and she'd been unable to resist the draw of a bulging wineskin he touted. Little risk, she reasoned, with not another traveller in sight and the man keen enough for the coin she offered.

She'd distracted Raif and Rose by buying them some honeyed nuts. When they excitedly moved away to eat them, she quickly grabbed the skin and handed the merchant a whole silver without thinking. An extortionate amount for what turned out to be the sourest wine she'd ever tasted. But it fulfilled its purpose, numbing the pain in her heart and head and limbs as she consumed it over the next two days. Her hand lingered over the empty skin tucked into her belt, shamed at her own inability to control her cravings. *And now the pain is all the worse for the withdrawal of it.*

"What's that?" Raif asked, pointing one hand ahead as he squinted towards the horizon. Evelyn followed his gaze, wondering how she hadn't noticed it sooner.

"Castleton," she said. "That's the ruin there, you see? On top of the hill. From what Bessie told me once, the king no longer resides there but it remains in place for the city named after it."

"I've never seen anything like it," Raif said. "Look Rose, d'you see? It's so *big*." Beside him, his sister nodded eagerly, pointing and smiling for all the world as though they were on an exciting adventure, a grand and happy destination ahead.

"Stay close," Evelyn said. "Try not to draw attention to yourselves." Her gaze lingered on Rose.

As they drew closer to Castleton, Evelyn felt a growing sense of bitterness for the life she'd led in Little Haven. Here, in this sprawling city weaving its way around the castle-capped hill, was more evidence of the sheltered life forced upon her. Safe, she was sure the village Elders believed. *Safe and lied to.*

"There are things you don't understand, girl. Things we Elders must ..." She gritted her teeth to recall those words. Should she tell Raif everything? She faltered, knowing her suspicions were not a confirmation of truth. *There's no need to worry him yet.*

Deep down, however, she was all too sure of their meaning—now more than ever. *They thought they could control us by hiding the truth.*

Her two years at the tavern had opened her eyes only a little; not enough to deal with this. *What am I doing here?* She gulped.

She looked up at Rose on Bert's back, bright-eyed and innocent—no sign at all she'd been responsible for two murders, that the powers within her caused any concern. *Had the Elders been aware of them? Did they know about mine? After what I did, they must have.*

Her hand drifted once more to the empty wineskin tucked into her belt.

What would Raif think if he knew of my cravings?

She glanced at him from the corner of her eye; he was tugging at the sleeve of his tunic, brow furrowed as he stared towards the city.

He doesn't know me.

Ha, and isn't that best? He'd never trust me if he did.

"Evelyn?" Raif's voice interrupted her inner torment. He pushed back the perpetually flopping piece of hair from his forehead. "What are we going to do once we reach the city?"

"I have some coin left. We'll find an inn and stable Bert. Then we'll see what we can learn about this Mak." She gave a weak smile. "Hopefully it won't be too difficult."

"*… be wary of who you ask. They have eyes everywhere.*"

"Mak," Raif said. "Maybe he'll find us." He beamed at her as though things were that simple. "Perhaps we'll be able to find out where our mo—uh, where our parents were taken. The rest of the villagers."

Evelyn shrugged, not sharing in his optimism. "We can only try." *What other choice do we have?* For now, she must focus on the most pressing matter: getting into Castleton without raising suspicion. In order to do so, they had to manoeuvre through a crowded market. Though she'd often dreamt of visiting such places, Evelyn was overwhelmed by the haphazard setup of eccentric stalls displaying an array of pottery, cloth, carvings of wood, stone and ivory, exotic coloured glass, and trinkets of every description.

To her relief, no one seemed interested in the three of them. Merchants vied for attention, individuals shopped for wares, and others, like them, simply sought to make their way into the city.

We're just travellers coming to Castleton, she told herself. *Nothing wrong with that.* She forced herself onwards, leading them to join those also moving forward, eyes down, jaw set firmly. Dog sniffed frantically ahead, darting through the crowd as he latched on to each new odour. The closer they drew to Castleton's western gate, the more crowded it became—and the faster Evelyn's heart raced.

"Evelyn," Raif said, eyes wide as he tugged on her arm. He pointed towards a red-cloaked soldier, standing in the space between two stalls. "They're—"

She shushed him. "Keep your head down," she muttered. "Don't look at them. Follow my lead."

Evelyn lifted her chin, lowered her shoulders, and walked with all the confidence she could muster. *We're allowed to be here, we're just travellers.*

As they approached the food stalls, the air was flooded with dizzying aromas and her stomach clenched with hunger even as a wave of nausea washed over her. Stall holders called to all who passed.

"Hot roasted chestnuts, blessed by the Powers!"

"Salted fish, straight from Taskan Bay! Personal favourites of the Grand Magister 'imself."

"Clay-baked bread, finest in all of Septima, by His Benevolent Powers!"

Evelyn walked past them all, eyes lingering only on the stall selling cheap spiced wine. *No, not now. I need a clear head.*

As they approached the city wall, her eyes were drawn upwards. A large red flag snapped in the wind; upon it, a golden crest depicted a great black owl, wings spread wide. Evelyn realised she'd seen it before in the tavern. She'd asked Bessie what it meant once and hadn't understood the dark expression that flashed across the woman's face. *"The symbol of the royal family,"* she'd said, snorting. *"Not that King Cosmo's protection means anything."*

Eager to leave the memory behind, Evelyn allowed her eyes to drift downwards. At first, she wasn't sure what she was looking at. She blinked, hoping she was mistaken.

Her stomach lurched. "Shit."

Ravens swarmed around the bodies, ripping bloodied meat from bone, rendering faces featureless, limbs fleshless. It was impossible to tell whether they had been men or women, young or old, rich or poor. One thing was clear: they were a warning.

"Evelyn, what—Oh, oh no." The colour drained from Raif's face.

She shook her head. "Don't," she said, tilting her head back towards Rose. "Come on. Best not to dwell on it. I'm sure they died for good reason." She almost believed her own lie.

Face tinged with green, Raif gave a too-vigorous nod. "I'm sure you're right."

At the gates, Evelyn's heart skipped a beat at the sight of yet more soldiers. *What did I expect?* she scolded herself. She glanced back at the roiling crowd behind them; no choice now. Turning back would draw more attention to them. She joined the queue, Bert's reins in hand, Raif at her side, and Dog at her feet, keeping a tenuous façade of calm confidence.

When they reached the front and were waved through the gate with barely more than a glance, Evelyn hesitated.

"What you waitin' for?" the soldier said, rubbing his eyes and casting her the briefest of irritated glances. "Move along." He stamped his spear on the ground, making her jump.

"Th-thank you," she said.

"Keep that fleabag under control," the soldier called after them.

Evelyn had little time to dwell on the strange ease of their entry before her senses were bombarded with the sights, sounds, and smells of the city. It was just as the market outside but much, *much* larger. She'd never seen so many people going about their day, even during the tavern's most popular months. All around, men and women were weaving back and forth, crossing each other's paths and calling out to each other; others kept their heads down and marched onwards, barely glancing up from their own feet.

The road along the city wall was occupied by further stalls. Farmers with cartloads of wheat, barley, and an assortment of fruits and vegetables made their way through the gates and along the streets, horses leaving fresh piles of manure on the already filthy cobblestones. Evelyn scrunched her nose, trying not to concern herself with what her worn boots were wading through. She walked on, letting herself be bustled along by those around them, not really paying attention to where they were going.

"Evelyn," Raif said after a short time. "Look."

Down a street to their right was an inn, a crude wooden sign depicting a bed and tankard creaking above its door. Glad of the chance for escape from the jostling mass of people, she tugged on Bert's rein to change their course.

"That's a fine beast you 'ave there," a nearby pie-seller shouted. "Plenty o' meat. I'll pay you most handsome-like for 'im."

Evelyn frowned. "He's not for sale."

"What about the little one?" The man was now greedily eyeing Dog who let out an indignant bark. "Might be small but you'd be surprised 'ow many pies he'd fill."

"No!" Rose shouted, glaring at the man from atop Bert.

Evelyn placed a hand on her leg. "It's okay, Rose." She turned to the pie-seller. "No. He's a beloved pet."

But the man didn't respond; his face had gone blank. *No.* Evelyn hurried them down the street towards the inn. She pulled Rose down from Bert's back and grasped her shoulders. "Not here," she said. "It's dangerous."

"What? What did she do?" Raif asked, turning from where he'd been distracted by a nearby row of market stalls.

Evelyn proffered her head back towards the pie-seller. "Used her ... you know, on him."

"Oh, Rose!" Raif knelt down to look her in the eye. "You can't do that, d'you hear? We have to be careful."

The young girl smiled. "Not having Dog," she said.

"Of course not," Evelyn said, patting her shoulder. "I'd never allow it."

She peered around the street, checking Rose hadn't drawn any undue attention, before glancing back at the man. He was rubbing a hand across his face, turning away from them. *He's fine.* Rose's powers hadn't touched him for long, they couldn't have done any harm—at least, she hoped so. *Nothing to be done about it now.*

As they entered the inn's stable, they were hit by the concentrated stench of mouldering manure. Evelyn stroked Bert's nose in apology. "It won't be for long," she promised.

The stableboy, evidently aware of his good looks and keen on preening himself, was picking his fingernails with a small knife. He glanced up as they entered, eyes roving over the group with a distinct air of disinterest.

Unimpressed, Evelyn cleared her throat. "We'll be staying for the night." The stableboy gave a lazy nod, waving her towards an empty stall. She sniffed with disdain, patting down Bert's saddlebags to ensure there was nothing of value being left behind, covering Raif's bow and arrows with Bessie's blanket.

"You'll want to leave him here too," the stableboy said, waving towards Dog with his knife.

Rose shook her head vigorously. "No." She placed a hand on Dog's neck. "No."

"They're quite attached," Evelyn said quickly.

"Suit yourself." The stableboy shrugged. "Don't say I didn't warn you."

Inside the inn, dust whirled thick in the air. The floor was littered with rushes and sawdust, though that did little to disguise the filth trodden in from the streets. The windows were stained with what could only be years of built-up muck, casting the room in shadow despite the hour. A central fireplace smouldered, the dense smoke it produced doing nothing to cover the strong aroma of rotten fish emanating from the kitchen. Despite all this, Evelyn was glad to be away from the roving eyes and curious gazes of those who could question their presence at any moment.

She waved Raif, Rose, and Dog towards a table in the corner. "Keep quiet." The room was empty apart from two hunched and dishevelled old men, engrossed in a dice game. Evelyn kept her eye on them as she moved towards the bar.

"Liar!" one shouted. A bony hand slammed against the table in apparent triumph.

"I think you'll find I have the Magister's protection," replied his companion, smugly uncovering the dice under his cup.

"You jammy bugger," muttered the first, tossing a meagre pile of coppers across the table.

It was then that the innkeeper snorted and spat on the floor. He was running a ragged-looking cloth around a tankard, his small, watery eyes appraising her every move as she made her way to the bar.

"Don't like filthy mutts," he said.

Evelyn swallowed. "He won't be any trouble."

"Don't like filthy mutts," he repeated gruffly. "They stink the place up."

She fought back a scoff, squaring her shoulders and meeting his gaze—a trick Bessie had taught her to deal with troublesome patrons at the tavern. *"Don't allow them to question you. Look 'em full in the eye, then they're more like to listen."*

"And I said he won't be any trouble. Our horse is in the stable. We're looking for a room for tonight. Nothing fancy."

"You've come to the right place then," one of the old men chimed in, cackling wildly.

"That's enough, Ed," the innkeeper growled. He snorted again, eyes running over Evelyn. "You got coin?"

"Yes," she said, placing a hand on her leather purse.

"Good," he said, small eyes following the movement. "It'll be three silver."

"That's—" Evelyn gaped. "No. We only need one room. We can share."

"Two silver then."

"One." She retrieved the coin from her purse, allowing the innkeeper to see it flash across her palm. At the glimmer of money, he darted his thick fingers out. She pulled back. "And the dog will stay with us."

The innkeeper rolled his eyes but jabbed his hand forward to take the coin. "One night." He spat on the floor again, confirming the conversation was over. Evelyn tossed the coin at him and turned, suddenly eager for some fresh air.

She joined Raif and Rose. "Let's go."

"Can we get something to eat?" Raif said.

"Let's see what we can find." Evelyn cupped her near-empty coin purse. *Shouldn't have bought that wine. A whole silver wasted.* She blew air through her lips. As Bessie had said to her countless times over the past two years, "*No point dwelling on what's done, girl.*"

Outside, the sounds of the city engulfed them once more.

"Where shall we start?" Raif's eyes were shining as he gazed from left to right. "Oh, I have a good feeling we'll find help here." He wrapped his arm round Rose's shoulder, grinning down at her.

Evelyn turned, unable to respond for fear of shattering his hopefulness. Her gaze was drawn to the unoccupied ruins of the castle at the city's centre. It loomed over the surrounding streets like a great squatting gargoyle, its mottled grey bricks seeming to absorb sunlight.

"I suppose we'll walk towards that," she said. "Stay close to me."

They wove their way through the city streets, market stalls and bustling crowds giving way to fine shops, clean cobblestones, lavish tea rooms and taverns. The air grew heavy with the scent of flowers, spices, and lady's perfume. Evelyn peered into the sparkling window of a nearby dressmaker, taking in the jewel-coloured gowns. She had never been one for dresses, even in Little Haven where the Elders had tried to force her to wear them. Why be bogged down with all those layers of needless fabric when a simple pair of trousers would provide far greater comfort? Even so, these were unlike any she'd seen before and some part of her was drawn to them, imagining being able to afford such finery.

Don't be so stupid.

She tugged her faded green cloak around her shoulders to conceal the stained tunic she wore, suddenly self-conscious of the brown woollen trousers that hung loose about her narrow hips. In the reflection, she became aware of the curious glances of the noble men and women who passed by, faces pinched, heads shaking, whispers of disdain hidden behind jewelled fingers as they took in her muddied boots, ragged clothing, the sword in its worn scabbard at her waist. Her envy intermingled with irritation—who were these people to judge her, Raif, and Rose? Their lives were easy, their clothes warm, their bellies full. She grasped for Rose's hand, glaring back at those who dared to meet her eye.

"Come on," she said to Raif. "Let's go this way."

They went down a side street and turned a corner, merging with a vast crowd.

"What's going on?" Raif asked, stretching on tiptoes to see over the heads of those before them.

Evelyn squinted towards the front of the gathering.

Gallows.

"Evelyn, I—" Raif swallowed. "I think they're—"

"Don't look," she snapped. She picked up Rose, made sure Dog was following. "Hold onto my cloak." Raif didn't argue.

There was movement atop the wooden platform. A red-cloaked soldier stepped forward, holding his hands up to silence the crowd. Try as she might, Evelyn couldn't block out the words he spoke.

"For the crime of treason against Septima, our beloved King Cosmo Septimus, and the sanctity and protection of the Commune, with activities directly seeking to contravene the Grand Magister's Benevolence and Wisdom ..."

She couldn't help looking up towards the gallows then, some compulsion that overcame her growing fear. The prisoner was gaunt and filthy. She couldn't see his face clearly, though his stance told her everything she needed to know. Despite the bruises mottling his starved body, the filth on his once-fine clothes, he held himself tall. She felt a flush of shame and sorrow on his behalf.

As she watched, he broke free of the guard holding him back and ran to the front of the platform. "I regret nothing!" he shouted, voice loud and clear despite his evident frailty. "The Grand Magister acts for himself, no other. You will die under the rule of that bastard. You fucking fools, you—" The man was punched in the stomach, a muffled cry escaping his lips as he buckled over. All around, there were jeers and boos from the gathered crowd. At first Evelyn thought they must be in support of the prisoner, angry at his mistreatment. When she listened to the words, however, she realised how wrong she was.

"Death to the traitor!"

"By His Benevolent Powers! Kill, kill!"

"Grand Magister! Commune power!"

With rising panic, Evelyn forced her way through the crowd, holding Rose close, Dog at her feet, and Raif at her back.

"Why are they hanging him?" Raif called. Evelyn ignored his question, leading them down a side alley and placing Rose on the ground. She fidgeted anxiously, crossing and uncrossing her arms, tapping her foot, fiddling with her braid, trying to process what they'd witnessed.

"Did they say treason?" Raif asked after an extended silence. "Against the Commune?" Rose looked up at Evelyn, expression grim, seeming to understand her brother's questions all too well.

"I can't be sure," Evelyn lied, dread pounding through her with every heartbeat. *What mess are we in? Oh, Bessie, why aren't you here?* "We must be—Wait." Her eyes came to settle on a tattered poster emblazoned on the wall of the alley.

"*Beware Veritas!*" it read. "*Traitors to the Commune, enemies of Septima. Extremely dangerous. Any sightings must be reported to the nearest soldier without delay.*"

"Veritas," she muttered, tracing her finger along the crumpled parchment. The individuals pictured seemed unthreatening enough; a man and a woman, evidently related, both with wide-set brown eyes, long brown hair and thin lips, and a man with green eyes, thick black hair and moustache.

"What is it?" Raif asked, coming to stand beside her.

"I think these are the people Bessie meant us to find," she said. She glanced at Raif, lips pursed. "It says they're traitors. Enemies of the Commune. This might be harder than we thought."

Raif studied the poster. "What shall we do?" he said.

Evelyn examined the faces on the poster for a moment longer. "Nothing to do but keep our eyes open. Come on." *Bessie, what have you got us into?*

As they walked through the affluent streets of Castleton, Evelyn's exasperation grew. They were increasingly conspicuous, their plain and dirty clothes a stark contrast to the deep reds, blues, greens, and purples around them. There were only so many nobles she could glare at before her resolve began to wear thin; this place was full of people who would sooner see them escorted away by soldiers than help them. She saw it in the upturned noses and sneers all around. It was surely only a matter of time before they were reported.

"Evelyn," Raif said, pulling her to a halt. "Look." He pointed towards a puppet show. Rose was entranced, drawn in by the lively entertainment. Other children—the first they'd seen since leaving the tavern, she realised with a jolt—

sat in front of the stall, giggling and cheering along. *It must be safe here,* she decided. Nearby, she saw a tavern. Now might be her opportunity to gain her bearings—perhaps have a drink to calm her nerves. *Just a small one. Just to help me think.*

"Can we watch?" Raif asked. "It might be good for Rose to be with other children."

Evelyn was torn, cravings pulling her towards the tavern. *What harm could one drink do?* The jeers of the crowd at the gallows echoed through her mind; the scene had unsettled her far more than she would admit. "Well, I s'pose so. As long as you stay there and don't move."

"Of course," Raif said.

"Here." She handed Raif a few coppers. "Buy some pastries and watch the show." She pointed towards the nearby tavern, the Golden Goblet. "I'm going to see if I can learn anything in there." She watched Raif and Rose sit in front of the puppeteer before turning, straightening her clothes, and entering the tavern.

She knew as she opened the door and the finely perfumed air hit her nose that she would not have enough coin to purchase anything here. Nevertheless, she made her way towards the bar, cravings driving her on. Perhaps she could convince the barman somehow. She cringed inwardly at the idea. *Leave, leave now before you're seen.*

But it was too late. The short, plump man was watching her, one thin eyebrow raised. "May I help you?"

Well, you may as well try. Evelyn put on her friendliest smile. "I'd like some wine," she said.

"And you've got money, have you?" His eyes roved over her ragged clothes, hovering on the bloodstain left by Rommy.

She coughed awkwardly. "Of course," she replied, tugging her cloak to try and cover the stain and giving her coin purse a jangle. "I could do with a drink. Terrible journey. Hunting accident."

"Hunting?"

"Yes, er, in the woods." *Stop talking. Now.*

The man gave her a look of pointed disbelief but poured the wine nonetheless; perhaps he sensed her need for it.

"One silver," he said, handing it towards her.

"Of course, let me just—"

"Please, Charles, allow me." A man sidled up, holding out a long-fingered hand decked with more jewellery than she'd ever seen before, on his middle finger a huge ruby sparkled like a pool of blood. She snapped her mouth shut and looked away.

"Thank you, my Lord," Charles said, taking the coin before moving away to serve another customer.

Lord? Why is a Lord helping me? The man's wealth was evident from … well, everything about him. Perfectly groomed, immaculate outfit. His skin was pale as milk, his hair black as pitch, eyes as blue and cold as ice. Evelyn was on edge in an instant, her tattered clothing and, though she'd tried to ignore it, the obvious smell of going far too long without a wash highlighting her inferiority. There was no reason a wealthy man, let alone a Lord, should take an interest in her. *Be alert.* She frowned, trying to make herself look unpleasant enough to dissuade conversation like Bessie had taught her to do with the tavern patrons who'd had too much drink, and turned her shoulder to him. She snatched up the tumbler of wine before he could take it away.

The man—*Lord, a bloody Lord!*—casually adjusted his billowing white shirt sleeves, amusement curving his lips. "What's your name?"

Evelyn drank some wine, revelling in the sweet warmth that spread through her. Its effect on her confidence was near-instant. She turned to face him and said, "My Lord, I thank you for the wine but I'm not here to make friends." She hoped her brusque tone would put him off.

It didn't.

To the contrary, he edged so close she could smell the sickening sweetness of his beard oil as he brushed a hand against her arm. She tensed, ready to spring from her seat and flee.

But she found she couldn't move if she'd wanted to. Her muscles were curiously weak, her body unresponsive, the feeling of his touch even more intoxicating than the wine.

The man picked up her braid, turning and stroking it between his fingers as he spoke. "Such beautiful hair. My mother had auburn hair. The colour of autumn, I always thought. It's all I remember of her, really." A strange mixture of sadness and anger flitted across his too-handsome face. He blinked and dropped her hair, studying her. It was all she could do to meet his gaze, unable to blink or speak.

"I haven't seen you in the city before. What brings you to Castleton? Are you here alone?"

Please go away, please. I don't want any trouble. But she couldn't say the words out loud. *Please.* She held the tumbler in her quivering hand, wanting only to gulp down the numbing liquid within.

The man rubbed a hand over his close-cropped beard, a scowl darkening his face. This hadn't gone as he'd expected, that much was clear.

What does he want from me?

And then, as fast as it had taken over her, the weakness passed. He stood, straightening his black doublet and glancing around as though only just realising they were surrounded by other patrons. "I can see you'd rather be alone," he said. "I shall leave you to enjoy your drink. Charles, another wine over here."

Before leaving, he left a handful of silver coins on the bar. He bowed curtly to Evelyn and headed to the rear of the tavern, where he disappeared behind some curtains. His scent still clung to her clothes, hair, and nostrils. She shuddered.

"Be careful of that one, girl," Charles said, leaning in close as he refilled her wine glass. "Lord Torrant is dangerous."

Lord Torrant. Evelyn scanned the back of the tavern, unable to shake the feeling he was still watching her. She downed the wine in an eager gulp. "I'll be fine," she said, and then as an afterthought, "Thank you." It was time to return to Raif and Rose. *Idiot, thinking I'd find help here. I'm lucky to be leaving without any trouble.*

As she moved towards the door, the barman called after her. She tensed as she turned back, worried there would be an issue after all. "Your coin," he said, holding his hand towards her.

"It's not mine."

"Take it." He pushed it into her palm. "You need it more than me. Get yourself cleaned up. You're likely to attract attention otherwise. The wrong sort." There was no malice in his words as he waved his hand over her dirty tunic. She took the money and left, relieved to be away from the place.

Outside, Raif and Rose were still enjoying the puppet show, tunics flaked with the remnants of their pastries, Dog nestled between them. Evelyn counted the coins in her hand. They had enough to eat a decent meal and that was something at least, though the encounter in the tavern had left a chill in her gut. She wouldn't forget those pale eyes. *Lord Torrant.* She moved towards the children, wanting to leave the area as quickly as possible.

"That's the king," Raif said as she approached, pointing towards a puppet with a mess of blonde hair and a lop-sided crown. "Like the scroll we found, isn't it? You know, in the …" He trailed off. "Anyway, I think people here might know something, Evelyn. I think we might be able to find help."

"Hmm." She nodded towards the other puppet, a red-robed figure. "Who's that?"

Raif's face dropped. "That's the Grand Magister," he whispered. She watched as the puppet, its face concealed, commanded and beat the little king. The other children at the show laughed and cheered and shouted at the puppeteer, but the adults walking past all shared shocked and disgusted looks with each other.

"He'll be taken away before long," one woman said to her husband as they walked arm-in-arm.

"Deserves all he gets, doing that so close to—" All around there were similar mutters and fear-filled glances. Anxiety spiking, Evelyn grasped Raif's shoulder.

"Get Rose," she said. "We're going. There's still lots of the city to explore."

8

Evelyn

Later that day, as the afternoon dimmed to evening, they made their way back towards the inn. Evelyn was doing her best not to feel demoralised after a fruitless day of searching. She knew from Bessie and the poster they'd found that they had to be careful if they were to locate Mak, or the group, Veritas. Evelyn had walked them through the streets with growing hopelessness, wondering how she might find who they needed to without drawing unwanted attention. At every turn in the street, she imagined they would be ambushed by red-cloaked soldiers. *How can I know who to trust?*

In the end, she'd decided it would be best to ask about the Commune's attack on Little Haven rather than mentioning Veritas or Mak and risking immediate danger. To her dismay, she found no one who would answer her questions, let alone help. One shopkeeper, a woman with squinting brown eyes, peered over Evelyn's shoulders the entire time they spoke.

"By the Powers, girl," she said in a hushed voice. "The Grand Magister is the King's most trusted advisor. The Commune acts for the good of the kingdom." She shooed Evelyn from her shop without another word, slamming the door shut in her face.

Evelyn rubbed a hand across her aching eyes. She was sure she'd be able to think more clearly after a hot meal. *And more wine.* Since the attack in the woods, her mind was a muddle of problems, past and present. Half-truths and unfinished suspicions from Little Haven all the way to the city and back ran rampant in her mind.

After a particularly nasty response that left a gob of spit from a stranger on the toe of her boot, Evelyn decided it was time to make a better plan. She was looking forward to a moment of peace in what had turned out to be a frantically stressful day. They made their way back to the inn, back on the first main road they'd walked that morning. Evelyn made sure Rose was distracted with Dog as they neared the pie-seller's stand, hoping he wouldn't recognise them. As they grew near she saw he was gone.

It was exactly as before, but the man himself was nowhere to be seen, his stall left unattended, the wares left out for anyone to help themselves to. As she watched, a bedraggled young woman with sunken cheeks and darting eyes hurried towards the stall, pocketed three pies, and ran back the way she'd come, nearly knocking the entire stall to the floor in her eagerness to get away. Evelyn held her hand up to stop Raif and Rose in their tracks, scanning down the street.

It was then she saw the armoured horses tethered beneath the creaking wooden sign of their inn. A man held their reins, his back turned to them, a red cloak draped across his shoulders.

They've found us.

Before she could react, the pie-seller emerged from the inn alongside another red-cloaked soldier.

"It's them!" the pie-seller cried, waving his arm in their direction, face contorted. "They're the ones."

The soldier followed his gaze. "You there! Stay where you are."

There was no time to think.

Evelyn grabbed Rose's hand and shoved Raif backwards. "Run," she hissed. Raif's eye's were wide, fixated on the red cloak. "Run!" Evelyn shook him once. He blinked and gripped Rose's other hand, pulling her away. They sprinted back into the crowd, Evelyn in front, Dog a black blur at their feet.

"Stop! In the name of the Commune!" called a soldier.

More shouts joined him as Evelyn led Raif, Rose, and Dog away from the inn, moving as swiftly as she could along the city streets. *Shit, shit, idiot.* She wished she had listened to her gut after the encounter at the tavern with Lord Torrant. She should've known the Commune would come for them. It had been too easy to get into the city, hadn't it? *A trap. Of course, they wanted us to think we were safe ... .* She couldn't be sure it was so, but something told her this had been coming all along. There could be no escape.

Should've been more careful.

This is my fault.

They kept running, running, running until the soldiers were lost in the crowd. She dragged Raif and Rose into a side street.

"Why are they chasing us?" Raif's eyes were wide as they crouched low. "Why can't they leave us alone?"

"The Commune." It was all the response he needed. Raif nodded, grim, resigned. Evelyn tucked away the strands of hair that had fallen loose from her braid and took a few moments to slow her breathing.

"What are we going to do?" Raif's voice was strained, his arm clasped tightly around his sister's shoulders.

Evelyn peeked into the street, hoping to gain some time to think. She immediately snapped her head back as a mounted soldier came into view. She signalled for Raif and Rose to stay crouched. She held her breath for a moment, expecting there to be a cry of recognition at any second. The three stayed frozen, even Dog remaining still in a point position beside Rose. When Evelyn heard the sound of beating hooves pass them by, she breathed again.

"We have to try and get out of the city." She closed her eyes, trying to visualise the quickest route to the gate. The roads were tightly packed, running a parallel square around the periphery of the castle. If they wanted to get back to the gate they'd entered—the only one she knew of—they had to head west.

"What about Bert?" Raif asked, wringing his hands. "I left my bow in his pack."

"I'm sorry," Evelyn murmured. Regret washed over her, thinking of Bert alone in that wretched stable. "We can't." Her voice trembled. "We can't go back. We'll get you a new bow."

"Oh." Raif's mouth twisted oddly. "I see."

But there was no time for comfort. She looked around the corner again and found the street clear. "Let's go," she said, urging Raif, Rose, and Dog down the sloping streets towards the city gate.

At the market, they were ignored by the remaining stall holders packing away their wares and readying themselves for homeward journeys. As darkness drew in, an evening flame-bearer began his rounds, lighting the torches lining the street. Ducking and weaving around carts, people, and market debris, Evelyn kept going. Heads down and feet quick, there was total silence between them. Perhaps they had lost the soldiers, the growing shadows allowing them some measure of concealment.

All too soon, a shout rang out from behind. *No!* As the galloping of hooves drew nearer, Evelyn's heart pounded, her breaths coming in short, sharp bursts. She dared to glance over her shoulder and saw a red-cloaked soldier closing in.

Fuck. Think fast, come on, come on.

She darted down a dark and narrow alley, littered on all sides with discarded crates and mouldering buckets full of rancid slop. They couldn't waste time climbing the debris. She drew her sword, still stained with blood, and swung it to clear their way. They scrambled desperately through the alley's piled rubbish.

At the end of the alley, the soldier had abandoned his horse and was clambering over the mess, his size and armour slowing him.

Suddenly, Raif cried out and stumbled behind her. "Evelyn, there's someone—there's a—"

"I see him," she said, despair threatening to engulf her. Ahead, a hooded figure atop a horse drew across the other end of the alley. *His cloak isn't red,* she noted. *He's not a soldier.* She wasn't sure if that was good or not. Their path was blocked in both directions—but surely they were safer running away from the Commune than towards them. It was a split-second decision; no time to overthink or question herself. Evelyn sheathed her sword, leant down, and picked Raif up, pushing him on. The soldier was close now, face full of fierce determination even in the enclosing darkness.

"Quick, quick." She ushered Rose and Dog on from behind. "Keep running." She was between the soldier, Raif, and Rose. The clank of armour and slap of boots against cobblestone rang through her head. She waved her arms at the horseman ahead, hoping he would understand her meaning. His head turned, facial expression hidden beneath the shadow of his hood, and he remained where he was, blocking their path.

"Move!" she shouted. "Please!"

Perhaps he couldn't hear her—perhaps his intention *was* to prevent their escape. Either way, there was nowhere to go. They were trapped.

A sharp pain shot across Evelyn's shoulder as the soldier's hand clamped down and tugged her backwards. She shrieked as she was dragged to the ground, a jarring pain coursing up her back and arms. "Get off me!"

"Silence, traitorous bitch," the soldier spat.

Evelyn ignored him, watching in horror as Raif skidded to a halt, turning back as though intending to try and help her. *No, you bloody idiot.* She shook her head, urging him on with frantic arm motions. He frowned, remained rooted to the spot. Beside him, Rose was watching everything, eyes darting between Evelyn and the soldier, Dog barking wildly at her side.

Evelyn thrashed against the soldier holding her down. He grimaced, leering down at her, the scent of his musky sweat filling her nose. She twisted, panic rising as his weight bore down. She glanced up, hoping Raif and Rose had fled but they were still there looking back at her. In her alarmed state, it took Evelyn a moment to notice Rose's face. The young girl's eyes had taken that focus once more. *Not again.*

"No!" she cried.

Too late.

Everything happened in a blur.

The grip on her arms loosened. The soldier lurched up and away from her. He drew the sword from his belt. For a horrible moment, she thought it intended for her. She fumbled for her own sword, knowing she couldn't draw it in time but needing to *try* nonetheless. And then she realised the soldier wasn't looking at her. His eyes were glazed as he turned his sword on himself, stabbed inwards into his own gut so hard it punctured his armour. He screeched, fell to the ground, head meeting cobblestones with a *crack*.

Evelyn barely had time to watch him fall before the horseman moved towards them from the other end of the alley.

Did he see what Rose did? Her stomach flipped. *Is he with the soldier?*

Raif stood aghast, eyes glued to the soldier at Evelyn's feet, apparently oblivious to the horseman at his back.

"Follow me if you want to escape," the man said.

Raif's trance was broken, turning to see the hooded figure.

Evelyn needed to reach him, to protect him, but first, she had to stop Rose. She stumbled on trembling legs towards the young girl, shaking her shoulders in a desperate attempt to break the intense concentration with which she still stared at the prone soldier.

Rose blinked, blue eyes clearing. "Stop," she whispered. "Had to stop him."

"It's okay," Evelyn said, letting out a quivering exhale. "You don't need to anymore." She picked the girl up and rushed towards Raif, now speaking to the hooded figure still atop his horse.

"How do we know we can trust you?" he asked as she joined them.

"You have no choice."

Evelyn narrowed her eyes. Though the man's features remained obscured, there was something about the shoulder-length hair that peeked out from beneath the grey hood that felt familiar. He was offering them help, and he hadn't reacted to the falling soldier. He couldn't be working with those red-cloaked bastards.

Evelyn's mind cleared and her thoughts finally aligned. Her eyes focused on the dark outline of the figure's face. They had nothing left to lose. "Are you from Veritas? Are you ... Mak?"

"Ah," he said, proffering his head. "You are clever."

Her eyes drifted downwards to the horse he rode, taking the animal in properly for the first time. *Bessie's blanket.* And beneath it, the end of a bow stuck out—Raif's bow. "That's our- that's Bert!"

"There's no time to explain," Mak said. "Come with me, or they'll take you before the Grand Magister himself."

Evelyn clutched Rose tighter. Where else could they go? The Commune was hunting them. What would they do to Rose, especially now that she'd injured one of their soldiers? Wherever the Commune was, they would be at risk. If Bessie trusted this man, they had to as well.

This was why they'd come to Castleton.

"We'll go with you," she said.

Behind them, the soldier on the ground groaned, stirring from unconsciousness.

"No time to lose," Mak said. "Lift the girl up here." Evelyn swung Rose up, seating her behind the hooded man.

"Come," he said. "Stay close." He kicked Bert into a trot, and Evelyn, Raif, and Dog jogged behind, leaving the awakening soldier.

As they made their way through the streets, Evelyn cast her gaze about in search of soldiers. For now, it seemed, they were safe from pursuit. Mak steered the horse down another alleyway near the city wall.

Mak dismounted and helped Rose from Bert's back. "In here," he said. He moved to open a rusted metal gate from a circular hole in the wall. "It'll lead us from the city."

Evelyn eyed it. The blackness inside the tunnel was dense, the smell of stale water, damp and mould almost overpowering. "Won't they follow us in there?"

The man retrieved a flickering torch from a sconce on the alley wall. "You'd be amazed how much goes unseen," he said. "Trust me. We won't be followed." He stepped inside the tunnel, waving them in. Raif glanced at her, an eyebrow raised. With a shrug, she nodded. *Bessie trusted him,* she reminded herself again. *We can trust him.*

She took hold of Bert's reins and followed them. Mak moved to close the gate. With the torch in hand, his smile was illuminated, crooked yellow-white teeth in a pale face. "This way." He waved the flame ahead. "We can rest as soon as we're away from this place."

Evelyn watched him walk on, Raif, Rose, and Dog at his back. She ran her hand through her tangled, sweat-matted hair, noticing how much had come loose from her braid in their flight. She combed it with her fingers and tucked it beneath her cloak before giving Bert a weary sigh. "Come on, boy."

Footsteps and hoofbeats alike echoed against the damp walls of the dark tunnel as they made their escape from Castleton.

9

Commander Sulemon

"We'll disregard how long this report has taken to get to me, Commander."

"Yes, my Lord." Commander Sulemon bowed his head, unable to meet Lord Torrant's scrutinising gaze. There had been a curtness between them since their encounter over dinner a few nights before. He couldn't help but wonder if his visit to the brothel had been discovered. He closed his eyes, trying to force away his unease. *Surely he would make it clear to me if he'd gained such knowledge.* He raised his head, looking upon the man he'd once known so well. *Or would he?*

Lord Torrant turned away, clasping his hands behind his back, navy shirt pulling tight across the muscles of his back. "Since we met ..." He cleared his throat. "I mean, since you came into my ... *service*, you have been of great value to me." There was a drawn-out pause.

The Commander shuffled on the spot before saying, "Yes, my Lord."

"By which I mean, you are of great value to the Commune." Lord Torrant moved to stare out of the window, scanning the streets of Castleton.

"Of course." The Commander stood tall, trying to take pride in the words even as they forced an ever-widening chasm between them. He was a soldier of the Commune—that was all he had been to Lord Torrant these past seven years. Loyal, obedient. *Fucking stupid.* He looked down at himself. That morning, he'd risen early, ensured his uniform was pristine, his breastplate polished, his face clean-shaven, and skin oiled. *He doesn't care about your efforts. Pathetic.*

"I'm sure you did all you could to find them, Jonah." Lord Torrant glanced over his shoulder, perfect brow creased into a frown. "Nevertheless, the search must not end. I've spoken to the soldier who was injured in the pursuit and his news was troubling."

A prickle of apprehension ran down Commander Sulemon's spine. "My Lord?"

"He spoke of a young girl, a *child*, using powers on him. Taking over his mind, controlling him with ease."

Commander Sulemon balked. "A child? She must be—"

"Incredibly strong, yes. And, we must assume, untrained." Lord Torrant sighed, breath steaming on the window. "Perhaps he was mistaken, delirious from the healer's potions." He shook his head, a tendril of black hair falling loose over his ear. "Nevertheless, a soldier of the Commune was injured. These children are traitors. Their threat cannot be underestimated."

"Yes, my Lord." The Commander beat his fist against his chest plate; he was nothing if not loyal—to Lord Torrant most of all. That was a seed planted from the moment they'd met.

Thirteen years …

How much had changed between them.

Would I have gone with him that morning, so long ago, had I known who he would become? Veritarra forgive me, I believe I would.

Guilt threatened to devour him at the thought. Despite all he'd witnessed in his homeland, despite the destruction he'd seen and the hatred he felt for those wretched, accursed powers, this man was his first—his only—love.

If we went back, I would do it all again. If I went back, I would not let myself be pushed away again.

The Commander scowled. To distract himself from the unwelcome memories, to reposition the barrier he'd nearly allowed to collapse in that moment, he studied the room in which his former lover was stationed. The dining table at which he had entertained guests was now cluttered with maps, scrolls, ink bottles, and quills. A half-empty bottle of wine and half-drunk glass sat beside an unfinished scroll, contents concealed from view. Above the crackling fire and marble hearth was a portrait of the Grand Magister, red-robed and hard-faced.

The choice of furniture was unremarkable, the inn clearly decorated by someone lacking any notion of an imagination. Against such plain furnishings, Lord Torrant shone all the brighter; it was in his choice of clothing and jewellery he excelled most of all. His outfit today was no exception: navy shirt and cream trousers tailored to accentuate his lean figure, brown leather boots polished to a sheen, matching the belt at his slim waist.

Commander Sulemon touched a hand to the pouch at his own waist, praying to the Goddess he should no longer worship. *Veritarra, give me strength to resist him.* The option was there, always. He could brush those scrolls and maps aside, throw him against the table, tear the clothes from his back.

He was mine once; why can't it be so again?

Always the thoughts were there, taunting him with what he could no longer have.

You really are a fool.

"Commander?" Lord Torrant had moved from the window to the table, an eyebrow raised, eyes flitting to the Commander's hand still resting on his pouch.

The Commander jerked his hand to sit on the hilt of his sword, clearing his throat. "Yes, my Lord?"

"I said, you must see to it that the innkeeper is punished for allowing the children into his establishment without notifying us. Three unaccompanied children." Lord Torrant picked up his wine glass, taking a sip of the dark liquid. "The man's either an idiot or a traitor. Either way, his failure has led to *this*." He waved the wine glass in the air.

"It is already done." The Commander inclined his head. "He put up quite a fight. My men had to use force to subdue him. He is in a cell awaiting execution."

"Excellent. I should have known." An approving smile played at the corner of Lord Torrant's lips. He placed his glass down, running a hand across his close-trimmed beard. "Such insolence cannot be tolerated. The man must be made an example of. The Grand Magister would expect nothing less."

Commander Sulemon nodded.

"Very good. Is there anything else, Commander?"

"Yes, Lord Torrant. We have the stableboy from the inn ready for your questioning." He signalled towards the door. "He is still conscious. He may be able to provide some information, if you would like to speak to him."

"Very well, Commander." Lord Torrant rubbed his jewelled hands together. "Bring him in."

Commander Sulemon moved to the door and instructed his awaiting soldiers to escort the stableboy in. The young man's face was coloured with bruises, his left eye swollen shut, nose bloodied and lip split—yet he still managed to look indignant as he was dragged into the room and thrown into a chair.

"I ain't done anythin' wrong!" he cried. "What d'you want from me?"

Lord Torrant stepped forward, waving the soldiers away and leaning down to face the stableboy, lips curled into a sneer. "You can shout all you like but you may as well know now—no one will come for you. We are doing the work of the Commune and that is recognised by all within Castleton."

A glimmer of despair flashed in the boy's eyes. He glanced towards Commander Sulemon, mouth dropping open. "But I—"

Lord Torrant opened his palm and struck it across the boy's face, the *slap* resonating through the room. The Commander gritted his teeth as fresh blood splattered across the wooden floorboards.

"Another word out of line and you will receive far worse," Lord Torrant said, retrieving a kerchief from the table and wiping the smears of blood from his palm with a look of disgust. "Do you understand?"

The boy remained slumped over, head twitching in a near-imperceptible nod.

"Good." Lord Torrant threw the soiled kerchief into the fire. "What's your name?"

"Sten," the boy croaked.

Lord Torrant smiled, patting the boy's shoulder. "Sten. Good." He moved aside, signalling the Commander forward. "I'm sure Sten here will tell us whatever we want, now that he understands the situation."

Commander Sulemon knelt in front of the boy, the metallic tang of blood filling his nostrils and hitting the back of his throat. He exhaled, wishing he could rinse his mouth clean of the taste. "Where did they go?"

Sten didn't respond. A string of bloodied saliva dripped from his down-turned face, running onto his torn tunic and staining the beige linen.

Commander Sulemon shifted, irritation growing. "Where did they go, boy? If you don't speak then—"

The stableboy grunted, wincing as he lifted his head. "Where did *who* go?"

Commander Sulemon clenched his jaw, sure he could still see a defiant gleam in the boy's eye. *Does he want to be beaten? Or worse?* "You know well who I am speaking of," he growled. "My men made it clear the first time they *questioned* you."

"Commander," Lord Torrant said, touching a warm hand to his arm. "Last chance. The boy needs to be *made* to respect us if he will not do so voluntarily."

The Commander gave a curt nod, stomach knotting. Lord Torrant's powers were always an option, of course—yet Lord Torrant also knew of the disgust, hatred, sorrow that overwhelmed the Commander every time he saw any powers used. In years past, where possible, this had been taken into account. Lord Torrant would rarely use them in front of him. But now, the Commander could see he had already decided. There was an excitement in his eyes.

Commander Sulemon licked his lips, moistening his suddenly dry mouth. "Answer the question, boy, or you will no longer have a choice."

Sten spat on the ground. "You almost killed the innkeep. Why should I tell you anythin'?"

"You stupid bastard!" Commander Sulemon lunged forward, stopping just short of throttling the boy. *Can't he see the danger he is in?* "That man was obstructing soldiers of the Commune. What happened to him was his own fault." He clenched his hands, pulling them back to his sides. It was a mistake, a show of weakness. Perhaps he should have beaten the boy—it was better than what was to come.

Sten's broken lips twisted into a semblance of a smile as he let out a wheezing laugh. "You won't hurt me, will you?"

"That's enough." Lord Torrant moved forward once more, grasping Sten's shoulder and stopping his laughter mid-flow. "You've had the chance to be truthful."

Commander Sulemon stiffened. "No, my Lord. I'm sure I can—"

"Hush, Commander. He's had his chance." He gave a wistful smile, performing perfectly as though he actually cared about the young man's life.

The Commander stepped away. *It is necessary*, he reminded himself. *The boy was given the option to speak.* Even so, he couldn't watch as Sten's mind was taken from him.

"Tell me what happened," Lord Torrant said, hand clamped on Sten's shoulder.

The stableboy began to speak in a slow, monotonous voice. "They had a horse. An old beast, brown, white flecks through his mane. Barely worth my time."

"The horse was gone, my Lord," Commander Sulemon said over his shoulder.

"There was a man," Sten continued. "Hooded, dressed all in plain clothes. I didn't see his face but he- he took the horse. By the Powers, my Lord, I- I swear, I couldn't stop him." The boy squirmed in his seat, the wood creaking as he shifted his weight.

Commander Sulemon scoffed, turning around despite himself. "Accepted a bribe, I expect."

"I …" Sten's one open eye scrunched closed. Lord Torrant lifted the boy's chin, running a finger along his jaw.

"Is that true, boy?"

Sten's eye glistened. He gulped, some part of him evidently still fighting against Lord Torrant's powers. "It's my mother, my Lord, she's- she's sick and- The man gave me coin. To help. Please, you have to understand. Please, please."

"Stupid child," Lord Torrant whispered, squeezing the boy's jaw between his fingers. "You've endangered every Commune-abiding citizen in this city, do you know that?" Sten could only blink back, an odd groan escaping his lips. Finally, Lord Torrant relinquished his hold, shoving Sten's face away in disgust.

"My Lord." Commander Sulemon moved to speak in his ear. "Could this man be one of *them*?"

Lord Torrant looked up at him, white teeth flashing in a satisfied grin. "Ah." He tapped a finger against his lips, blood-red ruby ring glinting in the firelight. "It's possible, Commander." He moved to the table and picked up a quill, scribbling a note on fresh parchment. "If they are involved, we need to move all the faster."

"Yes, my Lord." Commander Sulemon cast Sten a pitiful glance. The boy appeared to have lost consciousness, his head lolling against his shoulder, breathing erratic. It was unclear whether he'd retain any of his sanity after this. The Commander swallowed, the bitter taste of bile burning his throat.

Lord Torrant held out a scroll stamped with the black wolf's head of his family crest, indifferent to his discomfort. "My orders for the pursuit of the children and this hooded man, whoever he may be. Their descriptions are included, from what the injured soldier could tell me. An older girl, auburn hair in a long braid. A boy, tall and slim, mousey hair. And the young girl with blonde hair, very small. She's the one to watch. Leave as soon as you can." As he handed it over, his finger stroked the Commander's hand. "And be careful. Consider them dangerous."

"Yes, my Lord." Commander Sulemon bowed swiftly, taking the scroll. He spared a fleeting glance for Sten. "And him?"

"He is no longer your concern."

The Commander saluted Lord Torrant and left the room. *He is already gone, his life all but forfeit,* he told himself. *I cannot help him.* Somehow, the lie helped to lessen the shame in his heart.

As he pulled the door shut, he heard sniggering from two soldiers in position along the corridor. He scowled, marching towards them. Their conversation froze as they stood to attention.

"That is hardly behaviour suited to a soldier on duty," he snapped. "What is so amusing?" They remained tight-lipped, staring straight ahead with blank expressions.

No respect. Never any respect. Commander Sulemon's fist flashed forward, punching the wall between them, splintering the wood panelling and causing them both to flinch. "You will tell me or you will both be on latrine duty and reduced rations for a month."

The two men looked at each other, faces paling. The one on the left, dark grey eyes flickering to the Commander's face then to the ground, saluted and stepped forward. "Commander Sulemon, we were just saying, uh, that Lord Torrant is sure to be glad of that boy's company. Despite, uh, despite all the rumours about the Grand Magister's ..." The man trailed off, looking somewhere past the Commander's shoulder.

"Rumours, Crowe?" Commander Sulemon glowered. "Care to enlighten me?"

"It's just, we've heard speak that the Grand Magister intends for Lord Torrant to marry a noblewoman, Commander. But his ... *preferences* seem otherwise engaged."

The younger soldier beside Crowe snorted, though his amusement quickly wilted under a hard glare from the Commander, his gaze dropping to the floor.

"Look at me!" he hissed, glancing between the two men. "How dare you? Speaking of rumours and hearsay. Lord Torrant is *one step below the Grand Magister himself*." He inhaled sharply, nostrils flaring. "I could report you both for such vile gossip."

"Please, Commander. We meant nothing by it," Crowe said.

The younger soldier nodded, joining his comrade. "It was a jest, Commander, nothing more." He saluted for good measure.

Commander Sulemon watched them shift uncomfortably for a moment, wanting them to suffer for their comments. Yet a part of him knew it was pointless; that such talk could never be stopped. A great wave of exhaustion washed over him. "Get out of my sight."

The soldiers saluted and bolted away, eager to obey. He waited until they were gone before leaning against the wall, running a trembling hand across his face.

Marry a noblewoman? Surely he would have told me if that were true. But he was finding all too often these days that the truth was no longer clear to him, especially when it came to Lord Torrant. He touched the pouch at his waist, taking some small measure of comfort from it. *Veritarra save me from this torment.*

He hesitated, considering going back into Lord Torrant's chambers, demanding answers. The stableboy would understand nothing said between them; the risk was minimal.

The scroll in his hand grew heavy. Lord Torrant had entrusted these orders to him and they must be seen through. He nodded to himself, turning away from the draw of the room and the man within. *Mere soldiers, spreading gossip and rumours. Nothing more. He wouldn't conceal such a matter from me.*

Decision made, he felt in control once more. Action, that was the way forward. The way to prove his worth. He straightened his cloak and, with a final glance towards Lord Torrant's door, set off for the city barracks. He had work to do.

10

Raif

Raif awoke sheltered in the remains of what must have once been a waypoint west of Castleton, its half-collapsed and rotting walls providing some defence against the bitterly cold winds blowing across from the ocean to the east. A rickety sign creaked in the gusts outside, still clinging on to its rusted hinges.

He sat up and held a hand to his forehead, his thoughts slow and muddled, mind unwilling so soon after waking to recall details of their flight from the city—making their way through the tunnel, running as fast as they could until they found their way here. He didn't even remember falling asleep. Raif winced as his hand brushed his right cheek, still tender and bruised from the attack in the woods. He stretched his aching legs, exhaustion weighing heavy despite the night's sleep. *But at least we found who we needed to.* Beside him, Evelyn was still resting beneath her green cloak, her freckled face creased into a frown as she slept.

Rose. His sister's absence sent a jolting panic through him. He leapt to his feet and rushed through the doorway into the open air, frantic.

The man who'd helped them escape—Mak—was leaning over a fire, long brown hair hanging forward. The cloak he'd used to cover his face yesterday was draped across a nearby tree, revealing an outfit of earthen tones—brown trousers, cream tunic, faded green wool waistcoat, topped off with well-worn brown leather belt and boots. As Raif studied him, the man glanced up and smiled, an easy expression that made his plain face open and friendly. Just like the posters around Castleton, he was pale-skinned and thin-lipped, though his brown eyes were full of kindness—not the pure rage that had been depicted.

"Have you seen my sister?" Raif asked, glancing about. "She's not in there and—"

"Oh," Mak said. "She's over there playing with her dog."

Just then, Rose dashed past, shrieking with laughter as she tumbled through the leaves with Dog. Raif steadied himself against the doorframe, dizzy with relief.

And then it came rushing back to him what Rose had done to the soldier in Castleton—or at least, what she *might* have done. The alley had been dark, after all. *Perhaps I imagined it. The soldier might have tripped on something, fallen back, injured himself.*

Tripped and fell on his own sword? Raif almost laughed at his own foolishness. *You know that's not true.*

"Are you well?" Mak asked. "I hope you got some sleep." He handed over a waterskin.

Raif shrugged. "Some," he said. He drank down the cool liquid, still uneasy. As his strength began to return, his eyes drifted behind Mak where a roasting duck was crackling over the fire, filling the air with the delicious scent of cooking fat.

"Perhaps we can speak over some food," Mak said, amusement tinging his voice.

Raif followed the man towards the fire, taking a seat in front of it and wiping a hand across his salivating mouth. *I haven't had fresh-cooked meat since …*

Mother, Father. Our final meal, the night before—

No. He became aware he was crushing the waterskin, cool liquid spilling down his hand and soaking his sleeve. He dropped it, exhaling as tears blurred his vision.

"Raif," Rose said, coming to stand beside him. She touched a hand to his arm. He immediately felt calmer, more grounded.

He wiped his eyes. "Morning, little bug." He ruffled her hair. "Sit down. Save your energy."

She giggled, giving him a fleeting hug before sitting at his feet with Dog in her lap. No sign of any powers, no inclination that she had strength enough to injure—*kill, she killed them*—a grown man. Raif pushed back his hair, wishing someone would give him some answers. Everything that had happened was building up like a weight on his chest, making it harder and harder to breathe or think straight.

"Ah, good morning," Mak said cheerfully, looking over Raif's head.

"Morning." Evelyn awkwardly straightened her dishevelled tunic and cloak before joining them in front of the fire.

"Well." Mak clapped his hands together, sending birds flying from the nearby trees. "I suppose we should start with introductions. Though you already know who I am, I think, but in case you don't, it's Mak Chetwynd." He gave a quick smile, moving to rotate the roasting bird.

"We know your name." Evelyn sat up, meeting the man's gaze in an almost challenging stance. "That's all. We were told you could help."

Mak tucked his hair behind his ears. "I see. And who told you that?"

"A friend." Evelyn hunched over, picking up the edge of her cloak. "Bessie, she ran a tavern with her husband near—"

"Bessie! Fat Bessie?" Mak beamed. "Delicious apple pies, if I remember rightly. How is she? And that husband of hers, Dick, wasn't it?"

Evelyn closed her eyes, shaking her head. "They're, um ..."

Mak's face dropped for the first time that morning. "Oh, oh no. I am sorry."

"She helped us." Raif leant towards Evelyn, hoping the comment might provide comfort. "No one else would, but she did. If it hadn't been for her, we would have been caught by the soldiers who ..." *Killed Father.* It was his turn to avert his gaze, jabbing the toe of his boot into the ground. "She helped us."

Mak nodded, expression solemn. "You've all been through a lot, I can see that. Veritas can help you. In fact, I insist that we do."

Raif glanced at his sister, barely daring to believe they might find somewhere truly safe. "Help? How?"

"I don't mean to be vague," Mak said, leaning over to turn the spit. "I'll be happy to answer any questions you have. About who I am, who Veritas are." He sat back on his haunches. "But first, I'll need to know your names."

"I'm Raif Huntsman," Raif said. "This is my sister Rose. And her dog, Dog."

"Aha, Hunstman, is it?" Mak smiled. "I noticed the bow and arrows on the horse." He nodded a head towards Bert. "I assume those are yours?"

Raif felt a flush of pride at the recognition of the name passed down in his family and a flush of shame that he should be so unskilled as to live up to it. "They are," he muttered, "but I'm not a good hunter."

"Nonsense," Mak said cheerfully. "Practice, that's all you need. You're young yet. There's time, boy. There's always time."

The words bolstered Raif and he sat up, giving Mak a reserved smile.

"And what's your name?" Mak asked, turning to Evelyn.

Evelyn sniffed, wiped her nose on her sleeve, and said, "I'm Evelyn."

"Evelyn … ?"

Raif was sure he heard the grind of her teeth as her jaw clamped tight. She let out a strange snort before grumbling, "Folksman."

"Folksman." Mak moved to examine the duck, no doubt processing the name that branded Evelyn an orphan, the false title given to babies whose parents didn't bless them with their own. He gave the crackling carcass a prod before tucking his hair back behind his ears. "I see. No shame in that, girl."

Evelyn jabbed at the ground with the toe of her boot and said no more, though her cheeks reddened.

Mak clapped his hands together again, drawing Raif's attention back to him. "Well, it's nice to meet you all—properly." He grinned. "Now, almost time for some breakfast." He retrieved a square of cloth from a bag at his feet, placing the meat down to cool.

"Been together long, have they?" Mak asked, inclining his head towards Rose and Dog.

It took genuine effort for Raif to pull his gaze away from the steaming bird. "Um, not really, no. We found him after our home was … After the Commune's soldiers, uh …" He shuffled, running his finger along the weathered bark of the log he sat on. "I was trying to hunt, find something to eat in the forest. I came back and there he was, panting and filthy. Stubborn thing wouldn't leave. And, to be honest, Rose wouldn't let him." He snorted, watching his sister stroke her beloved pet. "They've been attached ever since."

"Ah," Mak said, as though Raif's statement made complete sense. "That was fortunate for you, I'm sure." He studied Dog a moment longer. "Well, shall we eat? Then we can talk properly."

Raif eagerly opened his palm to receive his portion of duck and honeyed oatcakes. He ate with as much decorum as he could muster, though he could as easily have inhaled it all in one scalding mouthful. Beside him, Rose shared her portion with a begging Dog, allowing him to lick her greasy fingers clean.

Once they'd all eaten and passed round the waterskin, Mak sat cross-legged on the ground. "So," he clasped his hands together, "I'm happy to answer any questions you have."

"You already said that," Evelyn said.

"Sorry, you're right. Go on, ask away."

"How did you get our horse? That bloody stableboy—I knew he was useless." Evelyn shook her head in disgust.

Mak laughed. "On the contrary, I think you'll find he helped you. More than happy to take a bribe, Commune's laws be damned. Else your horse would still be in Castleton, wouldn't he?" There was a playful glimmer in his brown eyes.

"Thank you," Raif said. "The bow you saw, it was my father's. It means a lot to have it back."

"Not at all."

"Wait, wait." Evelyn waved her arm in the air. "No, that's not an answer. How did you know he was ours? Why did you take him in the first place?"

"I'm getting to it, don't worry." Mak grinned. "Impatient, aren't you girl?"

Evelyn scowled, unimpressed by his jesting.

Mak continued, unperturbed. "So, my friend and I—Hector, he should be with us soon—we came into Castleton with the mission of learning what we could about the Commune's plans. Our scouts had seen evidence of them carrying out raids on the western villages. We were—"

"Yes," Raif said. "They did, they attacked our home."

"I'm sorry to hear it." Mak picked up a stone and threw it into the surrounding forest. "Heartless bastards, the lot of them."

Raif raised an eyebrow.

Mak gave an unapologetic shrug. "It's true. Anyway, I was keeping watch for anyone unusual coming into the gate. And what should I see but three children—"

"I'm not a child," Evelyn snapped. "I've seen eighteen summers."

"Right you are," Mak said. He ran his hand over the dry mud of the forest floor beside him, scraping through the dead leaves. "But even so, it was unusual to see three *so young* on their own. Round these parts, it's unheard of. So, I'll admit, I followed you."

"That much is evident," Evelyn muttered.

Mak paused, picking up a crisp, yellow leaf and twirling its stem between his fingers. "Didn't you say you were looking for me anyway? Seems to me I simply shortened your search time."

Evelyn pursed her lips, cloak twisting round her hands.

Raif sat forward. "If you were following us, why didn't you help us right away? You could've saved us some effort trying to find you. And we might not've been discovered."

"Ah, yes." Mak dropped the leaf. "Well, I wasn't following you for that long actually."

"You weren't?" Raif said.

"Why not?" Evelyn snorted. "Not very good at accomplishing your mission then."

Mak hesitated, brushing the mud from his fingers before responding. "Look," he said. "I can see how much pain you're in, but I'm not your enemy. Veritas can help you if you let us. We're fighting against the Commune."

Evelyn turned her face away, shoulders slumping. "Yes, okay. Sorry. It's just been hard. Really hard."

"I'm sorry, Evelyn." Raif was sure Evelyn's thoughts were still on Bessie. "If we hadn't come to your tavern, Bessie might still be ..." He swallowed back the useless words.

"No," she said. "You don't need to say that. It's not your fault. Let's be clear, the Commune are the ones to blame." She released the edge of her cloak, laid her hands flat on her lap. "We're on the same side, aren't we?"

"We are," Mak said. "I can promise you that."

"Okay." Evelyn sighed. "Tell us."

"So, as I said, I was following you for a while. You were heading for that inn. Then I saw something unexpected." He ran a hand through his hair. "What you did to that pie-seller ... Well, let's just say it was a surprise."

Raif flinched. *Rose's powers. He knows.*

"That was me," Evelyn blurted.

Mak raised his eyebrows. "I see." Raif was sure his eyes briefly flicked towards Rose, though the glance was so fleeting he might have imagined it.

"It was a mistake," Evelyn continued. "We wanted to avoid trouble but doing that, I only caused it."

"Ah." Mak bowed his head. "Well, perhaps it worked out in a way. It led me to truly notice you."

"Mm," Evelyn said. "That's true." She gave Raif a sideways glance.

"I wouldn't worry about it now." Mak smiled. "Once I saw that, I knew you weren't just three *young people*, I knew I had to help you—though, of course, it wasn't that simple. My comrade, Hector—where *is* that old fool?" He peered behind them, scanning the trees. "Anyway, I had to let him know. Took me half the bloody day to track him down. By the time we returned to the inn, that pie-seller was gone."

"Gone?" Evelyn tapped her leg, agitated. "Yes, he'd gone to report us."

"Yes." Mak pinched his lips together. "But like I said, no use dwelling. What's done is done. We knew we had to find you all and get away from the city. That's when I took your horse. As I mentioned, stableboy was open to a bribe. That was the easy part. Then we had to search the streets. Unfortunately, we have to keep to the shadows somewhat in Castleton." He pushed his hair behind his ear, giving a snort of derision. "You might have noticed the posters."

"We did," Evelyn said.

Raif chewed his lip, remembering the gathered crowd, the public hanging just before they'd discovered the first poster. "Why do they do that? Kill people so openly?" he asked, unable to hold the question back. "Everyone watching as if it was a- a puppet show."

"Saw that, did you?"

"And those bodies outside the city," Evelyn whispered.

"Mm." Raif grasped for his sister's hand, seeking comfort.

Mak glowered. "The Commune—that's what they do."

"I know," Raif said. "They destroyed our village. Took everyone. Our parents, our home. Rose and I, we're …" *Alone.*

Father. He inhaled slowly, breath shuddering through him. *Can't tell them yet. Need to protect Rose. She can't know.* He gulped, that horrible lump in his throat stubborn as ever. *Can't know how I failed him.*

"Took everyone? Hmm."

Raif glanced up. "Do you know where? Our parents, we might find them if we knew where to go."

"I can't be sure," Mak said. "The Commune's compound is in Taskan. It's likely where the villagers and your parents have been taken. First to be tested for powers and then—"

"Powers?" Raif frowned. "There it is again—*powers*. We didn't even know about them. Did we, Evelyn? Not until after we'd fled the attack! No one in Little Haven—" He stopped, recalling his father's words once more.

"Protect Rose … They want her."

"They lied to us, Raif," Evelyn muttered. "I think they knew."

His mind reeled. Rose's powers had been a secret from him, but his father had known something. Raif wanted to be furious. He wanted to condemn all who kept these secrets, to distance himself from the lies he didn't know surrounded his childhood home, to leave it all in his past.

He was still our father. He wanted to protect us—Rose most of all.

As quickly as it had come, Raif's impulse to hate was gone. He couldn't be angry. He couldn't forget Mother just because she'd hidden Rose's powers, nor the other villagers who might still be alive. He wouldn't pretend to be happy about the secrets they were uncovering, but no one else needed to die.

"What can we do to save them?" he asked. "The rest of the people from Little Haven."

Mak's lips tightened. "It's too risky for you to even try. I'm sorry."

"What do you mean?" Evelyn stood, clutching the hilt of her sword. "That can't be right. I thought you said Veritas were fighting the Commune. We came to find *you*, to *fight*. We can't- we can't do nothing!"

"I understand it's difficult to hear," Mak said. "Believe me, I've seen the children who have been torn from their families, the scars left behind. You aren't the first and you won't be the last."

"There must be something we can do," Evelyn continued, either not hearing or not caring about Mak's comments.

Mak watched her for a moment. "They won't be killed if that's any measure of consolation. Those with powers will be permitted to serve in the Commune's ranks. Soldiers, perhaps. Acolytes of the Grand Magister. If their powers are weak—or they have none—they'll be farmers, cooks, carpenters, labourers, maids, servants, in various estates around Septima. Nobles gladly take on those discarded by the Commune. Free workers for their extensive properties. There's very little chance of escape or rescue. I'm sorry."

Mother. Raif looked at Rose, tried to stop his lower lip from trembling. *There's no hope, is there? It's just us now.*

"No," Evelyn said. "That's not good enough." She kicked the ground. "What do the Commune want? Why are they attacking villages now?"

"It's hard to say," Mak said. "The truth is, we've been hearing rumours for some time now. Villages like yours being attacked suddenly, without warning. Once, the Grand Magister held an agreement with the noble families: any children born with powers would be handed to the Commune, no question. And there was a sort of balance, I suppose. True, children were still being taken prisoner, but it was with the approval of their parents."

Raif gawped at Rose, imagining his parents sending her away.

"And now?" Evelyn leant against a tree and crossed her arms, eyes fixed on Mak.

The man held his hands up, half shrugging. "I wish I could tell you for certain. It's clear the … offerings from noble families are not enough for him anymore. He's spread his searches, hunting down as many with powers as he can. Taking them in so the Commune can grow stronger and stronger."

How can this be fair? Raif couldn't even bring himself to question it, despite the indignation burning in his gut. He turned towards his sister, knowing he had to keep her safe no matter what.

"If those soldiers had caught you, you would have been taken to the Commune, too." Mak smiled. "I'm glad I found you when I did."

"What about the King?" Evelyn's amber eyes blazed. "How can he support this?"

"Cosmo Septimus," Mak spat the words. "That useless bastard is as much under the Grand Magister's control as the rest of Castleton and Taskan, Cragside and Ambleside—any city you can think of, in truth. Used to be that those outside the cities were safe—too poor and lowly for the attention of such a great man. We were fools to think it would remain so."

"Shit," Evelyn muttered, swinging her fist backwards against the tree. "We should never have gone to Castleton. You say the cities are the worst. Why would Bessie send us there?"

"I haven't seen Bessie in some time, and things change quickly nowadays. She couldn't have known. She sent you there in good faith," Mak said gently. "And think about it. You found me, didn't you?"

Evelyn slumped her head back. "I s'pose so."

"She did what she thought was best, Evelyn. I'm sure of it. But the Commune has been in place for a hundred years. Its loyalties run deep. These days, the support of the nobles is near unquestioned. What's the sacrifice of one child compared to protection for the realm, for their family title and land? And now, this third Grand Magister provides free labour as well?" Mak scoffed. "The commoners, too, see more and more that their safety is ensured if they do as they are told. And so the Grand Magister's hold on Septima tightens."

"Blind idiots," Evelyn said. "We're all in danger, aren't we? The Elders at Little Haven must've believed they were beyond the Commune's reach. Look where that got them."

A silence hung between them, dark and heavy as the clouds above their heads.

"What can we do?" Raif asked. "How can anyone fight against that?"

Mak gave him a measured look. "These powers are what the Commune seeks above all." He lowered a fist to the ground, grinding it into the mud. "What if they could be turned against the Grand Magister?"

Raif narrowed his eyes. "Powers," he muttered. "I've heard that word too much and I still don't really understand what it means."

Mak nodded sympathetically. "There are different levels of powers," he said. "At the most basic, they allow an individual to sense a nearby animal, to feel their thoughts, emotions, instincts. Others can change an animal's mood, calming an agitated beast or riling up an animal for attack."

Raif's heart skipped a beat, though he tried not to let it show. Rose had always been comfortable around animals and the animals, in turn, more content when she was near. *It's true then—she's always had them.*

You knew it already, don't pretend otherwise. He imagined his father saying those words, tone gentle but unrelenting.

"At their strongest and rarest," Mak continued slowly, "there are those who can control people."

"Control people?" Raif's vision swam, the blood roared in his ears. *Like Rose did to hurt that soldier. To kill those men.*

Evelyn looked at Raif, shaking her head so slightly he almost didn't notice. She moved back to the fire and sat down beside him. "How does this link to the Commune? And to you? Turning the powers against the Grand Magister, you said. How?"

Mak held his hands out, palms open to face them. "Two sides. On the right, we have the Commune. They take in those with powers in order to use them. Once in their grasp," he snapped his right hand into a fist, "you will work for and at the mercy of the Grand Magister. You will bend to his every whim; he will use your powers for whatever he wishes. Protectors of the realm, they believe themselves. Do not be mistaken, the Grand Magister is a ruthless man."

Raif barely registered the words. He pulled Rose tight, leaning his cheek against the top of her head. How could this be true, any of it? *How can I shield you if you lose control of these powers?* Dog looked up at him, dark eyes shining, ears pricked back.

"Veritas." Mak extended his left arm, hand open, palm raised. "We do all we can to spread the truth and to rescue those who would be taken by the Commune, though it's getting harder these days. We also provide training for those with powers. We believe those who have them must be taught to control them, to hone them. And then, when our ranks are strong enough, we will rise up against the Commune and free the kingdom."

Raif stared at Mak's two hands. One clenched, knuckles whitening, the other flat, relaxed. "You can help those with powers?"

"Train them, strengthen them. Keep them safe."

Relief washed over him, the tightness in his chest loosened. He clasped his sister's shoulder.

"We'll come with you," Evelyn said. "I think it's—"

"By the blasted powers, what a night." A gruff voice sounded from behind, followed by the rustling of leaves. Evelyn jumped to her feet, hand on her sword, placing herself in front of Raif and Rose.

"Ah," Mak said, smiling once more. "About time."

A short, bedraggled, and rather hairy olive-skinned man emerged from the trees, guiding a black horse by the reins, a white cat at his feet. "That was a rough night. And this bloody horse of yours is as stubborn as a soldier." He ran a finger over his thick black moustache, glinting green eyes drifting towards the three of them and Dog, then back to Mak. "Well, well," he said, bushy eyebrows waggling. "Looks like I owe you some coin."

"That you do, my friend." Mak gave him a commiserating slap on the back. "Twenty silver, if I recall correctly."

The man harrumphed, muttering under his breath as he brushed a hand through his black hair, thick and unruly as his moustache.

Mak paused, taking a moment to look behind the man. "Did anyone need our help?"

The man shook his head. "It's as Arturo and Griff said. The Nomarrans are gone. Into hiding, my contact reckons."

Mak sighed. "Of course. I trust they'll find their way to us, if they need to."

"Who will? What is it?" Evelyn asked, looking between the two men. "And who's this?"

"Oh." Mak turned to them, giving a sad smile. "Let us worry about such things. Now, let me introduce you to my good friend." He patted the short man aggressively on the back, earning himself a scowl. "Everyone, this is Hector Haralambous, a fellow member of Veritas. Hector—this is Raif and Rose Hunstman, Evelyn Folksman. And Dog, Rose's … pet."

"That so?" Hector's face immediately softened. "Pet, eh? Could be a companion. Does the lass have powers?"

"What?" Raif balked. "No, no, of course she doesn't."

Mak met Hector's eyes though said nothing.

"Companion?" Evelyn frowned. "No. We haven't seen anything."

"She's young. Might not have shown them as yet. Dog, is it?" Hector let out a brief, hearty laugh. "Course that's his name." He glanced at Rose, who was regarding him with wide-eyed curiosity. "Meaning no offense, lass." He waved his hand towards the white cat at his side, who watched them with cool yellow eyes. "My companion there is called Cara. Cats have names to suit, you see. Being the far superior creatures."

Unconcerned by the comment, Rose squatted down in an attempt to gain Cara's attention while Dog hid behind her legs, sniffing the air to determine whether this new arrival posed a threat.

Mak, who had been rummaging through his horse's saddlebags, pulled out some bundles of clothing, much the same earthen colours as his own. "I thought you might appreciate some clean clothes." He passed a bundle to each of them. "They're thicker than what you've got. Linen and wool, to keep you warm. You'll need it where we're going. Men and women dress alike in our camp." He eyed Evelyn up and down. "Though I see you're already accustomed to wearing trousers."

Evelyn bristled, running a hand self-consciously over her legs. "And where *are* we going?"

Raif coughed to hide his laughter at the sudden flush of irritation across her face.

Mak pointed towards the distant mountain range on the western horizon. "The Crystal Mountains." He moved to pack up the camp, extinguishing the fire. "Best get going."

"Wait," Evelyn said, stepping close to Raif. "We need a moment. To change."

"Very well, lass," Hector said, steering Mak away. "Be quick. We should get away from the city."

Evelyn signalled for Raif to follow her.

"What do you think?" Raif asked, pulling the brown woollen trousers on top of those he already wore. "They seem … nice. Though I am worried what it could mean for Rose if we—"

"Go to their camp," Evelyn said.

Raif glanced towards the two men. They appeared relaxed, Mak rolling his neck and stretching his arms idly, Hector surveying the trees as they spoke. As Raif watched, Hector stiffened and shot a sombre look at Mak, shaking his head briskly before quickly re-relaxing his posture and directing his attention to the forest again. Mak repeated the same arm stretches as a moment before, whilst Hector picked at an imagined piece of lint on his trousers. Raif realised then what was happening and felt anger burn in his gut. The men were putting on a show, doing everything they could to seem unbothered, casual, as if they were simply discussing the next time they thought crops would see rain—not civil unrest, not the prisons they'd be kept in if caught, not children capable of murder. *We're still nothing more than children in their eyes. Even after all we've been through—they wouldn't believe us even if we told them.*

Evelyn watched them as well. "I don't see that there's anything else for us to do. Bessie trusted them. That makes me think they're truthful when they say they want to protect us."

Raif swallowed. "But what about Rose's powers? And why are they so interested in Dog?" He eyed the white cat at Hector's feet.

"I'll do what I can to protect you both," Evelyn said. "I'll keep Rose's powers secret while we find out more, don't worry. I think that'll be safest. But maybe … well, you heard what they said. She's strong, Raif. Too strong. She'll need training, won't she? We can't keep her powers secret for long as it is. From anybody. She needs help controlling them, so she doesn't—"

"I know," Raif said. "No training right away, though. Not yet. I need time to think about it. She's only a child, Evelyn. If you're sure you can convince them it was you, if you can pretend, just for a bit—"

"Raif!" Rose jumped up behind them, still wearing the dress Bessie gave her. "Can we go to the mountains?"

Evelyn shared a glance with him before kneeling down. "Come here," she said. "Let's get this dress off you and some nice warm trousers on."

Rose grinned as Evelyn dressed her, Dog waiting beside her.

"You want to go with them, Rose?" Raif asked, pushing back some hair from his forehead. "Really?"

She nodded eagerly. "Dog wants to see the mountains," she said, beaming down at the black spaniel who barked his assent.

"Does he?" Raif chewed on his lip, looking ahead to the Crystal Mountains on the horizon. "I suppose that's where we'll have to go then, isn't it? Got to keep Dog happy."

Rose let out a gleeful cheer. "Come on, Dog!" she cried, running ahead to join Mak and Hector, new trousers and tunic making her look part of their group already.

Evelyn gave him a brief smile. "I think this is the only choice we have," she said. She moved to join the others, leaving him to stand for a moment longer. Raif knew she was right.

Veritas. A place to keep Rose safe at last.

11th Day of Solstice
13ᵗʰ Year of King Cosmo Septimus
33ʳᵈ Year of Grand Magister Quilliam Nubira Antellopie III

For the eyes of His Benevolence
Grand Magister Quilliam Nubira Antellopie III

Grand Magister,

Though this report comes later than I had hoped and without the tidings for which I would wish, I wanted to ensure that you were kept appraised of the state of affairs in Castleton.

Our patrols continue. Posters have been displayed about the city, not only spreading word of your benevolent wisdom but also alerting the citizens of Castleton to the identity of the Veritas members who we have—as you know—sought to capture for some time. For now, I must report that they continue to evade our grasp, though we have interrogated and rightfully punished those we suspect of being sympathisers to their cause.

I must advise you that three unaccompanied children entered the city. It is unknown from whence they originated, though it has been reported that their clothes were ragged and their appearance that of paupers. Perhaps I might guess at their provenance, given the recent raids you have permitted in the west of our beloved kingdom, but I do not feel it is important at this time. What is important is what ensued.

One of these children has immense powers, of that I have the word of one of my soldiers who was injured in pursuit of them.

They were almost captured though were able to flee the city with, I believe, the aid of a Veritas traitor.

Almost. It pains me to write the word.

I can only write as your humble servant and ask that you trust I will right the situation as soon as possible.

These children will be brought under our control—their powers will be confirmed, and they will be assigned positions within the Commune's ranks. If they prove to be lacking in powers and are unable to further your benevolent cause, their lives will be forfeit. On this you have my word.

Your ever loyal and faithful soldier,

E.T.

11

Commander Sulemon

"Lord Torrant has made it clear that these children and their accomplice *must* be caught. They are dangerous, with at least one of them using powers without the Grand Magister's knowledge or training. There are three—a girl with auburn hair, a boy with brown hair, a young girl with blonde hair. Travelling with a black dog, last seen with a hooded figure on horseback.

"There may be some who try to conceal the children from us. Veritas sympathisers, traitors, or plain fools." Commander Sulemon glared at the soldiers before him. Many stared at their feet, likely those with family and friends in the city—the same family and friends whose homes would be searched, for they could leave no building unchecked. Either way, their concerns were nothing to him. If their families were loyal to the Commune, their worries were unwarranted. "We must be prepared to punish those who defy the Grand Magister. By His Benevolent Powers."

His men muttered the words back to him and saluted before filing out of the barracks. As he watched them leave, his eyes crept towards the ruined towers of the castle looming over the courtyard. A shiver ran down his spine; a symbol of what could happen if those with powers were left unchecked. He knew all too well what could happen, his own childhood memories a constant echo in his heart. His hand stroked the pouch on his belt. The sacred token from his homeland, as always, filled him with a renewed sense of righteousness. *Veritarra lead me to the truth.*

"Commander Sulemon." A stableboy approached with his black stallion, a gift from Lord Torrant.

"Thank you, boy," he said, taking the reins. With a final look towards the castle, he spurred his horse through the gates of the barracks, continuing his search of the city.

Later that morning, Commander Sulemon rode his horse towards a group of soldiers ransacking the house of a merchant in the market quarter of the city. Despite his humble home, the man was dressed in fine clothes, a ruffled white shirt with billowing sleeves topped with a navy silk waistcoat such that Lord Torrant might wear—though this man's was straining across his belly. *Not fitted to him like Lord Torrant's clothes. Finery made for someone else.* Commander Sulemon's lips curled into a sneer. *Ideas above his station.* The merchant was shoved to the filthy cobblestones, eyes boggling at the Commander.

"Please, good man," he called, voice quivering with indignation. "I am loyal to His Majesty, t- to His Benevolence, the Grand Magister." He bowed his head, bald pate shining with sweat.

As he begged, a Nomarran woman was dragged from the man's home by a soldier, dressed in little more than a thin cream shift that hung from her slim frame. Commander Sulemon gasped, glaring at the merchant. Too young to be his wife, surely. He tried to catch the woman's eye but her gaze remained on the ground as she huddled her arms across her body, shivering in the cool morning air.

"Let go of her, Crowe," Commander Sulemon barked.

"Yes, Commander."

Be calm. Do not let them see your anger.

The Commander took a long breath in and out, climbing from his horse and motioning Crowe forward. "Hold the reins," he said, walking towards the woman. As a last minute thought, he clicked his fingers at the soldier. "Give me your cloak."

Crowe frowned, though obeyed without arguing, handing the thick red cloak across to the Commander who snatched it away and turned his attention back to the woman. As he approached, she peered up at him. Commander Sulemon's Nomarran accent was all but gone, while his cloak and armour showed him as a Commune soldier. He saw her recognise him as one of her own people, though her dark eyes remained cautious, glistening with tears as her lower lip trembled. He tried a smile but she visibly flinched.

"Please," he whispered, leaning down beside her. "What is your name?" Up close, he saw the bruises swelling her arms, sensed the tangible fear radiating from her. He held the red cloak out but her gaze remain downwards.

"She doesn't speak much," the merchant said. "But rest assured, soldier, I've got the papers to show she's mine. Took her on at the harbour, straight from the ship, employed as my personal maid. After the Grand Magister's latest decree, there were few else who wanted her ..." His eyes widened as he realised who he was talking to. "Er, begging your pardon, soldier. The decree, y'see ..." He shrugged, giving an unapologetic smile.

Commander Sulemon ignored the ramblings, focusing on the woman. It was in that moment he noticed. He scanned her clothing, sure he must have missed it—but where could she keep it in such a scant outfit? "Where is your ..." His heart skipped a beat. She didn't have it. He rounded on the merchant. "Where is her pouch?"

The man frowned, confused. "Pouch?" His eyes dropped to the Commander's waist. "Oh, you mean *that?*" He smirked. "Not all are as privileged as you, soldier. Nomarran immigrants must be shown their place in this new—"

The Commander punched the man, the dull smack reverberating across the street. "You will address me as *Commander*. And you will not say another word unless spoken to," he said, eyes blazing. The merchant tentatively wiped blood from his broken lip, saying nothing.

Commander Sulemon turned to the woman, trying to still his trembling hands. "What is your name?" he asked in Nomarran. His tongue felt clumsy, too big for his mouth—it had been some years since he'd spoken his native tongue. *Too long, Goddess forgive me.*

"The man calls me only 'whore'," she said, mouthing the word with hesitation as though she didn't truly comprehend its meaning. Commander Sulemon's fists quivered as he fought against the urge to beat the merchant senseless.

"What did your mother call you?" he asked, voice hoarse.

"Imarra," she said. She blinked and tears rolled down her cheeks, glinting in the meagre sunlight.

How many others has this happened to?

He already knew the answer to that, though he'd gone too long ignoring the reality before him. This decree—he needed to learn more about it. No more excuses. He'd allowed himself to be distracted by duties and orders. Perhaps he knew, deep down, what was happening; perhaps that was why he never pressed Lord Torrant to confirm the truth of it, afraid of what he already suspected.

He shook his head; he could't change what had happened now. If he could help this woman, he would. Then he would speak to Lord Torrant. He smiled, pleased to have a plan. "Imarra," he repeated. "Named for fertility and good health." Though the wariness remained on her face, the corners of her mouth twitched upwards. He held the cloak towards her and, this time, she took it gratefully, shrugging it over her shoulders. "Which island are you from?"

"Samalah's Isle," she whispered.

"Ah," he said. "I am from the Isle of Veritarra myself. Though it has been—"

"Commander Sulemon." A blonde-haired soldier approached, holding a hand against his breastplate.

The Commander exhaled. "Yes, Auras?"

"The merchant's home is clear. No sign of the children. What are we to do with him?"

Without hesitation, the Commander said, "This man is a traitor to the Commune, to the Grand Magister, and to Septima." He felt a distinct sense of satisfaction seeing the colour drain from the merchant's face. All that remained was a dark red welt where the Commander's fist had met his cheek.

"Yes, Commander," Soldier Auras said, moving to pull the man upwards.

"I am no traitor," the merchant cried.

"Come with me, Imarra," Commander Sulemon said, leaning down to help her stand.

"She belongs to me." The merchant's voice rose further as he thrashed against Soldier Auras. "I told you, I have the papers!"

"Get that traitor under control. Now."

Crowe joined Auras in restraining the merchant with a few swift punches. The old bastard cried out with each blow but still tried to fight, flailing and kicking, eyes bulging as he strained against the soldiers holding him.

"This is unfair! Unjust!" he shouted. "The king will hear of this. I am loyal to His Majesty. Do you hear me? I am *loyal.*"

Commander Sulemon was aware the scene had quickly grown out of hand. Merchants, stallholders, and shoppers alike had stopped to observe with interest. Such a scene was a treat—it might even result in a public hanging. Once the merchant had been secured within the wagon, the Commander nodded his head at Auras and Crowe, the latter eyeing his cloak around Imarra's shoulders but saying nothing. *Some respect at last.*

The Commander turned, chin up. *Perhaps this has worked out for the best.* He led Imarra to his horse and encouraged her to climb onto the animal's back. "He is a gentle beast despite his size," he said. "Do not be afraid. You can climb up." Imarra's movements were hesitant but she did as he said. The Commander sat in front of her, eager to be away from prying eyes. He did not look back as he heard the merchant's incessant cries fade away. The man would not live to see the sun set on another day.

He drew the horse to a halt at the intersection. For a moment, he wondered whether to take her to Lord Torrant. She was a Nomarran, one of his people— she deserved a safe home in Septima as he had been given. But in his gut, he already knew the reception she would receive. This was not a matter for the Commune. He would confront Lord Torrant once Imarra was safe. He would no longer accept half-truths and distractions.

There was only one place he could take Imarra.

As he rode, he found his mind wandering. He'd heard rumours of the treatment of his people and done nothing, convincing himself he couldn't possibly change the course of action chosen by the Grand Magister. *The decree. More powerful words do not exist in the Kingdom. What has the Grand Magister done?* He swallowed, suddenly feeling very helpless. He was only one man— what change could he possibly bring about? Besides, his place was by Lord Torrant's side. After seeing the devastation the accursed powers had wrought in his homeland over twenty years before—with his own father as one of those responsible—he'd known he couldn't stay. The uprising had been quelled with

Veritarra's aid, but at just sixteen years old, he'd seen the ill-concealed fear in the eyes of any who looked at him—the resemblance to his father a constant reminder of what had taken place. And so he had boarded a ship for Septima thirteen years ago, buried away the memories and pain, forgotten the boy he used to be, and found another place to call home.

He ground his teeth, angry at himself for ignoring what lay before his eyes. He inhaled slowly, calming himself as best he could. *You are doing what you can against the powers. That must be enough.* In the Commune, under the command of Lord Torrant, he could do what he'd been unable to do as a boy, watching helplessly as his home was all but decimated.

The Commander felt Imarra shift behind him on the saddle, bringing his mind back to the present. He had to get her away from here, of that he was certain. Other concerns could come later when he had time to think. They moved through the streets of Castleton. When they drew close to their destination, the Commander began to question his memory. Surely this run-down building wasn't the place he recalled.

He jumped from the horse, hand on his pouch. He took in the filthy street and abandoned shops all around. *What has happened here?* This street, the southernmost in Castleton, had once been filled with Nomarrans—shops and stalls and homes. True, he was usually posted in Taskan but it hadn't been so long since he'd last visited, had it? He shook his head, a strange pain tugging at his heart.

He moved to the building, running a hand over the mud-stained door and … Yes, there it was, the barely discernible outline of the delicate white flower of Veritarra. A crude imitation of the temples in the Noman Islands, but a place where the Nomarrans here could worship their beloved Goddess nonetheless. He pursed his lips, wondering if he'd made a mistake bringing Imarra here, but then the faintest scent of sweet, floral incense reached his nose and he knew there was still hope.

"Come," he said, helping Imarra to the ground. He pushed open the creaky door and led her inside the ramshackle temple. As his eyes adjusted to the dark, he took in the wreckage around him—broken benches, ruined tapestries, smashed pottery and statues.

He pushed open another door and led Imarra into a back room, silently praying he hadn't imagined the incense and that there was still someone here who could help.

To his relief, they found the room lit by a single lamp upon a small wooden table. The incense was stronger here, though it did little to conceal the pervading smell of damp and dust in the air. A hooded figure shifted on a stool beside the table, letting out a low, sing-song hum.

Imarra gasped, reflexively reaching for his arm.

"Do not be afraid," he said in Nomarran.

"It's been some time, Jonasaiah." The figure spoke in the King's tongue, heavily accented. "But I had a sense you might come today."

Jonasaiah. So long since he'd heard his birth name. Commander Sulemon swallowed. "I have been busy, *Samalah*," he said, knowing better than to make any further excuses. He bowed his head. "Forgive me."

The figure let out a light, lilting laugh. "No matter, a'laha." The hood was removed to reveal the woman's wrinkled old face. Her eyes twinkled in the lantern light, ethereal, full of wisdom. Beside him, Imarra let out a wordless exclamation, clasping her hands across her heart.

"This is Imarra. She needs your help."

Imarra kissed her thumb and lifted it to the ceiling. "*Samalah, Samalah,*" she said, shuffling towards the old woman.

"You may leave her with me, Jonasaiah," *Samalah* said. "She will be safe."

"Thank you," the Commander said. "Will you take her away from this city? I understand the Grand Magister has …" He found himself unable to complete the sentence, the red cloak at his back suddenly feeling like a betrayal to all he should be.

Samalah nodded slowly. "Fear not, a'laha. We are safe."

A'laha. My son. Sulemon's knees nearly buckled at the weight of such a greeting. *As though I still deserve such a welcome.*

The old woman smiled as though reading his thoughts before saying, "Arrangements have been made. There are those who have not forgotten what our people did for this kingdom, who continue to aid us."

Commander Sulemon could hardly contain the sigh of relief that passed his lips. *Safe.*

No thanks to me.

"There is still a place for you, a'laha. Always. You need only—"

"No, *Samalah*," he said, nervously peering towards the door. "Please, do not ask it of me. I cannot leave this place." He approached the old woman. She cupped his hands in her own.

"I trust you will find peace, my son." With a final knowing smile, *Samalah* led Imarra into the deep shadows at the back of the room, the red cloak over Imarra's shoulders the last thing he saw. He watched the space they had occupied for a moment.

Would it be so terrible to return to my own people? To return to my mother, Goddess pray she's still alive, to allow myself to be who I once was?

But, as ever, Lord Torrant's face flashed into his mind, the thought of leaving him like a dagger to the heart. *I cannot rip myself away. It would kill me.*

He would speak to Lord Torrant about the treatment of Nomarrans in Septima. Perhaps he *could* make a difference, if he tried.

He forced himself to slowly breathe in and out, straightened his cloak, and made for the door. It was time.

Commander Sulemon forced himself to keep his nerve as he approached Lord Torrant's door. *I am doing nothing wrong,* he reminded himself. *Simply learning what I must.* He ran his hands down his front, dusting away some imagined dirt before knocking a fist to the door.

"Enter," came Lord Torrant's voice. The Commander's heart skipped a beat. He pushed open the door, head down.

"Ah, Commander," Lord Torrant said, standing from his seat at the dining table where the usual scattering of scrolls lay. "Come in. I was just wondering how your searches were faring. Any sign of the children?"

The Commander met his eye, swallowing. "No, my Lord."

"No?" A flicker of irritation passed across Lord Torrant's face. He moved from the table to stand in front of the Commander, looking up to study his face. "Well then, why are you here? The searches must continue until those children are apprehended. I thought I made that clear."

"You did, my Lord. It's just …" Commander Sulemon hesitated. Was now the right time? Were his concerns really so important? But then he recalled the bruises on Imarra's arm, the removal of her pouch, the desecration in the Nomarran temple, and felt the heat in his gut once more. "On my search, I found one of my people. A Nomarran woman, treated appallingly by the merchant who offered her … *employment*."

Lord Torrant raised an eyebrow. "What of it, Commander?"

"The other night, at dinner, that woman, Lady Cragside, she mentioned a decree."

Lord Torrant smiled. "Now, what did I tell you about her, Commander? Why concern yourself with the ignorant views of—"

"I heard mention of it again today, my Lord. Saw what remained of the Nomarran homes in this very city. Where have they gone, the people who lived there?"

The smile fell away from the man's face. He turned away from the Commander, facing the crackling fire in the hearth. For a handful of heartbeats, silence engulfed the room. Commander Sulemon stood tall, determined that he would not lose his nerve. *Not this time.*

Lord Torrant's shoulders rose and fell as he let out a long exhale. "The decree," he said finally. He glanced at the Commander over his shoulder before walking back to his table and absent-mindedly sorting through some scrolls. "The Grand Magister has run out of patience."

Commander Sulemon frowned, unsure how to respond.

"Your people refuse to share their secrets with us, yet the Grand Magister speaks of his growing fear of late that another rebellion could be on the horizon. Think of those Veritas traitors. Could there be other groups like them, waiting for their chance?"

"Secrets?" The Commander's hand touched his leather pouch. "My Lord, Veritarra's Gift is sacred. It was given in aid to Septima a hundred years ago, yes, but it is not a weapons or supply cache hidden to—"

Lord Torrant's gaze snapped towards him, eyes pale as shards of ice. "Think of how quickly the Commune could take in those with powers with its help. These commoners who *choose* to hide from His Benevolence." He eyed the pouch at Commander Sulemon's waist. "You know how that *flower* can turn the tide in our favour. Power withheld from the Commune is a threat *to* the Commune. In *every* instance. You remember what harnessing that simple little plant did for your own home."

The Commander closed his eyes, the briefest glimpse of his father's face flashing into his mind, the sound of the noose creaking in the breeze a haunting echo in his mind. He'd been just thirteen years old when he'd watched his father hanged for the betrayal he had wrought upon his own people. "Of course I do," he whispered. "But what of the Nomarrans in Castleton? Why have their homes been ruined?"

"They have simply been moved northward," Lord Torrant said casually. "For their own safety. If the nobles of this city found out that they'd chosen to deny their aid … Well, I dread to think of what might happen to them."

"Northward?" The Commander frowned. "To Alpin?"

"Alpin, yes." Lord Torrant gave a quick nod, turning aside from the Commander to peer from the room's sole window. "The recent raids have proven to us that there are far more commoners than we ever believed possessing powers. We were foolish to think otherwise. Willfully ignorant. The previous Grand Magisters allowed the oversight to go on for too long. His Benevolence has seen the wisdom in spreading his control over the villages across Septima." Lord Torrant sighed, retrieving a half-full glass of wine from the table and swirling it in his hand. "Not to mention those god-fearing idiots in Nook Town, hiding behind their oath."

The Commander blanched. *God-fearing.* Is that how he would see me, if he knew of my ongoing love for my Goddess?

"Too long we've relied on the noble families sacrificing their children." A strained tone entered Lord Torrant's voice. He audibly swallowed before looking up, scowling slightly. "I thought you, of all people, would understand the importance of this. Perhaps I was mistaken about your loyalty to our cause."

The Commander's heart lurched. "No, my Lord. I mean, yes, of course, it's just …" He clenched his teeth. He could push for more information, learn all he could, but where would that leave him? He ran a hand over his hair, closed his eyes, wanted to scream. A warm hand came to rest on his arm.

"I know this is important to you, Jonah," Lord Torrant said softly. "But there is no more to say on it. You know I would not hide the truth from you, don't you? You know you can trust me."

Commander Sulemon nodded, though doubt nestled within his mind, barely acknowledged by his conscious thoughts.

"Good." Lord Torrant smiled as he pulled his hand back. "Perhaps you'll share some lunch with me before you return to your duties?"

The Commander returned the smile, feeling no warmth. He kept a carefully even expression as he said, "Yes, my Lord."

And so they ate, and for a time, things were as they had once been. Lord Torrant talked no more on the subject, and the Commander asked no more questions. He chewed slowly, drank slower, and let his heart, his loyalty, his dedication to being who he was supposed to be keep him silent.

Inside, he was torn apart. The voice in his head would not be repressed any longer. It told him, even as he grinned and laughed and spoke of trivial matters, that something truly immovable had shifted.

That looking the other way would kill him before it ever gave him peace.

Later that day, as dusk settled over the city, he carried out an inspection of the northern market.

"Commander Sulemon!" Soldier Auras called.

"Auras?"

"Commander, this man says he saw the children escape." Soldier Auras moved aside, revealing the man in question—brown skin stained with filth, white hair clinging to his scarred scalp in greasy clumps, dressed in a long, muddied tunic with no shoes on his calloused feet.

"*You* saw them?" Commander Sulemon could barely conceal the revulsion from his voice.

"Yes, Commander," the man said, bending into an over-exaggerated bow.

"Stand up, man," the Commander snapped. "Tell me."

"They went that way, I'm sure of it. By 'is Benevolent Powers and all that." The man guffawed, pointing a gnarled hand towards an alleyway behind the Commander. "I'm certain, y'see, as this 'ere is me usual begging spot. If I position meself jus' right—"

The Commander stopped listening to the man as he headed for the alley. "With me, Auras," he said, marching ahead and leaving the old man to his incoherent muttering.

"A reward, kind soldier?" The beggar called after him. "From one such as yourself, you must understand how awful the clench of hunger can be."

Commander Sulemon stopped abruptly. He took a deep breath before responding, not wanting the man to know how deep a wound he had prodded.

"Your reward, beggar, is not being arrested for failing to report this sooner. Some might call that treason." Commander Sulemon turned away from the man's grumbling.

"Do you believe him, Commander Sulemon?" Soldier Auras asked, jogging to keep up with the Commander's long strides. "Seems a little too good to be—"

"I'll remind you, soldier, you will speak only when spoken to," Commander Sulemon said, still reeling from the beggar's comment. He held a hand over his nose, wishing he'd brought one of Lord Torrant's scented kerchiefs. "Now, tell me what you see."

Auras studied the dead-end of the alley, brow creased. The floor was littered with debris and mouldering wooden crates, dumped by nearby merchants. The crumbling wall was sealed off with a metal grate—some long-forgotten city entrance, no doubt, disused since the Uprising over a hundred years ago.

"I-I can't see anything, Commander." Auras's eyes flitted around.

"Yes, Auras. Exactly." Commander Sulemon frowned, examining the wall around the grate. He shook his head in disgust. "How dare that filthy man lie to my face."

"Commander?"

"Back to your duties, Auras." Commander Sulemon stalked back towards the street and the beggar. *I'll show the old bastard what it means to—*

"Commander Sulemon!"

"What is it, man?"

Soldier Auras had moved to stand beside the grate in the wall. "Look, Commander," he said, pointing. Commander Sulemon narrowed his gaze, seeing nothing at first.

But then he noticed it. Near invisible in the growing dark and caught upon the dark metal bars, a clump of auburn hair.

"Are you looking forward to seeing the camp?" Griff asked, standing beside her with a friendly twinkle in his blue eyes.

Evelyn pursed her lips. "I s'pose so."

"It's nice to see new members of the group coming in. It's been a while." The young man smiled broadly, a genuine gesture, so unlike Arthur.

Still, the likeness between the two gnawed at her, leaving her unable to relax—could it be a sign? She didn't respond, watching as Griff moved ahead down the jetty.

Don't be stupid. A sign of what?

She took a moment to regain herself, straightening her clothes, tucking her braid beneath her cloak, running a hand across her forehead. "Time to go," she muttered.

Hector climbed from the boat as she approached. "See you at the camp, lass," he said, giving her a nod. The white cat at his feet rubbed herself briefly against Evelyn's leg as she passed. She paused as a strange sense of calm washed over her.

Perhaps things would be okay after all. Perhaps this boy who looked like Arthur wasn't an omen.

Perhaps.

A short time later, the group reached the far side of the Crystal River. Mak and Griff set down the oars and the boat was tied up to a wooden post on the shore.

"Well, now, that wasn't so bad, was it?" Mak climbed from the boat and stretched.

"Could we take a moment?" Raif croaked, his face an unnatural shade of white, a sheen of sweat on his top lip.

"Why, what's—oh." Mak chuckled. "Of course. We can gather ourselves before we move on."

Raif stumbled from the boat and leant against a nearby tree, gulping in breaths of air. Rose and Dog rushed over, one giggling and one barking. All he could do was groan in response.

"Leave him be, Rose," Evelyn said, though she couldn't quite conceal the amusement from her own voice. She turned to Mak and Griff, rolling her neck. "How long will the rest of the journey take?"

"Two days or so," Mak said. "We'll be at the camp soon."

"Not soon enough," Griff said, tugging a knapsack from the footwell of the boat.

"You've done well, boy." Mak passed him a waterskin. "Avanna will be pleased with your efforts."

Evelyn focused on the snowy peaks of the mountains looming ahead. "Avanna? Who's that?"

"My sister," Mak said. "The leader of Veritas."

Evelyn nodded, placing a name to the second painted face they'd seen in Castleton. "She looks like you—if the Commune got the posters right."

Mak snorted. "About the only thing they *did* get right."

"Sorry 'bout that," Raif mumbled, moving to join them with a weak, lop-sided smile. "First time on a boat."

"Not to worry," Mak said. He rummaged in his cloth satchel, pulling out a small package. "Here, chew this. It will settle your stomach." He handed over a green leaf.

Raif sniffed it before placing it in his mouth. "Oh!" he said. "Mother used to make tea with this." He chewed, the colour slowly returning to his cheeks.

"Here," Griff said. "Don't forget this." He held out Raif's bow. "You know, Arturo could teach—"

"I've already told him, Griff," Mak said.

"Thank you." Raif hooked the bow across his torso.

"Arturo's very good," Griff continued, rolling his eyes at his friend's back. He walked ahead with Raif, Rose, and Dog, mimicking a bow shot with his hands as he spoke animatedly about the archery teacher.

Evelyn waited for Mak to finish checking the boat before falling in stride with him. She pulled on the edge of her cloak, twining it between her fingers. "Mak," she said. "Will we, um … Is there any danger of the Commune finding us at the camp?"

Mak blew air through his lips. "They've tried to find us for over ten years. They haven't succeeded so far." He smiled at her, full of confidence. "You'll be safe with me. With Veritas." She searched his face, wanting to find a reason to disbelieve him. But she had to admit that maybe—just maybe—the camp might be the best place for them. Raif certainly seemed keen on the idea of a place that would provide the training Mak promised; a place where Rose could be monitored, once her powers were revealed to these strangers.

Bessie trusted Mak. The constant reminder ran through her head, fighting against the ingrained inability to trust that had been at the core of her being for much of her life.

"Okay," she said finally.

"Come on." He motioned her to follow as he marched ahead to join the others.

Evelyn glanced back in the direction of Castleton one last time, a long sigh escaping her lips. "No going back now."

They camped that night at the foot of the Crystal Mountains. It was significantly colder already, the ground sprinkled with light snowfall. Mak showed them into a small cave to shelter from the incessant winds blowing down from the white peaks. Griff set about constructing a campfire to warm them while Mak retrieved some hard sausage, cheese, sweet brown apples, and bread from his satchel.

Evelyn nibbled at the food, watching Rose and Dog as they curled beside the fire, too exhausted to stay awake any longer. Companions, Hector and Mak had called them. She'd known that's what Dog was as soon as she saw Hector and Cara. *Linked by Rose's powers. But she can do more than influence animals ...* Evelyn frowned as Mak's earlier words returned to her. "Wait," she said. "You told us there are different strengths of powers." Raif paused mid-chew, listening intently.

Mak nodded, looking caught off guard at the sudden question and taking a moment to swallow his mouthful of bread. "Been thinking about that, have you? There are. Griff, here, has a way with animals."

"Well, it's unreliable at best." Griff gave a bashful smile, cheeks flushing.

Mak elbowed him gently. "Nonsense." He lifted his chin towards Evelyn. "Why do you ask?"

Evelyn picked up a piece of cheese, crumbling it between her fingers. "If some people with powers can only influence animals, what is the Grand

Magister afraid of? Why does he want to control them? For *the good of the kingdom*? What danger do they pose?"

"Ah." Mak brandished a piece of bread at her. "You make the mistake of thinking the Grand Magister is a man who acts out of fear."

"He doesn't care about the good of Septima," Griff muttered, aggressively pulling apart his own bread as though he wished it were the Grand Magister himself.

"That's right, boy." Mak waved his hand around, flinging crumbs across the fire. "Perhaps that's why the Commune was started—some notion of aid for a kingdom ravaged by war. But it's not about helping Septima, not anymore. It's about control, plain and simple."

"Control?" Evelyn watched the fire consuming the logs carefully placed by Griff. "He's trying to take as much of it as quickly as he can."

"Of course," Mak said. "There's something desperate about his recent actions, don't you think? He wants *everyone* with powers in one place, under his watchful eye."

"Why now?" Raif moved away from his sister, voice hushed. "What's changed?"

"That's the question," Mak said.

"What about the rumours?" Griff said. "What you and Arturo spoke of when—"

"Now, boy." Mak scowled. "Superstition and hearsay, nothing more. None of us can be certain of what he's doing."

Griff's eyes dropped to the fire. "Sorry."

Evelyn raised an eyebrow at Raif, whose expression confirmed her suspicions: Mak said they could ask anything, but it seemed there were some things he was reluctant to reveal to them. This wasn't the moment to push it, though. She would bide her time and keep her ears open. *For now, agree with the obvious. Keep Mak happy.* She sat up. "So, what you're saying is we have to do everything we can to stop him," she said decisively.

Mak slapped his hands against his knees. "That we do. And you're coming to the right place, I promise you that." He stood and dusted the crumbs of food from his lap. "Now then, Griff. You and I will—"

"I'll take the watch," Evelyn said, standing and stretching her hands above her head. "I need some fresh air."

Mak eyed her. "You're sure?"

She nodded.

He shrugged, forcing an air of carelessness though Evelyn got the feeling he wanted to argue. "Well, don't stay out there too long. You'll be surprised how quickly you can chill to the bone. And wake me if there's any problems." He let out a jaw-cracking yawn. "In truth, I'm exhausted."

Evelyn gave a fleeting smile, pleased he seemed to want to keep things on friendly terms, too. "Get some sleep," she said. "I'll be fine."

If she was honest, she was drained—so tired her eyes ached—but she had too much to think on.

She wasn't sure how long she had been adrift in her thoughts, staring up at the shimmering lights in the dark night sky, when Raif came to join her.

"You should rest," she said, shuffling over on the rock outcrop she leant on. The warmth of his body beside her was a reassuring presence. *Damn. You care about him. About Rose. Dog. Even more important to stay vigilant.*

"I will," he said. "I just wanted to check on you." He raised his eyebrows at her. "You know, there's no shame in wearing the clothes Mak gave you. This waistcoat is very comfortable—though, between you and me, it just smells a bit … musty." He wrinkled his nose and Evelyn snorted.

"I'll wear mine. Don't think I'll have a choice soon. It's getting bloody cold."

Raif grinned for a moment before dropping his gaze to the ground, toeing a small pile of snow at their feet. "I've been wondering something."

"What's that?" Evelyn asked, watching him from the corner of her eye.

"Your reaction to Griff," he said. "I noticed he kind of looks like Arthur, doesn't he?" He turned towards her. "The day you left Little Haven, there was a hunting accident. I remember you bringing him back injured." He scrunched his face, as though embarrassed to say his next words. "You were gone soon after that. There were … rumours. About what happened. Why you left."

Evelyn's vision narrowed to a pinpoint, speckling like the stars above. "Raif, I—"

"No, it's okay." He held a hand up. "You don't need to tell me anything about what happened."

There was a pause, and Evelyn didn't know whether she should speak. Her mind raced, images from that final day in Little Haven flashing before her eyes.

"Your son, he- he forced himself—"

"Enough! You are to be married. That's the end of it."

"After you left, there was talk. About you and *him*—Arthur."

"Yes." Evelyn rubbed her throbbing eyes. "I'm sure there was."

"You were meant to marry him. He told everyone you'd hurt him when he asked." Raif shifted on the spot, a white cloud of breath drifting from his mouth. "I just want you to know, I'm on your side. I never liked him. Well, *Rose* never liked him—always avoided him around the village." He gave her a lopsided smile, bereft of any notion of joy. "I suppose she must've sensed something about him with her powers. Never realised at the time that was why but …" He shrugged, his arms slapping against his sides.

For a moment, their eyes met and some level of understanding passed between them. Evelyn's heart bloomed with gratitude. She nodded, not trusting herself to speak through the thickness in her throat. Of course, if he knew the truth, perhaps he wouldn't be so eager to offer his friendship. Rose had powers, true, but she was his sister. Evelyn had no such blood ties to protect her from his judgement.

No one can know. My powers, they were out of control.

A violent response, but it was justified after what Arthur did—wasn't it?

And now they elude me when I need them. She smiled bitterly to herself. *Useless, as ever.*

Finally, Raif pushed himself up from his perch. "I should try to sleep. Shall I wake Mak to relieve you?"

She shook her head. "No, I'll stay up for a while longer," she said.

"Okay," he said. "And Evelyn?"

"Hmm?"

"I'm sure you did the right thing—running away rather than marrying him."

Evelyn couldn't respond. She bit her lip and tried to smile, though was sure it must have been more of a grimace. Raif appeared not to notice, retreating back into the cave and settling down beside Rose.

Marry him. If only that was the worst of it. Evelyn closed her eyes, saw Arthur's face, his eyes gleaming with amusement, his lips upturned in a self-satisfied smirk.

He deserved far worse than what I did to him.

Evelyn knocked herself on the forehead, slapping away the unwelcome thoughts. She couldn't allow herself to sleep, not with such memories flowing so close to the surface.

She moved into the cave and sat before the fire, staring at the flickering flames, wanting only to burn away the images in her mind. There was still some time before morning.

13

Commander Sulemon

Commander Sulemon and four of his soldiers drew to a halt at the bank of the Crystal River. On the opposite shore was tied a rowing boat, bobbing with the flow of the water.

"Shit," he muttered, swinging his horse round. "Bede." He waved the man forward. "Do the tracks end here?"

Soldier Bede leapt from his mount, squatting to the floor. The man's small brown eyes were keen, darting about, taking everything in. "Some do," he said, hands trailing along the churned mud leading up to the river. "Footprints on the jetty there, you see. They must've used the boat to get across."

The Commander climbed from his stallion. He ran a hand along his chin, feeling the stubble starting to grow through. *I can't have lost them. They are far too dangerous to be free.*

"Once you have caught them, do not waste time bringing them back to Castleton. Head for my family estate. I shall finish my business in the city and meet you there." Lord Torrant had rubbed his hands together, pale blue eyes gleaming with anticipation. *"They'll be quite a catch, Jonah. Yes, that young girl's powers will be mine to present to the Grand Magister personally."*

Commander Sulemon was determined to be the one to bring them to Lord Torrant, to see the satisfaction on his face. Perhaps this was the chance to make things right between them. Not to go back to what was before, but to create a new path. A better one.

"Commander? I think … hmm." Soldier Bede moved about on his haunches, brow furrowed.

"What is it?" he asked, leaning over the hunched soldier.

Bede stood, brushing the dirt from his knees. "The horses seem to have been taken that way." He pointed south along the river.

The Commander followed his arm, squinting against the midday sun. "How many with them?"

"Just one," Bede said, scratching his balding head. "A man, looks like, from these boot prints."

"Veritas," the Commander muttered. "The one who helped them escape." He stood for a moment, considering their options. Could it be a coincidence, someone unrelated to the children travelling here? Something told him it wasn't so; that following his gut, this lead, was the best choice. Besides, the river was too deep for them to cross with their horses. He had nothing to lose by going south.

"Commander." Soldier Auras climbed from his horse. "Shouldn't we return to Castleton? Report our findings to Lord Torrant. The children's trail has run cold. How can we be sure that any tracks we follow from here will lead to the children we seek?"

"No. We go on. I believe we will find what we're looking for if we follow this trail." *Veritarra guide me.*

"But, Commander, surely—"

"You speak out of turn, Auras," he said, glowering at the young soldier. "You will stay here, keep watch. If any come to use that boat, apprehend them. They may be with Veritas."

Soldier Auras saluted, though he couldn't quite hide the glimmer of irritation in his eyes. "Yes, Commander."

"Bede, Crowe, Neston, with me." He moved to his horse and leapt into the saddle. "Bede, follow the tracks. Lead the way. If we move quickly, we may catch up with this Veritas traitor." He inhaled deeply, nostrils filling with the earthy scent of the riverbank. "I have a sense we may yet find these children."

The tracker saluted his commander, climbed atop his horse and moved southward at a brisk pace, eyes on the ground.

I will find them. Commander Sulemon gripped his horse's reins. *I will prove myself worthy of his service—of him—once more. I have to.*

What else do I have?

At the back of his mind, the voice whispered, *You have your people. The love of your Goddess*—yet it was all but drowned out by the thundering of hoofbeats as he spurred his black stallion onward.

14

Evelyn

Evelyn awoke the next morning unrested and irritable. She pressed her fingers into her eyes, hoping to banish the demons from her nightmares. *Demons. As if you don't know who it was, every dream.* She shook her head, knowing the truth.

Arthur.

Frustration boiled within her, an unwelcome companion to the anxiety that had taken hold ever since she'd fled the tavern with Raif and Rose. He'd finally made his way back into her mind, the defences she'd built for two years cracked.

You'll never amount to anything.

Arthur had been right all along.

She heard someone approach and lowered her hand from her face.

"Good morning," Raif said cheerfully. She had no energy to respond, giving him the barest hint of a smile. Since meeting Mak, Raif's hopefulness appeared fully kindled. She daren't voice her concerns and smother his optimism. If he continued to get too close to her, she'd drain it from him like a leech.

"Are you looking forward to seeing their camp? Perhaps we might be able to—"

"Not now, Raif," she snapped. His mouth flapped open before shutting again. He turned and left her alone without another word. She regretted it immediately, tried to think of the quickest apology but no words came. She stayed silent and seated. *What good would it do anyway? Let him see the real me. Then he'll realise he doesn't want to be my friend.*

I don't deserve his friendship.

She sat alone for some time before Mak came to sit beside her, rubbing his hands over the blazing fire.

"Once we reach our camp, there'll be plenty of warm food," he said.

She rolled her eyes, too short-tempered for his endless smiles and light-heartedness.

When she didn't respond, Mak said, "You care for them, that much is clear." As if to underline his point, he inclined his head towards Raif and Rose, happily playing outside with Dog.

"Yes, Mak, I do," she said, voice low.

"Well, where we're going, they can be children without fearing for their lives." His tone mimicked the one she used whenever reassuring Raif. "You don't need to protect them anymore."

"And yet, I will." She stood, the strength of her own conviction in those few words surprising even herself; a deep-seated stubbornness to prove herself to this man and everyone else. "I will continue to protect them."

I'll show you, Arthur. I'll show everyone.

She walked out of the cave, ignoring Mak's bemused stare.

That afternoon they made their way along increasingly snowy paths. Evelyn pulled her green cloak tight around her, eyes drawn upwards to the vast mountains at either side. She stamped her feet, trying to loosen some of the snow lodged on her boots—though they would soon be clogged again—hoping to bring the feeling back to her toes. The air even *tasted* cold, prickling against her skin, her tongue, making her eyes water and eyelashes freeze.

Mak, seemingly unperturbed by her gruff exit from the cave earlier, remained his irritatingly cheerful self as he and Griff walked ahead with Rose, discussing the local wildlife. Dog trotted alongside them, clumps of snow clinging to the black fur on his belly.

"You've been quiet today." Raif had fallen in step beside Evelyn, gaze glued firmly ahead. His brow was furrowed, lips set in a straight line.

"Yes, Raif, I'm—"

"I understand you're not responsible for Rose or me. Or Dog. Just 'cause we're from Little Haven too, I know that doesn't mean you care about us. But I wanted to say thank you for what you've done for us. Since we left the tavern." He spoke fast, his hands wringing together. Evelyn stopped walking.

"Raif, I didn't *help*. I froze when those men attacked—" She leant her head towards him, realising how loud her voice had become. "They attacked us and I couldn't do anything," she whispered, hand brushing the pommel of her sword. "I couldn't stop Rose from doing what she did. I'm …" She bit her lip. *Useless, don't know why I even carry a weapon.*

"You were there. What might've happened if you weren't?"

Evelyn shrugged.

"It's just this morning, you were angry with me. I'm sorry if I did something wrong." Raif stared down at the snow.

"Raif," she said, reaching to touch his shoulder before thinking better of it. "I- I should be the one saying sorry. It's hard to explain. I- There was a lot on my mind. Some things are best left unspoken because once they're out, it's-they're—"

"Real," Raif said with a brief nod. "Can't be taken back."

"That's right." Evelyn tried to keep the surprise from her voice. "They can't." She sighed and looked ahead just as Mak, Griff, and Rose turned a corner. Evelyn elbowed Raif gently, finally drawing his attention. *I have to know.* "Do you trust them?" she asked. "Mak, Griff, Veritas?"

"Do I trust them? Oh, I—"

"Evelyn, Raif!" Griff's voice was sharp.

Raif's mouth was half open, distracted from his words by the call. Without hesitation, he and Evelyn rushed forward. Her mind ran through everything that could have gone wrong in the seconds Rose had been out of their sight.

As they barreled around the corner, Raif lost his footing for a moment in the snow and Evelyn shot out her arm for him to take. Raif grabbed it just above her wrist and she pulled him upright, skin strangely warmed by the touch of his palm. Yet she couldn't dwell on the fact that she'd allowed him to touch her, that her guard had been down—where was Rose?

They passed Griff and found Rose giggling, Mak holding her on his shoulders, pointing at the view below.

"Come and see," Griff said, grinning inanely. "There she is—Veritas."

Mak beamed with pride as they approached the edge of the overlook. Evelyn willed her heartbeat to slow, adrenaline still forcing her to look for some danger as she scanned the view at their feet. Slowly, as her eyes adjusted, she saw it: deep in the snow, nestled perfectly in the valley, a levelled basin surrounded on all sides by mountains and scatters of dense, green fir trees. To the northeast of the camp, a great frozen lake. And at the centre of the basin, dozens of huts. Black smoke rose from campfires, a stark contrast to the perfect white of the steep mountainsides. A thrill ran through Evelyn's body at the sight of it— though whether it was from excitement or dread, she couldn't be sure.

This was a hidden place. Veritas was so perfectly concealed by natural barriers, she couldn't believe the mountains, the trees, the frozen lake hadn't been intentionally placed by those within the camp. Veritas was the secret, the protection, they'd been promised. And they were being trusted with its location.

What would be expected of them in return?

"Another half a day and we'll be there. I'm sure you're all looking forward to some hot food, a hut to sleep in, furs to keep you warm," Mak said, lifting Rose down and tickling her under the arm as he spoke. She let out a shrill giggle, eyes dancing with joy. "That sounds good, doesn't it?"

"Yes," she said, laughing. "Hot food and furs!" She danced around, chanting the words as Dog barked at her feet.

Mak chuckled. "It's nice to see some excitement," he said. "Come on. Let's find somewhere to camp for tonight and we'll set off at first light."

By the time they found another cave, the sun had set. The sheer whiteness of the snow-blanketed ground reflected the moon's glow, lighting their path. Inside, the cave was dark but Mak and Griff knew their way from memory. They retrieved a small stack of supplies—some salted meat, pots and pans, and dried herbs for brewing tea, all well-wrapped. In the cave's centre was a circle of stones and a pile of firewood ready for lighting.

"We keep caves like this all over the mountains, in agreement with the mountain tribes. In case any of our people get stranded in a snow-storm on their scouting missions." Mak set about preparing the fire. Rose and Dog helped Griff unpack the food. Evelyn took the opportunity to peer out at the path ahead from the cave mouth, arms folded against the biting cold.

"Rose seems happy," Raif said, moving to join her. He gave a sad smile over his shoulder. "It's good to see."

Evelyn nodded.

Raif pushed back his hair, exhaling. "No," he said.

She turned to him. "No?"

"I don't really trust them. It. Veritas. I want to, I really do." He peeked over his shoulder again, speaking in a hushed voice. "But after everything that's happened, it just seems too good to be true, doesn't it? But what choice do we have? Mak mentioned training and I think that's what would be best for Rose after, uh, you know. If we decide to tell them about her, that is." He rubbed his hands together in front of his mouth, blowing into them. "I need to help her. We have to go. At least find out what they have to say. Then we can make a decision."

"I know," Evelyn said, looking up at the moon. Somehow, hearing Raif say exactly how she felt didn't comfort her the way she thought it would. It just made her tired. "It's all we can do. We just have to make sure we keep our—"

"Who wants something to eat?" Mak called.

Raif patted her arm. "I know. Come on."

They moved inside, taking a seat by the fire. Tomorrow, they would reach Veritas. Evelyn's earlier excitement at seeing the hidden camp fading, she tried to ignore the growing knot of trepidation gnawing at her stomach.

False kindnesses, she reminded herself. *Every smile can turn.*

Raif looked back to her, smiling over his shoulder and glancing between her and the heaped ration of food Mak had presented him and Rose with. She grinned warmly, unwilling to shatter his moment of joy. *I'll have to see the truth before they do.*

15

Hector

"Damned headstrong beasts," Hector grumbled, tugging at the reins whilst doing his best to influence Bert and Hazel into obeying.

I think you might be out of practice, Cara observed. *Or your powers aren't as strong as you thought.*

"Hush," he muttered. "You know that's not true."

Cara brushed past his legs, purring.

Since the morning, they'd ridden at little more than a crawl. Hector had pulled to a halt as much from frustration as the need for a break. He stretched the stiffness from his limbs. Rolling his neck, he peered back over his shoulder. "I'm sure I can still see the bloody boat, you know."

He retrieved a waterskin from Hazel's saddlebag and took a deep swig, internally cursing himself for losing his bet to Mak. *At least I can rid myself of that debt,* he supposed. *Saves those silvers.* Though, at this point, he'd much rather pay the money and be done with it.

At that moment, Bert lifted his tail and released a vast pile of manure. Hector puckered his mouth, waving a hand to stave off the smell of fresh shit. "So undignified."

Cara gave him a sardonic stare. *I've seen you do worse.*

Hector cast her a scowl. "I can hardly see how that's relevant." He turned away from Cara, sucking on his teeth as he stood in front of the two horses. "Look you two," he said, glancing from one deep brown eye to another. "The quicker we get back to the camp, the quicker we can all eat a decent meal.

Perhaps even a good groom for the likes of you. Not that you deserve it." He stroked them both. Hazel whickered in return; Bert remained silent.

Grumpy old sod, Hector thought.

Takes one to know one, Cara noted.

"Pah," Hector grunted, digging out an apple for each horse.

"Right then. Let's try this again, shall we?" He grasped both sets of reins and encouraged the horses onwards, allowing them to set the pace for a time.

See, it's not so bad. Cara darted ahead, chasing some unseen prey.

"Mayhap." He smiled, lifting his face to enjoy the breeze gusting across the river, tendrils of black hair whipping about his face. Perhaps a slow stroll was what he needed after his exerts in Castleton.

Take it easy, old man. Cara whipped past, a blur of white.

"Quiet, cat."

Later that day, Hector sat on the riverbank enjoying some sweet brown apples and cheese. The horses seemed to be warming up to him—at bloody last—and the day had passed without event, though he still couldn't wait to be home. He'd have his bed to sleep in, sweet honeyed ale, crusty bread fresh from the oven, hot stew with—

You're trying to distract yourself from thinking of the girl.

Hector jerked, his daydreams of the camp drifting away like a puff of cloud. "And what would you know of it?" He raised an eyebrow at his cat, whose sardonic stare told him he was fooling no one—least of all his beloved companion. After all their years together, he should know better than to try and hide anything from her. He bristled with irritation, hardly ready to acknowledge his own feelings on the matter, let alone voice them to her.

But as always, she knew what was best.

"What d'you think, is she like me?" he asked. "That dog of hers ... Dog." He chuckled, twirling his moustache. "Seemed they had a connection."

You know they do. Cara moved closer, sitting next to him and following his gaze out towards the river. *Now admit I'm right about the girl.*

He exhaled sharply. "Never met anyone else like me. Only ever heard of them. And then ..." Cara purred, rubbing her head against his hand. Hector swallowed, fighting against the sudden pressure at the back of his head. "And yet, there was something different about her, wasn't there?" He stroked his bristled chin, recalling the feeling of *nothingness* surrounding the lass.

Cara blinked up at him. *Could she be shielding herself?*

"Hmm, perhaps. Hiding something, might be. Though how she could do that so effectively, so young ..." Hector pursed his lips, unease gnawing at his gut. "Bugger. Too many questions. Should've gone with them, shouldn't I? I doubt Mak realises how strong she is, if he knows at all." He punched a hand into the grass and mud. "Seen near fifty winters and I'm still fool enough to be distracted by a blasted bet. I should've—"

Too late for that now. The white cat stood, stretching out beside him. *We should get back to camp as soon as possible and—*

"Wait, what's that sound?"

Hector leapt to his feet, wiping the damp grass from his trousers. Cara was alert, ears twitching. *Horses.* She turned to him, yellow eyes wide. *Soldiers.*

He already knew it, his powers automatically roving outwards, allowing both of them to scan their surroundings. The minds he sensed were like dim lights in the periphery of his vision, weak but growing stronger by the second.

The Commune.

"Oh, fuck."

He scooped up his companion in one hand and leapt onto Bert's back, sturdier and surer to outlast Hazel in the pursuit to come.

"Find your way home, girl," he said, slapping Hazel away.

They're coming, Hector.

"I know, my love. I know. Powers be damned, I'm too bloody old for this."

He tucked Cara neatly down the front of his tunic and kicked Bert into a gallop, becoming aware of distant shouts.

Come on, come on. He gritted his teeth, leaning forward in the saddle, riding as hard as he could. If he made it to the mountain trails, he should be able to lose them.

He had to get back to Veritas, to Avanna, tell her about the lass. As he rode, he became more and more sure that she was something he'd never encountered before.

16

Raif

They arrived at the Veritas camp the next afternoon. As they made their way through the huts, Raif clutched for his sister's hand, hoping she wouldn't notice the trembling of his fingers or the tears in his eyes. He glanced at Evelyn, wondering if she saw the similarity too, but her gaze was down, brow furrowed.

Raif peered around, taking in the camp and the central hut around which it was arranged. He looked up at the plume of smoke billowing from it, drifting away towards the mountain peaks. All around, people called to each other, laughing amongst themselves, even those performing the smallest tasks did so with a gleam in their eye and a spring in their step.

Just like home.

"Keep up," Mak said. "We need to report in before anything else."

Rose's fingers twitched in his hand. He swallowed, giving her a tight smile. "We'll be safe here," he said. His sister nodded, though she frowned as she took in the scenes all around. It must be overwhelming for her, he reasoned.

It is for me as well. So like Little Haven, yet so different too.

The weight of the last two weeks sat heavy on him.

Rose's powers.

The Commune.

What would we have done without Evelyn?

What will happen to Rose? How long should we keep her secret?

He needed answers, and as they walked closer and closer to them, he imagined the very best and very worst possibilities.

As they walked, a group of children ran towards them, waving and grinning towards Rose. "You're new!" a scruffy young boy called to her in a shrill voice. Rose stiffened.

"Is that your dog?" asked a dark-haired girl. In response, Dog let out a bark, tail wagging. Rose, however, remained tense at Raif's side. At home, she'd always been shy with the other children, preferring the company of animals. She stared down at the ground, flushing under the probing gazes of these new children. Soon growing tired of her lack of response, they returned to their play. Raif watched them move away, chasing and giggling without a care in the world.

"You might like to play with them once we're settled in," he said to his sister, giving her a nudge. She nodded, wide blue eyes reflecting the bright sky. "We might have to stay here for a while."

"Okay," she said.

"Would you like to stay here?"

Rose shrugged, scuffing at the floor with her shoe. "I like Mak."

"He's nice, isn't he?" Raif eyed the man who hurried ahead of them. *I hope we can trust him.*

He so wished he could be sure, yet something in him continued to hold back. A roof over their heads, a bed, a fire, that would have to be enough for now. Trust could come later.

In any case, they had no choice but to stay here until they knew more about Rose's powers, about the villagers taken from Little Haven, about the Commune.

As he ran through the list in his mind, repeating the questions over and over, already afraid he'd forget one, his father's face flashed into his mind. His stomach clenched, though he did his best to hide it.

"Raif?" Rose peered up at him.

"I'm fine," he said, trying his best to sound cheerful. "Just hungry." He looked away, afraid his eyes might reveal the truth.

Father.

An image of his face entered Raif's mind again—this time with such clarity, he physically flinched, accidentally pushing his sister away. The image instantly disappeared. He gasped, realising that somehow Rose had caused it.

He'd been hiding the truth about their father's death—but how much did she already know? Guilt and shame flooded into his mind, nearly knocking the breath from him. He swallowed, watching Rose from the corner of his eye—could she see into his mind? *Does she know what I've hidden? How I failed Father?*

He frowned to himself. His pain was intense, a constant burn in his heart always threatening to burst forth. *Can she sense it?* Was he a fool for thinking they'd keep the immensity of her powers a secret? He tentatively touched her arm and felt nothing.

"Raif," she said, pointing. "Look."

Ahead, Mak had come to a stop outside the central hut. They moved to join him and stood before two men, swords strapped to their waists. A flurry of apprehension bubbled up within Raif. If this was a friendly place, why were there guards?

"Wait here," Mak said. "I will enter first." He disappeared beneath the hanging canopy door of the hut.

A few minutes passed. Evelyn stood behind them, absent-mindedly fiddling with the end of her braid.

"Evelyn," Raif said, keen to know her thoughts on the camp. She didn't respond. "Evelyn." He touched her shoulder.

She jerked back, scowling. "Oh," she said, blinking. "Raif." Her lips curved upwards, a smile that didn't touch her eyes.

"What's wrong?"

She cleared her throat. "I'm fine. Just didn't sleep well."

"Okay." He leant his head close, eyeing the guards at their back. "Remember our promise."

"Promise?"

"About Rose. We have to keep what she did between us. I, uh … I'm scared she'd be in trouble if we told anyone. *Real* trouble."

Evelyn nodded. "Of course."

"Thank you. I need to think about whether to tell these people about her … you know."

"I know." She gave him a brief smile. "Don't worry."

Before long, Mak's head appeared from the doorway of the hut and he waved, summoning them in. Raif bowed his head, pushed away his doubts and ushered Rose forward. It was time to learn about Veritas.

17

Hector

For a day and a night, they'd ridden. The sun was high again, and Hector's whole body ached, his stomach empty, eyes dry, muscles tight. Cara was now tucked behind his back while Bert panted beneath him, his coat gleaming with sweat. Hector patted the horse, feeling his growing exhaustion. *A little further,* he willed through his powers, hoping to reinvigorate him, asking for just a little more each time. And, to his relief, Bert kept on responding, kept on going.

Still, the soldiers maintained their pace. They were dogged in their pursuit. Though Hector lost sight of them more than once, they always reappeared, forcing their own horses ever onwards.

As they approached the treacherous mountain paths, Hector risked another glance behind.

"Ahead, Commander Sulemon! I see him!" one soldier shouted.

Commander Sulemon. The Nomarran in Lord Torrant's service.

"Stop! Hector Haralambous! I know your face, traitor!"

Shit.

Hector knew he could lead the soldiers through the mountain trails for a time but he would eventually have to fight them. *Better sooner than later,* he decided. *While I still have reserves left to defend myself.* He began to steel himself for it had been some time since his powers had been called upon for such a task. He hadn't killed a man since …

He shook his head—this was not the time to think on past regrets.

Cara peeked her head over his shoulder. *They're close.*

"I know, girl. I need to get to a clearing. Then we'll make our stand."

The cave.

He didn't need to respond; Cara knew his mind and oftentimes he spoke aloud from simple habit. The cave she suggested was closer to the camp than he would have liked, but she was right; it was his best chance. It would provide shelter if he was injured—and would allow for someone to find his body should the worst happen. He let out a shuddering breath, trying to calm his rising nerves and the fluttering of his heart.

I'm here. You're not alone.

He smiled tightly, appreciating Cara's attempt at reassurance. Unfortunately, there were some things she could never truly understand. How it felt to kill a man, no matter the circumstance, would always be one of them.

The mountain air grew colder as he ascended the paths, the snow thick beneath the horse's feet. The soldiers cried out behind him, shouts of encouragement passing between them. To them, it must have been a game. Away from the confines of the city, they could test themselves. Prove themselves worthy of the Grand Magister's approval, perhaps even make a name for themselves. He knew that if he reached his powers outwards, he would sense their thrill, excitement, determination. But their powers would be nothing compared to his, of that he was sure.

They are weak, Cara confirmed. *Barely detectable.*

Hector allowed himself a small smile. That, at least, was something in his favour. He kicked his heels into Bert's sides. The old horse was surefooted on the snowy paths, kicking up flurries as he ran, snorting heavily with every hoof beat.

The cave was close now. Hector hardly registered the scratch of the fir trees as they lashed against his arms. He allowed muscle memory to take over, ignoring his surroundings. Completely absorbed in readying himself, he didn't notice the soldier closing in on him until Cara's urgency broke through his concentration.

Watch out!

Hector unsheathed his sword, turning awkwardly in the saddle and meeting the soldier's blade, his teeth jarring. The clash of steel rang out, echoing through the stillness of the mountains. At the clang, the soldier's triumph turned to bewilderment in his small, brown eyes; perhaps he had believed this would be weak prey, an easy kill.

I won't give them the satisfaction of dying so quickly.

Before the soldier could react, Hector reached out with his mind. The man's eyes grew dull in an instant, his arm falling to his side, his sword dropping to the ground with a snow-muffled thud.

The use of his powers, once unleashed, was as natural for Hector as breathing. He directed the soldier to ride his horse into a nearby ravine between two diverging pathways, hidden by deep snowdrift. The man didn't make a sound as he fell to his death, though his horse let out a scream that Hector wouldn't forget.

Two more deaths to my name. Cara purred and nuzzled him, though it did little to ease the ache in his chest.

"You monster." The voice came from behind, full of vehemence. As Hector turned, distance finally closed between him and his pursuers, the Commander jutted out his jaw. "Go," he said to his remaining men.

"Yes, Commander Sulemon."

Hector didn't wait, spurring Bert on. As the cave mouth came into view, Hector leapt from Bert's back, directed him to stay around the side of the entrance, and hurried inside. It was low-ceilinged, running deep into the mountainside. He hoped he would have the advantage here, his stature allowing him to reach the rear of the cave largely unimpeded. He placed Cara at his feet.

Who'd have thought you'd be glad of your shortness for once.

He snorted. "True." He flicked his head towards the cave entrance. "Now go," he said. "Keep your distance."

She watched him for a moment as though thinking to argue before trotting away, camouflaging herself against the snowy ground.

Hector held his sword in a defensive stance, waiting for the men. The two soldiers came first. He reached into each man's mind in turn, gauging their feelings, seeking out their weaknesses. With the Commander there would be no such tactic, for it was well known that many Nomarrans held a Goddess-granted immunity to powers. He'd have to beat him physically, or not at all.

Focus.

"Damn it, Cara," he muttered, glancing around to check she wasn't too close. But she *was* right, as always.

The soldiers stood in unison, blocking Hector's path out of the cave. They were both young, brown-haired and fresh-faced, their armour well polished, unmarked and undented, their eyes glimmering with a mixture of determination and wariness. Their first real fight, perhaps. The excitement of the chase had thawed, their friend had fallen, and they were left with the realisation that Hector truly was a danger.

The blue-eyed one stepped forward and attempted to use his pathetic powers, visibly straining as he did so. No matter—even in his exhausted state, Hector knew he was far stronger. Without a second thought, he took over the man's mind. The soldier's eyes widened and dulled in a second. At Hector's unspoken command, he faced his fellow soldier, sword poised for attack.

"Jack?" The unnamed soldier edged backwards. "Snap out of it! What've you done to 'im?" His glare towards Hector was ferocious, yet his trembling lip gave away his fear. "Jack? Jack!" The soldier pressed himself against the cave wall, fumbling and dropping his sword. He groped about desperately, grasping for a fist-sized rock on the cave floor.

"I'll attack, Jack! You'll give me no choice," he squeaked.

Without a flicker of emotion or recognition, Jack attacked. It gave Hector no satisfaction to hear the unnamed man's screams echoing through the mountain air.

He'd done all he could. He would leave them to kill each other.

Hector shifted his attention from the fight—though still maintaining his control over Jack's mind—and onto the Commander. The Nomarran stalked into the cave like a hunter waiting for his moment, unperturbed by the plight of his men, dark eyes fixed on Hector with an air of undeniable hatred. Unlike his soldiers, he was largely unarmoured, with only a gleaming iron plate across his chest, curving with the line of his ribs, decorated with a golden crest. His black undertunic, trousers, and boots were form-fitting, outlining the broad musculature of his chest and shoulders. The red cloak at his back was stark against the whiteness of the snowy ground outside, his hand rested on the golden grip of his sword, the muscles in his arm taut and and ready for attack. He was much bigger than Hector, his movements slow and lumbering.

Careful. Considered.

Shut up, Cara.

"You are truly an abomination," the Commander spat, grinding his teeth as though holding back a flurry of further insults. He pursed his lips, looking down his nose as his nostrils flared with evident disgust. "We've hunted you for a long time, Veritas scum. Your actions go against the very kingdom you profess to love."

Hector raised an eyebrow. "Says the man who stands by while his fellow country folk are terrorised by the Grand Magister, forced from their homes— lives ruined." He pointed his sword at the Commander. "*We* have provided them shelter and safety. Are we traitors to them too?"

For a moment, Hector imagined he saw a glimmer of hesitation in the Commander's eye—some unspoken doubt that his words had sparked. Seconds later, it was gone. Commander Sulemon growled, thrusting forward with his sword such that Hector barely had time to parry the attack.

"You think you can control me with words. Do not mistake me for my weak-minded men," the Commander said, circling Hector. There was an amused flicker in his dark eyes, though his face was an expressionless mask, his voice little more than a whisper. "I'm afraid you will have to use other means to fight me."

With that, the Commander darted forward again, as fast and graceful a fighter as Hector had ever seen; he realised the earlier thrust had been a feint, a taunt, a mere fraction of the man's true ability.

Hector knew then he was unlikely to see the sun set on another day.

Still, he forced himself to dance with the man, meeting every sword swing, using his agility to his advantage as best he could. If he kept defending, it might be the larger man would tire. *Ha, you know he won't, old fool.* Hector cried out, batting away another sword strike, infurirated by his own self-doubt.

But there was something at the edge of his mind even as the clash of steel echoed through the cave, as sweat formed on his brow and ran down his back, as the Commander lunged and parried and jabbed.

Cara. She was trying to speak to him. Her thoughts prodded at him, though he pushed them away, afraid to remove his attention from Commander Sulemon.

They circled each other, again and again. Within the periphery of his consciousness, Hector noted the fighting soldiers had grown silent. He risked a glance towards them and noted a slumped body, the red of blood spreading across the snow-covered ground.

Snapping himself back to the Commander's leering face, Hector met another sword slash, the slam of the impact numbing his entire arm.

Shit.

In his panic, he tried to manoeuvre the fight towards the back of the cave, hoping the sloped ceiling would impede the Commander's movements. But his opponent anticipated his every move, expertly steering Hector back towards the entrance, fighting without sign of slowing.

Hector.

"No," he groaned. "Cara, no."

"What? No? Had enough, traitor?" The Commander sneered.

Hector blinked the sweat from his eyes, entire body shaking as he dashed away another sword stroke.

"Speak if you mean to, monster."

Jab, slash.

Hector couldn't respond; his thoughts were blurring together, his movements awkward and jerking. His time was coming to an end. There was no way out.

"Come on then," he growled. "Be done with it."

Commander Sulemon nodded, a strange sort of respect passing over his face. "Very well," he said. "You meet your death like a—"

Suddenly, there was a darting movement at the corner of his eye.

"No!" Hector cried, pivoting.

He realised too late that the Commander had the opportunity for unimpeded attack. His sword slashed upwards. The steel met Hector's thigh, biting into flesh. A scream erupted from his mouth as his left leg buckled, blood gushing from the wound.

As he collapsed to his knees, he watched his beloved companion leap at the Commander's face. He couldn't stop her. She screeched an otherworldly sound. The Commander dropped his sword, scrambling to remove her from his face, his cries muffled by her lithe body.

"What is this, monster? What—argh!"

Hector grimaced, dizzy from through the pain. Cara was giving him a chance, he had to help her. He pushed himself up, vaguely aware of the blood pulsating from his left leg, pooling on the ground. He moved as though in a dream, throwing his weight at the Commander without thinking.

The man lurched backwards, arms flailing. His head hit an outcropping of stone on the cave wall with a sickening thud. He stopped fighting Cara, arms slumping to his side as he fell silent.

Hector's beloved companion slinked away from the unconscious Commander, his face a mess of bloody scratches. Hector slumped to the floor beside him, breathing hard and fast. Painfully slow, he removed the belt from his waist and tightened it round his leg.

My love.

Cara purred.

The horse, Cara.

She darted from the cave, finding Bert and winding between his legs.

Get help, she said, using Hector's own powers to influence him. The old horse obeyed without delay, galloping away.

Hector blinked around, taking in the scene before him—the Commander motionless. And amidst the churned red snow nearer the entrance, one body.

One.

"Oh, Cara," he croaked.

Yes. One got away.

He propped his head against the cave wall and clung to his waning consciousness.

18

Evelyn

Evelyn straightened her clothes, brushed back the wisps of hair from her face. *Time to get some answers.* She nodded to Raif and Rose, and the three entered the hut.

Inside, the air was heated to an almost uncomfortable level by the central firepit. Smoke billowed upwards, drawn through a chimney. Evelyn squinted against the brightness of the flames as her eyes adjusted. There were animal furs on the floor and lining the walls, varying in colour from tan-beige to deep black. It was larger than expected too, with a smaller room separated from the main hut, a fur hanging across the doorway and blocking anyone from seeing inside.

At the centre of the main room, a woman sat on a wooden chair behind the fire. Her face was obscured by the dancing flames, features flickering in and out of visibility too quickly to get a full image. Despite this, Evelyn had the sense she was being watched.

"This is my sister, Avanna," Mak said, arm held out. He introduced them each in turn.

"Welcome to the camp," Avanna said, standing and holding her hands out in greeting. Like her brother, she had wide-set brown eyes and shoulder-length hair. However, where Mak might have worn an easy, friendly expression, there was an uneasy air to the smile she gave. She was trying to emulate her brother's natural warmth and failing. She wore a similar outfit to her brother too—much like everyone in the camp, it seemed, with brown trousers and cream tunic, though her wool waistcoat was dark blue rather than green and was considerably less faded. It was clear she took pride in her appearance and held herself as such as she moved round the firepit to stand in front of them. Evelyn couldn't deny she had a certain presence about her; she drew the attention of all as she cleared her throat to speak.

"My brother tells me you've had a long and stressful journey," she said. "Please, take a seat. Some refreshments will be here soon." She directed them towards a cushioned seating area in the corner.

Evelyn sat beside Raif and Rose with Avanna and Mak opposite. Dog scratched at some of the furs before circling twice, lying down, and promptly falling asleep.

"You aren't the only ones to seek shelter here," Avanna said, eyes drifting over them all—hesitating a moment longer on Rose. She turned to Mak. "We had some more arrivals while you were away. Nomarran men, a few women, and children. I'm sure they won't be the last."

Mak nodded gravely.

"Nomarrans? We passed some on the road ourselves. And there was one … There was a man in the tavern where we- where I—" She glanced at Raif and Rose, gulping.

Avanna's gaze was intense—sympathetic and measuring both at once. "These are trying times for many," she said, bowing her head. "But enough of such talk. You are safe now. Tell me about yourselves. Or if you have any questions, you may ask them."

Raif chewed his lip. "*Will* we be safe here?" he asked. "My sister and I, we need- We've lost everything."

Avanna nodded. "I am sorry," she said. "I can assure you that we will do all we can to protect you. My brother wouldn't have brought you here otherwise." She smiled widely and Raif smiled back. For some reason, it irritated Evelyn. She jiggled her leg, watching the woman closely. *She says the right words but …*

Before any more could be said, a dark-haired girl arrived, carrying a wooden tray stacked with fresh bread, bowls of lamb and vegetable stew, tankards of mulled ale.

"Ah, here we are. Thank you, Flo," Avanna said, clasping her hands together. "Don't be shy. I'm sure it's been a while since you ate something hot and fresh."

time when we rescued you. You saw the posters around the city. We're well known." Mak gave an uneasy smile before continuing. "The villagers will have been taken there—to Taskan, the Commune's compound."

Raif sniffed. "What will happen to them?"

Mak shook his head, unwilling to meet the boy's eyes. "The Grand Magister, he—"

"He needs workers for his land," Avanna interjected. "They will be there, kept as servants within the Commune's compound. But do not give up hope. We might be able to think of a way to rescue them yet, along with others who have been taken."

Evelyn raised an eyebrow at her sharp interruption of Mak. *Did Raif notice?* She watched him nod, clearly believing Avanna's words.

"Mother might still be alive," he said to Rose.

Evelyn watched as Raif and Rose allowed themselves a shared smile. Evelyn bit her lip. She would not be the one to shatter the hope growing here. She would bide her time, learn what she could, keep Rose's secret, as she'd promised Raif.

And question Avanna until she finally speaks in full truths. But not today. Today was about making friends, allies, securing their safety.

"Tell us how we can stop the Commune," she said. "What can we do here and now?"

Avanna's mouth drew into a tight line. "That is precisely what we are working towards. It will take time. First of all, you must learn," she said. "We offer training to those with powers." Her eyes flitted to Rose, to Dog at her side. "There is other training available too. Fighting, cooking, hunting."

"And what in return? What do you expect of us for this promise of protection?" Evelyn was no fool. Bessie taught her to never accept a promise without knowing the cost.

"Evelyn." Avanna laughed gently, and Mak cracked a smile.

He leant towards his sister, feigning a whisper. "What did I tell you?"

Avanna shook her head. "We expect nothing from you. You are welcome to stay here. We can help you to train, should you need it. That's all."

Evelyn refused to look at Mak, instead glaring at Avanna. In that moment, however, she could find no reason strong enough to accuse her of lying. She bit her lip again, fighting to stop herself from saying something she might regret.

"Tell me," Avanna said. "How long has Rose had her companion?" She nodded towards Dog as though there could be any doubt as to who she meant.

"Companion?" Raif asked, voice straining a little too much. "Dog? Um, we found him just after the attack on Little Haven. Well, Rose did, didn't you?"

Rose nodded, hiding behind her brother's arm as she shied away from Avanna and Mak's direct attention.

"Said his name was Dog." Raif puffed out his cheeks and rolled his eyes. "Couldn't get rid of him after that." He smiled at his sister.

Avanna and Mak shared another look—another piece of the picture held back from them. Evelyn stared, bristling with irritation. *We are not naïve children.*

Evelyn watched the pair. "What does it ... Why do you ask?"

"Oh," Avanna said. "Perhaps it's nothing. But there are those whose abilities are unusually strong. They attract certain animals. A companion. They become connected in a way imperceptible to the rest of us."

"And you think Dog and Rose are ..." Raif's brow furrowed.

"It may be. At the least it's possible. Which would make training Rose all the more important." Avanna raised her eyes to the ceiling of the hut, runing a hand along her chin. "Has she shown any significant powers?"

It was Evelyn and Raif's turn to share a wary glance. They shook their heads, just barely, in unison. "No," said Evelyn. "Nothing unusual."

"If we find out she does need any ... Well, I'd like any training to be discussed with me first," Raif said. "She's my sister. I'm responsible for her."

"Of course," Avanna said, bowing her head.

Rose sat in silence, bright blue eyes reflecting the firelight as she cuddled up to Dog.

"When do you plan to fight the Commune?" Evelyn asked suddenly, hoping to catch Avanna off-guard.

A scowl passed over the woman's face before she regained her composure, smiling once more. "It is important you understand what we are offering. Training is needed to ensure everyone's potential is discovered and controlled."

Evelyn swallowed; she abruptly got the feeling she shouldn't share how she'd discovered her powers. She shrugged, trying to appear nonchalant. "All this talk of training. But we have to do *something* about the Commune in the meantime, don't we?" She needed Avanna to agree, needed to know there would be *something*, even a promise of *one day* they'd fight. A promise she'd be able to prove herself.

You'll never amount to anything. Evelyn couldn't help hearing Arthur's words in Avanna's avoidance of her question. *I'll show you, bastard.* "We can't just do nothing. How long will we be here?"

"I will have to monitor Rose closely to determine her powers. I know you're frustrated and seeking answers but—"

Evelyn stood and began to pace, restlessness coursing through her body. "How long?"

"You ask as though there's a definitive answer. Weeks, months," Avanna said, shaking her head. "It's not possible to say yet."

"No, no, we can't wait that long. We have to fight them. We have to help those who were taken from Little Haven—from who knows where else." Evelyn's voice rose. She was sure that fighting the Commune—rescuing those taken—was the right thing to do. Why wouldn't Avanna just *agree*?

She stared hard at Raif, trying to make him see how disappointing this was, but his face was pure confusion. Dog watched her with dark eyes, head tilted to the side.

"And we will, child, but we have to be prepared," Mak said, moving towards Evelyn with an outreached hand. She slapped it away.

"I am not a child," she said, storming from the hut. "If you won't help us, we can fight them ourselves."

So much for diplomacy.

Later that day, Evelyn made her way back into camp. She'd taken herself for a walk to calm down, though the chill in the air and the winding mountain paths soon drove her back the way she'd come. Her stubbornness didn't go so far as to risk her own life and leave Raif and Rose alone in this place.

Nothing but a bunch of cowards. Bragging about their past adventures, heroic days long behind them. They're hiding here.

As she moved through the camp, she saw Raif was already beginning his archery training. Mak was inside the ring alongside an older man with a scarred face and long grey hair pulled into a horsetail. As the man spoke, Raif's eyes returned repeatedly to Avanna's hut.

She must have Rose, Evelyn realised. *Selfish, selfish! Leaving just as they started to question about Rose. You promised Raif.* She hurried towards the hut.

As she neared, she heard Avanna's muffled voice from within, though could not make out her words. The guards outside the hut blocked her way as she tried to enter.

"Avanna has not requested your presence," said the first, a grey-bearded man.

"I need to see her," Evelyn said, trying to push through them. "She has my friend."

"You haven't been sent for," said the second, a ruddy-cheeked young man with short brown hair. "And your friend is busy. Leave it, child."

Child. He's barely older than me! She glared but the guards ignored her, unmoved by her anger. She had to get Raif—this wasn't right.

As she made her way back towards the archery ring, she knew she had to get Raif's attention without raising Mak's suspicions.

Bessie trusted them.

Yes, but why? They're treating us like idiots.

No answers, only more questions. She had promised to help Raif and Rose. She dug her fingernails into her palms, utterly at a loss.

"Evelyn!" The voice called out from behind. *Ugh, not now.* She kept walking. If she didn't respond, maybe he would move on, let her go.

"Evelyn." He was nearer now, footsteps crunching on snow.

A hand clamped on her shoulder and it took all of her might not to lash out.

There he was, so like Arthur.

"Didn't you hear me?" Griff said, grinning.

"No," she replied. She crossed her arms, her whole body tensed to flee at the slightest threat, but she was glued to the spot by his gaze.

"Mak asked me to fetch you," he said.

"To *fetch* me?" It was difficult to make eye contact with him without her stomach churning.

Griff's smile didn't flinch. "He's asked you to go to the archery ring," he said. "I think he's got Raif there as well, so—"

"I know where he is," she snapped, irritated by his ease in mentioning Raif.

"Griff?" A woman's voice called from a nearby hut.

"I must get back to work. I'm showing the new group around—Nomarrans. Did Avanna tell you?" His eyes sparkled with excitement. "I've never met anyone from the Noman Islands before. I'm going to try and help them settle in here, I'm sure it must be strange for them being here in the mountains." He paused as though waiting for Evelyn to say something. When she didn't, he gave a small shrug and smiled. "Well, see you around soon, I hope!" She imagined she saw a flash of something else—his true intentions—for a moment and thought she might implode with fear and hatred. "Bye, Evelyn."

She watched him walk away, hands clenched, unable to move.

"You're lucky to have someone like me interested in you, you know. An orphan dumped in the forest."

She closed her eyes and focused on her breathing, trying desperately to break through the iron vice tightening around her chest.

"You should consider yourself privileged."

As she stood, immersed in the memory of that awful morning two years ago, she became aware of the distant sound of hoofbeats drawing ever closer.

She blinked and turned just in time to see Bert galloping through the camp. He nearly overshot her, barely stopping in front of her and tossing his neck, pants billowing steam from his nostrils.

"What the ..." He bumped his nose against her arm. "Why are you alone? What's happened?"

He whickered, nostrils flaring, eyes wide. She ran a hand along his neck, slick with sweat. "Where's Hector?" She'd never seen Bert like this, not even on the night they'd fled the tavern. She took hold of the horse's reins, leading him at a jog towards the archery ring.

"Mak," she called. "Bert just arrived—unaccompanied." Raif was focusing on firing an arrow under the watchful eye of the grey-haired man. Mak looked up, grin melting away when he saw her.

"Hector could be in danger," he said. "I'll gather some men, search for him. Take Raif, go to my sister. Tell her what's happened."

"Is it them?" Evelyn struggled to keep the tremble from her voice.

Mak's mouth pinched with worry. "I can't be sure," he said. "I must go."

"Evelyn," Raif said, approaching. "What's going on?"

"I- I'm not sure," she said. "I think maybe Hector's in trouble."

"The Commune?" Raif's mouth dropped open.

Evelyn swallowed. *Have they found us already?* "I don't know," she admitted. "Let's wait and find out before jumping to conclusions."

"You're right," he said, though his face was drawn.

Evelyn nodded and nudged his arm. "Of course I am," she said, offering a weak smile.

Internally, however, she was in turmoil. She'd been a damned fool. She watched Mak until he was out of sight, guilt heavy as she thought of what could have befallen his friend because of their decision to help. *And I was an ungrateful wretch to him and Avanna earlier.*

"Evelyn." She snapped back as Raif tugged on her arm. "Shall we go?"

"Yes, sorry," she said. She was still clutching Bert's reins, leather twisted tightly around her knuckles. She gave the horse's nose a stroke, a sense of calm returning to her. Where Bert was, she still had her link to Bessie.

To home.

What would Bessie do? And Evelyn knew immediately. *She wouldn't be a bloody brat, and she'd help the people who were promising her the same.*

"Let's go to Avanna. We need to find out what's happened to Hector. We need to try and help."

15th Day of Solstice
13th Year of King Cosmo Septimus
33rd Year of Grand Magister Quilliam Nubira Antellopie III

For the eyes of His Benevolence
Grand Magister Quilliam Nubira Antellopie III

Grand Magister,

I write with grave news.

The soldier of whom I previously wrote, injured by a young girl's untrained powers, has lost his life. Though it was believed he would recover from his wound, a fever took him in the night.

This, of course, means that the girl in question is now a murderer. She has willfully and unlawfully taken the life of an innocent man—a Commune soldier. There is no telling what else she might do without the wisdom of your benevolent gaze.

Rest assured, Commander Sulemon has led his men in pursuit of these children, these criminals. He will not cease until they are in our hands and this girl has answered for her actions. I am sure of this.

Meanwhile, I am pleased to report that no fewer than 21 traitors have been hung from the city walls of Castleton—a reminder to all that the Commune's power is present, its justice swift.

I will report again as soon as I have news.

Your ever loyal and faithful soldier,

E.T.

19

Evelyn

It was the third time Arthur took Evelyn out hunting. It was mid-morning and he'd promised her they would catch a rabbit that day so he could show her how to build a fire, then skin and cook their kill.

It was a welcome distraction. Of late, she'd grown restless in Little Haven, her mind often wandering as she longed for a life far more adventurous than what she'd come to know. She knew the village Elders were content to have her away from the other young girls in learning their "womanly duties"—and Evelyn didn't mind missing the lessons in the slightest.

She'd always been an outsider in Little Haven—an orphan, alone, abandoned as a young child by parents who didn't want her. She didn't even know her true age, though the Elders guessed she couldn't have been more than two years when she had been left outside their hut that night, wrapped in the green cloak she still treasured to this day. They had taken pity on her, vowed to bring her into their community. But in the years since, she'd grown more and more aware that this was an impossible task. She simply didn't fit in with the contented family life of Little Haven. Without a family, she couldn't.

As such, she couldn't bear to be around the other girls, so prone to giggling and gossiping and fluttering their eyelashes at the boys—Arthur most of all. It gave her a small thrill of satisfaction to see their crestfallen expressions as she and Arthur paraded by; she with her battered sword—a gift from the village smith Tomas, second-hand but much cherished—and he with his hunting bow and arrows. She'd smirked at them, full of foolish pride.

As they left the village, Evelyn realised Arthur was conducting most of their conversation. The people of Little Haven had always been polite, but never truly tried to bring her into their circles, their families, and she'd adapted to the quiet. She'd hoped she could make up for her clumsy socialising, prove one way or another she had been the right companion for Arthur to choose on these excursions.

Evelyn soon found she had a natural aptitude for hunting; she learned much quicker than she ever had in the lessons on clothing repair, animal-keeping, or food preparation. She was thrilled—there was something much more instinctual about this. Even more satisfying, she was actually beginning to enjoy the time with Arthur, despite telling herself that such infatuations were for the silly young girls in the village.

She peeked at him now as they lay stomach down on the crest of a hill, concealed within some shrubbery, observing a rabbit-grazing spot. His face, tanned from days out in the sun, had some of the softness of youth, but she had begun to notice his strong jawline, currently clenched in concentration, and the deep blue of his eyes, focused on their target. He brushed back his short blonde hair and winked at her, placing a finger over his lips. She snapped her eyes back down to the rabbits, hoping he wouldn't notice the flush of colour in her cheeks.

"They're sensitive to noise," he whispered, his head leaning close to hers. "That's why we have to stay still for a while. Allow them to get used to our presence."

Her flesh prickled as his breath tickled her ear, their shoulders touching. She smiled at him and he smiled back. Her stomach fluttered. *Pull it together,* she told herself.

With an expertise she had grown to admire, he hopped to his feet without making a sound. He poised himself in a low squat, pulling an arrow from his back and positioning himself to shoot. She saw the truth in his words; they had remained still and patient, taken their time, and now the rabbits were eating contentedly, unaware of the danger. With a slow exhale, he released his arrow. Below, it found its target and the other animals fled.

"Our lunch," he said with a grin. She stood and watched him retrieve the kill, not sure if her dizziness was from getting up too quickly or his perfect, self-satisfied smile.

Arthur instructed Evelyn on the best way to build a campfire, observing her attempts with ill-concealed amusement. When he moved forward to adjust the firewood, their hands brushed together and Evelyn flinched back, fingers tingling at the contact.

"Sorry," he said, though she could see from the mischievous glint in his eye that he didn't mean it. She gave him a nod and poked at the growing flames, suddenly embarrassed.

For a while, they remained in silence. Evelyn watched Arthur prepare the rabbit, using a sharpened knife to remove its skin with ease. Once the animal was roasting above the fire, he moved to sit beside her once more, smears of dark red staining his beige tunic.

"I've enjoyed spending time with you," he said. It was so unexpected, Evelyn almost choked on the water she was drinking. Arthur's face twitched with irritation, perhaps believing she was laughing at him. His brow creased, anger flashed across his eyes.

"I mean it," he said, shuffling closer. Before she could respond, he reached up and tucked some loose hair behind her ear, his hand lingering on her cheek. Evelyn's heart was hammering so hard she thought he must be able to hear it.

She swallowed. "It's been … nice." She liked him, true, but this was only their third time alone. She was still shy, reserved, unsure why he'd chosen her. *What does he want me to say?*

"Yes." His face was getting closer, his breath warm on her cheek. She could hear the rabbit spitting over the fire, the smell of roasting meat filled the air.

"Should we turn the—"

Before she could finish speaking, his lips were pressing against hers. His hands were on her back, pulling her closer. She stiffened, a moment of shock, before trying to pull away.

"Don't you want to?" His face remained in front of hers, his grin more like a snarl.

"I, er … Shouldn't we—"

"You should learn to be more grateful," he growled.

"Grateful?" She couldn't fully grasp what he meant, her mind a muddle at his sudden change in demeanour. When she tried to edge away from him, he only followed. She knew then with an abrupt, horrifying clarity that if she tried to flee, he would chase her.

He laughed, a harsh sound. "You're lucky to have someone like me interested in you, you know," he spat. "An orphan dumped in the forest. A *Folksman*. You should consider yourself privileged." He drew himself up, rolling his shoulders. "Like I said, learn to show some gratitude." Without warning, he lunged towards her. His breath was on her face once more, stale and hot. She tried to put her arms up in defence but he preempted her movement, clamping his arms around her in a suffocating embrace.

"You'll never amount to anything," he said into her ear casually, as though he was commenting on the weather. "You should be flattered I want you. No family, no generations-honoured name. I'm the best option you'll ever get."

"Please, Arthur," she said, desperately flailing.

She could see in his eyes he no longer cared what her response was. He had made his mind up; perhaps he'd known before they'd left that morning what he'd wanted to do. Arthur would have hunted one way or another. Evelyn was the chosen target, she saw now. He'd been patient with her, bided his time, waited for his moment.

Now he was taking his shot.

In a flash, he moved his hands to her front, shoved her backwards. She fell to the forest floor, too shocked to stop herself, and he followed, pressing the weight of his body on top of her.

And Evelyn did what had come so naturally to her in Little Haven: she stopped. Stopped speaking, stopped moving, stopped attracting attention. She was still. The pounding of her heart seemed to slow, her vision becoming a pinpoint as her mind retreated from itself.

She scrunched her eyes shut, waited for it to be over. Retreated further, further. The pain was inescapable but distant; her own sobs barely registered in her ears.

And then, something began to happen.

So slowly at first, she barely even noticed it.

But as the seconds stretched, she felt a change. A fire burned inside her, deep and hot, growing stronger and stronger, more furious every second.

Still, she didn't open her eyes.

Still, Arthur held her down.

Then, without warning, the flames surged. Her whole body grew impossibly rigid and *it* flew from her. With a harsh cry, Arthur lurched away from her. She didn't look up. *Please. Please be over.* She prayed to every deity she could imagine, despite believing in none.

"What the—" Rustling above her. "What was ... Did you burn me?" He sounded unsure—afraid, she thought, but couldn't believe it, not yet. She couldn't move, refused to look at him. Without a response, he grabbed her shoulders and shook her. "Evelyn, did you hear me?" She remained still, hoping he would leave.

He didn't.

His fear must have passed, perhaps satisfied that whatever had happened was a trick of the mind, and he knelt over her again.

No!

She snapped.

Evelyn wasn't sure what happened next; a part of her was still separated from itself, a graceful barrier formed around her mind.

But some part of her was in control. A screech broke free of her lips; the fire inside was too much. It was burning higher. She needed it to stop, needed everything to stop. Evelyn did the only thing she could—she forced it away.

Arthur staggered away again. A loud *snap* filled the air; he screamed in agony, the kind Evelyn had never heard before. "Evelyn! What is this?" Another snap, another cry of pain. Whimpers, screams, almost a howl. "What are you doing? I know this is you! I know this is *you!*"

She still didn't open her eyes, couldn't look at what she'd done. Whatever had come from her—she was sure he was right, she *had* done it—had burned out. *Not yet, don't leave me yet,* she prayed. And as she waited, for the fire, for the terror, for Arthur, Evelyn heard it. Sobs, soft at first, then more desperate, shorter breathed. Arthur was crying, and she was glad.

Your turn to be hunted, she thought, and, as she heard him slump to the ground, heard the cries stop, she closed her eyes and allowed her mind to go blank.

Evelyn sat up in bed gasping for breath, a cry she couldn't hold back echoing across her room. Her face was slick with sweat, dripping with tears. Her whole body was alight, hot, burning again, only, this time, with fear and shame. *It's over, it's passed. Little Haven is gone, he's gone.* No matter what she told herself, Evelyn couldn't calm her breathing. She sat straight up in bed, refusing to accidentally slip back into sleep, focusing on the low-burning fire across the room.

The door creaked open. She pulled the blankets around herself, tensing in the darkness. *He's come for me …*

"Evelyn?" A sweet voice.

"B-Bessie?" Relief washed over her, extinguishing any last remnants of that awful, all-consuming fire.

"You okay, girl?" The woman made her way to Evelyn's bedside, the oil lamp in her hand causing shadows to shift across her round face. "I heard a shout."

Evelyn rubbed her arms, brushing away the bumps of cold on her skin. "Just a dream," she said, smiling weakly.

"Hmm." Bessie leant close, reaching a hand out towards her. "You're shaking, girl." Her dark eyes were soft as she studied Evelyn's face. After a moment, she spoke, "When you first came here, I saw the hurt you carried. Someone caused you pain. An inhuman pain. So much, you 'ad to run. I just want you to know, whatever 'appened wasn't your fault."

Evelyn nodded, not believing the words.

Bessie squeezed her hand. "You'll believe it one day, girl. Trust me." She stood, pulling the blanket up round Evelyn once more. "Now, get some rest. Early rise tomorrow to get those damned animals fed."

Before she left, Bessie kissed Evelyn gently on the forehead. "You're safe here. You're with family. We Folksman, we stick together, don't we?"

Overcome with emotion, all Evelyn could do was give a brief nod.

"Remember that, my girl." Bessie patted the blanket down one last time. "Rest now."

Evelyn watched her leave, allowing a tiny smile to flicker over her lips. Those words, at least, she could believe.

What would I have done without you? The only family I ever knew.

Lost in her memories of Bessie, Evelyn didn't hear anyone approach.

"Evelyn." A hand clasped her shoulder, jerking her back to the present. "Evelyn. They're back."

She tensed, turning away from the firepit into which she'd been staring, blinking. "What? Who?"

"Mak's back. With Hector," Raif said.

"Oh." Evelyn rubbed her eyes. "Are they okay?"

Raif's mouth twisted with worry as he moved to peer through the doorway. "I'm not sure." Rose came to take his hand, Dog at her feet.

Something was wrong.

"What is it?" Evelyn asked, moving to join him. Outside, an unconscious Hector was being carried away by two men. His white cat followed behind, padding across the snowy ground. "Who's that other man? Tied up on Mak's horse? Is he Nomarran?" Before Raif could answer, she saw the red cloak, the blood-stained breast plate. Her mouth went dry. "A Nomarran who works *for* the Commune?"

Raif shared a glance with her, seeming to read her mind. "It is them then." His eyes brimmed with ill-concealed tears as he tightened his clutch on his sister. "They've found us."

"It's one soldier. Perhaps he was alone," Evelyn said, though the words sounded empty and weak even to her own ears. She watched as the red-cloaked man was removed from Mak's horse, saw with a jolt he was able to stand on his own, though he was hunched over and swaying. *He's alive. They'll question him.* She drew herself up. "I'm going to get us some answers," she said. "Don't worry."

"Bring him to my hut," Avanna said, voice ringing across the campsite.

"Come away from the door," Evelyn said to Raif.

As Avanna entered, she barely seemed to see them. Her eyes were glazed and downcast.

Evelyn gave her a moment, then stepped forward. "Is Hector well?"

The woman flinched. "Oh." She smiled tightly. "I don't think this will be suitable for children," she said, looking at each of them in turn. "You should occupy yourselves for the afternoon. Raif, perhaps you could show Rose where you've been learning to—"

"I want to stay," Evelyn said. "I'm not a child. You don't know what I've been through, I—" She stopped herself from saying too much, reminded herself Avanna was the one needing comfort, needing help, and squared her jaw. "I want to stay. Please."

Perhaps Avanna was too weary to argue. Perhaps she finally saw something to believe in Evelyn's eyes. Either way, she gave a brisk nod. "Very well, but only you." She waved towards Raif and Rose. "You two are too young."

Evelyn put a hand on Raif's arm in reassurance. "Look after Rose," she said. "I'll see you both later." *I'll tell you everything.* She hoped Raif saw the promise in her eyes.

"Be careful," he whispered, then led Rose and Dog from the hut.

The soldier stumbled in between Mak and Griff, hands bound behind his back and a gag in his mouth, seemingly on the brink of losing consciousness. He was a tall, well-muscled man, and they struggled to hold him up. Evelyn stepped out of their way, watching as Avanna guided them to place the man on the floor against the far wall of the hut, to the side of the seating area. As he was lowered to the ground, the man blinked around. Evelyn edged back into the shadows, afraid to meet his dark, angry eyes.

"That will be all, Griff," Avanna said. "Thank you."

Without question, the young man bowed his head to her and left.

Once he was gone, Avanna spoke to Mak. "How many soldiers were there?"

"Two dead. And him." Mak jutted his chin towards the soldier. "Signs of another that got away."

"Got away? We must send men in pursuit."

"I have," Mak said. "Alon and Lark. They went straight from where we found Hector."

"Good." Avanna moved to study the soldier at her feet. The man glared back at her, though the effect was somewhat dampened by the swelling round his eyes and the bloodied scratches marring his black skin.

No more than he deserves, Evelyn thought.

"Do you think it was an ambush?" Avanna asked, unperturbed by the man's evident disdain. She held her chin high, and there was no trace of the worry in her eyes from a moment before. *She looks powerful.* Evelyn knew without question that she was witnessing exactly why Avanna, not Mak, not Hector, not anybody else, led Veritas.

"I would expect more if that were the case." Mak joined his sister in front of the soldier. "No, I don't think so." He pursed his lips. "Even so, Hector was almost overpowered."

"Mm." Avanna waved her hand in the air. "Remove his gag."

Mak leant down so his face was at a level with the soldier's. "Don't waste your energy crying out," he said. "No one here will help you." He removed the rag from the man's mouth. The soldier's lips were cracked and broken. He winced as his tongue moved to moisten them.

"Water, Mak," Avanna said, crouching down, radiating control. "Do you know where you are?" The soldier remained silent. The corner of Avanna's mouth twitched with amusement. "You may know us as Veritas."

"I know who you are," he hissed. "Traitors. You desecrate the Goddess of my homeland." The soldier spat on the ground for good measure.

"Goddess?" Avanna raised an eyebrow, glancing at her brother. "Yes, Veritarra, isn't it?" She stood again and began to pace back and forth, hands clasped behind her back. Evelyn couldn't take her eyes off Avanna. There was a physical aura radiating from her. *A commander.* Avanna continued, "She was something of an influence when I chose the name, I will admit. Her stories go back generations in the Noman Islands, don't they? And She has not been without Her fanatics here in Septima. Her values of truth, wisdom, and *kindness* are openly followed in our camp. Indeed, we have some of your own people seeking sanctuary within this place. Driven away from the homes they'd built in Septima by the very man you work for."

The soldier's mouth dropped open, his lower lip trembling. "You lie," he whispered.

Avanna halted, head cocked as she regarded the soldier with a mocking smile. "Are you so blind to the Grand Magister's intentions? Which reminds me, surely you are not permitted to worship Veritarra anymore, given your work for the Commune? My understanding is you are forbidden to do so. Especially given that bastard's latest *edicts.*"

The soldier scoffed, his eyes blazing. "*You* are what we are fighting against," he rasped. "My prayers are irrelevant to you. The Grand Magister would not … He is a benevolent man!"

"Is that so?" Avanna smirked.

"By the Grand Magister's grace, we hunt those who use their powers unsupervised. Unchecked. Endangering innocent lives. You dare speak of my Goddess, but what of the other? Of the abominable God Ezzarah's final, dark hold on us—on these *children* you pretend are harmless." He coughed, clearly in pain, yet his air of defiance seemed to grow stronger the more he spoke. Avanna nodded to Mak who knelt and carefully poured some water into the man's mouth. He seemed to try and reject the drink at first, but gulped twice before Mak moved away again.

"And what is your name, soldier?" Avanna continued as blood-reddened water dribbled down the man's chin, leaving streaks on his stained and dented breastplate.

The soldier lifted his head, drawing his shoulders back in what might have been a dignified position had he not been seated so awkwardly. "*Commander* Jonah Sulemon, a sworn soldier of the King and Commune," he said. "I am here by the orders of Lord Torrant, a sworn and powerful agent of the Commune."

Lord Torrant. Evelyn balked, moving for the first time since Avanna had spoken. The man from the tavern in Castleton.

"Ah, Commander Sulemon. I should've known. You are the only Nomarran in the Commune's service, are you not? Yes, and Lord Torrant's own loyal *man*." Avanna let the word hang in the air for a moment before continuing. "We know him well. He is a faithful servant of the Grand Magister, that's for sure. Faithful and cruel."

"Do not proclaim such condemnation as truth," the Commander said. "You know nothing of Lord Torrant. He is a good man. A man sworn to—"

Avanna laughed—a cutting, sharp sound Evelyn couldn't have previously imagined coming from this woman—and Commander Sulemon's speech stopped immediately. "He has you well trained. Doesn't he, brother?" She shared a look with Mak, eyes dancing with fury concealed as false merriment. She leant down and touched a finger to the golden inlay on the Commander's breastplate. "The Royal Crest," she muttered. "King Cosmo and the Grand Magister, can there be a worse union for our beloved Septima? What's that saying they're so fond of amongst the ignorant? 'By His Benevolent Powers'?" She swiped her finger down, the smallest of movements. And yet, Evelyn swore the Commander flinched. Avanna's smile stayed. "Benevolent, indeed."

"You know nothing of the Commune's work," Commander Sulemon said, though his voice had lost some of its fervour.

"Perhaps so, Commander," Avanna said. "But let us return to you. What led you to these mountains?"

Commander Sulemon's gaze drifted to Evelyn, where she stood in the shadows behind Mak. When her eyes locked with his, her body jolted at the undiluted disgust she met.

"Auburn hair," he muttered. "So I have found you after all."

"Commander?" Avanna no longer smiled.

"My soldiers and I were searching out that girl and her travelling companions, two children. They have high crimes to answer for." His narrowed eyes moved to Mak. "A hooded horseman rescued them from Castleton, just as my soldiers attempted to take them into the Commune's care."

"Perhaps your men should have been better able to carry out their orders, Commander," Avanna said scathingly. "But it makes no matter now. What crimes do you put at this girl's feet?"

"Do not mock the Commune's work, woman," the Commander spat. "It is vital for the safety of Septima."

Avanna slapped Commander Sulemon's cheek, spraying droplets of blood across the floor. Evelyn had to look away, yet Avanna didn't even glance at the red blood speckled across the white skin of her palm. "I am not interested in hearing your propaganda," she said coldly. "If you don't answer my questions, I have no further use for you. I'll ask again: What crimes do you place at this girl's feet, Commander?"

Commander Sulemon's face remained the same, an unmasked show of contempt. It broke for a moment with a grimace as he shifted, straightening his spine as best he could, then was back. He did not speak.

Answer. Answer her! Evelyn needed to know. The attacked soldier? The men in the woods? Simply existing? What was she accused of? What did they know of Rose? Avanna remained still.

And finally, she could not stand the silence. Evelyn moved forward. "My friends and I did nothing to you, yet we were hunted down by your men. We only wanted to find somewhere safe to stay in Castleton." Avanna's head snapped towards her, and Evelyn nearly cowered beneath the fire in her eyes.

"Ah, she speaks," the Commander said. "If you had nothing to hide you should have handed yourselves over to my men. I don't think I need to tell you what happened to the soldier who tried to apprehend you." Avanna's gaze was hard, demanding, but now almost curious.

Evelyn turned her back on them both. *The soldier. Does he know it was Rose? Mak must have seen, must have told Avanna.*

"You see?" Commander Sulemon's tone was triumphant. "You cannot face what you have done."

Arrogant bastard. Evelyn turned back, widening her stance and turning up her chin as Avanna had.

"What happened?" Avanna finally spoke. Her eyes darted between the Commander and Evelyn, brows slightly raised, cheeks flushed with— excitement? Anger? Shock? All of them?

What does she want? Evelyn tugged on her cloak, suddenly wishing she were not in the hut. *You wanted to see this, you made Avanna agree.* She stopped fidgeting and waited for someone else to speak. She would not reveal anything she didn't have to.

"I think a soldier was injured," Mak said slowly. "It was dark. I didn't see what happened."

Commander Sulemon laughed. "She did not tell you. Are you ashamed of what happened in Castleton, girl? You should be." His eyes were on Evelyn's face once more. She fought to remain still, not to run. *Don't mention Rose, please.* In that moment, she was unsure who she was most afraid of.

"I will not warn you again, Commander Sulemon," Avanna said. "You are the one under questioning. So eager to speak yet so deft at providing nothing with your words. Tell me what happened."

"A soldier, as he said." The Commander inclined his head towards Mak.

"No," Evelyn whispered.

"Let him speak," Avanna said, shooting her a cold glance.

"One of the Commune's soldiers was injured as this girl and two children were tracked down in Castleton."

Not Rose, not Rose. The soldier couldn't know.

"It was self-defence." Mak frowned. "Your soldier hunted them like prey."

Commander Sulemon stared at him, unblinking. "There are laws to be obeyed, you fool. Those soldiers were carrying out their duty. That man did not ask to be impaled on a sword."

Shut up, shut up!

Mak and Avanna shared a glance.

"Lord Torrant spoke to the soldier and he was able to reveal it was—"

"No!" Evelyn shouted. "He's one of *them*." She moved, stood between Avanna and the Commander, desperate to keep Rose's secret. *Not yet, not yet. I promised Raif. We need more time.* "Surely you know he'll say anything to further his," she searched for the word Avanna used before, "*propaganda.*"

"'Truth and wisdom,'" Commander Sulemon quoted Avanna in turn. "You are not worthy of the Goddess you claim to emulate."

"Stand aside, Evelyn." Avanna moved her with a gentle push, though her eyes were fierce. "What did the soldier reveal?"

"A young girl, blonde hair. She used powers on him, compelled him to stab himself." He turned his gaze back to Evelyn. "The soldier was gravely injured."

Evelyn watched on in horror, helpless as the Commander undid everything she'd promised Raif she'd protect.

Mak sucked in a breath. "Sister," he said. "I didn't know. If I had—"

"Silence." With a word, Avanna stilled the hut. She knelt before the Commander. "You're sure of this?"

He gave a curt nod. "Now, you see as I do. I have seen with my own eyes the danger these children pose," he said. "No matter the sides we stand on, you must understand they need to be brought under the control of the Commune for the good of the kingdom."

Avanna stood and turned away from him again. "You believe your own words, that much I understand."

"You are as much a fool as your brother if you do not listen," the Commander snarled. He took a deep inhale, eyes closed for a moment. When he spoke again, his voice was calmer, more confident. "This young girl who has such powers, who caused such injury, she poses a risk to all who come into contact with her—you and everyone in this camp included. It is not a question of *belief.*"

Avanna remained silent for a time. Evelyn watched her, waiting for anger, for betrayal, for condemnation, but instead she was certain she saw a glimmer of satisfaction on the woman's face.

Evelyn thought of every rebuke for the Commander's accusations she could, desperate to hold true to her promise to Raif. But the longer the quiet stretched, the more she was certain Rose's powers were now indisputable. Would it be better to confirm the truth to Avanna—to confess and apologise? Could it be their best hope of safety and protection?

"I believe I've heard enough," Avanna said finally. She signalled to Mak. "Take him to the prison hut. Strip him of his armour and possessions. Commander Sulemon, you have been courteous in answering my questions, but I cannot forget that you and your soldiers attacked one of my men, perhaps fatally. You will answer for your crimes."

Again, the man was strangely obedient as Mak dragged him up, despite being a head or more taller than his escort. Resigned to his fate, perhaps. Knowing there was no use trying to run in a camp filled with those who would happily see him dead.

As he was taken from the hut, Evelyn avoided his gaze. His hatred was palpable enough without seeing it again in his eyes.

As soon as they were alone, Avanna turned to Evelyn. "Is it true?" She held a relaxed posture, a gentle and comforting smile, eyes wide with innocent curiosity, an air of patience. There was no trace of the militant leader she'd been moments ago, and somehow this made Evelyn even more reluctant to answer.

Think. Think then speak. Think then speak. Evelyn pinched her lips tight, heart racing. *Perhaps Avanna could help Rose.* Even as she thought it, doubt stabbed at her.

But if they stayed here, Rose would be trained to better control and conceal her powers. Raif could continue to learn archery. Evelyn realised how desperately she wanted to be the only one who could provide that for them—a life, a home—but she had already seen how incapable she was of protecting them. How she may need the help of Veritas as much as Rose did.

Could I learn more about my own powers? Discover what they really are? Finally get them back?

"Come. I know this must have been a difficult experience for you," Avanna said gently, moving closer. "Interrogation always presents hope. Yet, sucessful or not, it is exhausting once done." Before Evelyn knew it, she was being led to the seating area, a tumbler of hot wine pushed into her hand. *Have to keep a clear head. Don't drink too much.*

Yet even as she cautioned herself, she took a sip of the delicious wine and found herself lulled into a sense of calm by the comforting warmth of the drink, the fire at her back, Avanna's unwavering, reassuring smile.

"You might have been shocked at the man's conviction and beliefs. I know I was when I first heard the words of a soldier of the Commune," Avanna said, cupping her own drink between her hands.

Evelyn drank deeply of her wine, giving herself a moment to gather her thoughts. *Just a little more. Just to calm my nerves.* "What did he mean about you desecrating the Goddess of his homeland?" she asked. If she couldn't keep Rose's secret anymore, she could at least delay the inevitable. *Divert, learn, drink,* she repeated to herself.

"Ah, yes," Avanna said. "Veritarra, a Goddess of the Noman Islands. Like I said, she stands for truth, for wisdom. I believed it an apt name for our group, fighting against the lies of the Grand Magister. And now that those from the Noman Islands are being exiled because of the Grand Magister's growing madness ..." She lifted her cup in a mock salute, lips twisted with bitterness.

"The Noman Islands." Evelyn had heard of them, of course, but never so much as in the past days. "That's where the Commander's from?"

"Yes," Avanna said. "I went there once in my youth. A place devastated by war. Of late, they've stopped outside visitors. A shame. All I can do now is try to help those who seek our aid." She shook her head and closed her eyes. "That man has obviously been persuaded onto the path of the Commune. He is blinded by his loyalty to ... well, at best, a cruel man."

"Lord Torrant?" Evelyn murmured. She recalled the man's cold blue eyes and immaculate dress, the strange sense of weakness he'd instilled in her. Her anxiety spiked and she took another long gulp of her wine. *It'll be fine. It's no stronger than what Bessie used to give me.*

"Yes," Avanna said. "He's been with the Commune since he was a child. Trained and controlled by the Grand Magister for too many years. I doubt he even knows his own mind anymore. A dangerous man, no doubt of it."

Dangerous. There it is again.

Avanna's brown eyes shone as she watched Evelyn over the rim of her cup. "I hope you come to realise what I aim to do here is to help men like that, and

212 – LUCY A. McLAREN

every other person, noble and peasant and everyone in between—anyone drawn in by the Commune's lies. We are working to overthrow the Grand Magister. We need all the help we can get." She sipped her wine, staring down at the furs on the floor as though deep in thought. "What the Commander spoke of … Such powers in one so young would help our cause immensely. It might be what we've waited for."

And in that moment, Evelyn saw with startling clarity the commander in Avanna once more. There was no demanding language, no forceful gestures—it was all spoken softly, casually, with only the slight furrowing of her brow to give away what she wanted. Evelyn swallowed, feeling powerless beneath the woman's gaze. "What- what you've waited for?"

Avanna placed her wine down and clasped her hands in her lap. "Did you know the Nomarrans speak of the powers as a curse inflicted by the callous God Ezzarah? The Commander mentioned him, and I daresay even I cannot question his fear of the God. Ezzarah used the powers as a way of creating imbalance and hatred amongst His people. Jealousy of an unasked for birthright for those inflicted, turning son against father, daughter against mother, for generations. An absolutely uncontrollable chance that's as unpredictable as the shape of a babe's nose or the colour of their hair. And it ripped their Islands apart. Ezzarah prophesied that the powers would grow in strength with the years and, with that fear—or hope, depending on one's hatred or worship or him—solidified His own hold over all Nomarrans. Ruling with equally powerful terror and admiration, much like the Grand Magister." She held up a finger. "Of course, thousands of years have passed and the powers are no longer solely contained within the Noman Islands. They're all over Septima, the Farring Isles to the west, the eastern lands of Norhia and Alphira."

Evelyn scrunched her face. *Careful, Avanna. I'm learning your tricks.* "And what's that got to do with what you're doing here?"

Avanna smirked, as though the answer was obvious and Evelyn simply wasn't trying hard enough to understand. "The Nomarrans were heroes when Septima needed them. And now the Grand Magister sees them as a threat. Wants everyone to see them as a threat."

"A threat?" Evelyn raised an eyebrow. "But they weren't one when his regime needed them?"

"Ah, but that was before the Commune was formed." Avanna leant forward. "A hundred years ago, they used their close-held secrets to help Septima put down the rebels during the Seven-Year War. Nomarrans have the ability to repress the powers of an individual with their Goddess granted gifts—*any* individual. It appears that, one hundred years later, the Grand Magister has changed his mind about such an alliance. He is a paranoid man, even more so than his father and grandfather before him."

"What isn't he paranoid of? Those who can't fight back most of all," Evelyn muttered, more to herself than Avanna.

The woman snorted. "You're starting to understand the situation, I see." She rested her elbows on her legs and her chin on her clasped hands, dark eyes studying Evelyn. "There was an uprising in the Noman Islands some twenty years back. Not on the same scale as the Seven-Year War in Septima, of course, but the *cause* was the same," she said casually. "Those with powers tried to take control of the Islands, to abolish the worship of the Goddess Veritarra. They believed they were preserving the rule of their precious God Ezzarah, doing what was best for the Noman Islands. Just as in Septima with the forming of the Commune, which was justified by claims of preserving the realm, protecting the throne, the safety of all citizens." Avanna raised an eyebrow. "After all, what is the easiest way for a leader to justify violence?"

Evelyn shook her head, unable to answer.

"By proclaiming its necessity to maintain peace, of course."

Evelyn felt cold. *The attack on Little Haven.*

Avanna spoke softly. "It's likely Commander Sulemon was still in the Noman Islands, in his home, when the onslaught happened there. Perhaps he lost people he loved, saw what those with powers could do if they chose the wrong path. All in the name of keeping the peace. It seems he's following the Commune for the very same reason. I wonder what Lord Torrant promised him."

Evelyn remained silent. *Wars created for nothing? And where does Rose fit into this?*

"The Nomarrans *cursed* with powers tried to rise up but were defeated by the protection granted by Veritarra. They underestimated the Goddess's gifts, you see," Avanna said. "It's a wonder the Grand Magister doesn't see that he and the remaining Nomarrans want the same: to be able to live a life unimpeded by the powers of others. But like I said, he is a paranoid man. He has no need for them. His own power grows and so he sees them as a threat, knowing what they could do if they so wished." The woman pinned Evelyn with a hard stare. "What do you think? Do you suppose the proclamation of a cruel god, prophesised millennia ago, could still come true?" Her eyes glimmered feverishly; Evelyn did not think Avanna even saw her sitting an arm's length away any more, her voice having taken on a strange, faraway tone. "The strongest of powers—imagine what they could do."

The strongest ... What does she—

Evelyn's stomach dropped. This was it. *Rose.*

Avanna tilted her head, a satisfied smile on her face as though she could read Evelyn's mind. "If there is a child who has such strength; one so young, yet so unquestionably advanced beyond those with decades of age and training over them. Powerful beyond comparison from birth. Just imagine what could be achieved."

Evelyn watched her for a moment, fought to process her words. "You think such powers could help fight the Commune?"

Avanna remained silent, a knowing look in her eye.

Evelyn chewed the inside of her cheek, thumbed the lip of her cup. *Rose can't fight a war. She's a child and will be for a decade to come. And yet ... what if Avanna is right?* She took a sip of her drink. *Raif wouldn't want her to know.*

Raif won't care, another part of her mind argued immediately. *I shouldn't care. This has never been Rose's war. But if she could help ... could train until she was strong enough, old enough.* Evelyn had a sick, unwanted sense of satisfaction. She'd known it back when they'd first arrived. *There's always a cost. She will need to fight.*

Avanna stood to refill her drink, offering Evelyn the same. Once seated again, she pushed her hair behind her ears. "The fact is, if the Grand Magister were to take into his control such an individual, he would want those powers for himself. For more false wars, promising Goddess knows what at this point, bountiful crops and endless wine to all." She raised her cup, sloshing the liquid within. "But *we'd* know the truth, wouldn't we? The terrible, unending danger." She let out a long breath. "Do you know what he does with the children he captures?"

"What- what does he do?"

"First, they're tested."

"Tested?"

"The Grand Magister has to know what powers each child has—if any. He doesn't do it all himself. Not anymore. He has agents everywhere—men like Lord Torrant. They do such menial work for him now. Of late, a child taken before His *Benevolence* must be proven to have powers. Anything less is a waste of his precious time."

Evelyn shuddered at the idea of standing before Lord Torrant, forced to perform or fail. *You would fail.* "What would the test involve?" she asked, shutting out the taunting voice within.

"I can't be sure," Avanna admitted. "But it will be some way of proving your powers, your worth to the cause as it were. Once they have been confirmed, the child will be taken before the Grand Magister himself. He will decide what use their powers would be put to, whether it be a simple soldier, an agent working to spread his word across the kingdom or something more."

"Something more?"

Avanna nodded. "We have long suspected the Grand Magister's own powers are waning. He is old, his body grows weak, and so his powers do, too. But there are old, dark ways to slow this. If he finds a child with unmatched, unique strength, he would take them over. Merge his mind with the child, keeping them on the brink of life while using them as a source of power. A child with such raw, unchecked strength as the Commander spoke of … Well, they would be highly coveted indeed."

"Merge his mind?" Evelyn's heart was racing. "But how can he …" Her brow furrowed. "Surely people can't believe that's … Is that even possible? How could … The people wouldn't let him get away with that!"

Avanna barked a harsh laugh. "He has the protection of the Commune. He *is* the Commune. And the Commune, in turn, offers a sort of protection to those who follow it." She leant forward again. "Do you see now why it's so important those with such strong powers are protected?"

"Y-yes, of course," Evelyn said.

Shit. Shit, shit, shit. Raif is going to be furious. Avanna wanted to protect Rose from such a fate. Any life but that must be better. *Raif will understand if I can explain what the soldier said about Rose, tell him what Avanna believes … won't he?*

"Evelyn," Avanna said in a hushed voice. "You can tell me the truth now."

Evelyn drained her cup, staring at the dregs of fruit sitting at its bottom, wishing she had far more wine to drink. They'd come here to help Rose. If she could be taught to control her powers, she wouldn't kill anyone else. *Unless she was asked to.* Evelyn realised with a wave of nausea that was precisely what Avanna wanted of Rose. *No, I can't allow that. But what other choice—*

"We can help you," Avanna said, interrupting her thoughts. "That's why Mak brought you here." She smiled broadly, her brown eyes once more soft and friendly and kind. "Was it Rose?"

Raif, oh, forgive me Raif. What, by all the damned powers, do I say? Bessie sent me to these people, she would have known.

But Bessie wasn't here; there was no one to tell Evelyn what the right thing was. She was on her own. She had to make a choice.

The words were sour on her tongue as she said, "Yes. It was Rose."

Avanna didn't seem in the least bit surprised. "You're sure?"

"Yes. It wasn't the first time …"

"Go on," Avanna said, then again, softer, like a prayer, "Go on."

So Evelyn described all that had happened—not just to the soldier in Castleton, but the two men in the woods as well. It was cathartic, for a moment at least. A weight off her shoulders that she hadn't known she was carrying.

"We don't want her to be in trouble though," she finished quickly. "Rose, I mean. I don't know if she really meant to- if she even truly knows what she … She's not a fighter—"

"It's no matter now. What's important is we can provide what Rose needs. The dog must be … Yes, as I thought." Avanna spoke quietly as though to herself.

"What can you do for her?" Evelyn asked.

"Hmm?" Avanna's eyes were glazed. "I will need some time to think. And you should get some rest. It's been a trying day for all of us."

"Oh." Evelyn was surprised at the sudden dismissal. "Okay." She placed her empty cup on the cushion beside her. She made to leave the hut when Avanna called to her.

"Evelyn?" She turned to meet Avanna's intense gaze. "You've done what's best," the woman said. "Leave it with me. I will speak to Rose."

With an icy doubt already spreading through her, Evelyn nodded and left.

20

Hector

"Father, you sent for me," Hector had whispered, creeping into the ill-lit bedroom. He'd held a lamp, casting a warm glow in the room that flickered upon the white walls. The air was stale despite the burning lavender incense.

"Son." His father's voice was a strangled, pain-filled croak.

Hector put his lamp down and moved to pour a glass of water before holding it to his father's lips, trying not to let his gaze linger upon the sunken cheeks, yellow-tinged skin, and bloodshot eyes.

His father sipped down the water as best he could. Hector mopped his stubbled chin dry, then sat on the stool beside the bed and waited. When nothing was said and his father's breathing began to deepen, Hector took his hand.

"Did you need something, Father?" he said, giving the withered hand within his own a squeeze. His father's eyes blinked open again, taking a moment to focus before they rested upon his face. They were no longer the keen emerald green they'd once been, their brilliance fading fast.

"Hector," he said with a weak smile. "You came." After a few laboured breaths, his father's eyes locked with his own and, within them, there was a light of clarity that sent a jolt through Hector's body. "I need your help, my lad."

"My help, Father?" Hector was shaken by the sudden sureness in his father's voice, as though a glimmer of his old self had returned.

His father closed his eyes and breathed deeply, filling the room with a wheezing crackle.

Behind, he heard the door open. Hector turned to see who had disturbed them, but no one was there. When he moved back to the bed, his father was gone, the sheets long cold.

"Father?" Hector glanced around, frantic. He scrabbled at the bed sheets, searching, needing. "Father!"

Hector jolted awake.

"Are you well, my friend?"

Avanna? He blinked open his heavy-lidded eyes, taking in the walls of the hut in which he lay, the furs layered over his weakened body. The dream was gone; the past was buried.

He took a deep breath and allowed the thought—and the image of his father's face—to drift away. He pushed back the furs, studied his bandaged arms, the wrapping across his left thigh. The burning in his leg was abominable. He instinctively moved his hand, clammy with sweat, in search of his companion. She leapt to his side and nuzzled against him.

"Avanna," he whispered. "Where am I?" Hector squinted against the lamplight.

"You're safe, Hector," she said. She moved closer and clasped her hand around his own, cool and comforting. "You're back at the camp. Mak found you. I dread to think what might have happened if he hadn't." She squeezed his hand, his fingers twitching in response.

"I was followed. One- one may have escaped." Hector tried to lift his pounding head. "The children—they're in danger. They—"

"I know. Hush, stay down." Avanna gently pressed him back onto the bed, brushing back his hair tenderly. "We must try not to dwell on such things. We must look ahead. You must regain your strength. The children, yes. I need your help, my friend."

Hector glanced up at her and saw the barely concealed elation in her face. "My help?"

"Yes," she said, beginning to pace the room, evidently unable to contain her restless excitement. "The girl, Hector. I believe she is strong. Unbelievably so. I had my suspicions when I first laid eyes upon her—the dog, her companion

… And yet, when I touched her, I could sense nothing from her. No powers, nothing to give away any remarkable strength." She stopped and turned to him with feverish intensity. "But from what the soldier has told me, and the girl too—well, the other girl. It's confirmed what I thought. Oh, Hector. This may be our chance. She is the one we've been waiting for, I'm sure of it. I have been in contact with Elussius Muelaman, the Nomarran in Nook Town. He's been coy about the work they do there but," she almost laughed, "what else would it be? Perhaps he will be able to help."

Cara shuffled beside him, staring at Avanna, her mind as fogged with pain as his.

Hector's brow creased, trying to make sense of his friend's words. "Nook Town?"

Avanna ignored him, nodding fervently to herself. "I think this could be it." She tucked her hair behind her ear, smiling at him. "Oh, here I am talking away when you need your sleep." He heard fumbling movements before she came to his side with a cup full of steaming liquid.

"Drink this. When I searched the Commander's belongings, I found- Well, no matter. But it will take away the pain, my friend, and that's what you need for now. I knew not to use much, don't worry. Just enough to let you rest."

The liquid inside had a strong, earthy smell. Some part of him knew the scent from long ago, fought against consuming it. But he was in too much agony for that tiny voice to take hold and he drank deeply.

"Sleep. When you're better, we shall talk again." Avanna wiped his brow, plumped up his pillow.

Hector groaned as he nestled back, already slipping into unconsciousness. He reached a hand for Cara as he drifted away.

Don't leave me.

Never, she purred sleepily.

His lips twitched into a smile as the fog overwhelmed his mind.

21

Evelyn

Shame burned in Evelyn's chest, rushed through her ears, sank claws into her mind and refused to let go.

Once she'd left Avanna's hut, she had avoided Raif and Rose for the rest of the day. She'd promised them answers, knew Raif must've been desperate for them, and yet at the mere thought of meeting his or Rose's eyes, she couldn't breathe. She busied herself with any small task she could find for the evening, sharpening her aged sword with a whetstone from one of the camp's smiths, braiding and re-braiding her hair, washing her hands and face in the basin of water in her room until it was cloudy. Finally, when it was dark enough, she slept, shamefully grateful she'd made it to the night without a knock at her door.

The next morning, she'd expected Avanna to send for Rose with the same eagerness and excitement she'd had while learning of the young girl's powers. Evelyn waited on edge and expectant until, at last, her luck ran out.

"Morning," Raif said, emerging from the side-room he shared with Rose. "Are you okay?"

She blinked at him, wondering what he'd do if he knew. "Yes," she said, though the word was unconvincing even to her own ears.

"What happened with the soldier? You never came to talk afterwards." He rubbed his eyes clear of sleep.

Evelyn shrugged in as nonchalant a manner as she could muster. "Nothing much," she lied, giving a disdainful snort. "But he *really* believes the Commune are good."

Raif's mouth twisted into a half-smile. "Well, we know at least a dozen reasons why that's wrong, don't we?"

Evelyn let out a weak laugh. "I s'pose we do."

She wondered whether to tell him about Avanna's strange talk of a Nomarran curse, her ideas about the powers. In all they'd learned these last weeks, that had somehow never come up. But she reasoned there would be time enough for that later. For now, she was unwilling to risk further questions that might cause her to reveal what she'd done. She'd decided just before sleep took her that until the choice was taken from her, she would do her best to pretend the events in Avanna's hut hadn't happened at all. To pretend she hadn't broken a promise or betrayed the trust placed in her by Raif. Until Avanna's intentions were clear, she reasoned that it was a protection of sorts. Keeping Raif and Rose free of the worry of Avanna's belief that Rose was the answer to defeating the Commune.

If she wished it hard enough, perhaps it would come to be true.

It was the coward's approach, she knew, but it was all she could do to shield herself from the knowledge she'd let down her only friend.

Rose appeared with Dog at her feet and she was saved from any more questions. Raif quickly began to talk about food, asking Rose what she wanted to do for the day. They were about to leave their hut for breakfast when a brisk knock came at the door. Evelyn faltered, palms clammy, the rushing sounds back in her ears.

"Uh," she uttered, frozen in indecision. *Should I just tell Raif what I did? Blurt it out now, better from me than someone else, surely?* Raif raised his eyebrow at her.

But then Mak called, "It's me," and the tension in her body eased a hair's breadth.

But what if he's come on Avanna's behalf?

"Come in," she said. *Please, please, please don't say anything.*

"Ah, you're all still here," he said, beaming. "Good. We could use your help round the camp."

Evelyn swallowed. "Help?"

"We're in the Solstice period," Mak said. "Lots to do to prepare for the colder months."

She could have cried with relief. "Ah," she said. "Of course."

"It was the same in Little Haven," Raif said.

"Most of Septima follows the old ways when it comes to marking the passing months, whether under the Commune's thrall or not." Mak smiled. "Come on."

The camp was busy. The leisurely walks and easy conversations seemed to have been replaced with business, everyone with a place to be and a job to do. After taking Rose and Dog to be with a group of other children who were being shown how to create decorative wreaths, Mak led Evelyn and Raif through the camp.

"Everyone will be glad of the extra assistance," Mak said. "When the Reaping period comes, there'll be a great feast." He grinned. "You're in for a treat."

"How is Hector?" Raif asked.

Mak's smile fell, halting in the midst of the surrounding hubbub. "He's recovering." He sighed, face lifting to the sky. "Those bastards almost killed him. But he's strong. Stronger than he looks." He recovered quickly, casting them a wink. "He'll be okay."

Raif pursed his lips, giving Evelyn a worried glance. "I think Rose likes him," he said. "Well, his cat at least."

Mak chuckled. "I'm sure they'll be able to spend more time together. Soon, I hope."

"So, what do you need us to do?" Evelyn asked, watching the people moving back and forth around them. The camp felt alive with purpose.

"I'll show you."

And so, the days afterwards had passed in a blur as they helped prepare for the feast to come. Evelyn began to allow herself hope that perhaps Rose's powers meant nothing to Veritas, that Avanna had decided Rose was not the one to fulfill some part of a millennia old prophecy, she was just a child. Evelyn imagined sharing knowing smiles with Avanna; what they'd spoken of would stay between them, the young girl would be safe. Raif would never know.

You know damn well that isn't true. Enjoy it while it lasts.

Raif continued to question her, and desperate for peace, Evelyn lied. One morning, as they worked to prepare food, she decided telling him about the Nomarran Curse might distract him. A story to keep his mind as far away from Rose as she could.

After all, how could he possibly suspect any link to his sister?

"Is it the Curse of Ezzarah, you speak of?" A woman standing nearby, helping to scrub piles of muddied root vegetables, paused to glance at them. Beneath her fur hood, Evelyn saw long black curls cascading round a black-skinned, full-cheeked face. The woman chuckled, hazel-brown eyes shining. "No need to look so worried. I am simply curious to hear speak of the Curse. I did not expect it so far from my home."

"Oh." Evelyn let out a strained laugh. "Of course. I was just trying to tell my friend here about it. I learned about it recently."

"Is that so?" the woman asked.

Raif cleared his throat, digging his elbow into her side. "I'm Raif. This is Evelyn." He gave her a disapproving look as though to scold her for her lack of manners.

"It is nice to meet you both. I am Sarhia. I came with my brother, Elias, and his wife, Jorenya. She is with child and we ... Well, our home in Castleton is gone. We got separated from our friends, had nowhere to go. We only found our way here out of luck—met another group of Nomarrans on the road who'd heard of a place of sanctity in the mountains. Everyone has been very nice here. Very welcoming."

Evelyn nodded and smiled, feeling absurdly guilty for the doubt a part of her still harboured towards Avanna.

"It's nice to meet you too," Raif said. "I'm glad you were able to find this place."

"Me too." Sarhia kissed her thumb, pressed it to her forehead, then lifted it to the sky. "Goddess, protect us all." Her hand drifted to a leather pouch secured to the belt at her waist.

"I hope she does," Raif said.

"Veritarra shines Her love on us all," Sarhia said. "The Curse was placed upon us by the wrathful God Ezzarah. A vicious test. It does not hold sway over us. We will not be brought to our knees by such an uncaring monster."

Evelyn wondered whether she was still talking about Ezzarah.

Suddenly, Sarhia's name was called from behind. A man with the same full face, hazel eyes, and black curls peeked his head from a nearby hut. He waved her towards him. "I must go," she said. "Goddess's blessings to you both."

Evelyn and Raif bowed their heads in thanks before sharing a glance.

"Protection and love—seems the opposite of what the Grand Magister's Commune offers," Raif grumbled.

Evelyn swallowed. "I think that's the problem, isn't it?" She viciously scrubbed the potato in her hand. "Damn them all."

The days went by and they continued to carry out their Solstice duties. Evelyn finished her story of the Nomarran Curse and Raif's curiosity seemed satisfied, at least for the time being. He began to wonder out loud what Avanna intended to do with the soldier—was there some link between him being Nomarran and Avanna's speak of the Curse? All Evelyn could do was nod along, ashamed to feel so pleased at his musings. They were nowhere close to the truth. That was all she could hope for.

But after two weeks of work, of hope, of deceit, the charade finally came to an end.

As they roused for the morning, Avanna's serving girl, Flo, appeared at the door of their hut, requesting Rose's presence.

"Rose?" Raif's brow creased. "What does Avanna want with my sister?"

The serving girl stared at the floor, dark hair hanging over her face. "I, um, I don't know. She- she just asked me t' fetch 'er. The young'un."

The sun had barely risen in the sky. They'd become accustomed to getting up early, working hard, sleeping well. Usually, the three of them would head to the feasting hut for breakfast before they began their chores for the day, Rose and Dog staying with the other children, and Evelyn and Raif finding Mak to direct them in the day's tasks.

Evelyn swallowed, looking between Raif and Flo. "There can't be any harm in it, Raif," she said, heart racing. *This is it.* "Perhaps she's decided to ask Rose about her, um ... She did mention training when we first came, didn't she?"

"I told Avanna she had to discuss that with me before—"

"Raif?" Rose and Dog emerged from their tiny bedroom. The young girl's cheeks were still flushed with the warmth of sleep as she looked up at her brother.

Raif knelt before her, grasping each shoulder. "Flo's here to take you to Avanna. But if you don't want—"

Rose nodded and Dog let out a bark. "Okay," she said.

Raif frowned. "Are you sure?"

Rose placed a hand over her brother's. "Okay, Raif."

"Well," Raif stood, not meeting anyone's gaze. "I suppose so. If Rose is content to go. But I'm going with her."

"Oh." Flo's head snapped up, dark eyes flashing with what looked unsettlingly like fear. "Avanna said it was t' be the girl alone. No one else."

Raif glanced at Evelyn, brow furrowing deeper still. "I'm not happy about this," he muttered, though Rose patted his arm in a remarkably adult way, and he didn't argue when she and Dog followed Flo from their hut. "What do you think Avanna wants with her? I wanted to discuss any training for Rose—she knew that. She doesn't know what Rose is capable of. I don't want to risk her finding out."

"I doubt it's anything to worry about," Evelyn said, trying her best to sound unconcerned. But something about her face must have given her away—the shame that had dulled mercifully over the weeks had returned, her stomach knotting into itself. Though she tried to remain impassive, Raif narrowed his eyes.

"Evelyn?"

She turned away, face burning. "She'll be okay. I'm sure of it."

"How do you know?"

Evelyn could almost feel the heat of his gaze and made herself meet it. His eyes were wide, his confusion palpable. *Better from me,* she reminded herself. She inhaled, bracing herself for the ruin of their friendship. "The soldier … When Avanna was questioning him, he recognised me."

"Why didn't you tell me?" Raif stepped closer. "And what does that have to do with Rose?"

She rubbed her forehead. "He … he knew about the soldier in Castleton, Raif."

"The soldier in—Oh." Raif's hand clamped over his mouth, he stared at the door.

"The soldier knew it was Rose who made him, you know … hurt himself."

Raif's nod was curt. "And you didn't think I should know?"

Evelyn gulped. "Well, anyway, um, he told Avanna. So …"

Raif's gaze snapped towards her. "So what?"

"Uh." Evelyn pulled on her braid. "I … confirmed the truth, is all."

"Confirmed the truth." Raif's soft grey eyes hardened. "I see."

The silence hung between them.

"Raif, I'm sorry." She was suddenly desperate to make him see she'd acted for the best. "You have to believe me. I had no choice. Avanna—I think she can really help Rose."

"Oh," he said. "Avanna. Mm." He slumped down onto his sleeping pallet, all energy drained away. "I suppose all that about a Nomarran Curse was what? A story to distract me?" He laughed bitterly. "Worked, didn't it?" He looked at her, eyes full of pain. "I didn't expect lies, Evelyn. Not from you."

"I- I'm sorry." She moved to sit beside him. "But you didn't hear the soldier. What he said. What he *knew*. Avanna had her suspicions—more than we thought. It was only a matter of time."

"Only a matter of time," Raif muttered.

Evelyn glanced up at him then down at her lap, hands pulling at the edges of her cloak. "I really am sorry. I know I promised you, and I meant it, but I didn't know what else to do."

After a while, Raif let out a long and weary sigh, far too laboured for a boy his age. His shoulders were squared, his body turned slightly away from her. "All I want is to protect my sister. I have to. It's what our father wanted. What he told me to do with his dying breath." He looked at Evelyn, expression unreadable. "I hope I can still do that now that people who aren't family have decided it's their right to make decisions about her without speaking to me."

"I'll help you," she pleaded, trying to place a hand on his arm. And then, a timid question. "Aren't … aren't we like family, after all that's happened?"

Raif stood. "I know you mean well," he said. "But *family* doesn't break promises. Now, I need to try and find out what Avanna's doing with my sister."

Evelyn watched his back as he left the hut, stomach sinking. She didn't know how long she sat there, wallowing in a sense of unshakeable despair. Eventually, she managed to push herself to her feet and move to the door, feeling as though she was fighting against the current of a river that was far out of her control.

She opened the door and took in the camp, going about its business without her. As though she didn't exist. As though she wasn't needed. *As it did before and will do after you. Like Little Haven.* She might have shuffled back to her bed and slipped into a numb sort of sleep had she not been spotted by a short, stout woman walking by with two pails of sloshing goat's milk.

"Girl," she called, setting her burden down on the ground while she caught her breath. "Give me a hand with these, would you? Before I spill half of it for the worms."

Evelyn reluctantly left the doorway and joined the woman. Once they started walking again, a pail each, Evelyn felt the woman studying her.

"You're new here," she said. "One of the arrivals from a couple of weeks back, eh?"

"I am," Evelyn said quietly, finding she had barely enough energy to place one foot in front of the other, let alone make conversation.

"Well, I'm Cassandra. Friends call me Cass." The woman beamed at her as though letting Evelyn in on a secret.

"Evelyn."

"Ooh, Evelyn! You know my son, Griff, eh?"

She grunted in response.

"Good boy, he is. Always running errands. We came here because he has those powers. I knew ever since he was young. Always had a strange way 'bout him. Friendly, but strange too." She studied Evelyn again. "You have the same air about you. P'raps that's my ability, sensing it in others." She laughed, a genuine, hearty sound that caused her round belly to jiggle up and down.

"No," Evelyn snapped, irritated at the woman's easy merriment. "I don't have any powers."

"Oh," Cass said, face dropping. "Well, could be I'm wrong …" She hesitated before speaking on. "My partner, Marnie, she tells me I should stop trying to pry so much. 'Let people talk when they want to, Cass,' she says." The woman smiled at Evelyn, an expression that lit up her ruddy face, made her small brown eyes twinkle. "Sorry if I said too much, girl."

Evelyn found herself warming to the woman despite herself. "No, it's not you," she said. "It's just … all so much, sometimes."

Cass nodded as though she knew exactly what Evelyn meant, though said no more. They continued in silence until they reached the rear side of the feasting hut. "Put the milk there, girl. That's it. Thanks for your help."

Evelyn placed the pail down, turning to leave.

"Well, if you ever need a task to do, we're always after an extra pair of hands in the kitchen," Cass called after her. "You've been a big help."

Evelyn waved in acknowledgement as she moved away.

Big help. Pah. She didn't deserve such kindness, she believed that without a doubt. She'd failed Raif and Rose.

To think I believed I might've been able to learn more about my powers here, to receive training.

Stupid. Stupid and useless.

You'll never amount to anything.

She clenched her fists and shut her eyes but still couldn't keep the agonised groan from escaping her lips, refusing to acknowledge the confused stares of those around her.

"Evelyn." She heard a familiar voice behind her and was strangely glad to find Hector approaching her. He leant heavily on a wooden stick, his face drawn, olive skin cast with a sickly pallor, but it was a vast improvement from when he'd first been brought back to camp. At his feet walked Cara, delicately padding across the snow-covered ground with tail held high.

"Are you well, lass?" He gave her a scrutinising stare. She felt weak and exposed under his gaze. As though he knew her innermost thoughts, he said, "I thought they'd have you training by now."

"Training?" She shook her head vigorously. "I, er … no. Not me. I don't need it."

Hector moved closer and placed his free hand on her shoulder. "Hmm," he said. At her feet, his cat rubbed against her leg. "Perhaps a warm drink is in order, child."

Evelyn glared at him. "Don't call me a child."

"Now, now, lass. I mean no disrespect." His voice was gentle, his eyes full of kindness. She didn't know why she had lashed out, the fury already subsiding and giving way to the usual sense of suffocating hopelessness.

Hector chuckled. "I mean, to me you are a child. I've seen more years than I care to admit." He patted her arm. "Perhaps you'd like a story to take your mind off things. I could tell you about my powers. How I discovered 'em, how I found my dear Cara here."

Evelyn gave a terse nod. *At least it would be a distraction.*

Hector's green eyes glimmered. "Come on," he said. "Let's go in then." He gestured to the hut. "There'll be a warm fire and a glass of spiced mead I'm sure."

Inside, the feasting hut was largely empty, though a cheerful woman delivered them both a full tankard of spiced mead, as Hector had anticipated. They sat at a wooden bench close to the crackling hearth.

Hector exhaled as he sat, his cat jumping up beside him and promptly curling herself up. "If Avanna had her way, I'd still be abed," he said in a hushed voice, casting his eyes about with mock conspiracy. "But I couldn't face another day of staring at those bloody walls. Need to get some exercise, clear my head." He grimaced as he shifted his healing leg.

"Did it hurt much?" Evelyn asked.

"It did at first. But you'd be surprised how quickly the shock dulls the pain. Can't complain though. Could've been a lot worse. I'll live to fight another day." He smiled at her, moustache twitching upwards.

"I s'pose so." Evelyn took a deep swig of her spiced mead. It was richly flavoured, warm and strong; just what she needed.

"Don't drink too fast, girl." Hector eyed her as he sipped his own drink. "There's no rush."

"I'm used to it." Evelyn shrugged. "I stayed at a tavern for a time and had wine most days."

"Even so." He rubbed the back of his hand across his mouth, wiping his moustache clear of froth. "You've nothing to gain from drinking yourself into oblivion."

Evelyn paused, tankard touching her lips. Then, to make a point, she took another long drink. If he wanted to ask about her drinking habits, he could do so and be done with it. She was growing weary of playing games.

Hector placed his tankard down on the table. "Stubborn one, aren't you?" His words were serious, though Evelyn could see a hint of amusement in his eyes.

"Well, we didn't come here to speak of such things. I promised to tell you my story. Where to start?" He ran a hand through his hair. "I met Avanna and Mak eighteen years ago, before Veritas was formed. I'd made my way to Taskan after some … misfortune drove me from my hometown." He tilted his head away, hiding his face.

Evelyn frowned. "Misfortune?"

When he looked back at her, his eyes were clouded with tears that he quickly blinked away. "It's long-buried now. Anyway, when I arrived in Taskan, I had nothing. I was desperate, alone. I knew about the Commune and I knew I wanted nothing to do with them. Their control never reached Nook Town, my home. They're protected by an oath, able to continue worshiping the god of their ancestors." Hector's lip curled, his entire body tensing.

"Are you okay?" Evelyn asked.

He released the grip on his tankard, puffing air through his lips. "Not a good place, Nook Town." He gave a weak smile. "Wouldn't recommend going there. The people may not support the Commune but that doesn't mean they support those with powers either. They have another way of looking upon those like me." He pulled his tankard close, staring into it with a glazed expression.

Evelyn raised her arm, waving for more mead. When their tankards were refilled, she sipped it gratefully. "So, what happened when you got to Taskan? How did you meet Avanna and Mak?"

Hector rubbed a hand across his forehead. "I wasn't used to the levels of suspicion in the city—soldiers everywhere, scrolls offering rewards for children handed into the Commune. It was impossible to find honest work; everyone in the city was suspicious of outsiders. I lived on the streets for a time and did some things I'm not proud of." He steeled himself with a swig of mead.

"That must've been hard," Evelyn said, a sudden affection for Bessie bursting into her mind. *Had I not found her when I left Little Haven, I'd have been in the same position.*

"It was," he said. "Not a time I like to relive. And then I met Cara. She wouldn't stop following me around—this ragged, filthy, little kitten. In honesty, I was annoyed. Barely able to feed myself—what was I supposed to do with a cat? And then, of course, the *voices* began." He waggled his fingers at her as though telling a ghost story and she couldn't help but chuckle. "I would do my best to block out the strange thoughts entering my mind. Was convinced I was going mad, truth be told. I did all I could to shake her off, tried to stop her following me, shouted, swore, threw stones. She always came back." He placed a tender hand on his companion who let out a deep purr. "But she knew before I did that we were bound together. Companions."

Companions. Evelyn was filled with an overwhelming sense of envy; what must it be like to find another being with whom you shared everything? *No use being coy anymore. News will spread soon enough.* "Like Rose and Dog?" she asked, voice strained.

"Yes, I think so." Hector turned to face her fully then. "What do you know of Rose's powers?"

"Oh, um …" Evelyn chewed on her lip. "Can't say I know much."

He eyed her for a moment before continuing. "She might be one of the strongest people I've ever met. I've never *felt* anything like it." He shook his head. "But that's no matter for now. The girl has time to train. For myself, I knew about my powers from a young age but I was strictly forbidden from using them. An abomination, they were called. Was told to deny them, by my father most of all. Made to consume … Well, no matter. They were forced away is the point. Looking back, it was easier. To be nothing, nobody, anything but someone with these powers I didn't really understand."

"I know how that feels," she muttered without thinking, surprised at her own honesty. And then she realised why the words had burst from her. *That's what I wanted when I left Little Haven.*

Hector grunted. "Hindsight is a strange thing, isn't it?" He looked at her expectantly, an almost satisfied gleam in his eye.

Damn. He wasn't just telling his story, he knew my past—assumed it at least— and now what? Is he waiting for me to say it aloud? To confirm his suspicions? Despite her annoyance at being led by his conversation, Evelyn couldn't ignore the small warmth of appreciation at his gesture. *Must be the mead,* she reasoned. For a moment, she considered admitting what she'd done to Arthur two years before. To share the weight with another who may actually be truthful when they replied, "I understand."

And then Raif and Rose's faces flashed into her mind. Could she have this with Rose as well? And Raif by extension? Evelyn shook her head, almost imperceptibly. It was different for Rose. The girl was only six; there was no responsibility to be taken, no solidarity to share with her seniors. Rose's powers were more evidence of a child's emotional outbursts than of choice. Evelyn had been sixteen, nearly a woman. And, what was more, she had been *glad* of the pain she'd caused.

He deserved it.

No, she couldn't tell the truth. She couldn't risk getting into any sort of trouble, being unable to help Raif and Rose. She braced herself with a clear, absolute thought: no matter Raif's anger, she would always be here for them.

"Hector," she said. "I don't have any powers."

His lips pinched tight, eyes narrowed. "That so, lass?" he said.

"I've never had them," she said, irritated that he wouldn't believe her lie.

"Okay," Hector said. "I just …" He sighed. "I suppose the point of me telling you about my past is so you can bear it in mind. Will you do that, at least? If you do what I did and deny a part of yourself, you'll never be truly happy. Curse it, you won't even be content. Besides which, if someone represses their powers—which," Hector held his palm up to Evelyn as she opened her mouth to deny it once more, "I understand no one here is doing. It can lead to them being used when you least expect it, like a waterskin full to bursting. Sooner or later, something has to leak out. It could be a tiny dribble, barely noticeable, but it could also be an explosion."

It's a bit late for warnings like that, she thought bitterly. To Hector she said, "I'll remember."

"Very well. That's all I can ask."

Evelyn gulped down more mead. "But that's not your whole story. How did you end up here?"

"At Veritas?" Hector peered around at the hut, a wistful smile playing at his lips. "Ah. That's a long story. Suffice to say, Avanna, Mak, and I formed it together all those years ago. I was alone in Taskan, like I said. Didn't have a place to go. And then one night, Avanna found me. I was huddled in an alley, cold, alone, afraid. The nobles there care nothing for the starving, the homeless, the desperate. They turn a blind eye. It's easy to ignore what you don't see. So, I was all the more surprised when she even *saw* me, let alone spoke words of kindness."

A pang of guilt coursed through Evelyn as she remembered the friendship Raif had shown her, his words of comfort, his *belief* in her. She sighed. She would have to speak to him again, to try and make him understand.

"Are you listening, Evelyn?" Hector said, not unkindly.

"Sorry. What happened when Avanna found you?"

"I was wary at first. How could I not be? But she told me she knew about my powers, could sense them. Could see the strain of hiding them. It was the first time I heard them described as something good. She knew how to avoid the Commune, she said. Wanted to help me. I couldn't refuse.

"She took me to Mak, who had been gathering intelligence about some children due to be transported to the Commune. And that's how we met. Of course, Cara followed. I told Avanna about trying to rid myself of the stubborn thing. She said I should never do that to one who was drawn to me."

"I see," Evelyn said, studying her near-empty tankard.

"I don't mean to chide you, lass. It's just … we don't always know what's best for us. Imagine if I'd succeeded in shooing Cara away. Well, I actually can't imagine. Not having my dearest companion? A terrible thought."

No, we don't always know what's best for us.

But if we could give to others what we wished we had for ourselves …

"Thank you for telling me your story, Hector," she said, running a finger along the wooden grooves of the table. "Will you promise me one thing?"

He raised an eyebrow. "Course. If I can, lass."

"If anything happens to me—"

Hector frowned. "What? Evelyn, you're safe here. This is the best pla—"

"Please." He must have seen the conviction in her face, for he nodded and didn't say another word. "If anything happens to me, you have to protect Raif and Rose."

Cara sat upright, watching Evelyn with her piercing yellow eyes. "Of course," Hector said. "If I ever need to, that is."

"Thank you." And Evelyn meant it deeply. She drank the last of her mead. "I'd best go and do some chores. Don't want Mak hunting me down and telling me how laziness leads to stupidity or something."

Hector laughed, waving a hand at Evelyn. "The man couldn't discipline someone if he tried," he said. "Don't worry about him."

And as Evelyn stood to leave, she saw Flo dashing towards them.

"Hector, Hector," the serving girl cried. "You're needed in Avanna's hut. Now, please. *Now.*"

Evelyn turned to Hector, eyes wide. "Rose was called this morning—"

Hector clutched her arm. "Never had a promise come round on me so quick." But Evelyn saw the unquestionable concern in his eyes. "Come on," he said.

Without a word, she helped him from his seat. Together, following an unnerved Flo, they hurried out of the hut.

22

Raif

Raif knelt beside Rose, cradling her in his arms. "It's okay, little bug," he whispered, stroking her back just like their mother used to do. *Will I ever feel her hand on my back again?* He shut the thought away before it could fully develop, afraid to allow it to take root in his mind. He had to focus on Rose; that was all he could do.

Though his sister was silent, her tears having stopped as he held her against his chest, he could still feel her trembling. He glared at Avanna and Mak, standing across the hut, heads together and voices hushed. The air was filled with the strange scent of scorched fur, though Avanna seemed to have done her best to cover it with the usual heady incense she burned in her hut. Dog whined beside him and he couldn't hold himself back any longer.

"Avanna," he said. "What are you going to—"

"Avanna." Hector burst through the door, Evelyn at his side. Raif avoided her gaze, continuing to comfort his sister.

"What's happened?" she asked, voice tense.

"Why did you send for me?" Hector limped to where Raif, Rose, and Dog sat, leaning down to them. "Are you okay, lass?"

Rose let out a gentle whimper. Cara jumped onto her lap, purring.

"Hector, thank you for coming," Avanna said. "We'd value your input in explaining to—"

"Go on, tell them," Raif snapped. "Tell them what you've done." He could scarce believe it himself, though he'd witnessed the aftermath. He'd been refused entry to the hut when he'd first demanded it that morning, but had hovered nearby, wanting to stay close for Rose's sake. And then, all of a sudden, he'd *known* something was wrong. Had Rose drawn him here with her powers? All he'd known was that nothing would stop him getting past Avanna's guards. He'd forced them aside, hearing his sister's anguished cries from within.

The woman gave him a measured look, letting out a weary sigh. "We're trying to help," she said. "Perhaps you don't see it because you're worried about your sister but—"

"What did you do?" Hector asked.

"There was never any intention to cause harm," Mak said, holding his palms up.

"You failed," Raif sneered, squeezing Rose's shoulder. *They promised us we'd be protected.*

If we're not safe here, where can we go?

Rose lifted her head to look at him, eyes bloodshot and cheeks blotchy.

I'm sorry I didn't protect you, he thought, meeting her gaze. She gave the tiniest nod of her head and touched his arm. She said nothing and he feared it may be some time before she spoke again.

"I think an explanation is in order," Hector said, frowning. "Shall we?" He held his arm out, waving Avanna, Mak, and Evelyn to join Raif, Rose, and Dog in the seating area.

Once everyone was sitting, Flo began offering around cups of hot wine and tea. Raif shook it away; he wouldn't be so easily appeased with offers of refreshments. He saw Evelyn take a tumbler of wine, sure her hand trembled as she lifted it to her lips.

He turned his attention back to Avanna and Mak, sitting opposite as they had that first day in the Veritas Camp. He sat tall, puffed out his chest. "You were using Dog," he stated, pointing an accusing finger towards Avanna. "Using him to get to Rose."

Evelyn almost choked on her mouthful of wine.

"*What?*" Hector reddened. "Tell me that isn't true."

"It isn't what you think," Avanna said, unabashed at the accusation. "I was trying to encourage your sister to use her powers. We need to train Rose for her own safety. I offered myself as a vessel to practice on but she refused. What else could I do?"

"I asked you to speak to me before you started any training on my sister," Raif said, voice low. "Why didn't you?"

Avanna's eyes widened. "You didn't even tell us about your sister's powers, boy," she said. "How can you expect such levels of respect when you keep such truths hidden from us?"

Raif bristled, furious at her causal accusations, her arrogant tone. "How dare you?!" he said. "My sister's powers are for me to—"

"Now, lad," Hector said, reaching for his arm, giving him a gentle nod. "Getting angry won't help here." He turned to Avanna. "Start from the beginning. I'm sure there's an … explanation for all of this." His hesitation spoke of his doubt all too clearly and Raif was oddly comforted by that. He breathed deeply, allowing his moment of rage to subside.

"Rose was brought here this morning so we could begin her training. After her powers were confirmed to me, I needed some time to make a plan. To work out how best to proceed with one so young. But Mak and I agreed it would be best not to wait any longer." Avanna tucked her hair back, meeting each of their gazes. "What if she's our only hope?" She looked to Mak expectantly.

"My sister speaks the truth," he said. "Rose wasn't showing any signs of her powers other than her relationship with her dog. You know that Hector. We've given her space, observed her, tried to sense them, but nothing. One thing is clear: she's different to all the other children we've trained. After we aked her to use her powers and got no response, we knew we had to use a different technique. So Avanna thought if we perhaps, er …" He cleared his throat, at least having the decency to seem embarrassed. "If we threatened the- the animal a bit, acted as though we might harm him."

"*Threatened?*" Evelyn exclaimed. "Animal? He's a dog! A harmless dog!"

Hector let out a bitter laugh. "And you wanted me here to help explain your actions?"

"We did it to help Rose, Hector. We never meant any harm," Avanna said. "It was to encourage the girl, that's all. I thought, surely, someone like you, with powers akin to the girl's, would understand how important it is for us to—"

Hector scoffed. "Oh, no. You don't get to use my powers to justify what you've done." He slammed his palm into a cushion. "Damn it, there are other ways, Avanna, you know that. Ways that don't involve harming Rose or Dog."

At Hector's words, Dog let out a low growl. Cara moved from Rose's lap, gently touching her nose to his. The animal soon quieted, laying his head on his paws. Rose let out a shuddering breath and leant against Raif.

"Perhaps we should talk away from the children," Mak said.

"No," Evelyn and Raif said simultaneously.

"Not again," Raif snapped. "Rose and I deserve to be here. To understand what exactly you think you're doing to *help* us. We won't be shut out anymore. Especially as you seem to think my sister is different somehow."

Evelyn nodded, trying to catch Raif's eye though he still refused to fully look at her. "You need to give us answers," she said. "You owe us that much. After what you told me about how important you think Rose is, it's the least you can do."

"What?" Raif asked, finally turning to Evelyn. She gave him a weak smile. He sniffed and turned aside. *How much did she keep from us?*

"You're right, both of you," Hector said. "After what's happened here, a full explanation is owed."

Avanna let out an exasperated breath. "I know I told you we had time to train and prepare to fight the Commune," she said. "The truth is, we've been waiting for someone like Rose for many years. What you confirmed to me after the soldier's interrogation, Evelyn—it could change everything. The girl clearly has a *lot* of untapped potential."

Evelyn shifted, cheeks flushing. Raif ignored her, glad of her discomfort. "I still don't understand why that means you hurt Dog," he said. Rose let out a quivering exhale, reaching to pet her beloved companion. His heart ached. *I should have been here. I should have insisted.*

"Mm." Hector absent-mindedly tugged at his moustache. "It's clear you've caused some serious distress. That is not the way we train. Never has been."

"We had no choice," Avanna said, steadfast in her defiance.

"There's always a choice," Raif muttered, glancing at Evelyn. Her head was clasped in her hands, her shoulders hunched. For a moment, he felt sorry for her. But then the feeling of betrayal returned and he knew she'd let him down. Let them both down.

"There is, lad," Hector said, lips drawn tight. "We'll get to the bottom of this."

"She refused to show her powers," Avanna said, waving her hand towards Rose. "We had to take … extreme measures."

"Surely she needs time." Evelyn lifted her head, scowling. "She's *six* years old. If she doesn't want to do something, she won't."

"You know that's always the way at first, Avanna," Hector said, voice pleading as he tried to calm the rising anger in the room. "We have to be gentle, coaxing, encouraging. You expected too much too soon. Why didn't you come to me about this?"

"This isn't like any other training we've done. It can't be. No other powers have come close to hers. No one else here, other than Hector, has shown any remarkable capabilities, but now …" Avanna's brown eyes seemed darker than ever as they lingered on Rose—a strange, hungry look that unsettled Raif. "We didn't know what else to do. We simply thought if the dog was in danger, that Rose, well, she might be more willing to show us her powers. The dog wasn't harmed. Some fur singed, that's all. Please, Hector, you have to understand." The woman's lips spasmed, as though she were struggling with her words. Finally, she sat up straight, looking directly at Raif and Rose. "I'm sorry. Perhaps we acted rashly."

"Perhaps?" Raif glared. *Half an apology. She doesn't care.*

Avanna gave him a pointed look, chin jutting forwards. "Yes."

Raif clawed his hands in his lap, trying his hardest not to scream. "You could have seriously hurt him," he muttered, nodding towards the sleeping Dog.

Avanna rolled her eyes. "He was never at any risk, don't you see that?" She looked at her brother for support again, though Mak appeared to be growing more uncomfortable by the minute. He shuffled, giving an awkward smile.

"We were never going to hurt him," he whispered. "Just thought if we held him *near* the fire, Rose would act quickly."

"Exactly," Avanna said.

Evelyn let out an indignant snort. "What the fu—"

Hector held his hand up to stop her. He took a moment to breathe in and out slowly. "This really isn't good enough, Avanna. I can't believe you—"

"Hush," the woman retorted, patience evidently run thin. "He's not in any danger, how many times do I have to say that? He never was. We needed Rose to be persuaded to show us her abilities. She could have taken over my mind and controlled me—she's done it before, has she not? With ease, apparently."

Hector's shoulders slumped. "As I said, it's not the way we train. As well you should know after all these years."

"What do we really know though?" Avanna asked. "This is unprecedented."

Hector shook his head. "There's no more to say on the matter. What you did was wrong."

There followed a silence, the only sound Dog's gentle snoring. Though it was clear the animal suffered no wounds, Raif couldn't ignore his sister's distress, the pain glazing her eyes.

"I don't want Rose trained anymore," Raif said. "I don't want you near her."

"Now, Raif, don't speak out of anger," Mak said, the usual passion back in his voice. "Rose needs help, otherwise her powers might overcome her. She might act without control again."

"You don't know what … She can't be held responsible for what she …" Raif turned aside, too frustrated to say more.

"I'd have expected such manipulation from your sister, Mak. But you … Can't you see this is wrong?" Evelyn crossed her arms, eyes blazing.

"Now, now, let's not speak rashly. Let's take some time to calm down," Hector said. "Raif, Rose, Evelyn. Take Dog. Get some rest. Leave me to speak to Avanna and Mak. This won't happen again."

"Come on," Evelyn said. "Hector's right." She touched a hand to Raif's shoulder. He stiffened but didn't brush her away. There was no use in arguing any longer. Rose and Dog needed to be away from these people—as did he.

Outside, he was shocked to discover it was still early afternoon. The sky was bright, the breeze crisp and cool in his face. He let out a long sigh, watching as Rose and Dog quietly made their way toward their hut. He dearly wished he could speak to Evelyn about what had happened. Perhaps they could make a plan together.

No. I can't trust her. Not yet.

"Raif," Evelyn called.

"What?" He turned to find her twisting her cloak in her hand. He couldn't feel bad for his curtness. His head was too muddled, his mind riddled with confusion. *Are we safe here?*

Are we safe anywhere?

"I can't tell you how—"

He raised a hand to cut her off. "That wouldn't have happened if Avanna hadn't found out about Rose's powers." The words were harsh, he knew, yet this was the easiest vent for his outrage.

"Raif, I—"

"I need some time to think. I need to protect my sister. She might be the only family I have left."

Evelyn's eyes glistened, she blinked quickly. "Raif, please, you two are ..." Her shoulders dropped. "I'm sorry."

He turned to follow Rose. "We just need some time alone, Evelyn." He walked away without looking back, afraid that if he did his resolve would crumble. He had to be strong—for Rose.

For the promise I made to Father.

23

Evelyn

You'll never amount to anything.

Evelyn gulped down the tankard of spiced mead. In the corner of the feasting hut, keeping her distance from those eating their dinner, talking and enjoying each other's company, she was able to wallow in her ever-deepening pit of self-despair. She thought back to the day, not so long ago, when Raif and Rose arrived at the tavern. Even in the short time they'd known each other, she'd felt a true connection—and they had, too … hadn't they?

You'll never amount to anything.

She drank more mead, wanting only for the pain to be dulled. When the second tankard was drained, she signalled for another, then another, the feasting hut slowly filling around her.

After a time, she noticed two men she recognised were sitting at the table behind her. *Who … I know their faces.* She watched them over the rim of her cup, slurping down more mead.

Ah! She smirked to herself, triumphant at remembering; Avanna's guards. They were deep in conversation. Evelyn sat up, running her hands down the front of her tunic. *Be inconspicuous, jus' like Bessie would've said.* She casually leant against her table, head in her hand as she tried to listen to their words. They were laughing and joking, sharing stories over their stew and ale. Her head lolled as she struggled to stay interested in their inane chatter. Just as she was beginning to think she should probably go to bed, she noticed the change in their tone. With all the grace she could muster—which was, admittedly, not very much—she edged closer still, stifling a hiccough as she tilted her head to hear them.

"I think this is it, Bo," said the grey-bearded one.

"Really?" Bo's voice was full of awe.

"I *know* it." The bearded man gulped some of his drink. He raised his voice, his tone boastful as he said, "I've never seen Avanna so excited. She's training the girl herself—when have you ever known her to do that?"

Evelyn's stomach lurched and she drank more mead to force back the wave of nausea. She turned to face the gloating man, mouth agape, and made eye contact. She prepared herself for a confrontation and was surprised when, instead, he raised his tankard towards her.

"You there," he said, smiling kindly. "Come, join us."

She awkwardly clambered from her bench and moved to theirs, waving at the nearby serving-boy for another fill as she sat. *I could learn something to regain Raif's trust,* she told herself. *Jus' listen this time, you've done enough talking.*

"But she's so young," Bo continued, giving Evelyn only the briefest of glances as she sat down. "And what about the soldier?"

"Yes, what of the soldier?" She wiped a hand across her top lip after a mouthful of fresh mead. "What *will* they do with him?"

"They can't let him leave here, can they, Tavin?" Bo's eyes were shining and wide, full of conspiracy. "Though I heard the other Nomarrans here, they tried to make Avanna—"

"Enough of that, boy," Tavin snapped, glaring at Bo. "No place for such talk."

Evelyn frowned, trying to maintain her focus. "If they- if they can't leave him here, what'll happen to 'im?"

Tavin bowed his head, regaining his composure. "Well, Avanna will learn what she can from him, but after that, in my eyes, there's only one option."

Evelyn blinked, trying to process what he could mean.

There was a silence before Bo said, "I've never witnessed an execution before."

Execution. Evelyn did her best to hold back a gasp, but couldn't control her expression. *Surely not. Executions are what the Commune do. Not ... not those who are against them, surely?*

"You're right to be shocked, girl," Tavin said. "Rare thing 'round here. Fear not, you're not likely to see it. Avanna isn't one for public shows like those Commune scum. If the man must die, then die he will, but it won't be for entertainment. He'll be disposed of discreetly. He may already have been dealt with."

"No more than he deserves, is it?" Bo asked, scratching at his alcohol-flushed cheeks.

"No more than he deserves, my boy." Tavin nodded sagely.

Evelyn frowned, strangely regretful at the idea of the soldier's death. He'd regarded her with more disgust and hatred than she'd ever felt before and yet there was a depth to his beliefs, a conviction to his actions that she couldn't forget. It made her want to know more. To try and understand why he so fervently followed the Commune. Could he unwittingly help them fight the very thing he served?

She stared into her tankard, thoughts fumbling and bumping into each other as she tried to form a plan. "Where's ... where's Avanna keeping 'im?" She asked the question before she truly knew why.

Tavin and Bo had moved on to a new topic while Evelyn was silent, they glanced at each other before the older man answered with an amused gleam in his eye. "Fancy a go at him before it's too late?"

Evelyn blanched. "S-sorry?"

Tavin chuckled. "Prisoners are a rare opportunity to practice your powers on another person. And a Noman Islander," he beamed at Bo, "that is a rarity. Those with abilities like to challenge themselves, in my experience." He peered around the hut before leaning his head closer to hers. "And it's well known a Nomarran is almost impossible to exert any control over. They've got protection, y'see. From their Goddess."

"Ah," she said slowly, doing her best to think before she spoke. "To practice my powers on." An idea, incomplete but strong, finally formed in her mind.

"It's sure to help." Tavin stroked his beard. "Practice on a Nomarran is sure to be a unique experience." He finished the ale in his tankard and banged it against the table for a refill before turning back to Evelyn. "He's kept in a hut to the rear of the camp, near the latrines. Comfortable enough. As comfortable as a soldier of the Commune deserves to be, in any case."

As Evelyn stood, he raised his fresh filled tankard towards her once more. "Good luck, girl," he said. "And be careful. He's an angry one—and that mead is strong." He shot her a wink and she pouted at him.

I can handle the bloody mead, she told herself, downing the last of her tankard before moving to the door. She focused on every footstep, determined not to falter or stumble. *Not drunk. Jus' got some confidence back.*

She stalked outside with all the bluster-filled determination of her mead-fueled, half-formed plan. As the night air hit her, nausea coursed its way up her throat. She took a moment to lean against the hut, shutting her eyes and breathing deeply. *Not drunk, not drunk.* Her mind swam, but a part of her knew she needed to speak to this soldier—now. "Execution," she whispered to herself, mouthing the word over and over again before spitting on the floor as though it were poison. *Now's my only chance.*

The frozen camp was quiet, Evelyn's breaths and pounding heartbeat seeming all too loud. She blinked up at the stars, watched them dance and blur together. She curled her hand into a fist and punched it into the top of her leg. *Pull yourself together.* She exhaled, a white cloud of breath hovering before her face. "Come on," she said into the night. "For Raif an' Rose."

With exaggeratedly careful strides, she made her way towards the latrines at the camp's northernmost point. Perhaps her fortunes were turning, for she encountered no one on her way and managed to keep her footing, even on the treacherously icy ground. *Raif'll be so pleased with me when I find out s'more stuff about the Commune,* she told herself, biting her lip as a choking lump formed in her throat. *Keep your head, stupid. Got to focus.*

You'll never amount to anything.

"Fuck you, Arthur," she whispered.

She *could* be something. A friend. A sister. A *good* person.

As Evelyn approached the latrines—doing her best to ignore the distant stench of stale piss—she saw the hut. Outside, a single torch was ensconced upon the wall. Some small part of her thought it strange there was no guard present, but she was too overcome with the prospect of reconnecting with Raif to notice. It was only when she drew close enough to hear the muffled voices that she paused.

She cocked her head and held her breath. Still unable to discern what was being said, she sneaked closer with all the subtlety she could muster and pressed her ear against the hut.

" … dare you ask me to reveal the secrets of my people?" *The Commander.*

"I see you are a man who recognises the need for caution." *Avanna!*

Evelyn pulled her head away from the hut for a moment, brows knitted. What was she doing sneaking around at this late hour? Then she shook her head and snorted gently to herself. *Exactly the same thing you are, idiot.* She covered her mouth as another hiccough escaped her lips, holding as still as she could for a moment to ensure she hadn't been heard. The words inside the hut continued. Satisfied she had remained concealed and more than a little smug that her plan had led to such an end—the Commander and *Avanna*—she settled against the wall once more.

" … no point in arguing. I've already been through your possessions, Commander. I know what this is."

The Commander's gasp of shock was audible.

"It's important to you, I see. I'm surprised the Commune allowed you to keep it, especially with the Grand Magister's increasing suspicion about your people." There was a pause and Evelyn imagined Avanna holding the curious object up for closer inspection. "Veritarra's Gift. Common in your homeland, is it not?" There was the sound of slow footsteps. Evelyn imagined Avanna pacing before the man, his dark brown eyes following her. "There are rumours that the Grand Magister is right to be cautious about its presence in the kingdom; that its use in the Seven-Year War went beyond providing protection against the po—"

"Fool. You speak of what you do not know." The Commander's voice was low, full of venom. "That powder is sacred. And it is *dangerous.* You have no idea what it could do to you, to *everyone* in this camp, in the wrong hands. In ignorant hands."

There was a momentary silence as though Avanna wanted him to speak on. There was an audible exhale before she said, "Everyone? Not just power-holders? How interesting. I've always wanted to know more about it. It seems there is a far greater use for it than I thought. Perhaps capable of stopping the Grand Magister himself. If you could tell me more … Well, that would warrant a great debt. One I'd be willing to repay."

"You assume I would forsake the Commune, all I am loyal to, because you crave the knowledge to bring him down."

"Come now, Commander, let's not play that game. You work for Lord Torrant, not the Grand Magister. Don't you want to see him again?" The silence was pointed, filled with an unspoken meaning that Evelyn couldn't grasp. Avanna sighed again. "You know full well the respect I have for the Goddess of your homeland. I don't hide it."

"You take Veritarra's name in vain," the Commander said weakly.

"I won't waste your time any longer, Commander. I will speak plainly." More footsteps. Evelyn held her breath, afraid Avanna might be an arm's reach from her current position—she could be exposed at a moment's notice. "You must be aware one of your soldiers escaped. I won't lie to you; we sent scouts after him but they never returned. Our camp could be in great danger. The soldier of yours, if he has reached Lord Torrant, has undoubtedly reported the location of the fight with Hector. He will lead more men this way and they will find our camp."

Evelyn's heart pounded. *An escaped soldier!* She massaged her forehead, trying to focus. *How many days has it been? How close could more be to finding us?*

The Commander let out a rasping laugh. "It is no more than your traitorous people deserve."

"That may be what you believe, Commander. It is of little consequence now. What I need from you is information. It's that simple."

The Commander scoffed. "There is nothing simple about your request," he said, though Evelyn sensed his resolve waning, his voice growing weak.

"Veritarra's Gift. Tell me all you know about it and I will let you go. You can return to Lord Torrant. That's what I'm offering you."

She's letting him go. Evelyn daren't move, even as her body alerted itself for the growing need to run.

"And you will return my pouch to me?" Evelyn wondered what could cause such an anxious strain in the Commander's voice.

"I am giving you your life and freedom. Do not push your luck."

Why is Avanna prepared to let him go in exchange for information about this Veritarra's Gift? And what possible reason could Avanna have for not alerting the camp to the escaped soldier, the risk of danger?

She was supposed to protect us!

Evelyn held a hand to her pounding head. Suddenly all too sober, she wondered what this could mean. Somehow these pieces slotted together. Her mistrust of Avanna might not have been unfounded after all—but *why?* She rubbed her temples, willing herself to connect the parts.

Too much bloody mead.

From the camp, she was sure she heard the sound of barking.

Dog.

It could have been some distant wild animal, not Rose's beloved companion at all, yet it was enough to jolt her into action as she pushed herself upright.

Have to tell Raif and Rose.

Have to get away from here.

They needed a head start on any soldiers who might, even now, be closing in.

Filled with a sudden sense of certainty, she lurched away from the hut. Her legs were numbed with cold and heavy with drink. She stumbled and fell. *Idiot.*

"Where do you think you're going?"

Evelyn didn't think her heart could beat any faster, but in that moment it threatened to burst through her chest altogether. Something pressed down on the small of her back—a boot? She tried to push herself up and Avanna dug her heel into Evelyn's back harder still. She grunted in pain and tried to reach down for her sword.

"Don't be a fool," Avanna said, leaving to remove the sword from Evelyn's scabbard before throwing it into the night.

"No," Evelyn whispered. "Please." She dragged herself on, scrabbling at the hard ground. *Pathetic.*

It was no use.

Avanna grabbed her shoulder. "Oh, child. What have you done?"

Evelyn lurched, threw the weight of her body forward, and for a moment felt the grip on her release. Then there was a hand on each of her arms, Avanna's breath near the base of her neck, the sadness gone from her voice as she whispered, "Didn't anyone teach you to stop fighting when you've been beaten?"

Evelyn fought to push down the nausea in her belly, mead and panic churning together in her gut, rising up her throat. Arms pinned behind her, elbows nearly touching, pain shooting through her shoulders, she tugged in every direction in her desperation to break free. She saw images in the dark, faces she knew weren't there, her mind trying to convince her the shadows would morph into Raif, into Rose, even into Dog barreling towards her, teeth bared. *I'm so sorry.*

Avanna pulled Evelyn to her feet, dragged her backwards into the hut, and the camp disappeared.

24

Raif

"Where is she?"

Raif sat up at the sound of shouting outside. He checked on Rose who still slept soundly on her pallet, Dog curled beside her.

"No, this is unacceptable." The shouts continued, the sound of the door opening was followed by scuffling. He dragged himself from his bed, shivering as his feet hit the cold floor. He quietly pulled on his socks and boots, not wanting Rose to be awoken. After the incident with Dog yesterday, she had been lethargic at best.

He stumbled into the main room of the hut, noticing first that Evelyn's bed was empty. He turned to the door, rubbing his eyes to be sure of what he saw. Avanna was in front, Hector tugging on her arm as though pulling her back. Mak stood behind them, mouth agape, a lamp hanging limply from his hand to illuminate the scene.

"What's going on?" Raif asked.

They froze in their struggle.

Hector peered round Avanna, smiling apologetically. "Good morning, lad. Is Rose with you?"

"Of course," Raif replied with a frown. "Why wouldn't she be?"

"It's that *friend* of yours," Avanna spat. She moved forward, freeing herself of Hector's grasp and gripping Raif's shoulder with fingers like claws. "Where has she taken him?"

Raif tried to shrug free of her hand. "Taken who? What are you talking about? Where's Evelyn?"

254 – LUCY A. McLAREN

Avanna's mouth dropped open, eyes flitting about as though hoping to find Evelyn hidden away.

"What's happened?" Raif frowned. "Where is she?"

Hector ran a finger across his moustache. "I'm sorry, lad. She's gone."

"Gone?" Raif's body jolted at the word. "What do you mean? Where? Why would she … ?"

"Last night," Avanna croaked. "She- she stole a horse, took the prisoner. I still can't believe … After all we did for her!"

"Now, Avanna, stop that. Anger won't serve us," Hector said. "It's clear the lad knew nothing of this. Do you know where she might've gone? Why she might've taken the soldier?"

"Took the soldier?" Raif said, his mind a whirlwind. "I, uh … I don't know." He sank to his knees, legs suddenly too weak to hold him up. *This isn't right. Evelyn wouldn't do this. She wouldn't leave me and Rose … would she?*

"Yes. The Commander. The enemy. A pawn we could have used against the Commune." Avanna's voice rose. But beneath the anger, Raif saw some indecipherable emotion within her expression—the way her eyes darted about, refusing to remain upon his face for long. The woman began pacing between Raif and Mak, hands clasped at her back. "What are we going to do?" Hector stepped towards her, placing a hand on her arm.

"Mak, take your sister to her hut," he said. "She needs to calm down. I'll speak to the lad."

Without a word, Mak handed the lamp he held to Hector and took his sister's arm, steering her away. Raif watched the door close behind them, trying to process the information.

Why would Evelyn leave us? Was I too hard on her?

And why would she help the soldier?

At the back of his mind, another thought sprouted, too quiet for him to pay much heed.

Why is Avanna so frantic? Raif couldn't remember a single time since arriving at Veritas when someone outranked Avanna, and yet she left the room without question.

"Come on, lad," Hector said, lifting Raif by the arms and steering him towards Evelyn's bed. Raif slumped onto it gratefully. When he was handed a flask by the older man, he didn't question it. His hands shook as he lifted it to his lips, wincing as the liquid fire spread down his throat and through his body. It filled him with a small modicum of strength, though he wasn't sure how long it would last.

"Where's she gone, Hector?" he whispered.

"I don't know, lad. It's a shock, I see that."

Raif nodded and let out a groan, holding a hand to his forehead.

"She was your friend and she's gone."

"Why would she help *him*?" Raif managed to say, voice hoarse.

"That I can't say. Sometimes people act in ways we can't fathom. Mayhap she had her reasons."

"They're going to find her, aren't they?" he asked, running a trembling hand through his hair. "Evelyn. They'll find her."

"They may send someone after her," Hector said, though his wringing hands told a different story. He swallowed before speaking again. "But the truth is, your sister is of the most importance here. Evelyn may not warrant the … Well, we can't afford to let people leave at the moment, with so much still to do around the camp in preparation for the coldest months."

"But …" Raif frowned. "No, Evelyn- She …" He bit his quivering lip, refusing to cry in front of Hector.

"I know. Have faith you'll see her again, though. I'm sure we will."

Raif inhaled deeply, trying his best to believe it.

From the rear of the hut, there was a rustling sound. Rose and Dog were waking.

"What am I going to tell my sister?" A lump swelled in his throat.

Was it my fault?

The thought wouldn't stop returning.

"Don't worry about that, lad," Hector said. As he spoke, Cara appeared at Raif's side, yellow eyes glowing in the dim light of the flickering lamp. She let out a soft purr and licked his hand with her rough tongue.

"Yes, I suppose you're right," Raif said, sighing. "We have somewhere warm to sleep and Rose has been … mostly content here."

"I know. And don't worry," Hector's expression hardened, "what happened to Rose won't be allowed again. I've made sure of it."

At that moment, Rose made her way towards them, blonde hair a mass of rumpled curls.

"Good morning, lass," Hector said in a loud, too-happy voice. "I've come to give Raif the good news. I'll be helping you with your training from now on, how does that sound?" Rose simply stared up at him, eyes groggy with sleep.

Raif laughed despite himself. He gave Rose a reassuring pat on the shoulder. "Dog will be safe now," he said.

"Of course." Hector nodded. "Cara here will make sure of it."

Rose studied both her brother and Hector. "Okay," she said. "Dog likes Cara."

"It's a wonder." Hector chuckled. "The old girl can be a bit grumpy at times."

Cara let out an indignant mewl.

"Well, it's early but what do you two say to some breakfast?"

Raif nodded, content to follow Hector's lead.

Raif and Rose dressed in warm clothes and together emerged into the rousing camp. All the while, Raif tried his very hardest not to think about Evelyn. She'd gone. She'd freed the soldier—their enemy. Whatever her reason, he had to focus on his sister now.

What else can I do?

And yet, his heart ached all the same. *Evelyn, why?* And then, a little softer, *Evelyn, come back.*

25

Commander Sulemon

A s they rode through the night, Commander Sulemon grew sure everything was as it should be. He pushed away the doubts gnawing at his heart—*You told that wretched woman your sacred ways? You betrayed your people*—and, instead, focused on his victory. He smirked as he felt the girl's torso bump against his, her chest to his back. She hadn't spoken in hours, not since her last attempt to leap from the horse's back led to nothing but a deft arm blocking her lurch, a mocking, scorn-filled laugh from him, and a strong kick to spur them faster. *Not so confident now that you're the prisoner, are you?*

True, she wasn't the young girl who'd attacked the soldier in Castleton, but he knew where that abomination was. He could instruct Lord Torrant on the whereabouts of the traitors' camp. They could return there together and burn that damned place to the ground.

For now, they would head for the Torrant Estate where Lord Torrant would await him. His heart soared. Even as the days passed by in that forsaken place, he had not lost hope. He couldn't help but feel that his path had taken him to the heart of the Veritas camp for a reason. His faith had been tested; that *woman* had questioned his own belief in Veritarra, told him that his own people sought shelter in that wretched place—*Lies, all lies*—but he had remained strong, held onto himself—to the truth. Even as he'd shivered and half-starved, choked with the unmistakable scent of piss and shit mere feet away, he'd remembered the face of the man he loved, his resolve strong as ever.

My faith has been repaid. The woman came to him that night, a strange gleam in her eye. Though a treacherous bitch, her offer was his only chance of freedom: information on Veritarra's Gift for his life. At first, he'd refused; there was no way he would share such sacred knowledge. But when the girl was dragged in front of him, thrown at his feet, and added to the deal … Well, that was *far* too tempting to refuse.

Lord Torrant was sure to approve of his decision.

His hand drifted to his waist and his stomach crumpled into a knot, remembering his pouch was gone. The last link to his home—to all he'd been before he'd come to Septima.

He straightened himself up in the saddle. *No matter.* The important thing was he lived to see another day. He would return to the Veritas camp with Lord Torrant, and the woman would return what belonged to him—he would give her no choice.

Though the snow-covered mountain paths were winding and hazardous, he'd managed to navigate well enough by moonlight, giving himself and the horse no chance for rest. He had to reach Lord Torrant as quickly as possible. Before his mind could wander, the girl stirred in the saddle behind him, pulling him back. Her arms tightened instinctively around his waist as her body tensed. Perhaps she had awoken from a restless sleep, recalled where she was. Her concern was understandable given the circumstances of her capture, the sweet and swift betrayal of her leader.

Despite his undeniable hatred for all she protected, he could not forget she was a child in a war she knew nothing of, and he'd done his best to ensure she was comfortable. He would not bind her hands unless absolutely necessary; that much decency he could afford her, though it was less than she deserved. *Now you see how your allies truly are—traitorous, merciless, liars. Soon, you'll see true power, true loyalty.* And so, imagining every kind word, look, even touch Lord Torrant may offer him when presented with this gift, he scanned the sky and inhaled deeply, satisfaction thrumming through his body.

As the sun rose above the eastern mountain peaks, Commander Sulemon stopped the horse and leapt from its back. He ignored the girl's burning gaze, patting the animal on the nose and moving to search the saddlebags for something to eat.

Ample supplies. The Veritas woman had been prepared for his departure, it seemed. A thought slipped into his mind: *She knew you'd agree. She knew she'd break you, that you would betray your people.* He ignored it. She'd been as good as her word, at least, even returning his red cloak and sword, though not his breastplate.

A slight she couldn't resist. He shrugged to himself. *It doesn't matter now. I am free and she'll get what she deserves sooner or later.*

As he fed the horse and drank from a waterskin, he turned his gaze to the girl still sitting stiffly atop the horse. "Are you hungry?"

She narrowed her eyes and crossed her arms but couldn't quite stop the flicker of longing on her face as he retrieved some bread and cheese from the saddlebags. He passed a slice of each up to her before retrieving a portion for himself. He turned his back on her, chewing on his breakfast as he observed the path ahead.

"Where are you taking me?"

The Commander finished his bread and took another drink of water before looking at her again. She was sitting straight-backed, jaw squared in what he imagined she thought was a defiant expression. *Stupid child.*

"You do not need to know," he said finally, giving her a hard stare, daring her to defy him.

Her lips pursed and her jaw clenched tighter still, but she didn't ask again. Instead, she gnawed on the hard bread he'd given her and pointedly ignored him, suddenly taking a great interest in the distant scenery.

He left her to sulk, focusing on the horizon to the east, mind drawn back to Castleton. Before he could stop himself, he found himself wondering about the young Nomarran woman, Imarra. He hoped she had been taken somewhere safe; he had no doubt that *Samalah* would ensure it was so. Still, he couldn't help the sense of foreboding that arose when recalling that ruined street. Where had the rest of the Nomarrans from the city gone? Could that Veritas wench possibly have spoken the truth when she'd said some of his people had found their way to that camp? *Offered safety by traitors.* He scrunched his face. How could it be so? What was it Lord Torrant had told him—moved northward to Alpin *"for their own safety."* Could some misguided Nomarrans have found their way to the Veritas camp, believing themselves safer there than under the care of the Commune?

At the back of his mind, the voice whispered, *The Grand Magister gave them no choice.*

"Shouldn't we keep moving?" The girl, having apparently regained her composure, had climbed from the horse. She watched him, brows creased and lips pursed into a ridiculous pout.

"You should learn to hold your tongue, girl," he said, taking the horse's reins in hand and guiding them onwards towards the Crystal River.

"Evelyn," she grumbled.

"What?" He glanced over his shoulder where she walked some steps behind.

"My name is Evelyn," she said, frowning. "Not 'girl.'"

Despite himself, he laughed at her brazen outburst. "Very well," he said. "You should learn to hold your tongue, *Evelyn.*"

To his horror, she sped up to walk beside him. "What should I call you?"

"I think you will find 'Commander' works fine."

"Okay, *Commander.*" She smirked, though her expression quickly dropped as she began to fiddle with the edge of her cloak. "Do you … Hmm."

He rolled his eyes. "What is it?"

"Is it true the Nomarrans call the powers a … a curse?"

He blanched, immediately on his guard. "What do you know of it?"

"Not much," she said. "It's just, er, I heard it mentioned that the powers are a curse on the Noman Islands."

The Commander frowned, irritated by her ignorance. *How dare she so casually mention my homeland?* "It is of no consequence to the likes of you. Enough insult to my people was done by your *leader.*" He snorted at her wince. "I will not tolerate it from you."

She fought to compose herself. "Is it why you follow the Commune? Or is it because of Lord Torrant, like Ava—"

He stopped walking, rounding on her. "Avanna. You still say her name with respect—the woman who traded you like a mule."

To his surprise, she did not shrink back. "And you think *you* are any better? The way you looked at me in that hut. As if my friends and I did anything but try to run from …" She hesitated, stamping her foot as she glared up at him, mouth dropping open and closed for a moment before she said, "My friends and I did nothing wrong. *You're* the monster! You and those bastards you work for."

"You protect those who betray you and condemn those who hunt you. Yet you know full well why the Commune sought you and your *friends*. At least the hunter shows who he is. Acts for a greater purpose—for the good of Septima." He looked her up and down. "You're weak. As I thought then, in that hut."

Evelyn squared her jaw. "And you're pathetic. You serve the Commune, yet they're treating your people like *vermin*. I've heard all about how the Grand Magister—"

Commander Sulemon closed the gap between them, voice booming. "You will hold your tongue girl—or lose it."

She shrunk back, and he discovered it gave him no pleasure to see the fear in her eyes. He uncurled his fists. "There is more at play here than you could possibly …" He sighed. "Do not speak of things you do not understand."

Her face reddened, eyes filled with scorn, but this time she heeded his word. She dropped back behind him, scuffing at the ground as she walked. *Let her be petty,* he thought. *It makes no difference to me.*

For a time, they travelled in silence. Commander Sulemon entered a trance-like state, his thoughts drifting to memories of Lord Torrant. He recalled the "reward" that had been promised to him before he left Castleton, heart soaring at the possibilities that ran through his mind.

He rubbed his stubbled chin, wincing at his imagined appearance. His bruises had faded, he was sure, but he could still feel the raised lines where the cuts on his face had healed.

And his *stench* was a whole other issue. He wrinkled his nose, tugging at his cloak in an attempt to cover his filthy tunic as best he could.

Deep in thought as he was, he didn't notice the girl approach and fall into step with him again until she said, "I need to … relieve myself."

"What?"

"We've been walking for hours. I need to piss."

"Hold it."

She shuffled on the spot. "We are *far* past that."

The Commander pointed towards a nearby copse of trees. "Go in there. Be quick."

She rolled her eyes at him before stalking away.

"Not much longer now," he muttered.

He watched birds flying overhead, envious of their speed, wishing he could fly straight to Lord Torrant, happy simply to see his face once more. He reached for a waterskin and refreshed himself, stretched his arms over his head, rolled his neck. And then, when the moments stretched on too long, he narrowed his eyes towards the trees.

She wouldn't try to run … would she?

He darted towards the area. "Evelyn!" he cried. *Damned headstrong girl.* He held his hands up to protect his face as he burst through the trees, branches scratching, scraping, tugging at his clothing and skin. He cast around, panic clenching at his chest. *No, I can't have lost her.*

He could already imagine Lord Torrant's disappointment. *His anger.*

"Evelyn!" He kept moving. The area wasn't large; she couldn't have gone far. How long had he been distracted?

Idiot. Fucking idiot, letting her out of your sight.

"Evelyn, where are you?"

"I'm *here*." She appeared from the trees behind him, adjusting her tunic. "What's wrong with you?"

He lunged forward, grabbing her arm. "You will stay where I can see you from now on," he said, face close to hers. "Piss or shit or *whatever*." She flinched back, cheeks flushing.

"What is wrong with you?" she said, snatching her arm free. She exhaled sharply, turned, and made her way back to the road, muttering, "Outside eyes would think you cared. Stupid oaf."

"Ignorant child."

They continued their walk as the day stretched on before them—past quiet farmsteads, smoke curling upwards from silent chimneys, abandoned buildings long-since picked clean of any signs of life, and barren fields.

After a time, Evelyn cleared her throat. "How will we cross the river?" she asked. "Aren't we going to Castleton?"

"That is not your concern," he said sharply, still agitated. "We cross the river when I say we do."

"You can't keep it secret forever," she said. "What if I refuse to go with you?"

"You'd be a fool. You walk free by my good grace. I will restrain you and throw you over the horse if I need to. Your choice."

She scowled. "Like to see you try," she muttered.

"Believe me, you would not."

She crossed her arms over her chest, grumbling incoherently to herself.

A short time later, they reached the bank of the Crystal River. The Commander retrieved their waterskins and moved to refill them from the cool, flowing waters.

"Castleton is over that way, isn't it?" Evelyn asked.

"Perhaps, but we do not need to cross here," he said, casting a gaze towards the direction she pointed.

"Will we cross further down?"

The Commander ran a hand across his eyes. *Incessant questions.* "We will go where I say we go," he said. He began to lead the horse southwards, following the river.

"When will we rest properly?"

He grunted in response.

"We might be travelling for some time, not that I would know," she continued, voice rising with frustration. "Perhaps you could answer me when I ask you something."

"Hmph. You are in no position to argue, girl." He pursed his lips and scanned the horizon once more. "We will rest at night fall." He glanced over his shoulder. "And save your anger. It is wasted on me."

He continued walking towards Lord Torrant's estate, certain the girl would follow.

That afternoon, they rode the horse at a swift pace and reached the outskirts of Haven Forest.

"We'll camp here," he said. "The trees should give some shelter from the chill."

Evelyn's irritating questions had ended some time ago. Her movements were unsure, an awkward, uneasy air radiating from her. Exhaustion had overcome him physically and mentally, the constant ache in his chest an endless distraction. He did what he could to push it away.

He handed the girl some dried ham and apples, ignoring her surprising disinterest in the food compared to her earlier complaints of hunger, and attempted to warm himself by the campfire.

Tired as he was, Commander Sulemon refused to allow Evelyn to take the watch. The night dragged by as he watched the crackling flames. He drifted and dozed throughout the night but always jerked awake and found the girl still curled up and sound asleep. *She is as exhausted as I am. And blessedly silent.*

The next morning, he rose with the sun, head pounding and eyes aching, driven on by their destination. They would continue south until the crossing at Taskan Forest. Two or three days away, if they set a decent pace.

Taskan Forest. He brushed his hand over his growing curls, recalling the time spent there with Lord Torrant some years ago. They'd gone to hunt, though they'd soon found themselves far too distracted to focus on such things. A smile played at his lips, a tingling heat spreading across his body. *So many years have passed. How young we were.*

"Good morning," Evelyn said behind him. "What's for breakfast?"

He pulled an apple from the saddlebag and threw it at her, irritated that she had interrupted his reverie.

"Oh, more fruit. Thanks," she said with mock appreciation.

"There is other food," he snapped. He slung a small sack down by the fire. "See for yourself. Perhaps you might start—what is the saying—pulling your weight."

She opened her mouth as if to respond.

He held his hand up to stop her. "You would be wise to do as I ask. We have a way to go and my patience is almost gone. Already."

"I thought soldiers—sorry, *Commanders*—were supposed to be tough. Can't handle a few questions?" When he glared at her, she waved her hand in the air. "No, don't worry. We'll be silent forever. Powers forbid a few words interrupt the nothing around us."

Sulemon dragged his hands down his face. "Just. Make. Breakfast."

"Just saying, high up servant of the Commune can't handle a little *child*— it's a wonder anything gets done …"

Commander Sulemon lowered his hands as she trailed off. *Perhaps her tongue fell out.* But as he opened his eyes, he saw her kneeling down to pull out some bread, butter, and hard sausage. Over the fire she softened the butter and toasted the bread, remaining silent until she handed him a serving.

He nodded his gratitude. "Thank you."

"You're welcome," she muttered.

They ate in peace, both, he thought, doing their best not to devour their first proper meal too quickly. He wiped his hands along the sides of his trousers as Evelyn licked her fingers clean, making a popping sound on the last few.

Finally, she looked at him, brows raised. "Now, are you going to tell me where we're going?"

The Commander began extinguishing their campfire, allowing his gaze to drift across the clear blue sky. At least the weather was pleasant for the season.

"Well?"

He sighed.

It was going to be a long journey.

26

Raif

"Draw your arrow."

Raif took a deep breath and aimed for the circular red target ahead. After four days and long hours of practice, he was quickly recalling his father's lessons, his confidence growing.

"Fire."

He let the arrow fly, almost shouting with joy as it hit the target. Not centre, but it was already a vast improvement. He grinned. *Father would be proud.*

"Well done, boy." The archery master, Arturo, patted him on the back. Raif beamed at him. The man's face was heavily scarred, weathered, and mean-looking, but Raif had soon learned he was an easygoing man with plenty of patience.

Arturo examined the sky and, though the sun was obscured by a heavy veil of cloud, concluded it was time to finish for the day. "You've improved a lot," he said. "You should be pleased with how far you've come."

"Thank you," Raif said, securing his bow across his back, rolling his already sore shoulders.

As he made his way to the feasting hut, his stomach let out an audible grumble. He'd been so focused on his shooting, he hadn't even thought of food since breakfast some hours ago. He hoped Rose and Dog would be waiting for him; he was eager to find out how her training had been going with Hector.

He paused for a moment, eyes absentmindedly drifting towards the fir trees lining the path into the camp. He knew what he hoped to see and that his hopes were futile. But then he blinked, frowning at what he did see. He ran towards the group. "Sarhia!" he called. Her brother, Elias, was leading the horse upon which his pregnant wife sat. They paused, turning to see who approached.

"Ah, Raif," Sarhia said, beaming.

"Are you leaving?" Raif looked at the bags strapped to their horse, saw their cloaks of fur and sturdy new leather boots.

Sarhia turned to nod at her brother and his wife. "We are. Avanna, she has arranged passage home for us, Goddess be praised. A town to the south and west of here." Her hand moved to her belt where her pouch should be and Raif saw that it was gone. She seemed to realise it at the same moment, awkwardly lowering her hand to her side. "She has been … most kind." The smile she gave was not so warm as usual. "There are others, friends of ours, who will stay here but for us … it is time to return home. Jorenya here longs to have her child on the shores of our beloved Isle of Veritarra."

"Oh," he said. "Well, I hope your journey is safe."

"Thank you," Sarhia said, Elias nodding behind her. "May the Goddess bless you."

He watched them leave, a strange feeling gnawing at his gut. And then his stomach gave its loudest grumble yet and he remembered his hunger. He turned and made his way back towards the centre of the camp, trying to shut out the disquiet in his mind.

As soon as he entered the feasting hut, Raif was overcome by the mouth-watering scent of roasting mutton. He scanned the tables for his sister's bright blonde curls. *Not here. Must still be training.* He moved to retrieve a bowl of thick stew, freshly baked bread and a tankard of honey-sweetened mead.

He found an empty table and sat, too impatient to wait for Rose to arrive. He wolfed down his meal, splashing gravy down his chin. Once the majority of his stew had been consumed, he slowed and sat back. He looked around, sharing brief nods or smiles with those around him. None stopped to speak and he tried not to take it personally. Since Evelyn had left, there'd been an air of suspicion towards him from others in the camp—proximity, apparently, making him an unwitting accomplice.

He chewed on some mutton and potatoes, willing Rose and Hector to hurry up and join him. Without distraction, he was prone to dwelling too long on Evelyn.

He tensed. *She made her choice.*

She never cared about us.

He gulped down his mead, wiping a hand across his mouth.

Then why am I so damn worried? He'd been, infuriatingly, unable to answer the question thus far.

He recalled the way Avanna had refused to meet his eye the morning she'd come to their hut. She'd been angry. She'd reminded him of Mother when she used to look over his head, unwilling to meet his eye when she'd caught him in a lie. But Raif knew he wasn't hiding anything. What could Avanna possibly think he was hiding? Or was it perhaps *she* who was hiding something? After what she'd done to Rose and Dog, he had too many questions about that woman for there to simply be no answer.

But who was he to question the leader of Veritas? He had to think of Rose; they couldn't lose the shelter they'd found here. So he'd decided to avoid Avanna as much as possible. Now that Rose was being looked after by Hector, he was satisfied that she and Dog were in safe hands. They just had to keep going, hope for the best.

What else can we do?

He heard a bark from behind and turned, grinning at his sister and Hector as they entered the hut. Dog scurried about, sniffing frantically at the floor until he almost tripped a heavy-set man with a thick, brown beard. Duly scolded, Dog skulked the rest of the way to the table with his tail between his legs.

"Stay here, boy," Raif said, patting him on the head. Dog tilted his head, letting out a gentle whine. Rose sat at the bench beside him, cheeks rosy with excitement.

"How was training?" he asked.

"Good," she said, smiling back at him.

Hector came to join them, placing a bowl of stew in front of Rose. "Eat up, lass," he said to Rose. "Got to keep your energy up." He cast her a wink and she giggled, picking up her spoon to eat.

Raif mopped up the gravy in his bowl with the last of his bread, ignoring the pointed looks from Dog under the table. "How is Rose doing?" he asked Hector.

The man finished his mouthful of stew before answering. "We're still at the beginning."

"At the beginning?"

"Your sister is … strong-willed, shall we say? I can't sense her powers at all yet." Hector snorted. "I don't think it's anything to worry about. It just may take some time before her true strength is known."

"Mm." Raif glanced away, unsure of how much Hector knew.

"What is it, lad?" Hector's bright green eyes bored into him.

He tilted his head close, unwilling for Rose to overhear him. "I'm just worried about how much control she has over … you know."

Hector thoughtfully chewed on some bread, handing the crust down to Dog. "Used them before, has she?"

He doesn't know. Raif chewed on his lip. "Once," he lied. "In Castleton, when we were being chased by soldiers."

"I see. Well, no danger here, lad. No reason for her powers to get out of control."

"I suppose so," Raif said, glancing towards his sister as she shovelled down her stew.

Hector gave him a measured look. "Don't worry, lad. I'll keep training her. I'll keep her safe."

Raif shuffled closer and whispered, "What about Avanna?"

The man's black moustache twitched. "I understand your fears, Raif, after what happened. But believe me, Avanna wants only what's best. She has her interest in Rose, as she does in all of those in the camp with powers. Rose is stronger than everyone else, true, but I don't think there's anything to be concerned about."

It was evident that Hector believed the words and Raif couldn't bring himself to show his doubt.

"There's something I do need to tell you, lad."

"Yes?" Raif raised an eyebrow.

"Evelyn, she …"

Raif sat up. "Evelyn? What about her?" He clenched his hand on the table's edge, knuckles white.

"Now, now, lad. Calm down," Hector said. "I don't know where she is, it's not that."

"Oh, okay." He gave a weak smile. "I just can't help but think it's my fault that she left."

Hector touched a hand to his shoulder and gave a gentle squeeze. "Evelyn did what she did, lad. No one else is responsible for her decision."

"I suppose not."

"But what you should know is, she asked me to take care of you and Rose— should she ever be unable to."

Raif gasped. "She did?" *She must have known she was leaving. She must've planned it.*

And she couldn't tell me. Raif couldn't work out whether that added to his frustration or quelled it.

"That she did. She cared about you both, I could see that. Anyone could." Hector signalled a nearby serving-woman to top up their drinks. Once she'd gone, he leant in again. "And I want you to know, I intend to keep my word."

Raif gulped down the lump in his throat. "Thank you."

I wish she'd told me her plan.

Hector bowed his head in acknowledgement. "Now then, it's time to get back out with Rose." He stood and stretched alongside his companion, who had been observing the conversation from atop the table, legs tucked neatly beneath her.

Rose and Dog stood as one, jumping from the bench and rushing towards the door.

As he watched them, Raif had a sudden, intense feeling that he didn't want to be alone—couldn't face an afternoon of being stuck with his own thoughts. "Can I join you? I won't get in the way, I just … It'd be interesting to see Rose's training."

Hector brushed back his hair. "Course," he said. "She's your sister. Mayhap if you're there, she'll be more open to letting me see her powers."

Raif swallowed. "Maybe." *Though that may not be a good thing.*

He gulped down the last of his mead and followed Hector and Cara from the hut.

27

Evelyn

After three days of travel, Evelyn's hopes of escape had all but extinguished. They'd passed a handful of small villages and quiet roadside taverns; there'd been pedlars, bards, and travelling merchants, farmers with wagons full of wares, even a small family who seemed to be moving all of their worldly possessions—which admittedly didn't amount to much—all travelling southwards on the road alongside them.

Surely one person will see what this is. Surely someone will help me.

That particular delusion had been short-lived.

In the eyes of every person they passed, Evelyn saw a flash of fear and horror at the sight of the Commander in his billowing red cloak. Even if she had tried to sneakily seek assistance from some hapless stranger, she knew then that none would risk the wrath of the Commune.

No, she was alone.

Betrayed by Avanna, torn away from Raif and Rose. She had to find her own way out of this, but it was becoming all too clear how impossible that was. She'd tried to run on the first day, but the Commander had apprehended her with ease, his agility and strength far outmatching hers. Since then, he'd been on high alert. *Stupid for thinking that would work.*

As they continued their journey, she tried ignoring and pestering the Commander in turn, flitting between sulking and asking question after question to irritate him. Strangely, he actually acknowledged her at times, giving what little information he undoubtedly deemed she was worthy of.

And then, just when she thought she couldn't sink any deeper into her mire of hopelessness, their surroundings began to look all too familiar. Her breath hitched in her throat. Yes, there was the bridge crossing the Crystal River—the very one she'd led Raif and Rose over what felt like a lifetime ago. She huddled her arms across her body, trying to repress the shudder of sadness that rippled down her spine. *Raif, Rose. I failed them. Foolish to ever think I could help them. You were wrong, Bessie.*

In the midst of her self-pity, Evelyn was also aware of what would soon appear on the horizon. Her mouth became dry, her throat constricted. "Commander," she croaked.

He turned, scowling as though she'd interrupted a private moment. "What is it?"

She waved her arm towards the bridge. "Aren't we crossing here?" she asked. *Please, please.*

The Commander squinted towards the direction of Castleton. "No," he said curtly.

"Why?" she pressed, trying not to sound desperate.

"Because I said so."

He'd avoided the question of where they were going for the past two days. It was only in that moment that she realised why. She swallowed. "We aren't going to Castleton, are we?"

He turned to face her fully, studying her face. Finally, he shook his head. "No," he said. "We are not going to Castleton." Before she could do any more, he took hold of the horse's reins again and marched onwards.

Shit. She brushed her clammy hands down the front of her tunic. She was going to have to face it then. She stumbled after him, struggling to keep pace with his long strides. All too soon, the building appeared ahead of them.

The tavern.

There was no smoke billowing from the chimney, no wagons pulled up outside, no patrons passing each other as they came and went through the green-painted door.

In their place was a half-collapsed, blackened shell.

She hadn't realised she'd stopped walking until the Commander called her name. "What are you doing?" he asked irritably.

Her mouth hung open, though she had no words for him. He wouldn't care even if she could answer. *It might as well have been him and his men who did this.*

Ignoring his question, she ran towards the ruined building, falling to her knees in front of it. Despite the fire damage, the front door remained in its frame. She imagined she could push it open and enter the bustling common room, filled with laughter and chatter and the smell of Fat Bessie's fresh-baked apple pie.

But, of course, that wouldn't happen.

Could never happen again.

"Girl, we need to keep moving." The Commander approached and stood behind her.

She sprang up at him, fists clenched and ready to attack. "How dare you?!" she screamed, tears blurring her vision. "This was *you*! Soldiers, they—" And then the wind was knocked from her; she had nothing more to say. Nothing would make this better. What use were words?

The Commander bowed his head, lips pursed. "You should save your energy," he said quietly. "Though you have yet to understand it, the Commune does what is needed for the good of the kingdom. You will learn once we reach …"

She didn't hear the rest of his words. Her eyes had drifted past him to the great oak tree sitting across the road from the tavern. For a moment, she was frozen. For a moment, she wished for death. The pain would have been far less, she was sure.

The vast tree had been in constant vigil for hundreds of years, Bessie once told her, watching the travellers who made their way along the road between the east and west of Septima.

Perhaps it was a fitting place for the woman to find her final rest—though if she was honest with herself, Evelyn knew that would never be true. She deserved far better than anything this life had ever given her.

On trembling legs, she made her way towards the tree. She brushed the tears from her eyes and blinked up at the thick branches. The nooses still hung where they'd been tied, swaying in the breeze. She forced her eyes to move downwards to the base of the tree, already knowing what lay there.

Bessie and her husband.

They'd been cut loose; left beside each other, unburied for all to see.

Their bodies appeared to have been picked apart by scavengers so that little remained of them, but Evelyn knew it was them. She knelt and picked up a scrap of royal blue cloth stained red with blood. *Bessie's skirt.* She clutched the fabric to her chest, letting the tears flow. She tried to take consolation in the fact Bessie had been beside her husband in death, though it did nothing to lessen the pain. In her mind, she heard Bessie's last, awful, blood-curdling cry.

She allowed herself a moment of silent crying, and then all she knew was rage.

"Bessie," she whispered, lips trembling. "I'm sorry. I did what you asked. I did." *Though if I hadn't, maybe I'd be here with you. I'd have died with my family.*

She crouched besides the bodies until her legs prickled and grew numb. There was no one to pray to, no peace to be found. She simply wished to memorise the scene. Finally, she wiped her face and tucked the scrap of blue cloth into her coin purse. She exhaled and stood, shaking her legs in an attempt to regain the feeling.

"Thank you," she whispered. "For everything."

She clenched her jaw and turned away. The Commune would answer for this.

With vengeance in her heart, she moved to join the Commander at the roadside. He didn't say a word as he held out a waterskin for her. She scowled, shoving his hand away. *As if water could help. Will it wash away what his superiors ordered? What they did?*

"Are you ready to go?" he asked.

Evelyn held trembling fists at her sides as she glowered up at him. "How dare you?"

This time, he had the decency to blanch at her vitriol. "What? I was merely asking if—"

"You see this?" She held her arm out towards the ruined tavern, towards the bodies of Bessie and Dick. "*You* are part of this."

The Commander blinked, as if finally connecting Evelyn with the tavern. "I'm sure the soldiers who did this had a good reason to—"

Evelyn spat at his feet. "*Fuck you,*" she said. "Fuck you and those bastards you work for." *He has the audacity to look offended,* she thought. *My words are wasted on this monster.*

She turned and stormed away, leaving behind the open-mouthed Commander, the tavern, Bessie.

She didn't look back.

The next day, Evelyn woke with anger still prickling through her whole body. What the Commune had done to Bessie and her husband had gone far beyond injustice, beyond cowardice.

As they continued their journey, she watched the Commander from atop the horse, whole body tensed. She took in the unreadable expression on his face as he walked, waiting for her moment. When she couldn't bear it any longer, she said, "How can you believe in the Commune? How can you think what they do—killing people in cold blood—is right?"

Her questions hung in the air between them. His shoulders tensed yet he didn't otherwise acknowledge her words.

Indignation pulsed through her with every heartbeat. "Didn't you hear me?" She leant forward in the saddle, so close she could see the beads of sweat glistening on his forehead. "I said, how can you—"

He turned with such suddenness, she jerked backwards and almost fell from the saddle. For a moment, she thought he might strike her, his eyes ablaze, knuckles tightening around the reins. "You will never understand the duty of the Commune," he said through gritted teeth. "You will never understand all they have done for this kingdom."

She returned his glare. "That's not an answer. Those were good people. She was my …" She bit her lip. *No, he's not worthy of knowing about Bessie.* "They didn't deserve to be *murdered*. They weren't soldiers in the line of duty or rebels falling for their cause! They did nothing but- but be good!" Her voice rose as tears welled in her eyes, and she swiped them away.

"You speak of good as though it is simple. As though people who deserve to live will do so, and those who deserve to die will get what is due. It is a child's understanding of life." When he faced her again, the rage had melted from his eyes. In its place was a deep well of sadness. "You do not understand the ways of the world, girl. Of the cruelty that prevails."

"But I—"

"Enough. Save your words, Evelyn." He focused his gaze ahead and quickened his pace. "They are of no use. Not to you, not to me."

"I'm going to stop them, you know," she said, and for a moment she was shocked by her own vehemence. "The Commune. The Grand Magister. They will see justice for what they've done."

He glanced over his shoulder and, for a heartbeat, she imagined she saw fear in his face. She sat straight in the saddle again, and neither spoke a word.

Later that day, as they rested the horse and ate their meal, Evelyn decided to try a different approach with the Commander.

"You say I don't understand the world," she said, watching him from the corner of her eye. He paused mid-chew, awaiting her next words. She spoke on, staring ahead. "I want to learn. If I'm to be taken to the Commune, perhaps I should know more …" She trailed off, hoping the man's sense of pride would will him to give her what she wanted.

He finished his food and brushed the crumbs from his tunic. She kept her mouth pinched closed, eyes meeting his with what she hoped was an air of innocent curiosity.

After an agonising moment, he spoke. "The Commune has long worked to right the atrocities committed during the Seven-Year War over a hundred years ago. Only during recent years has the Grand Magister's influence allowed for the kingdom to prosper once more."

Evelyn raised an eyebrow. "What of your people? I was told that—"

"You speak out of turn," he snapped. He took a deep breath, running a hand through his short black curls before speaking again. "You act as though you are the only one who has been wronged. But it is as I said earlier—you know nothing of the world."

Evelyn bristled, doing her best not to become angry. She was quickly recognising it achieved nothing with this man. "Tell me then. What do I need to know about the Commune?" She sat forward, forcing him to meet her gaze. "Why do they take children?"

"I would have thought that was a question you could answer yourself. You have seen the threat posed by untrained children, have you not?"

Tread carefully, Evelyn. He knows about Rose. "I- I would appreciate hearing it from someone like you, who has experienced the Commune's … benevolence first-hand."

"Hmm." He stood. "We should keep walking."

She reluctantly did so, scolding herself for pushing too quickly, convinced she'd receive no further responses from him. But when they began trudging southwards once more, he bade her walk beside him.

"As I said, the Commune was formed following the Seven-Year War. Since then, the Grand Magister, his father, and his grandfather before him have worked to bring balance back to the kingdom. The war only came about because those with powers were left unwatched, uncontrolled. The king ignored them, let them live out their lives however they willed. It was a mistake. They formed their own group, rising up in an attempt to take hold of Septima for themselves, killing many hundreds of innocent people."

Evelyn frowned. "But surely that was a select few. It wasn't everyone with powers who chose to start a war, was it?"

The Commander gave her a measured look. "Believe me, I have seen myself that once one rises up, the rest soon follow. Those with powers are naturally more inclined to seek control. It is …" He sighed. "It is simply how things are."

Evelyn suddenly recalled Avanna's words when they'd spoken after the Commander's interrogation. *"… the Grand Magister doesn't see that he and the Nomarrans want the same."* She held her tongue on the matter, afraid it would end the conversation in an instant. "So, the Commune was formed after the war?"

He gave a brisk nod. "In order to prevent such an uprising from occurring again, the first Grand Magister decreed—with the king's approval—all children from noble families who displayed powers were to be sent to the Commune for training." He grunted. "Foolish to believe that would be enough. The Commune were to form their own army of those with powers to fend off any peasants who sought to rebel again. But the current Grand Magister understands that the Commune must take control of *anyone* with powers, or risk the safety of all in Septima."

Evelyn's stomach dropped. He spoke with such conviction, with such perfectly rehearsed words; she was sure he'd memorised the speech for just such an occasion. The word from Avanna flashed across her mind again: *propaganda.*

Even as she thought it, she also had to admit the logic behind the Commander's words. After all, hadn't she witnessed Rose's powers, her uncontrolled violence, in action? The very realisation sent a chill through her heart.

Even so, she couldn't accept that the cruel and violent ways in which the Commune enacted the Grand Magister's edicts were the only option.

She watched Commander Sulemon from the corner of her eye. Even with the bravado, there'd been moments where she'd seen the man beneath. Not quite kindness but some meagre attempt at it. Couldn't he see the faults in the Commune? "Surely what you're doing—attacking villages, taking people from their homes—that can't be right."

Commander Sulemon let out an exasperated sigh, as though he'd expected just such a response from her. "The Grand Magister has the support of many in Septima who see the value of his presence and protection." His dark eyes bored into her. "Any who do not understand that are selfish, ignorant, or stupid."

Evelyn had to hold back a scoff of disbelief. *And am I to decide for myself which one I am? Or will he choose for me, just as his precious Commune chooses what is crime one day and justice the next?* It was confirmed to her then: the Commander's speech was nothing more than propaganda. "I see," she muttered.

The Commander must have taken her lack of argument as a sign of progress. "There is much to learn," he continued. "But for now, we must not waste our energy on such things. We must focus on reaching our destination. I'll ride with you." He motioned for her to slide back, and leapt atop the horse in front of her. "Hold on." She reluctantly clasped her arms round his waist, revulsed by the physical contact.

A waste to even question him. How can a man defend his own ignorance so completely? And then, a moment of clarity: *A mind that is blind to such lies will never give you truth.* As they rode, that final thought seered itself into her mind, and she repeated it, feeling it become a mantra she would not forget.

They journeyed on for three more days, but Evelyn was unable to gain any more information from the Commander. In truth, she couldn't bring herself to ask, knowing she'd only hear more blatant deceit—whatever lies had been fed to him by the Commune. By Lord Torrant.

She rolled her head from side to side as she walked, her shoulders stiff from days sleeping on the ground, and scanned the afternoon sky. They'd been lucky so far, the grey clouds barely producing any rain and the weather mild with only a slight wind cutting across the banks of the Crystal River. Her eyes roved down and across the fast-flowing water. Seeing an unfamiliar tree line, she decided to finally break the ongoing silence.

"Which forest is that?" she asked.

Commander Sulemon stared across the river, his shoulders rising and falling with a heavy exhale. "Taskan Forest."

"I've never been this far south."

The Commander glanced back at her, lips downturned. "I have spent time there," he said. "Some years ago."

"Did you hunt?" she said, glad to have a conversation not involving the Commune.

A tiny smile flickered across his lips. "The forest is famed for its rich hunting. The estate nearby ... I was a guest there and, on occasion, yes, I joined the annual wolf hunt."

"Wolves?" Evelyn gasped, scanning the dark tree line. Wolves had long since been driven from Haven Forest, and she'd never seen one herself, though she recalled the Elders' hut displayed fine furs from great black, grey, and white beasts hunted generations before.

Commander Sulemon stopped in his tracks. "We'll rest here," he said abruptly. "We aren't far."

She might have imagined it, but Evelyn was sure a ripple of apprehension passed over his face. Sensing his guard was down, she took the opportunity to ask him again where they were going—to finally receive an answer, or simply to annoy him, she wasn't sure.

He gave her a measuring look. "Telling you now won't make a difference, anyway. We are going to the Torrant Estate, girl." He pointed an arm ahead. "The crossing isn't far. From there, it's not half a day's walk."

Torrant.

Evelyn's heart skipped a beat.

She gulped, hand wandering to the waterskin at her waist, wishing it was wine.

Commander Sulemon followed the movement, brow furrowed. "Come, let's sit."

He walked towards a moss-covered log beside the riverbank. Surrounded by high grass and reeds, there was an unusual air of peace and stillness as Evelyn tied the horse's reins off and joined the Commander. The rush of the river filled her ears, the scent of autumn in her nostrils and for a moment at least, she was contented. It didn't last long.

Dangerous. She couldn't forget the word or the man towards whom it was directed; his cold eyes as icy clear as the flowing river before her. He'd frightened her even before she learned who he was. The Commander's focus was evidently elsewhere, eyes glazed, hands clasped tightly in his lap. She suddenly recalled Avanna's words.

"You work for Lord Torrant directly, don't you?" she asked, speaking in a moment of boldness. *Why didn't I put the pieces together sooner? Bloody idiot.*

He jutted out his jaw with evident pride. "Of course," he said. "I am a Commander under Lord Torrant." His fist drifted to his chest, the ghost of a salute. "He is a loyal agent of the Commune."

"And what does he want with me?"

He turned to her, expression unreadable. "You will be tested. The Grand Magister's time cannot be wasted. Lord Torrant will bear that task."

Dread clamped across Evelyn's chest. *What will happen when they discover my powers are useless?* She could do nothing but bide her time and hope some opportunity to save herself might yet present itself. She cast an eye across the river and the forest beyond. *Would it be so hard to get lost in such a place? I could—*

"There is something I feel it is important to say. For you to know."

She frowned, interrupted from her daydream of escape. "What is it?"

"The powers did not start in Septima. Trying to control them did not truly start with the Commune. Believe me when I tell you, those who have powers must be monitored, trained, protected. The Commune provides one way of doing so—of ensuring those without powers are kept safe. Perhaps there are lives lost because of their work, but it is a small price to pay. There have been innumerable unnecessary deaths caused by the greed, corruption, and ignorance powers can cause. Too much lost."

"Do you mean in the Seven-Year War?" she asked, curious as to his sudden change in tone.

"What?" His eyes darkened. Then he ran a hand over the stubble on his chin, taking a moment to calm himself before speaking on. "No, girl. I do not mean the Seven-Year War. My home. I mean my home."

"You lost … ?"

"Everything."

Evelyn didn't know what to say. She grasped at the edges of her cloak, listening to the sound of the river. She hadn't even thought of what he might've experienced, the life which had led him to join the Commune. She couldn't understand why she finally felt he'd spoken without the Commune whispering through him, nor why he would allow her such a tiny snippet of the truth—his truth—in that moment.

But does that make his hatred of those with powers justifiable? No. It can't.

"Come." Commander Sulemon's voice broke through her thoughts. "We must reach the estate by tomorrow morning. We will ride through the night if necessary."

Evelyn followed. Within the day, she would meet Lord Torrant once more.

28

Hector

Cara's bright yellow eyes bored into him, shining in the darkness of his hut. Hector stared at the ceiling, doing his best to ignore her.

But, of course, he couldn't. She was right, as always.

"That doesn't make things any easier," he muttered, rubbing a hand over his tired eyes. Stubbornness and pride were two of the qualities he actually quite liked in himself, but now it seemed foolish to follow them.

"If anything happens to me, you have to protect Raif and Rose."

He'd made that promise gladly, already feeling somewhat responsible for the children since meeting them on the road from Castleton. However, he'd been naïvely unaware of just how quickly he'd be required to fulfil it.

You can't avoid it. Not anymore.

He shot his companion a glare, unwilling to accept the truth of her words. "Why can't things be bloody simple?"

Cara nudged him with her nose. He gave her a wan smile before sitting up on his pallet and rubbing the scar on his leg. The ragged line was pink, the skin puckered, not yet healed beneath the tight, upper layer. The Commander had fought hard, pushed him to the edge of his physical capabilities—the soldiers, too. He hadn't used his powers to such an extent for some time. He'd allowed himself to get rusty. Mayhap that was why he was taking things so slowly with Rose.

You know that's not true.

"You're testing me this morning, my love," he grumbled. She turned her backside to him as she leapt to the floor. Almost as an afterthought, she rubbed herself across his legs and let out a short purr before stalking out of the hut through the small flap at the bottom of his door, leaving him alone with his thoughts.

He groaned, easing himself to his feet, careful not to put too much weight on his recovering leg. He moved to the wash basin to ready himself for the day, all the while thinking of the lass. As Cara suspected, his caution with Rose was not because of his own lack of practice. He'd been gentle and encouraging with her. He'd trained children before; none as young as her, nor with as much apparent potential but it was enough to understand what was needed. Yet it was becoming all too clear that Rose wasn't like anyone he'd trained before, child and adult alike.

"I knew it all along," he muttered.

From the first instance he'd met the lass, he'd felt an emptiness surrounding her. Yet the emptiness somehow had *form*, a shield around her mind, impossible to penetrate. With any other individual, he would be able to sense their powers, or lack thereof, with ease. Connect with their mind, just for a moment, and peer in, perhaps even see things they didn't know they held themselves. He had always hated doing so, and each time quickly severed the link, knowing the devastation a prolonged connection could cause. With Rose, though, that option never appeared possible. He could not tell then whether it was because there was simply nothing there to detect, or if it were a mental armour, so perfect and smoothly developed that even on his best day he could never find a foothold. The longer he had trained the lass, the more he became sure it was the latter. And he still hadn't the faintest idea what it might mean.

He'd hidden his concern as well he could, especially around Raif. The lad had been through enough. Hector wouldn't tell him. Not until he had something to give Raif that wasn't simply more questions, more fears.

Hector had hoped if he proceeded with Rose's training as normal, her powers would eventually become apparent. He was convinced he could somehow break through her defences given enough time. She had powers, that much was known. They'd been witnessed. Once they were past this first barrier, he'd understand the strength she possessed, be able to teach her how to control the immense strength that simmered beneath the surface.

Yesterday afternoon, however, those hopes had been all but shattered. He prayed the child hadn't told her brother yet. That should be Hector's duty: to inform Raif of his failing. He laid awake most of the night, wondering what would come next.

There was a knock at the door and Hector jumped. "Oh, Florence." He gave Avanna's serving girl a weak smile. "It's early, lass. What brings you here?"

"Hector," she said, dark hair hanging over her face. "Um, Avanna sent me to fetch you."

"Avanna?" Hector's stomach lurched. She'd want to talk about Rose. About what had happened. He gave a curt nod. "Tell her I'll be there soon."

He watched Florence leave, letting out an exhale that hung in the air.

As he dressed himself, layering a woollen vest and jerkin atop his tunic to shield against the increasingly bitter cold, Cara darted back inside. *Going to see Avanna?*

"It would seem so."

Cara purred.

He tugged on his well-worn leather boots, both fearful and curious as to what Avanna would have to say.

She found you there yesterday. After—

"I know what she found," he snapped. And then, softer, "Just got a strange feeling, is all." If he was honest with himself, it had been there ever since Avanna had chosen to torture Rose's poor dog.

Perhaps speaking to her is what we've needed all along.

He ran a hand across his moustache. "Hmm, you could be right. Mayhap I'm overthinking it. Least, I hope I am."

Cara twined round his legs as he stood, retrieving his walking cane and bracing himself for the early morning air. "Come on. Let's find out what she wants."

The camp was still, early enough for most to still be abed or only just stirring. His eyes were drawn to the vast mountain range on the horizon behind Avanna's hut. Icy peaks that sheltered them from the outside world had kept them safe from discovery for so many years; but he knew the camp couldn't hide anymore from what had been brought into its midst.

Hector let himself into Avanna's hut, glad for once of the roaring fire she kept burning day and night.

"Hector." The woman appeared from her bedroom, a small chamber connected to the main hut. She smiled, though her wide, brown eyes were underlined by dark smudges and her face was paler than usual. "Thank you for coming so quickly."

He bowed his head, removing his fur cloak and jerkin before following her to the cushioned area. Once they were seated and he'd been handed a warm mug of tea by Florence, Hector turned his attention to his friend.

He cupped the tea between his hands, allowing the spiced and floral scent to wash over him. "What do you need from me, Avanna?"

She regarded him over her own mug, brown eyes gleaming. "I think you know well what we need to discuss."

His stomach dropped. "The lass," he said quietly. By his side, Cara's gentle mewls gave him strength. "I know the incident yesterday caused you some concern. I've been thinking and—"

"*Some* concern?" Avanna's eyebrows shot up. "Hector, I've never seen anything like it. You were knocked unconscious. *You.* The strongest member of our camp. If I hadn't been there, I dread to think what could have happened."

He stared into his tea, unsure what to say.

I shouldn't have tried to use my powers on her, he'd told himself. *She perceived me as a direct threat.* Somehow, he couldn't bring himself to speak those words aloud. There was something in Avanna's eyes that told him she hadn't brought him to listen, but to support some already decided upon plan.

"My friend," she said, voice softening. "You and I both know that Rose is … different. Special. Ever since that Commander confirmed the injury she caused to his soldier. To be able to control the minds of others at her age, untrained. It's just …" She waved her mug in the air. "We both know that's unheard of."

"Mm." Hector stroked his moustache and gulped down some tea. The flavour wasn't his usual choice, though it was pleasant enough.

"Don't be ashamed that she was able to fight back against your powers. You are strong, but she is stronger."

He shook his head. "I'm not ashamed. I'm—"

"Scared." She nodded. "I understand. We have to think of the whole camp."

Hector frowned. "I have a feeling our fear is not the same," he said. "I am scared *for* the lass. It's clear she doesn't know her own strength. She barely seems to register what she's capable of, though that doesn't stop her from—"

"Come now, Hector." Avanna tilted her head. "You really believe she isn't a threat to the life we have here?"

"A threat?" He fervently shook his head. "No. She has a way with animals, with the other children, she is nothing but kind. The only problem is ..." He shrugged helplessly. "I ... I don't think I can train her."

Avanna smiled, as though he'd said exactly what she hoped he would. Hector sipped his tea—the flavour was growing on him, the spices a subtle tingling against his tongue—and waited for her to speak on.

"So, we're in agreement," she said at last. "The girl is beyond our help. Whatever her powers are, we are unable to control them here. We cannot train her—after all, you admit your inability and I have been ... asked not to continue my own attempts. Our options are too limited to do right by this girl. And yet, I can't help but feel she is the one we have been waiting for."

Hector narrowed his eyes, sure he'd heard those words before yet the memory was vague, the words a distant echo. "The one we've been waiting for?" he asked.

"Ah, Florence." Avanna waved her serving girl in. The room was filled with the delicious scent of blackened bacon and fresh bread. Despite himself, Hector's stomach let out a grumble. Florence handed him a plate of food and a fresh mug of tea, which he gratefully received.

"Thank you, Flo." He chewed on a piece of bacon, washed it down with more tea. It really was a delicious brew. After having a chunk of bread with a generous helping of butter, he glanced up to find Avanna watching him closely.

"I hope you'll be in agreement for what I have planned, my friend."

"Planned?" He swallowed his mouthful of bread, wiping his greasy fingers on his trousers. "What plan? For who?"

"The harvest festival will be bigger than ever this year, I've heard."

Hector fought not to roll his eyes. *As if I don't know you well enough to recognise your favourite diplomacy tactics.* The abrupt subject change was jarring, as it usually was when Avanna executed one, though Hector nodded in agreement, willing to show his friend the kindness of conversation. "It will. There's an air of excitement I've never felt before." He sipped his tea.

"Do you remember when we first began? How few of us there were?"

Hector chuckled, his mind bringing up the fond memories. "Course." His tongue felt clumsy, though the feeling wasn't entirely unpleasant. *Perhaps the lass's powers knocked you even harder than you thought. You truly are getting old.*

"A change from your home, wasn't it?"

Hector flinched, unprepared as he was to think of that place. "Nook Town," he muttered. "You know well how much of a change it was, Avanna. To find people like you and Mak, who allowed my powers to flourish rather than seeking to repress them." He gave a fleeting smile. "It meant everything to me."

Avanna bowed her head. "Repressed your powers, yes," she said. When she lifted her eyes to meet his, there was a curious glimmer he couldn't quite understand. But then she blinked and it was gone, a smile playing at her lips. "Sometimes, I like to reminisce. To think of all we've seen together, Hector. All we've been through."

"Eighteen years," he said, nodding. "Feels so much longer, doesn't it?" He snorted, head lolling slightly. He fought to keep his eyes open, a sudden weariness overcoming him.

She beamed at him, apparently unaware of his tiredness as she spoke of harvest festivals of years past. The words washed over Hector, who enjoyed the warm nostalgia the memories brought him, and he grinned at his old friend.

For a brief time as they sat and Avanna chatted, it was as it had been when they had first moved to the mountains, when their numbers had been fewer, their existence harder, their community more close-knit—a true family. He delighted to hear Avanna talk of their successful harvest, their ongoing fur trade with the mountain tribes and plans for the festival this year. He felt absolutely consumed by the joy of the simple conversation, a welcome and cheerful break from the tense tactical meetings and mission reports that had overtaken his and Avanna's relationship in recent years.

His attention was broken by a sharp nip on the hand. He frowned down at Cara. She rarely behaved in such a way; he realised she must have been trying to alert him for a while, but he had not heard her before the bite. He shook his head, his thoughts slow and muddled. He reached for his companion, movements awkward and slow as though he were pushing through treacle. His head seemed heavy yet light at the same time. Perhaps he was coming down with some winter chill. The weather had been abominably cold of late.

Hector, snap out of it. Cara laid her paws on his lap, butting her head against his chest.

All he wanted to do was stroke her silky-soft, white fur. *How lucky I am to have found you.*

Hector, listen to me, you—

But he was distracted by the sound of people entering the hut. He watched Florence leading Raif, Rose, and Dog in to join him. At sight of the young lass, he recalled Avanna's words. "What we've been waiting for," he whispered, brow furrowed. He turned to where the woman had been seated, but she'd disappeared. He rubbed his eyes, trying to shake away the cloud shrouding his thoughts. There was something wrong, but how could something be wrong when he felt so *free*? As though he was floating, as though all of his worries were drifting away.

The feeling was familiar to him, some part of him knew—yet in that moment he couldn't have recognised from when or where if his life depended on it.

"Ah, you're here." Avanna reappeared from her bedroom, securing a pouch to the belt at her waist. "Some more tea, Florence."

"Come, children." Hector held his arms out. "It's time for breakfast."

Raif raised an eyebrow, moving to sit beside him. He checked to ensure Rose was content before leaning his head in, so close Hector could see the downy hair beginning to sprout on his top lip. He moved a hand to his own bushy moustache and chortled. All the while, Cara was pacing about, occasionally pawing at his legs.

"Hector," Raif whispered. His grey eyes were brimming with worry, darting about Avanna's hut. "What's going on? Why have we been—"

"You needn't be worried, boy. I simply wanted to share breakfast with you all." Avanna clasped her hands over her lap, smiling that charismatic smile of hers.

Tea, Cara's voice broke into his mind.

"Yes, some more tea would be lovely," Hector said, turning away from the confusion on Raif's face.

"Here, have something to eat. It's not long been cooked." Avanna placed a plate in front of Rose and Raif. Dog took an instant interest in the bacon, though Rose's focus was intent on the woman in front of them.

Hector laughed to himself. *Such a serious little thing.*

Tea.

"The tea is delicious," Hector said to Raif with a wink. The lad's eyebrows raised, though he took what was offered without question. Hector happily helped himself to more bacon as the lad tried to entice his sister.

As he continued to enjoy his food, Hector noticed Cara again. This time, she was circling Rose, rubbing her arm, flicking her tail across the lass. At first, he was annoyed. *Bloody well talk to me if you've something to say.* Rose didn't need another companion, she had the black dog, always at her side.

Some quiet voice in the back of his mind, however, realised how unusual this was for Cara. He screwed his eyes shut and tried to concentrate. Why was it so hard to think clearly? Again, an unplaceable sense of déjà vu crept into his mind.

Tea. Bad.

The thought was there and then gone in a flash. He struggled to grasp its meaning or to hold onto the unquestionable panic from his beloved Cara.

"Hector, are you okay?" Raif put his breakfast down and moved close again, frowning.

"I ... Yes, I ... Cara," Hector managed, pointing a finger towards his cat who was licking Rose's hand.

Tea.

Hector looked down at the empty cup in his hands. "Have you drunk the tea, Raif? Rose?" he asked. The lad was clasping the steaming mug in his hand. Rose turned to him, face creased with concentration.

Was time moving faster than usual or was he simply too slow?

"Yes, I ..." Raif's face dropped, his eyes became pained. He dropped his mug, splashing tea across the furs upon which they sat. "Oh." His head lulled onto his shoulder and his body slumped to the floor with a gentle thud. *No.* Hector reached out, desperate, relieved to find the boy still breathing.

Hector turned to Rose. The lass was glaring at Avanna, an unblinking, piercing look far too furious for a child. He lurched forward awkwardly, though

his body didn't respond as it should. He dropped face first to the ground—
powers be damned, bloody idiot—and turned as best he could to lay on his back.

"Rose, no," he croaked. "Cara, the lass. Rose ... please, stop." He reached
an arm out but found he could move no further. Avanna was sitting perfectly
still before him, her face a blur. He blinked but his vision didn't clear.

"Do you remember telling me how they repressed your powers in Nook
Town?" he heard her say. "They use Nomarran secrets, do they not? Forced to
consume a flower from the Noman Islands, your powers were dampened to
nothing, that's what you told me."

"Veritarra's Gift."

Tea.

"Yes, that's it. Recently, I wrote to a Nomarran living in Nook Town. I was
keen to learn more. Who better to ask? Elussius Muelaman. He was reluctant to
reveal any information at first. But when I wrote to him, just after Rose arrived,
and told him of my suspicions about the girl ... Well, he promised he could
provide all I required and more, I simply had to take the girl to him."

"She is the one we've been waiting for, I'm sure of it."

Shit. Hector's half-conscious mind brought back Avanna's words, the first
evening he'd awoken after his fight with the Commander.

"I had faith, Hector, that my work here would not amount to nothing.
That I would find a way to prove myself once and for all. And now I happen to
have my own supply of Veritarra's Gift. Imagine my luck, having a whole group
of Nomarrans enter the camp in close succession. Some refused to part with it,
of course. But for others, the bargains I offered were too sweet to pass up. Two
pouches. Not much, but enough. Remarkable, it really is."

"B-bargains?" Hector wheezed. It was becoming harder and harder to force
his body to obey him.

Cara, my love. I know what she's done. He couldn't sense his companion
anymore, their connection interrupted by the potency of Veritarra's Gift he'd
consumed—though there was a flitting movement beside his leg.

There was the sound of footsteps. Avanna's face appeared above him, a hand
stroked his cheek. "I have to thank you, my friend. For telling me about your
home. Now that all the pieces have slotted together, I know what must be done.
This is about more than Veritas now. This is for the good of our beloved Septi-

ma." She stood. "The girl is coming with me."

Hector groaned, tried to move—no use. His vision darkened.

Oh, Cara—what's happening?

Stupid old fool. Why didn't you listen?

He couldn't tell whether the thought was his own or Cara's. It didn't matter anymore.

On the edges of his mind, Hector felt a growing *rage* within the hut as Dog's barking filled the room.

There was a thud, a whine, a young girl's screech.

"If you fight me, I will kill your companion. Don't make me do it, girl."

Dog whimpered.

Silence.

Rose!

"Florence. Help me bind her."

Hector shut his eyes, drifting into nothingness.

29

Commander Sulemon

Commander Sulemon's patience had worn dangerously thin.

He set a swift pace for the final part of their journey, forcing them onwards through the dark of night, arriving as the rising sun bled crimson in the east. His entire body ached with restlessness; he couldn't be still until he'd seen Lord Torrant, when his sacrifice would feel justified—celebrated, even.

As the fields and farms surrounding the Torrant Estate came into view, he slowed the horse. "We go on foot from here," he said, passing his eyes across the workers already toiling to harvest the crops. None of them acknowledged his arrival, their blank faces and black robes a clear signal of their status.

A nervous apprehension coursed through him. He tugged at his cloak, rearranging his ragged clothing as best he could. He ran a hand across his stomach and chest, noticing for the first time how his ribs protruded far more than they had before leaving Castleton.

They strode along the dirt track towards Lord Torrant's home in silence. He watched the girl from the corner of his eye, feeling a stab of annoyance as she dragged her feet.

"You should feel honoured to be here," he said, tilting his chin towards the mansion in the distance. *He's inside. So close now.* He stopped and turned to Evelyn, irritated at her lack of response. "Did you hear me, girl? I said you should feel honoured."

She kicked fiercely at the ground, eyes ablaze. "Honoured? Why?"

He pounded a fist against his chest. "Lord Torrant is the Grand Magister's own—"

Without warning, Evelyn bolted forwards, grabbing fistfuls of his red cloak. Though her head barely reached his chest, he had no doubt in that moment she would kill him given half a chance. If he had been vulnerable to any powers she might possess, he might be intimidated. As it was, he allowed her a moment to vent the anger that had clearly been building up for some time, pounding weak fists against him. Eventually, she fell away, gulping for air, face reddened by the sudden exertion.

"Do you know what he'll do with me?" she asked quietly.

The Commander looked down at her with pity. "It is as I told you before. You must be tested for powers. If you have them, you will be taken under the Commune's control. You'll take an honoured position in the Commune's ranks. It is what is best."

She scoffed. "You are such a—wait." Her eyes widened as she glanced behind him, towards the peasants toiling around them. "What about these people?" she said, waving a hand across the fields. "Were these people given an *honoured* position in—" Her arm dropped, mouth slackened. She peered up at Commander Sulemon, mouth hanging open. "What is this?"

He followed her gaze, frowning. "What do you mean?"

"Is this … Did you arrange for this?" She moved close to the nearest farmer, who was gathering bundles of straw leftover from the wheat harvest. "I know this man."

The Commander narrowed his eyes. "What do you—"

"And that woman … and those over there. What have you done? They're, they're all from Little Haven." Her voice rang out across the fields, growing shrill, yet still the farmers remained focused upon their tasks, seemingly unaware of her presence.

Evelyn approached the nearest man, tugging at his arm. "What are you doing here?" He blinked at her, eyes blank, before freeing himself from her grasp and continuing with his work. "What's wrong with you?" Her voice cracked. She ran to the next man, again receiving no response or recognition of any kind.

She moved back to the Commander. "Why won't they answer? What's been done to them? Did *you* do this? Make me see them? Now, before- before …"

Her eyes darted about, her hands pulling at her hair so frantically he thought she might tear it out.

He gave an exasperated sigh. *She understands so little.* "The Commune's work is best for the whole kingdom," he said, steadfast in his righteousness. "Villagers who ignore the Commune's decrees must be punished for their treachery. These people were tested and found to have no powers, as is the way of it. In his benevolent mercy, the Grand Magister has granted them—"

"Ignore the Commune's decrees? The villagers—*they didn't know!*" Evelyn cried. "We weren't told anything about the bloody pow—" She stopped as though the wind had been knocked from her. It took her some time to form her next words. "No, the Elders knew." She put a shaking hand to her forehead. "The Elders knew. I've known that ever since …" She trailed off, shoulders slumping as she turned to watch the farmers. "But these people aren't to blame."

He moved to stand beside her. "This is the only way to make people see," he said. "The Commune's laws must be obeyed." He watched the workers for a moment, unsure why he felt a sudden unease. Then he shook his head, stood tall, and said, "These people were traitors and so their minds have been … *opened*. They will never be disloyal again."

Evelyn remained frozen, staring into the field, eyes brimming with tears. Perhaps she was finally realising the futility of fighting. Perhaps she *was* beginning to understand.

He gave her a gentle nudge and she snapped her gaze towards him though remained silent, her usual fight gone.

"Come," he said. "Lord Torrant is waiting."

Without another word, he led them onwards. The scene had left a sour feeling within him; his excitement evaporated by Evelyn's outburst. He was suddenly anxious, worried that Lord Torrant wouldn't want to see him after all—would find some fault in his actions and turn him away. As they approached the mansion, his stomach knotted tighter still.

Once, he had been familiar with this place. He studied it, wondering how he'd ever been content here. The girl had unsettled him, but in truth the house had always set his nerves on edge with it's black-bricked walls, windows of darkened glass, its sheer, indomitable presence at the heart of the estate. He tensed all the more when he thought of everything that had transpired here. He closed his eyes, the memories playing at the periphery of his mind impossible to ignore.

"Commander Sulemon." The voice called from the direction of the mansion. He opened his eyes to see a gaunt, white-haired servant approaching. "Lord Torrant told us to expect your arrival."

The Commander cleared his throat. "Clim. He is awake?"

"Yes," Clim said. "Always the early riser." He cocked his head, regarding Evelyn as she stepped out from behind the Commander. "You have company, I see. Who is—"

"That is not your business."

"Very well," Clim said, though his watery eyes lingered on the girl. "Follow me. Lord Torrant will receive you in his study."

Commander Sulemon grabbed hold of Evelyn's arm, digging his fingers in harder than intended. "Do not speak unless you are addressed, girl," he said. "This is what's best for—"

Evelyn snatched her arm away from him, rubbing it furiously. "I remember."

He watched her for a moment longer, hoping she would heed his words for her own sake. "Come," he said, marching towards the house.

Inside, the mansion was much like he remembered. The same dark oak walls hung with portraits of the Torrant family, the same wooden floors carpeted with rich red rugs of the finest wool. And yet, for all of its outward luxury, the place also had an air of neglect. The smell of mould tinged the air, the paintings were faded, the ornaments layered with dust. Lord Torrant spent little time here; the house was as much a source of discomfort to its owner as it was to the Commander.

As the door to Lord Torrant's study was opened, the blood roared in his ears. He took deep breaths, trying to calm himself as he stepped inside.

At first, the room appeared empty. Above the hearth was a portrait of Lord Torrant's father: pale-faced, sharp-cheeked, cold-eyed. A stark difference to the man he so desperately wanted to see—yet at times, the ghost of an unwanted expression had presented an eerie likeness. He shuddered, glad he'd never had the misfortune of meeting that man, knowing full well the cruelty he'd inflicted on his own son. He was suddenly grateful for the heat of the blazing fire.

Take hold of yourself.

He clenched his jaw, watching as Clim leant down to the armchair facing the window.

"Commander Sulemon has arrived, my Lord."

"Some refreshments, please, Clim."

The Commander's heart leapt, his whole body alive with energy yet weak enough to collapse. A jewelled hand waved to dismiss the servant who bowed and retreated from the room in silence.

"Commander," Lord Torrant said, that same hand waving him forward.

He stepped in front of the chair, signalling for Evelyn to remain where she was before bowing deeply. "My Lord. I am glad to finally be back with you." When he looked up, his breath caught in his throat.

It couldn't have been so long, surely, since he had last seen Lord Torrant and yet a marked change had come over the man. His usually well-trimmed and oiled beard was unkempt and wiry, eyes ringed by dark purple circles, usually impeccable clothing scruffy and stained.

"Oh, Jonah." Lord Torrant gave a weak smile. "You were … I thought I'd … Well, I was beginning to lose hope of your return. But you're here now. Sit, please." He motioned a hand to the armchair opposite. The Commander did as he was bid just as Clim came back into the room, placing a tray of wine beside them before leaving.

Lord Torrant raised an eyebrow at the Commander, long fingers hovering over the bottle despite the early hour.

For a moment, the Commander was tempted to take a glass …

His eyes darted to Evelyn. No, there was other business to attend to first. The girl stood beside the door with her head down, hands clamped together. He wanted this done as soon as possible.

"No, thank you." He ran a hand over his jaw. "My Lord, the children …"

"Ah, yes, Commander." Lord Torrant's expression hardened. "Tell me what happened." His eyes scanned over the Commander's missing breastplate, the stubble on his chin, the filth on his clothing. "When Soldier Auras returned to report to me, he told me you left him at the Crystal River."

Commander Sulemon tweaked his red cloak, doing his best to cover his disgusting tunic. "I did, my Lord. At the opposite riverbank, we saw a boat tied up. We were unable to cross ourselves, but Soldier Bede, my tracker—he saw prints leading southwards, a man and two horses heading along the riverbank."

"Ah." Lord Torrant nodded. "No mere coincidence, I think."

"As I thought as well, my Lord. I followed my gut and we were soon rewarded. We located a member of Veritas, Hector Haralambous, as we followed the river southwards. We pursued him and he led us into the Crystal Mountains."

"We've long suspected their camp lay somewhere within that range." Lord Torrant's fingers interlocked, pale eyes glimmering with satisfaction.

"Yes, my Lord." The Commander's brow furrowed. "We had no choice but to fight the traitor. He was very strong. His powers …" He shook his head. "My men were overwhelmed. Two were killed, Bede and Neston. I was told one escaped, Crowe. I had hoped he would come to you, my Lord. Report what happened."

Lord Torrant frowned, eyes growing distant as he stroked his beard. "A soldier, you say? No such report reached me, Commander. Soldier Auras is the only man from your party who I saw after your departure." He pursed his lips. "I'll send word to Castleton. If Crowe returned to his post, he will be punished for such an oversight. Word of what happened should have come to me straight away. I'd have sent men to find you, you know that." For a moment their eyes connected. The Commander nodded, unable to speak. Lord Torrant lifted the wine bottle and poured some of the dark liquid into a glass. "Please, continue."

Commander Sulemon bowed his head. "As I said, the traitor was stronger than I had anticipated. I almost overcame him in a swordfight. If he'd been alone, I have no doubt I'd have killed him. As it was …"

Lord Torrant sat forward, sensing his hesitation. "What happened?"

"He had some kind of … demon."

He heard a muffled snicker from Evelyn and squared his shoulders, holding his head high.

"Demon?" Lord Torrant's lips pinched together. "Come now, I doubt—"

"It was white. A blur. It came from nowhere."

"Perhaps a companion. An animal of some kind."

"Perhaps so, my Lord. It attacked me; claws or- or talons scratched my face. Before I could throw it off, the man was upon me. I underestimated him. I was beaten to the ground. I tried to stop him but …" He rubbed his hands across his arms. Before he'd blacked out in the cave, he'd believed he would die there. He didn't want to admit to either of the listening parties that his last conscious thought was of Lord Torrant.

"The next I recall, I was being led to a hut," he continued after a brief silence.

"At the Veritas camp?"

"Yes, my Lord. I was prisoner there for a time." Commander Sulemon thought he saw a flash of concern upon Lord Torrant's face, but it was gone so quickly it might as easily have been the shifting of shadows.

"I knew there must have been something … unavoidable delaying you." Their eyes locked and Lord Torrant almost looked sad—almost. "How did you escape?"

Commander Sulemon motioned Evelyn forward. "I was able to come to an arrangement, my Lord."

Lord Torrant's pale eyes reflected the firelight as the girl approached. "Auburn hair," he muttered, tongue flitting across his lips. "Excellent work, Commander. You've done well."

Commander Sulemon allowed himself the ghost of a smile.

"Mm. Very well indeed. An arrangement, you say?"

"Yes, my Lord," Commander Sulemon replied, hand drifting to the belt where his pouch had once been secured. "It is of little importance now. But it was the only option I had. The only means of escaping with my life."

"I see." Lord Torrant stood, eyes glued to the girl. "Do you speak?" he asked, leaning down so their faces were inches apart. She didn't respond. He strode back and forth in front of her, lean and proud, in full control. He came to a stop, regarding her with all the power and authority of his station, and she met his gaze. The Commander felt a stir of something unexpected in that moment—surprise, respect even?—that she could return the look so calmly.

Lord Torrant laughed. "Well, I know you can, girl. You were all too happy to show me your disdain when we met in Castleton."

Met in Castleton? Commander Sulemon's eyes darted between their faces.

Evelyn remained silent, jaw clenched, chin lifted.

"Speak, girl," Lord Torrant spat. "What is your name? I dare say you have no grounds to refuse me now."

The girl's amber eyes were full of hatred as she muttered, "Evelyn."

"What? Speak up, girl. And you're to address me as 'my Lord.'"

Her fists clutched at her green cloak. "My name is Evelyn … *my Lord.*"

"Evelyn," Lord Torrant repeated, smiling. "You must be tired after your journey." He called for Clim. "Show Evelyn to the guest room. Ensure she has food and water." He looked her up and down, nose wrinkling. "And perhaps some fresh clothes."

Commander Sulemon watched in silence as Evelyn was escorted from the room, curiously concerned that she should be taken so abruptly.

"Jonah." Lord Torrant's voice drew his attention back. "You must rest. I see how exhausted you are. Perhaps you might join me for dinner tonight?"

Commander Sulemon's heart soared—Lord Torrant using his first name so softly, the invitation of privacy, the simplest sentence offering him everything he'd wanted since leaving Castleton. It was enough to push the girl, the camp, Veritarra's Gift, the travelling exhaustion from his mind. He did his best to keep his face still, to not betray the elation he felt. "It would be an honour, my Lord."

30

Raif

R aif gasped, his whole body jerking awake. Beneath his face, the ground was warm and coarse, fine tufts of fur tickling his lip as he breathed. His throat was dry, his tongue seemed too big for his mouth, his head throbbed.

Where am I? He forced himself to remember.

It was early. They'd been summoned for breakfast.

Avanna's hut.

Hector was there.

And …

Rose. He wanted to say it aloud though his body refused to obey him.

Breakfast. Hector. Avanna. Rose.

He concentrated all his might on moving, his head shifting awkwardly. His eyes batted open, taking far more effort than it should.

Did I fall asleep? No, that isn't right. It was early, yes. He'd been tired, they'd just arisen. *But to drift off like that? No.*

He fought to sit up, moaning as his sluggish limbs started to respond.

"Raif."

"Hector," he croaked. He moved a hand up to awkwardly rub his eyes, trying to keep them open. He turned his head to see the man's blurred outline. "What happened?" he slurred. "Rose okay?" He groped to his right where his sister and Dog had been and found only a cold, empty space. Confusion turned to icy fear.

Hector crawled towards him, placing a clammy hand on his arm. "A fool, lad. Damned fool." Cara stalked about the hut, tail held high.

Raif didn't understand Hector's words, but as he followed Cara's movements, their reality set in. "Where's Rose?" he said, heaving himself to his knees, grimacing as he tried to stand.

"Lad, save your energy. Slow down," Hector said. "She's gone."

Gone? Fear turned to suffocating panic. He ignored the man's plea, stumbling to his feet and lurching around the hut, heart racing, blood pounding through his quivering body.

She must still be here. She wouldn't leave me.

Not Rose as well.

He reached Avanna's sleeping area and found it empty. His legs buckled beneath him, unable to support him any longer. He cried out. "Hector." He looked back. "Where is she?"

"Oh, forgive me." Hector covered his face. "I'm sorry, lad. It's my fault. I should've known."

A surge of adrenaline forced Raif to his feet once more. "We have to find her, Hector." He grasped the older man's arm, trying to heave him up.

Hector pulled Raif back down to sit. "Stop, lad. Your body's not recovered from what we've been given. You'll be back to yourself soon enough. My powers will … well, they'll take a bit more time."

What we've been given … ? And then Raif realised—the tea, the food, all of it maybe. But there'd been something in it, something that had not only knocked him out, but Hector, too. Avanna had needed them both out of the way. *As if we haven't enough enemies from the Commune, but our own friends, our family …*

He slumped backwards, losing all will to fight. "What are we going to do?" Tears filled his eyes and he blinked hard, forcing them away. "Where's Rose? It was … Avanna took her? Why would she … ? We have to find her." His lip trembled and he bit down on it, not wanting his emotions to overpower him—not yet.

Hector watched Raif, seeming satisfied he was seated at least for the moment. "I know where she's gone." His voice was low and quiet.

"What?" Raif narrowed his eyes. "Why didn't you say?"

"Wanted to make sure your bloody legs could hold you first." Hector almost smiled, then seemed to think better of it.

Raif sniffed, wiping his hand across his nose. "Where's my sister?"

Hector let out a long, weary exhale, eyes glazed with pain. "She's going to Nook Town. My home."

Raif frowned, unsure of the connection. "Your home? But why?" He shook his head. *Doesn't matter.* His mind was clearing by the second, the feeling returning to his body. "We've got to go after them. Now. They can't be far ahead!"

"You're right, lad. Few hours at best, I'm hoping. There's only one reason we haven't yet. I need you to swear to me, before we leave this hut, that you're up to this. I won't let either of us leave this place until I know you're well enough. If I'm to protect you, I'm going to start doing a damned better job than I have been. I swear it."

Raif placed a hand on Hector's arm. "I'm getting my sister. And I need—I *want*—you to help me."

Hector clambered to his feet, steadying himself against the wall. "Right then. Let's get some supplies. Leave the food and horse to me. Get what you need from your hut. I'll meet you there."

"Okay." Raif stood. Hector seemed uneasy, almost off-balance, his usual authority and sureness dampened. Raif felt, despite his terror and panic for Rose, a need to say one more thing. "I know you weren't a part of this."

Hector's shoulders drooped. "Well then, lad." He cleared his throat. "That's … Thank you."

Raif nodded, darting away. *No more time to delay.* Outside, he held a hand up to shield his eyes against the blinding sky, running as fast as he could towards the hut he'd shared with Rose. He ignored the stares of those going about their daily tasks, finding himself all too suspicious of everyone around him.

Do they know what Avanna's done?

As he ran, he wished desperately for Evelyn. They would have worked through this together.

Raif crashed through the door to the hut and dashed about the two rooms without really thinking, grabbing items of clothing and throwing them into a pile on Evelyn's empty sleeping pallet. Finally, he retrieved his father's bow and slung it over his head. Arturo had gifted him a new quiver and arrows to practice with, and he secured it alongside the bow on his back.

He glanced around a final time. Satisfied there was nothing else he needed, he folded Evelyn's long-cold woollen blanket around the clothing and tied it off. Behind him, the door opened.

"Hector, I think I'm—"

"Good morning, Raif," Mak said, grinning broadly. *Too cheerful.* Raif felt as though the wind had been knocked from his lungs. *He knows.*

"Mak." He spoke as evenly as possible. "I can't help today. I'm, er … Hector's taking me somewhere."

"He is?" Mak's eyebrows shot up. "And where might—"

Just then, Hector bustled through the door, cheeks flushed. "Right, lad, it's later than we—Oh, Mak."

"Afternoon, old friend," Mak said, flashing another grin. "Raif here tells me you're going somewhere. Thing is, I came to ask if—"

"Let's not play that game, Mak." Hector's eyes darkened. Though shorter than Mak, Hector stood strongly, shoulders back, gaze even. Raif was almost scared of him. "You know as well as I do that Avanna wouldn't have done anything without discussing it with you first. Was a time you'd both've come to me as well, but it seems those days are behind us."

Mak's smile faded, eyes flitting between Raif and Hector. He ran a hand through his long brown hair and sighed with all the weariness of a man who wasn't sure he could have lied in the first place. "I'm sorry it had to be this way," he said quietly.

"What?" Raif cried. "You're *sorry*? Sorry doesn't do a damned—"

Mak held his hand up. "Now, boy, I understand your anger but listen to me, please. Avanna is doing what's best. She has a plan. There's a man in Nook Town who can help with Rose's powers. Make them *stronger*, even." His lips twisted into a sad half-smile. "I can't let you go after them. I've got to insist you stay in the camp."

Hector scoffed. "What nonsense has she told you?" He shook his head with disgust. "There isn't a living soul in Nook Town that has an interest in making powers stronger. They want the bloody *opposite*! Think, Mak, for once without your sister's words in your ear! You bloody fool." Hector's voice deepened as he spoke, his words ending in a near growl.

Mak's mouth fell open, he held a finger in the air and quickly dropped it again. "My sister ..." he began. Then he appeared to take strength from something, inhaling and drawing himself up. "Like I said, I'm going to have to insist you stay here. Both of you."

"I'm afraid we can't do that, old friend." Hector's voice was still deep, though now thick with sadness. "The lad and I'll be leaving. With or without your permission."

Mak's shoulders slumped. "Hector, no. We can talk this through, can't we? Like we used to. Come on, both of you. Let's go to Avanna's hut and—"

The rest of his sentence went unspoken. Hector lunged forward, grabbing Mak and ripping him away from the door. "Go, lad!" he shouted.

But Raif was rooted to the spot as the two men fell to the floor, grunting with effort as they wrestled each other. He should have moved, he knew that—this was his chance to get away, to get to Rose—yet some part of him almost immediately recognised that something was wrong.

Hector would be overpowered. Mak was bigger and undeniably physically stronger. Hector would need to use his powers. But nothing happened. Raif watched in horror as the man tried—and failed—his face scrunching with the effort, teeth grinding. Raif had no time to consider if Hector couldn't bring himself to use them on Mak, or if whatever Avanna gave him was still wearing off. Even Cara watched, seemingly frozen, from the doorway.

As the men rolled, Mak quickly gained the upper hand, pinning Hector to the floor. In that moment, Raif's arms acted almost with a mind of their own. He pulled his bow free, retrieved an arrow and nocked it, aiming for Mak's heart. He'd practiced—maybe not enough to meet the exact target but enough to know he'd meet flesh. In that moment, he wanted to make Mak *hurt*.

"Stop," he said, voice far calmer than he felt. "Get off him."

The two men were still. Mak lifted his arms from Hector's shoulders, holding them high. "Now, boy, don't do anything foolish."

Something in that moment—Mak half-crouched in a surrender, Raif with absolute power over him—made Raif hesitate. His breathing deepened, his pulse slowed. *You're not like this. He's lost.* He relaxed the bow, looking to Hector for—what? He wasn't even sure anymore. Reassurance? Permission to shoot, perhaps. The man heaved himself up and away from Mak, straightening his clothing, visibly shaken. "Just let us go. There'll be no trouble."

Mak let out a mirthless laugh. "It's not that simple, Hector. This is something my sister has waited for. Her plans—you may not understand but they *can* help! We might actually have a chance at—"

Raif's hands shook, fingers rubbing raw against the bowstring. *He still defends her. He's watched everything Avanna has done, found excuses every time. He's no better than her. He just wants his hands clean.*

"Don't be a bloody fool, Mak. She's a damned liar and you of all people should—"

"She is trying to save us!"

"You can't save a people by becoming what hunts them—"

"We've no time for this," Raif said. He tautened the bowstring again. "He won't listen." He aimed his arrow and—

"No, lad!" Hector cried.

Raif's arm jerked just as he released the arrow; it shot through the short distance and, a heartbeat later, Mak cried out a yelp and buckled forward, collapsing to his knees. Cara darted back out the door. Hector dove down and held a hand to Mak's neck. He repeated Mak's name, checked his wrist, pushed aside the curtain of hair that had fallen over his eyes, shook his shoulder. There was a tiny groan but Mak remained still, slumped against the wall of the hut, the arrow jutting from his body, though the angle made it hard to tell where it had hit. Raif watched, unmoving. The arrow should have pierced somewhere beneath the heart or lungs, an injury that could be survived. But he *was* still learning.

"Hector, we need to go," Raif tried. The man didn't move. "Come *on*, Hector!" He grabbed his bundle of clothes and made for the door. To his relief, the man followed close behind, though his face was pale, lips drawn tight.

Outside, Bert was waiting with Cara at his feet, saddlebags bulging with supplies. "Let's go," Raif said, climbing onto Bert's back. Hector nodded, giving a brief glimpse back towards the hut.

"Okay, lad," he said, voice quivering as he brushed back his hair, eyes lingering on the door of the hut.

"Hector?" Raif said impatiently. "Shouldn't we go?"

Hector cleared his throat, not meeting Raif's eyes. "Yes," he said. "We'll take one of the less used paths. Avoid the patrolling scouts. Can't be sure who knew about Avanna's plan. She may be trying to avoid the main roads as well. With any luck, we'll cut her off along the way." He took hold of Bert's reins and began walking briskly towards the treeline that marked their exit from the camp.

As they reached the outskirts, Raif heard his name called. He stiffened in the saddle, breath catching in his throat. *We've been caught already. I'll be punished for what I've done.*

"Raif!" Griff marched towards them, puffing heavily. "There you are! I've been trying to find you."

"What's wrong?" Raif asked, trying to sound as casual as possible, panic simmering within. "Is it Rose?"

"Rose?" Griff's brow furrowed. "No, sorry. Haven't seen her."

"Speak your purpose then, lad. We've training to attend to," Hector said a little too brusquely.

Griff raised an eyebrow. "Oh. No, it's, um, it's just the dog." He pointed over his shoulder. "I found him tied to a tree on my rounds. He wouldn't follow me, though. Seems to be waiting for something."

"Or someone," Raif said, glancing at Hector. "Take us to him."

As Griff walked ahead, Raif leant down to Hector. "We'll have to take the main path after all, won't we?"

Hector's moustache twitched. "I think so. Though Griff doesn't seem to know a thing, poor oaf. Starting to think it was just Avanna … and Mak."

Raif nodded, unsure what to say, sensing once more the depth of betrayal Hector was grappling with. "If we have Dog, he might help us find Rose," he said, trying to believe the words.

"Hmm, he might at that," Hector said, though he turned his head away.

Raif hardly noticed Hector's hesitation. He'd only one thought in his mind, and he willed all the powers he knew to carry it to his sister: *It'll be okay. We'll find you, Rose.* Nothing else mattered anymore.

31

Evelyn

Lord Torrant's home was as terrible as the man himself. Something about the dark walls absorbed the last shred of strength from Evelyn, draining her energy and any fight she had left. No matter what stone in the wall she studied, what window she gazed out of, she couldn't forget the blank faces of the Little Haven villagers she'd seen in the fields around the estate. Was Raif and Rose's mother there?

Was Arthur?

Is that what awaits me?

It was likely, it seemed, if her powers refused to show themselves again. No powers meant no use to the Commune, except as a mindless servant for some noble bastard. She clenched her hands into fists until they shook, trying to quell her rising terror by focusing on her anger.

And yet, overwhelming everything else was the feeling that she didn't truly understand what any of it meant. Bessie once taught her a board game, King's Gambit. She'd never been much good at it; she'd simply tried to keep as many pieces on the board as possible. But Bessie had explained the rules over and over again—how the King only appeared to take risks by losing soldiers, how he always kept the advantage, how the nobles shielded him, sacrificing themselves for the *greater good*. She was beginning to see the pieces at play here, see the way the Grand Magister threw away the smaller players and how the nobles and soldiers defended their leader despite being sacrificed themselves. Yet for all the sudden clarity the memory afforded her, Evelyn still couldn't work out the game as a whole. She felt herself poised on the board without a single clue as to where she'd be pushed next. Which play would move her along and which would end her turn?

She shuffled back and forth in the small bedroom she'd been sent to, hands wringing together. Awake or asleep, she'd been consumed with what the Commander had told her would come: prove the worth of her powers or join the Little Haven survivors as another empty puppet.

Even if I could use them again, would I want them to end up in the hands of the Commune? What violence might I be compelled to carry out? She paused in her pacing, nausea rising up in her throat as she recalled what had happened the one time her powers had shown themselves.

The sound of his bones breaking. She shivered then quickly hardened herself. *He got what he deserved.*

She sat down again, leg tapping with restless energy. What good was dwelling on the past anyway? Whatever had been within her then was gone now. *Pushed away for too long,* she thought. *Held inside. Or maybe burned away the first time I used them.*

"It doesn't matter now," she muttered, staring into the flames dancing in the hearth. She poked the tray of food on the floor with her foot, the soup long-cold. At the thought of eating, her stomach clenched. She longed for a glass of wine, a tankard of mead, anything to calm her nerves, quiet her mind.

Evelyn leant back on the bed, feeling the cold stone wall sapping away the last of her heat. She thought back to all that had led her here, everything in and outside of her control, feeling a deep, unquestionable understanding of how small, insignificant, and helpless she really was.

Lord Torrant is dangerous.

She jolted upright, the words shooting fresh fear through her.

Under Lord Torrant's gaze, she'd felt frozen to the spot, just as when she first met him in Castleton. He had the upper hand here in his own home. He could do whatever he wanted with her.

There's no way out.

She stood up again, moving to stoke the fire, doing what little she could to banish the icy chill. The sun had risen high since their arrival, the light from the windows almost white in her room, and yet the day remained cold. She felt as though she was observing herself from afar, unable to prevent anything that might happen, capable only of watching and waiting. She moved towards the washbasin and splashed water over her face, eager to cleanse away such thoughts. When she studied herself in the mirror, she barely recognised the sunken features and blank eyes of the girl reflected back. She snorted, disgusted by her own weakness.

She untied the leather cord in her braid and allowed her hair to come loose. It fell to her lower back, thick and wavy. She wished she could take a knife to it—to the the girl she'd been. She almost laughed at how foolish she'd been to think she could help Raif and Rose all those weeks ago.

She took a deep inhale and dunked her whole head into the basin, letting the bubbles rush from her nose and mouth. She held her breath, rubbing viciously at her scalp.

When at last she lifted her head, she took great gulps of air, wiping the water from her eyes, blinking the tears from her vision. She rang her hair out, winding it round and round until it was tight as a rope. She let it drop, feeling nothing.

She met her own eyes in the mirror. "You'll never amount to anything," she whispered.

She stumbled towards the bed and picked up the fresh clothes provided by Clim. The undershirt, tunic, and trousers were black wool, the cloth far more durable than what she was used to.

Like the servants wear, she realised bitterly. *A chance to get used to my new position.*

Finally, she re-braided her wet hair and laid back on the bed. Alone with the crackling of logs, Evelyn's thoughts soon drifted away and she entered the black depths of sleep with surprising ease.

In her dreams, Evelyn was in Little Haven once more. She was leading Arthur back after their hunting trip. He clasped his broken arm to his chest, whimpering as she urged him on. She didn't meet anyone's curious gaze as they headed for the Elders' hut. She couldn't separate any emotions—fear, anger, and grief all muddled together; a repressive mix that threatened to crush her altogether. She frowned, trying to recall what had happened. Her eyes flitted to Arthur's arm; the skin was strangely swollen, red, and shiny. Had she *made* him do that to himself? It had felt like it in the moment, a fierce fire bursting forth from her entire being, wanting only to hurt him. But how could that be so?

Inside the Elders' hut, Arthur's mother, Elder Alwyn, rushed forward to her son. "What happened?" she asked, eyes fierce as they ran over Evelyn's dishevelled clothing.

Arthur's mouth twisted into a horrible grimace-like grin. "I fell," he said. He looked at Evelyn. *There,* his expression said.

No, that's not right. Evelyn's heart hammered in her throat. She wanted to scream. She wanted to run. She could do neither.

Later, she was summoned to the Elders' hut. Elder Alwyn sat on a great, carved, throne-like chair, raised high on a stage as though Evelyn was on trial.

"Arthur was badly injured," the old woman said. Her blue eyes—so like her son's—full of suspicion. "Is it true, what he said? That he fell?"

Evelyn nodded numbly.

"Mm." Elder Alwyn clasped her hands across her lap, studying Evelyn. "Well, whatever happened, I have summoned you here because my son has told me he wishes to marry you. He told me you'd discussed it between you. That an agreement was—"

"What? No!" Evelyn cried, unable to stop the words from gushing forth. "We did no such thing."

"Excuse me?" The Elder blanched. "My son wishes to marry you, and it shall be so. There are things you don't understand, girl. Things we Elders must …" The woman shook her head, grey hair falling about her wrinkled face. "Suffice it to say that being my daughter by law is a protection you'll benefit from, should the *truth* of what happened ever emerge."

Evelyn's hands trembled as she balled them into fists, too angry to be ashamed at the woman's knowing gaze. "No," she whispered. "Your son- He … There was no … He forced himself on me and—"

"Enough! I will not hear such lies." Elder Alwyn slapped her palm down on the wooden arm of the chair upon which she sat. "You are to be married. That's the end of it."

And then a crowd of black-clad villagers came to stand around Evelyn. They pointed at her, accusing, disbelieving. Evelyn tried to speak but her lips wouldn't move, her voice was silenced.

Please! You don't understand what he did, what he can do again. Don't make me marry him.

Please believe me.

But they couldn't—*wouldn't*—hear her. They stared and stared with judgement burning in their eyes, pressing in on her until she fell to her knees, trampled beneath them.

Evelyn jolted upright, body drenched with sweat. She sat up, rubbing her eyes. The fire needed stoking, then she would—

"I trust you slept well."

Her heart skipped a beat, though she managed to keep her voice calm as she said, "Lord Torrant." She pulled her legs up to her chest, a useless shield against him.

The glare from the windows was gone, the faint glow of sunset illuminating the man before her. "I could have done anything while you slept, girl. Do not take me for a common man at the mercy of wanton perversions." He waved his jewelled hand, as though tired of the conversation already. "My Commander tells me he has prepared you for the test that awaits you."

Eyes adjusted to the darkness, Evelyn was able to make out the lines of Lord Torrant's face, the close-cropped black beard outlining his jaw, the sharpness of his cheeks. She bit her lip and remained silent.

Lord Torrant smiled, running a hand across his chin. "Speak or not, it makes no matter, girl. I will take the measure of your powers and know what lies inside." He poked a finger towards her chest. "In the morning, I will send for you."

"I'll never reveal anything to you," she spat.

Lord Torrant laughed. "You'll have no choice." He casually straightened his shirt sleeves. "It's best you get some rest. You will require all of your energy tomorrow." His voice was calm, and she saw him for what he was with stunning clarity: a predator biding his time before making the fatal blow.

She barely took notice of him leaving the room.

As she clutched her knees to her body, she felt an intense longing for Raif and Rose. She'd done all she could since escaping with the Commander not to think of them, of what Avanna may have told them, of how they must hate her. And now in the dark, they were all that was on her mind.

Hector, you'd better have kept your promise. Raif, Rose, please be safe.

She wrapped her arms tighter around herself to still the trembling in her body.

In the morning, Lord Torrant would decide her fate.

32

Commander Sulemon

"Jonah," Lord Torrant said, sweeping into the dining room. "I trust I haven't kept you waiting for too long."

Commander Sulemon stood up from his seat at the table, brushing down the front of his fresh black tunic. "Not at all, my Lord." He glanced up at the man entering, mouth suddenly bone dry. Since that morning, Lord Torrant's appearance had improved remarkably—the dark smudges beneath his eyes were faded, his fine clothes restored, his beard trimmed and slicked with oil. He'd replaced his stained shirt with a crisp white one, the neck slit open to reveal the coarse, black hair beneath. The Commander tore his gaze away with a great deal of difficulty.

"Very good." Lord Torrant moved to the head of the table, waiting for Clim to pull his chair out. "Come, sit beside me, Jonah. Like old times."

The Commander's stomach fluttered. He bowed his head to prevent his eyes from betraying him, obediently moving to the indicated chair. Behind them, the fireplace crackled, the table was set for dinner, the room felt almost homely.

But this place was never home for me. For us, the Commander realised bitterly. His eyes drifted to the family portrait behind Lord Torrant—all dead now, except the man before him. The parents and sons shared the same ice-blue eyes, the same air of pride and strength; he was only a boy then, just before he was sent away to the Commune, he'd once told the Commander.

"Before I knew how much my father truly hated me. How little I meant to this family."

The Commander averted his gaze, the memory too stark a reminder of what he and the man before him had once been.

Ignorant of his internal struggle, Lord Torrant signalled for Clim to fill their crystal glasses with red wine. He took a generous mouthful and let out an appreciative sigh. "You must try the wine, Jonah."

He picked up the glass and sipped from it delicately. "Thank you, my Lord."

"Don't you recognise the taste?" Lord Torrant's eyes gleamed in the dancing light of the candelabrum at the table's centre.

Commander Sulemon frowned, holding up the glass to examine the contents.

Lord Torrant chuckled. "Has it been so long? It's one of the last bottles from your home. I kept it all these years." He raised his glass before drinking. "Come now, Jonah. I had it brought in especially for our dinner. We have cause to celebrate, don't you think?" A smile played at the corner of his lips.

"Thank you, my Lord," the Commander muttered, gulping down the contents of his glass, barely tasting it. *You betrayed your home, you betrayed your people, you are a shame to Veritarra herself.* Did Lord Torrant somehow know of the roiling conflict within him? *Does he do this as some kind of cruel mockery?* Once he would have denied it could be so; that his former lover could be so cold.

He found he was not so sure of anything anymore.

What is wrong with me? I should be content simply to be here. With him. As it has been these thirteen years past.

When Clim stepped forward to refill their wine, Lord Torrant waved him away. "Leave us alone until dinner is ready to be served." The servant bowed and shuffled from the room.

As soon as he'd left, Lord Torrant lifted the wine bottle, leant across the Commander, refilling his glass. Commander Sulemon tilted his head away to avoid the floral aroma of beard oil, but the scent reached his nose all the same.

Lord Torrant sat back in his seat, giving a smile. The Commander had no doubt he knew what reaction such physical closeness had caused. He shifted in his seat, desperate to push away the longing. *Shouldn't be drinking wine*, he thought to himself, even as he picked up his glass and drained it, willing it to numb him. *He means only to taunt me. Veritarra forgive me, I have allowed it all these years.*

Lord Torrant held a kerchief to his lips, coughing lightly, bringing the Commander's attention back to him. "I'll admit, I was glad to leave Castleton behind."

Commander Sulemon snorted, trying to be glad of the change of subject. "Yes, my Lord. It was … an acquired taste, was it not?"

Lord Torrant laughed. "It was." His nose wrinkled. "The smell clung to my clothes long after I'd left. And the *people*." He rolled his eyes and shook his head.

The Commander paused, hand halfway to his wine glass. *The people. Did that sneering jibe include the Nomarrans? Displaced by the Grand Magister's decree.* Something about his time in that Goddess forsaken camp made him more determined to speak on the subject. Time alone to think on it had convinced him there were truths still hidden from him. *I must know what they are.* He pulled his hand back and wiped his clammy palm across his front, steeling himself. "My Lord … Might I speak honestly a moment? About Castleton?"

"Of course, Jonah. Always."

"I told you while we were there that I'd heard tell of the Grand Magister's decree … Seen the ruin of the Nomarran homes in the city." He hesitated, unsure how Lord Torrant would respond at his broaching the subject again.

Lord Torrant raised an eyebrow but gave a brief nod. "Go on, Jonah."

"I fear now it is the case for my people all over Septima." His lip curled; saying the words aloud made his repressed rage surge to the surface. "I even heard vile gossip from the leader of Veritas, though I would not believe a word that came from her mouth, about my people seeking shelter amongst those *traitors*. I wondered if you might—"

Lord Torrant reached out, touching a warm hand to the Commander's forearm. "You are angry, I see that," he said. He gave a soft pout, perfect pink lips stained red with wine. "But this is talk for the morrow, surely? Once the girl is dealt with."

Commander Sulemon nodded, though he struggled to comply with the clear command he'd just been given. He inhaled deeply. "Very well, my Lord." He lifted his wine glass, staring into the deep red liquid within. He drank it down, smothering the flames of frustration alighting in his gut.

Lord Torrant squeezed his arm before withdrawing his touch. "It's important to you, I see. I will listen, Jonah. You can trust me."

The Commander gave a fleeting smile, stomach cramping into a knot. "I do, my Lord." *Fool,* the voice whispered in his mind.

A gentle knock at the door indicated the arrival of dinner. A line of servants, all clad in black, entered the room and laid out dishes of roasted beef and pheasant, crisply cooked potatoes, blackened onions, honey-glazed carrots and parsnips, freshly baked bread—the line went on and on.

This is for me, he realised. *My reward.* His knuckles tightened around his fork. *You should not have expected any more than this.*

Lord Torrant gave him a broad smile. "You've done well, Jonah," he said. "It's the least I could do."

Commander Sulemon swallowed back his despair. "Thank you, my Lord."

"Shall I serve, my Lord?" Clim asked.

Lord Torrant shook out a clean white napkin and placed it on his lap. "Yes, Clim."

Dinner was piled high on their plates and they were, at last, left alone again.

The Commander stared at his food, wondering if he dared ask the next question that entered his mind. He drank his wine, growing more and more emboldened. "While I am speaking honestly, perhaps I might ask of Lady Cragside?" he said. "Have you seen her again? While I was in Castleton, I heard a rumour … the expectation of marriage placed upon you by the Grand Magister." It took him a moment to be able to look up, to meet Lord Torrant's gaze.

"Lady Cragside and her cousin have given their pledge to the cause. Funds for the Commune. But marriage?" Lord Torrant arched an eyebrow. "Never. You know my feelings on the matter." He lifted his glass again, peering towards the window as he took a gulp. "Perhaps you saw the new servants toiling the field? From the recent raids along the west coast. Damned peasants thought themselves safe hiding away in Haven Forest. They were shown the only mercy they deserved."

"Of course, my Lord," the Commander said, confused by the flush of remorse he felt at those words. The girl said she knew some of them, hadn't she? That they were innocent, honest people. Yet what Lord Torrant said was true—they deserved their fate … didn't they?

"Anyway, Lady Cragside and Lord Ambleside were very happy to receive the … overflow. Don't worry. We have what we need from them. Lady Cragside will need the occasional *flirtation*, no more."

"And what did you …" The Commander bit his tongue, afraid to speak the words.

"What?" Lord Torrant smirked. "You never used to be so careful with me. There was a time you'd have spoken your mind, consequences be damned."

Commander Sulemon swallowed, heart thudding a fierce beat that drove him on to speak the words he'd longed to for seven long years. "There was a time when we were much more than we are."

Lord Torrant paused, a forkful of food halfway to his mouth. He lowered it back to his plate and dabbed his lips with a napkin. "Jonah, I …" He smoothed the front of his shirt. "I don't know what—"

The Commander held up his hand, his nerve fleeing as quickly as it had come. "No, please. Forget I said anything." He pinched the bridge of his nose, trying to still his dizzied mind. *I should not have had so much wine.*

"Jonah?"

"Yes, Ei—my Lord?"

Lord Torrant's lips curled upwards, stained red with wine. "Tell me. How was your first journey into the mountains?"

Commander Sulemon let out a relieved exhale. Though some part of him wished he'd allowed the conversation to continue, he was also deeply afraid of where it would lead. He stroked his freshly shaven chin. "I must admit, I did not care for the cold."

Lord Torrant chuckled. "No, I'm sure you didn't."

"Have you been, my Lord? To the mountains? Before we … before we met?"

"No." He leant forward with a satisfied smile. "But soon we shall ride there together and tear down this camp in which you were imprisoned—of that I can assure you."

"Yes, my Lord." They clinked their glasses together and the Commander drank down more of the dark liquid.

"Now, enough talk of such things." Lord Torrant sat back in his chair, pushing away his empty plate. "We have the girl. You deserve some rest. You've done well to bring her to me."

Commander Sulemon's cheeks flushed, though he could not say whether it was caused by the praise or the wine. He ate a final mouthful of beef, enjoying the way it melted on his tongue. It had been a while since he had eaten so well.

As though reading his mind, Lord Torrant said, "I must admit, I have missed this. These last weeks have been a strain, Jonah. I wasn't sure I would see … that you would return to me." He sipped his wine, glancing about the room. "I've rarely returned here since we … since what happened those years ago. It isn't a welcoming place when I'm alone." There was a pause before he spoke again. "Do you remember the hunts?"

Commander Sulemon almost choked. "The wolf hunts? In Taskan Forest?" Though he tried to conceal it, his voice trembled as he spoke.

"Yes." Pale blue eyes met the Commander's, the heat between them burning as fiercely as the fire at their backs.

"Your brother was … unimpressed with our lack of success in the hunt. A Torrant returning without a kill—unheard of."

Lord Torrant grunted with amusement. "He was *very* unimpressed, wasn't he?" He let out a long sigh. "A different time. For us. For the kingdom."

Commander Sulemon studied his plate, pushing a scrap of potato around with his fork. "Yes, my Lord."

Lord Torrant slammed his glass down, sloshing the blood-red liquid onto the table. "Come now, Jonah," he said, scowling. "Is that all I am to get from you? *Yes, my Lord*? After all we've been through?"

Commander Sulemon watched him across the table, a thousand possible responses flitting across his mind. But he knew he daren't say any of them—the moment had passed, his courage fled. Instead, he drank the last of his wine and held his tongue.

Lord Torrant scraped his chair away from the table, threw down his napkin, and moved to the window, observing the darkness outside. For a horrible moment, Commander Sulemon thought he would be asked to leave; a pang of regret gnawed at him. *Coward.*

But a louder part of his mind spoke up, surging a sudden and powerful energy through his body. *Act now. It's not too late.*

"My Lord," he said, standing, moving closer, stretching his arm out. "Come back to the table."

"Can I not inspect my own estate, Commander?" Lord Torrant said, not glancing back.

"I—" The Commander's tongue felt too big for his mouth. "I'm sorry, Eir—my Lord Torrant." His words stumbled over one another, clumsy and awkward.

They were close—almost close enough to touch. Before he could stop himself, the Commander moved to stand at Lord Torrant's back.

"Please." Placing a hand on his shoulder, turning him around, he pulled Lord Torrant closer still. His fingers clasped with an iron grip, desperate to hold on to this moment. The Commander stared down at Lord Torrant, heart hammering, heavy breaths filling the room.

"Do you remember why we failed in the wolf hunts, my Lord?" he whispered. "What we were doing while your brother and the others were slaying the beasts?"

Lord Torrant's licked his lips. "Of course I do." His shoulders slumped, a long exhale escaping his mouth. Still, he did not move. The Commander knew this game, knew how the Lord always made him move first, made him reveal his play at the start while keeping his own secrets until the last possible moment.

He knew it was a game, knew he was a disposable piece on the board and yet—

Goddess forgive me.

Commander Sulemon closed the gap between them, pressing his lips to Lord Torrant's, feeling rough bristles scraping against his skin. His lips parted and, for an exultant moment, he felt a response. Soft lips that tasted of wine, a gentle tongue.

"Eirik," he rasped.

A groan in response.

He shoved Lord Torrant against the wall, tearing at his fine white shirt. He stroked the warm flesh and coarse hair beneath, felt the heat between them, bodies drawn together.

He pressed forward, closer still, wanting to engulf Lord Torrant completely. His hands roamed over the lines of lean muscle and soft skin he'd once known so well. Lord Torrant, in turn, ripped at his tunic, pulling it up, reaching beneath. Warm fingers brushed across his stomach, over his chest.

This was all he'd wanted for seven years. All he'd hoped for. One more time. He peppered kisses along Lord Torrant's jaw, down his neck, inhaling the mixture of sweat and floral beard oil.

He paused with his hands on Lord Torrant's hips, looking into his eyes. He hesitated; in Lord Torrant's face, there was hunger, yes, but something else too.

Afraid of that look—knowing when he'd seen it before—the Commander shifted and clasped him by the shoulders. *Speak, before it's too late.* "Eirik, what—"

Suddenly, there was a knock at the door.

Without prompting, Clim entered. A gasp echoed across the room, the Commander was shoved away.

"Clim," Lord Torrant snapped. "You were not summoned." He pulled down his shirt, ran a hand through his hair.

"My apologies, my Lord," the servant said, lips quirking into a strange half-smile. "But a scroll arrived for you from the Grand Magister and—"

"A scroll?" Lord Torrant paled. "Very well. Leave it and go."

Clim placed the parchment on the table beside Lord Torrant's wine glass before retreating silently to the door.

"Eirik." Commander Sulemon tried to reach for him, but it was too late. Lord Torrant had retreated once more. His face was blank as he moved to the table, reached for his glass with a trembling hand, and lifted it to his lips, drinking deeply.

He didn't look at the Commander as he picked up the scroll, slipped a finger under the wax seal, and popped it open. His brow furrowed as he read the message, though his face gave nothing away as to its contents.

"My Lord." No response. "Eirik?"

Lord Torrant jolted upright, his fist clenching in on the paper in his hand, scrunching it into a ball. He blinked, as though remembering he was not alone. "Oh," he said. "Jonah."

With a sudden, dizzying rush, the Commander was back in this very room seven years ago. Lord Torrant had been pale, his expression drawn much as it was now. He'd held a scroll in his hands, the contents hidden, much as they were now.

"You can't stay here any longer, Jonah. It's for the best."

The Commander shook his head, bringing himself back to the moment. "I'm sorry. I acted out of turn." He stood tall, holding his shaking hands behind his back.

Lord Torrant gave a sad smile. "No, Jonah. You acted precisely as I ..." He rubbed a hand across his eyes. "No matter. It is late. Perhaps you had best get some more sleep. We test the girl in the morning."

"I ... Eirik, I ..." Commander Sulemon bit back the words that almost formed on his tongue. *There's no use.* "Yes, my Lord." He made his way across the room, head down, bile rising in his throat.

"Jonah."

The Commander froze, hand slick upon the door handle. "My Lord?"

"Please send Clim in."

"Of course." Swallowing back the lump in his throat, he opened the door and came face-to-face with the servant. "He'll see you now," he said, avoiding the man's smug gaze as he marched away.

He walked, the smell of Eirik's floral oil still clinging to him, bottom lip trembling.

"It's from the Noman Islands, Jonah. A scent to remind you of home."

Stupid, worthless fool.

He bit his lip, lifting his chin high as he made his way through the hallways, ready for any eyes that might find him. He met none. He closed the bedroom door, leaning his forehead against it, recalling the look on Clim's face, the gasp of shock, Lord Torrant's rapid withdrawal.

He's going to wipe Clim's mind. He can't afford for us to be seen together. He waited for the familiar guilt, the uneasy pain in his gut that always followed Lord Torrant using his powers, even for justified work. That night, he couldn't force himself to care in the least.

You have lost sight of yourself, Jonasaiah. The voice was a gentle whisper in the back of his mind. As it spoke, fresh tears prickled in his eyes.

He clenched his fist, grinding his knuckles into the hard wood of the door until the skin tore, and barely felt a thing.

37th Day of Solstice
13ᵗʰ Year of King Cosmo Septimus
33ʳᵈ Year of Grand Magister Quilliam Nubira Antellopie III

Lord Eirik Torrant
Torrant Estate

My faithful servant,

It has been some time since your last report, though it has been confirmed to me that you left Castleton shortly after writing. It concerns me greatly that you have not seen fit to keep me appraised of the situation in the days since.

I am sure that, had your Commander Sulemon been successful in capturing the children you wrote of, your report would have been sent to me forthwith. I have told you previously of my doubts about one of his nature and origin, though you have continued to keep him in your service.

I have allowed you to keep him on in gratitude of your loyalty, but it is becoming clear to me that this is to the detriment of all. Can you be sure he is truly loyal to you, to our regime, given his Nomarran blood? I would urge you to reconsider his position and believe you will make the right choice regarding your relationship with the man, as you did seven years ago.

You may be surprised to learn that a soldier who was travelling with him has returned directly to Taskan, revealing the man's incompetence in tracking the children. Thankfully, the soldier was also able to provide directions leading to the camp of the Veritas traitors. I enclose a map and expect you to lead your own men to this place without delay. The justice of the Commune will be felt by those treacherous fools once and for all, and the hunt for the children will recommence.

Of all people, you understand that taking in every child with powers is of the utmost importance for the future of the Commune and the kingdom—even more so with one as powerful as the young girl who murdered our loyal soldier.

Do not fail me.

Your Benevolent Master,

Quilliam Nubira Antellopie III

33

Raif

It was the middle of the night and the moon beamed down, casting the world around them in a ghostly white light. Raif let out an exasperated sigh, shuffling in the saddle in an attempt to warm himself.

"We can't keep going much longer," Hector said. "Cara's eyes are good but I fear we're putting ourselves in danger if we—"

"No! We have to keep going," Raif demanded. "What about Rose?"

Hector halted Bert, twisting towards Raif with a frown. "Now, lad, be reasonable," he said. "We know Avanna's path. She's not so far ahead of us. Rushing and breaking our necks won't help, will it?"

Raif crossed his arms and huffed, though he could see the truth in Hector's words—besides which, he longed for a fire to warm his numbed fingers and toes. "Okay," he muttered.

"Good lad." Hector rubbed his hands together, spurring Bert on. "There's a cave near here. We can camp until morning, set off at first light. We've made good progress already. Will be out of the mountains before long, I'd say."

Inside the cave, Hector set to work retrieving some firewood while Raif unpacked some food from Bert's saddlebags. Dog stood at the entrance, staring out into the night, quietly whimpering. "Come here, boy," he called, but the stubborn creature ignored him. Raif rolled his eyes; he'd soon come when he realised there was food being served.

Rose would have shared her dinner with him, he thought. And then, before he realised what was happening, tears were falling down his cheeks. He dropped the food he was clutching and sunk to his knees.

"Oh, now," Hector said, bending to heave him up. "Some hot tea and rest will see you through. In the morning, everything will look better."

"W-will it?" Raif asked, stuttering through his sobs. "W-what if- if we c-can't catch up with her? We were asleep longer than we thought, Hector. Who knows how far Avanna's got?"

Hector walked him towards the pile of firewood and sat him down beside it, wrapping his grey fur cloak round Raif's shoulders. "Listen to me. I promise you we will find her. D'you hear me? I *promise*. Let's get this fire lit and I'll see about that drink." He leant over the wood and struck a flint. Before long, it was crackling healthily. Hector began his tea preparations, humming to himself.

Raif wiped his face on his sleeve and held his palms out over the flickering flames. Cara came to rub herself against his leg, purring softly. Despite everything, a sense of calm settled across him.

"Thanks, I guess," Raif mumbled to her. She butted his knee.

When Hector brought him some tea, he took it gratefully.

"Get some sleep, lad," Hector said, stoking the fire. "I'll keep you safe."

Raif didn't have the strength to argue. He blew to cool the drink and sipped it down. He laid himself out on the blanket and drifted into a dreamless sleep.

The next morning, they set off in a world dappled with a warm orange glow. Raif could almost have appreciated such a view if the circumstances had been different. As it was, he'd woken with a heavy heart and pounding head. He numbly accepted his breakfast from Hector, climbing onto Bert's back. "We shouldn't have stopped," he said. "Avanna must be miles away."

"Now, lad. That's no way to talk about a good night's rest. Move back, I'll ride with you." He climbed up in front of Raif. "We had to stop for our own good. Avanna's human too, y'know. She'll have needed to stop much as we did. And don't worry; this old beast can handle a bit of a sprint—he's done me well before."

Raif grunted.

On the ground beside them, Dog sniffed at Cara excitedly, his whipping tail sending up flurries of snow. Cara, evidently unimpressed with her new travelling companion, let out a curt *"Miaow,"* and leapt up to Bert's back, tucking herself into Hector's tunic.

"It's okay, Dog," Raif said. "We'll find Rose soon and you won't need to make any other friends."

Dog barked his agreement and trotted ahead. Hector nudged Bert forward. Together, they left the Crystal Mountains and Veritas camp behind.

Later that day, Raif walked ahead with Dog to stretch his aching legs and back, going over everything that had happened in the past few days, searching for some clue as to Avanna's plans—some hint as to what had transpired yesterday morning and *why*. Perhaps he'd missed something—been blind to what was right in front of him. There was one thing he still didn't fully understand though. He paused, waiting for Hector to catch up with Bert and Cara.

"Tired already, lad?" he joked, though Raif barely noticed. He chewed his lip, fumbling for the words.

"Hector, um, that wasn't what I … well, um …"

Hector looked at him with knowing green eyes. "What do you need to know?"

Raif scanned the sky, watching a flock of birds flying overhead. "Avanna told you she was taking Rose to Nook Town," he said. "And Mak said something about them making her powers stronger."

Hector bowed his head, tugging on his moustache.

"You told Mak they'd want the opposite in Nook Town. Where- where exactly is Avanna taking my sister?" Raif steeled himself for the answer, fearing the worst.

The man scraped back his unruly hair, features tight with apprehension. "I grew up in Nook Town. They're outside of the control of the Commune, but that doesn't mean they're any better than them."

Raif narrowed his eyes. "What do you mean?"

"They look on those with powers with a deep suspicion. *Hate* them, truth be told. There's no way they'd want Rose any stronger. I fear they might …" He blew air through his lips. "I fear they've laid a trap for Avanna and she's taking your sister right into it. Foolish bloody woman. If she'd spoken to me before

I might've been able to …" He gave a vicious shake of his head. "Ah, no use thinking such things. In honesty, I can't be sure what they want with Rose, but I am sure it won't be for her good."

Raif swallowed. "We have to get to her before they reach Nook Town, Hector."

"I'm doing my very best to make it so, lad."

"She said she was going to help us, made us believe we were safe. And all along this was her plan." Raif clenched his fists, screwed his eyes shut, and bit down on his tongue—anything to stop him from screaming.

"I'll do everything I can to make sure we get your sister back," Hector said firmly.

Raif nodded. "Okay." He tilted his chin upwards. "Hector?"

"Yes, lad?"

He squared his shoulders. "When we do find them, will you kill her?"

"Kill her?" Hector's voice was low, full of tension.

"Avanna," Raif said. "She has to die." He met Hector's gaze, feeling surer of that than anything. "She betrayed us. After all Rose has been through, I don't think Avanna ever cared about helping her, or any of us. She betrayed everything she claimed to stand for—everything Veritas was built around."

Hector hesitated, mouth hanging open. But Raif knew he was honourable— he'd make a promise to save Rose, no matter the cost. His mouth clapped shut and he grimaced, taking his time with the next words. "If it comes to it, lad. Only if. Our priority is to save Rose."

Raif considered pushing on, trying for a more definite response, but decided to let it be. He gave a curt nod. "Good. Let's go then. My sister needs us."

He didn't wait for Hector to respond. He straightened his cloak, held his head high, and marched onwards.

I'm coming, Rose.

I'm coming.

34

Evelyn

At the sound of the door unlocking, Evelyn clenched her jaw with defiance—even though her heart was beating so fast she could scarce focus on anything else. She'd barely slept after Lord Torrant's visit.

He'll soon know my lack of powers and I'll be a slave to the Commune.

She shuddered, unable to repress the trickle of fear running down her spine.

When the door opened to reveal Clim, she breathed a sigh of relief. At least she had a few more moments before meeting Lord Torrant's cold, calculating eyes again. The servant bowed his head to her and proffered a hand towards the open door.

"This way," he said. "My Lord is not a man to be kept waiting."

Evelyn gulped, shuffling from the room on leaden legs. The walk back to the study felt far longer than yesterday, yet not long enough to gain a hold over her fraying nerves. As they approached, she heard hushed voices inside. The talking stopped as soon as the door was opened. She glimpsed Commander Sulemon moving away from the table, red cloak draped over broad, proud shoulders as he stared out of the window. The room was filled with the sickeningly rich smell of breakfast; on the long dining table was set more food than she'd ever seen, even in the village feasts at Little Haven. Her stomach clenched as snakes of nausea coiled up her throat.

Lord Torrant gave her a hollow smile. "Evelyn," he said. "I trust you slept well." She drew her mouth into a hard line and said nothing.

Clim stepped to Lord Torrant's side and whispered into his ear. Once finished, the servant was waved away and left the room.

"I'm told you haven't eaten." Lord Torrant ushered her toward the table. "It's important you get your energy up in preparation for displaying your powers." He smirked.

Evelyn glared at him as he pulled out a chair and shoved her down. She stared blankly at the plates before her—all manner of eggs, a platter of ham slices glistening with honey, fresh bread and spiced potatoes, pots of tea steaming and fragrant, a spread of fruits sliced and piled high, milky oats mixed with berries, bacon and sausages that were crisp and fragrant. She swallowed, mouth filling with the bitter taste of bile.

"Eat," Lord Torrant said, standing to her side. She kept her hands in her lap, head raised, staring directly ahead. She saw, with a wave of satisfaction, his growing agitation—one hand clenched at his side whilst the other moved to rest on her shoulder; he clearly wasn't used to being ignored. *Good.* She tried to shift away but he dug his fingers in.

"Oh," she sighed. The sound was involuntary, little more than an exhale, as a strange feeling began to flow through her. Without wanting to, she began to pile her plate with food. Perhaps she was hungry.

"Is that really necessary?" Commander Sulemon's eyes blazed as he strode to the table.

"I don't believe that's your concern," Lord Torrant retorted.

"The girl doesn't need to be forced, I'm su—"

"Commander Sulemon, you are speaking out of turn." Lord Torrant let go of her and faced the soldier. Evelyn gasped, the dominating pressure leaving her body and her own control returning like a flood of ice through her veins. She dropped the slice of bread she'd been holding. *Is that what it feels like? It's that quick?*

Is that how Arthur felt when I—

"I'll let her starve, Jonah. Will that make you happy?" Lord Torrant lifted his chin, daring the Commander to challenge him further. Their eyes were locked. For a long moment, a strained silence hung between them. Evelyn couldn't tell which man would break first.

Finally, Commander Sulemon bowed his head. "I spoke out of turn, my Lord," he said. "Forgive me."

Something about the defeat made Evelyn pity him, the feeling sitting like ice in her gut; she did not like holding anything other than hatred for a

Commune soldier. She cleared her throat. "I'll eat," she said, shovelling some potato and eggs into her mouth. She chewed with growing disgust, the rich flavours turning to ash on her tongue. She struggled to swallow, reached for her glass, and found it empty. Noticing her discomfort, Commander Sulemon filled a mug with spiced tea and handed it to her. She drank the steaming liquid.

"Sit, Jonah," Lord Torrant said. "She's capable of retrieving her own drink."

The Commander sat to Lord Torrant's left, Evelyn to his right. The air crackled with tension as they ate, pressing down with suffocating heaviness as the silence stretched. Trying to ignore her discomfort, Evelyn ate, gulping down food she didn't taste, afraid of triggering another show of dominance between the men.

After forcing down what she could, Evelyn set down her cutlery.

"Well," Lord Torrant said abruptly, standing and straightening his shirt sleeves. "Shall we?" He waited for Evelyn and Commander Sulemon to rise before walking towards the door.

Evelyn focused on placing one foot in front of the other, legs trembling. It was happening. The chance for escape was gone—had never really presented itself. *How did I end up here?* At the back of her mind, a niggling voice whispered the response. *By trusting Mak. Trusting Avanna.* She'd known from the start. Wanted to speak her fears to Raif, but too consumed with protecting him and Rose, she'd ignored the concern in her heart, and now there was nothing to do but pay for it.

Even as she vowed to never ignore her instincts again, a stronger fear took over: soon, it wouldn't matter anyway.

Lord Torrant led them back in the direction of her bedroom, stopping outside a door she hadn't noticed before, almost indistinguishable from the dark wood panelling of the walls.

Clim emerged from the shadows behind them, clutching a flickering oil lantern in one hand and a large brass key in the other. From his own waistcoat pocket, Lord Torrant retrieved a similar key. He placed them into two adjacent holes in the door and turned them in unison, locks clicking open as he did so.

"Make sure we are not disturbed," Lord Torrant said to Clim, taking the lantern from the servant's hand. The gaunt man nodded, melting back into the shadows.

Lord Torrant pushed open the door and stepped inside, waving his hand for Evelyn and the Commander to follow. Evelyn glanced down the corridor for what she imagined would be the final time, then stepped over the threshold.

She was hit immediately by stale air as she began descending a flight of stairs. She did her best not to cough, afraid to inhale the suffocating odour. Their footsteps echoed too loudly from the walls around them. She fought back a shiver, wrapping her arms around her chest.

Before long, they came to the bottom of the staircase. Lord Torrant held the lantern up, illuminating half of his face. "You will speak of this to no one."

Evelyn wasn't sure whether Lord Torrant's words were meant for her or Commander Sulemon. It didn't matter.

Lord Torrant pushed open another creaking door. The air inside the room washed across Evelyn's face and she twisted her head away, sickened by the rotten stench. She had a flash of memory from Little Haven. The cows had been taken by sickness one summer. She'd helped to burn the carcasses, the whole village working together to purge the plague from their livestock. Before the flames had been lit, the bodies lay in a haphazard pile outside the village. The smell hitting her now was as it had been then: disease, decay, death.

Lord Torrant shook out a kerchief and held it over his nose before stepping inside. She stood at the doorway, afraid to go any further into the foul-smelling darkness. The glow of the oil lamp moved around the room as Lord Torrant lit candles within sconces upon the damp stone walls.

Gradually, the room was illuminated. The furnishings were few; a mouldering straw-filled mattress bundled with a pile of rags in one corner, a small wooden stool beside it. Her heart pounded. She'd expected opulence, a gross show of wealth as with the rest of the mansion, a smoke screen to imply prestige in her trial, a great honouring of the Commune and its work.

The room was nothing of the sort.

Her eyes darted around, waiting for the dim candlelight to reveal something—anything—that might make her fate clear. She became aware of Lord Torrant's eyes upon her.

"There's no use in standing out there, girl," he said. "Come in."

She wilted under his gaze, taking tentative steps into the room. Breathing deeply to steel herself, she shuffled closer to the mattress. Lord Torrant sat on the wooden stool, watching her as she drew nearer. Perhaps he wanted her to lie down upon it ... Was this part of the test? She found herself too afraid to ask.

Fleeing the tavern, escaping Castleton, being exiled from Veritas—Evelyn had thought she'd felt true dread these past weeks. Yet in this filthy room, she was gripped by a terror she'd never experienced before. Her body shook, her legs threatened to collapse, she couldn't speak if she'd wanted to. *This is it,* the voice in her head repeated. She faced Lord Torrant and began to lower herself down.

"No!" Commander Sulemon cried. She froze, waiting to be punished for whatever she'd done wrong. "What is this?" He stepped forward, expression a mixture of horror and despair.

I didn't know. No one told me what to do! Where do I— And then she realised his fury was directed at Lord Torrant, his hand pointing towards the mattress. Evelyn felt a stab of apprehension; what had she missed? She turned slowly.

As her eyes adjusted, she gasped, hand flying to her mouth. A pile of rags ... No, though at first it had appeared so. As she gazed down at them, the rags shifted. They shuffled and jerked, and she began to see shapes, still uncertain of what they were until they barely moulded into the loosest semblance of a human form. Evelyn couldn't even scream. She'd never seen a body so mangled. Whatever—whoever—it had been, they were broken, skeletal, half-dead. She would have assumed them to be a corpse, were it not for the twitches—the tiniest proof there was still breath left.

"Who- who-" she stuttered, stumbling backwards.

"Don't you recognise him, Jonah?" Lord Torrant said coolly. "I'd have thought you would, given how *intimately* you came to know one another."

"No, no," the Commander muttered, dropping to his knees beside the mattress. He reached a shaking arm towards the broken form, strangled half-sobs coming from his throat. "What have you done?"

Lord Torrant laughed, slapping his leg with what was somehow genuine merriment. But when he stood, the pleasure was gone from his face. He leant down to speak into the Commander's ear, though Evelyn heard every word in that all-too-quiet room.

"Did you think I didn't know? He got what he deserved. Now keep your mouth shut, *Commander*, or face the consequences."

Commander Sulemon's head dropped. He took a moment to calm his ragged breaths, arm dropping to his side. "Eirik," he croaked. "You didn't—"

Lord Torrant turned his back on him. "Silence. Your words mean nothing now."

Silently, the Commander stood, walked away from the mattress, and positioned himself in front of the door. His face was blank, his breathing shallow. He beat his fist weakly against his chest—one final sign of obedience.

Evelyn was frozen. The men didn't seem to see her at all. No part of her mind could make sense of this. All she knew was that she was a witness to a truly awful deed. *And witnesses don't often live to tell their secrets.*

As she looked between the Commander and Lord Torrant, she realised the prisoner—*a man, perhaps?*—was shifting, groaning. She allowed her eyes to rove over his broken body once more. His limbs jutted out, mottled by cuts and bruises. He was missing two fingers on his left hand, three on his right. As she watched, he held up a disfigured arm to cover his face as though somehow through the pain, he still knew to be ashamed of his appearance.

"H-h-h—" The broken man's mouth flapped open and closed. He moaned, perhaps with frustration, and Evelyn suddenly came back to herself. She took a step forward, waited to be stopped. When she wasn't, she moved to the mattress and knelt down.

"Who ... who is he?" she whispered. She looked to Commander Sulemon. He didn't seem to hear her.

"I hardly think that matters." Lord Torrant sniffed. "It's time for your test, girl."

"My test," she said, trying to gather her focus even as her vision swam. She wanted to look anywhere but at the decrepit body before her.

"He can't hurt you." Lord Torrant's voice was almost melodic, his lips curled with amusement. "He can't hurt anyone. He barely knows you're here." He shoved Evelyn so she fell forward onto the mattress. "You should have no problem using your *powers* on him. If you have any, that is."

She gasped, pushing back from the man. His legs splayed out from beneath him, bones clearly outlined beneath his pale skin. He rested awkwardly to one side, breathing fast and ragged. Last of all, she forced herself to see his face. Black hair clung to his scalp. His face was bruised and broken, misshapen as though bones had been shattered and allowed to heal in the wrong places. His pale blue eyes were unblinking, watery and bloodshot; within them, she could see nothing.

"I …" She looked over her shoulder, saw the expectant delight on Lord Torrant's face. Part of her wished she could prove him wrong—that she had Rose's powers.

I'd kill them all. Every last one. Even as the pity turned to rage, she knew the truth. Every day since she was taken from Veritas had been counting down to this moment, to her test. She'd fail, her mind would be taken over, and she'd be thrown in a field, unable to remember her own name. *My time has run out.* All she could do was try and fool Lord Torrant into thinking there were still a few seconds—a few precious moments—left.

Evelyn took a deep breath and reached for the man. His scabbed lips were slightly parted, drool running down his chin. *Just put on a show,* she told herself, clasping the bony fingers remaining on his left hand.

Please, please, please … She scrunched her eyes shut.

Nothing.

How long could she keep up this ruse? Minutes at the most.

She centred herself, trying to recall what she'd done to force her powers the first time. But she knew, of course, *she* hadn't even really done it—they'd been ripped from her. *Please, just another minute.*

"What's taking so long?" Lord Torrant's breath prickled against her neck, making the hairs stand up along her arms.

"I- I need to concentrate," she said, frowning over her shoulder. He sneered but backed away. Taking another long inhale, Evelyn faced the man once more.

Raif, Rose and Dog. Hector and Cara. Bessie.

Avanna and Mak.

Arthur. Elder Alwyn.

She reached for them—living or dead—wherever they were. She imagined herself connected to them, blocking out what they were, forcing the good and bad to lose shape and blend into unified energy. *Please just something, something,* she begged.

She reached for the mind of the man before her, desperate for forgiveness from him, tortured and half-dead—forgiveness for even trying, for disturbing what little rest his broken body might still be able to find.

It's now or never, the voice in her mind whispered. *He won't wait much longer.* She felt furious at the voice, knowing it was her own; at Arthur and the heartless village Elders who refused to believe what he'd done to her; at Avanna and Mak, Lord Torrant and Commander Sulemon, and every damned red cloak she'd ever seen. Most of all, that her final thoughts were on them—perhaps the last thing she'd ever remember.

No. Not them. Evelyn felt the thought like a slap, absolute and sure, and steeled herself. *They won't take more of my life.* She reached further—past the fear and anger and sorrow. She thought of Hector, his foolish jokes at the worst times; of Raif, so bloody hard-headed but loyal to his bones; of Rose, young and innocent yet so powerful; of Bessie, a friend and protector above all else; of Bert, of Dog, of Cara, of …

Keep going, the voice urged. *Just a little bit more.*

And then, all at once, as if it had always been there, she felt it. Something inside of herself, something warm. A fire, but a crackling comfort—not the raging blaze she'd released before. And within it, another thought, another mind that was not her own. It was dim, distant, but within reach.

Reach. It was confused, afraid, weak, but it was there. What was more, she was sure it *knew* she was there. Like the candle flames around her, it flickered and wavered but stayed steady and even glowed brighter as she grasped for it.

She'd never felt anything like it—it was *within* her but separate too.

What is this? She asked herself, and the response that came was from that *other.*

H-h-help m-me.

Her eyes shot open—for a second, they met the blue ones before her, and she saw where the voice had come from, knew what had happened, and—

Lord Torrant grabbed her arm and twisted her round, shattering the connection in an instant. She tried to cling to it, to hear the voice again, though she didn't know how. She thought of Rose, Raif, Hector again, but nothing.

"Pathetic," Lord Torrant said, spittle glistening on his lip. "Weak. Just as I knew you were the first time I met you. That's why I didn't take you in that tavern. I knew your value then—or lack of it." He squeezed her arm even harder and she yelped. On the mattress, the man let out the most anguished moan yet.

"How does it feel, girl?" Lord Torrant's face was ablaze. "You've sealed your own fate, I can assure you." His breath washed over her face, hot and sweet-smelling. She tried to pull away, but he was too strong.

"Please," she whispered, tears blurring her vision. *I was doing it, I felt it, I didn't fail, please, please.*

"Lord Torrant," Commander Sulemon said, moving for the first time since being disciplined. "Let me escort the girl upstairs."

"What?" Lord Torrant let out a bark of laughter. "Grown fond of the bitch, have you? You always were a fool."

The Commander flinched, but he remained steadfast. "Let me take her to your study. We can discuss what is best for—"

With his free hand, Lord Torrant whipped a back-handed slap across the Commander's face. Blood splattered across the floor; Commander Sulemon held a hand up to his split lip. Evelyn watched, new waves of fear for what the men would do rooted her to the spot, until something clawed at the back of her leg. She cried out in shock and jerked to the side, pulling Lord Torrant with her. The broken man was face down, half off the mattress, his arm stretched out, his remaining fingers clawing open and closed.

"H-he-help," he wheezed.

Before Evelyn could respond, Lord Torrant shoved her to the ground. She landed on her side, the wind knocked from her lungs.

Lord Torrant left her where she was, leaping towards the man on the mattress. "No one said you could move," he spat. He shoved the man backwards, causing his head to hit the wall with a *crack*. "You whore." A slap to the face. "You disgusting piece of filth." A punch to the stomach. He lashed out with such violence, Evelyn was shocked that he'd retained any modicum of control before now. The unnamed man seemed to have, mercifully, lost consciousness, yet Lord Torrant continued the beating.

"No!" Commander Sulemon shouted. "Stop!" He grabbed hold of Lord Torrant, pulling him away from the mattress.

"Come to protect your *lover*, have you Jonah?" Lord Torrant's face was splattered with dark splotches of blood, his eyes wide, teeth bared. He thrashed wildly against the Commander's grasp, wordless cries echoing around the room. He managed to wriggle free of Commander Sulemon's grip, lunging towards

Evelyn where she still lay on the floor. He pinned her down, hands wrapped around her throat, and she felt waves emanating from him—crashing, violent, inescapable, pure rage drowning her, tumbling her over and over. She tried to break her head above the current, just one breath, one gulp of air; it was impossible.

Her mind went blank.

You'll never amount to anything.

She made a cage—locked herself away, saving herself from whatever came next. She watched through almost disconnected eyes, as though floating above her own body. She saw Commander Sulemon heave Lord Torrant away from her, slamming him into the wall beside the door, holding him suspended. Lord Torrant's legs dangled above the floor, his face reddening.

"Evelyn!" Commander Sulemon shouted. "Run!"

She couldn't. There were no hands at her neck and yet the crushing waves were still too strong, her arms refusing to push her up. She wanted to scream, yet couldn't find the breath. She watched as Lord Torrant thrashed against the Commander, eyes bulging, mouth twisting with breathless curses. The air suddenly felt heavy with a growing, crackling pressure. It pressed down on her, suffocating, smothering, strangling.

"Evelyn," Commander Sulemon yelled again. His voice cracked. He leant backwards and slammed Lord Torrant into the wall once more.

The waves receded; Evelyn gasped, her arms flying up, suddenly freed from some invisible weight. She lunged forward, landing painfully on her hands and knees.

The man on the mattress uttered a low gurgle as bloody drool ran down his chin. It was dark, black, thick. She couldn't help him. No one could.

She scrabbled towards the door, tearing her fingernails on the filthy ground, ignoring the sharp pain in her ankle as she sprang to her feet. The air grew heavy again, the waves of power trying to pull her back in, the currents making her legs stiff and leaden. She looked to Commander Sulemon.

"Go!" he screamed.

She ripped the door open, sprinting up the stairs.

35

Commander Sulemon

Commander Sulemon watched Evelyn finally stumble to her feet. He grimaced, pushing his arm harder. Lord Torrant bucked against him, face reddening, eyes widening and almost bulging from his face.

"Jonah," he wheezed, laying a hand on the Commander's shoulder. He knew what Lord Torrant was trying to do. It was pointless—he was immune to powers thanks to the protection of his beloved Goddess. Lord Torrant knew it too, yet still he desperately flung his powers outwards, trying to control whatever he could. The Commander gritted his teeth and pushed back against the warming sensation running from Lord Torrant's touch, feeling it reach the impenetrable wall in his mind.

Lord Torrant cried out, punching his fist into the Commander's arm. In response, Commander Sulemon tightened his grip, pinning him back harder still.

Evelyn was at the door. She hesitated, glancing towards him. *Stupid girl.* "Go!" he cried. She pulled open the door, disappeared into the darkness beyond.

At last, he turned his full attention to Lord Torrant. He held his grip just long enough to give Evelyn a fighting chance before slackening his hand, allowing Lord Torrant's feet to touch the floor, though still keeping him pinned to the wall with a forearm.

"You said one day we would be together again. Did you ever mean it?"

Lord Torrant's eyes widened. "The Grand Magister," he wheezed. "He made me see ..."

The Commander tightened his hold again, the anger he'd contained for so long finally unleashed. "What?" he cried, shoving Lord Torrant's head against the wall. "Made you see what?"

Lord Torrant closed his eyes, face purpling, breath whistling in his throat, yet Commander Sulemon would not let go. He'd been lied to, kept in blind ignorance, betrayed his people, been loyal to—in love with—what? A man he might have never known. Working for a regime that exploited the very powers he despised.

Veritarra forgive me, I have been so blind.

He forced his former lover against the wall one more time, then backed away. Lord Torrant dropped to his knees, slumping forward, taking great gulps of that awful, stale air.

For a time, all that could be heard was his choked breaths. Then he stood and leant against the wall upon which he'd been pinned, rubbing a hand to his bruised throat.

"Don't go after her," the Commander growled.

"What a mess we've made, Jonah," Lord Torrant croaked. "Why? Why let her go?"

We. Never able to take the blame. Commander Sulemon's fury peaked again, threatened to consume him altogether, and he took a moment to calm himself before nodding towards the unconscious form behind them. *Cole.* "You know why," he said, trying his best to keep his voice from quivering. "You would have killed her for knowing a secret you forced her to see."

Lord Torrant straightened his clothing, regaining his usual air of aloof control as he coolly observed the straw mattress. "You always were naïve, Jonah," he said. "I will confess though, when I found out about him," he waved his arm towards Cole's slumped form, "I was surprised. I never took you to be a man who would *pay*—"

"You have no right," the Commander snapped. *Naïve. As if that is what caused this to happen.* "Seven years have passed. When you sent me away that day, you broke me. Then you summoned me back, promising we would one day return to what we were. *One day.* Always just *one* more. You have expected me to stand by your side, remain loyal, never ask questions—to serve you." He shook his head, sneering—as disgusted with himself as the man before him. "Always you."

"And yet, this is because of you," Lord Torrant said calmly, rationally, as if the words he spoke were the height of reason. He let out a resigned sigh, moving towards the mattress. "I couldn't let him live."

"You haven't let him die."

Lord Torrant glanced over his shoulder, eyes gleaming. "No. He took what was mine. He had to be punished."

The Commander closed his eyes, exhaling slowly. *What was mine. I've always been a possession to him.* He opened his eyes reluctantly, watching Cole's broken and bloodied form for a moment. "What have you done to him?"

"It's nothing I haven't done before. You know, it's truly remarkable what a person can be made to do to themselves with enough focus. My powers have been honed remarkably."

Commander Sulemon's heart skipped a beat. "What?"

Lord Torrant shook his head. "It's like I said, Jonah. You always were naïve." He tugged at his shirt sleeves, smoothed down his waistcoat. "Why do you think I sent you away all those years ago? You never would have allowed such … *ruthless* behaviour, but it was what was needed. The Grand Magister helped me to see that. How do you think I came to inherit my family title, this house?"

The Commander's brow furrowed. "But you … Your brother. There was a hunting accident. You sent me away, told me there was something you needed to do …" He held back a choke as understanding dawned on him. "I … I see." Seven years … *And you never even suspected. So blind. So fucking stupid.*

Lord Torrant laughed, the sound filling the room, bouncing off the walls. "Oh, Jonah. Yes, now you see. A hunting *accident.* No, no. My dear Ythan was a skilled hunter; he would never have succumbed to anything so predictable. He deserved what he got, just like this one. Worse, really, but my brother's body gave out far quicker than this, this … *whore.*" He spat the word, momentarily dropping his cool façade. He pushed back his black hair, scraping it away from his face, regaining himself. "Surprising, really, given how young and delicate he is."

The amusement in his voice was too much. Revulsion stabbed through the Commander's gut. "How could you, Eirik?"

"How could I?" Lord Torrant said, turning on him. "How could *you?* After all we've been through, you seek the pleasure of some pathetic little …" His

346 - LUCY A. McLAREN

nostrils flared as he stared up at the Commander. "You belong to me, Jonah. *Me*. What do you not understand about—"

The Commander smashed his fist into Lord Torrant's face. The anger coursed through him, pumping through his veins—his whole body shaking, burning, crying out with it. He stared at the man before him as though for the first time. "I have waited for a partner," he growled. "Not a master."

Lord Torrant held a hand against his nose, blood pouring over his lips and into his beard. "I have done all I can to protect you, Jonah," he said, voice a cracked whisper. "After all we've been through, you must know. I have loved you since that first day, so many years ago. Two people—such different lives— finding one another."

The Commander's hands were clenched so tight, they trembled at his sides. *Love. He truly thinks that is what he feels.* He breathed slowly, unfurling his fists, rubbing his pounding temples. He glanced between Lord Torrant and Cole, hoping the poor man's body had finally given out and allowed him the release of death. But then he saw the shallow flutter of Cole's chest and he couldn't stand to be in that place any longer, to see the suffering continue. He turned his back on Lord Torrant.

"Jonah. Don't you understand why I've done this? It's for you—it always has been."

The Commander had no doubt he truly believed his own words.

"Jonah, please."

Commander Sulemon felt the pull between them, tugging at that hollow spot beneath his ribs where his heart had once been, beckoning him back.

"Don't leave. I didn't want you to leave then—those years ago. I had no choice. I don't want you to leave now. And, this time ... this time is different. I have more authority than before. The Grand Magister will listen. Please."

The Commander turned around to find Lord Torrant closer than anticipated, already reaching a hand up to caress the Commander's cheek. It stayed there for a moment and he allowed himself to cherish its warmth. *No.*

The Commander groaned, finally seeing the test he had been put through, seeing the pieces fall into place. Lord Torrant had waited—weeks, months?—to reveal Cole. To corner him. Waited for a clear sign—*the perfume, the wine, the memories, they were all baits, to make you believe there was something left.* And last night, he'd made the Commander reveal, one more time, his dedication, his feelings, his struggles. *Just to show you today that it would not matter.*

"You gave me this red cloak, Eirik," he said, the name tasting rotten on his tongue. "Since then, I have been your commander. At *your* order. Nothing more."

Lord Torrant nodded. "I couldn't tell you the truth. I feared what you would think." His face leant up, moving so close their lips almost touched. "A red cloak to remain by my side. It was all I could do. But I love you, you must know. You've always known."

"I was so proud when you sent me my cloak," the Commander said. "But it was a contract—a purchase—not a promise."

Lord Torrant flinched, brow creasing with agitation. "No, Jonah," he whispered. "Now you know the truth; there are no secrets. We are- are equal, finally. We can go back."

Commander Sulemon did not answer.

"Jonah, we'll find the girl. I understand why you let her go, but she must be taken under the Commune's control. She cannot be free—not after what she's seen. And then we shall make our move against that traitorous camp where you were imprisoned. The Grand Magister will see our worth, both of us, *together.*"

The Commander knew he could have been persuaded then. He could forget what he'd been told; he could turn away from the Commune's—from Lord Torrant's—cruelty and continue his service—continue as he had been these past thirteen years. Wouldn't that be easier?

But then a groan filled the room. Cole—or what remained of him. It was sorrowful, pain-wracked, and it shattered any illusions Commander Sulemon had left. *Easier, yes. Lies are always easier.*

"There is nothing to go back to." He pushed Lord Torrant away. Without pause, he moved towards Cole's unconscious form on the mattress. "I'm sorry," he whispered. He lifted the young man's head—light as a feather—and twisted with as much force as he could muster, hearing the telling crack of his neck breaking. There was a final, wheezing exhale before the broken form fell still.

It was the least he could do for the poor fool whose only crime had been to resemble the man he loved.

"Jonah." Lord Torrant's voice was quiet and pleading, almost a whimper.

He didn't turn, instead striding for the door, twisting the handle, sweaty palms slipping over it.

"Please, Jonah."

He opened the door and stepped out into the stairway before his resolve could leave him. He waited for the cries to turn to shouts, for the rage to take over. He prepared himself for hands on his back, for blows to his legs, for another desperate sweep of power over him. There was none. The Lord had sacrificed all his pieces at once; he was alone, and there was no one left to use.

The Commander's vision blurred, but he push himself onwards. *Veritarra guide me.* As he walked up the stairs, legs slow and heavy, he unfastened the silver brooch securing his red woollen cloak. He let it fall around him, releasing the position that bound him to Lord Torrant.

Veritarra, thank you.

36

Hector

Ever since Avanna had taken Rose, Hector had tried to stay strong for Raif. As they continued on their journey to Nook Town, however, his own guilt became more and more overwhelming.

How could I not see what Avanna had planned? The question circled round his mind, taunting him, tormenting his every waking moment. *The talk of Nomarrans, her interest in the prisoner …*

How could you have known? She kept her full plans hidden from you. She knew you'd try to stop her. Cara's comfort did little to ease the heaviness in the pit of his stomach.

All he could do was lead Raif onwards in the hope they'd catch up with Avanna and Rose sooner rather than later.

With a sturdy horse like Bert, they'd managed to make good headway. The day after leaving the camp, they'd trotted at a steady pace until early afternoon. As he walked beside Bert to stretch his legs, Hector knew they would need to stop again soon, though he sensed that Raif wouldn't want them to slow. The lad's desperation was evident the longer they travelled—eyes darting about for any sign of his sister or the woman who had taken her, though they'd discovered nothing so far. Hector reasoned that this was nothing to be concerned about; Avanna might have taken a different road, after all. Ultimately, that road would converge with theirs. If necessary, they would follow her all the way to Nook Town.

He knew he had to keep a clear head for the lad as well as for his own sanity. *I've made too many mistakes, missed too many things. No more.*

He pulled the horse to a halt and climbed down, ignoring the lad's pointed glare. "We need to rest and eat," he said. "And this poor, old sod," he patted Bert on the neck, "deserves a break as well." He held a hand up to help Raif from the horse's back.

Raif accepted the help, though his tight-lipped expression made it clear he wasn't happy with Hector's decision. As he landed beside Hector, his eyes roved towards the tree line on the horizon, face paling.

"Haven Forest?" Hector asked. *We have made good time.*

Raif's nod was curt; his expression was guarded, eyes glossy.

"I'm sorry, I didn't realise we were so close to your home."

Raif shrugged, turning away to hide his face. Hector left him alone for a short time, busying himself feeding Bert. Cara weaved round his legs with a low purr before trotting towards the distant treeline, a white blur amongst the rich colours of autumn.

"Where's she going?" Raif asked, gaze lingering on the forest.

"To find some food," Hector said. "She's a good hunter."

Raif puffed out his lips. "Father tried to teach me to hunt in that place." He laughed, eyes dancing with joy for the briefest of moments. "Tried. I was too stubborn to listen to him. And now …" He gulped. "Now it's too late."

"I'd say he'd be proud of how far you've come with your shooting," Hector said, realising too late the implication of his words. *Mak.*

Raif fiddled with his tunic. "I didn't want to kill him, you know," he said. "He just …"

Hector swallowed. "I know," he said. "We had to get away. You did what you thought was best." He turned away so the lad couldn't see the disappointment in his eyes. *Another mistake. Another impulsive action I couldn't see until it was too late. Mak, you fool. Why didn't you let us go? You'd better not die on me.*

Hector had thought constantly of Mak since leaving Veritas. He'd played it over and over in his mind, convincing himself he was sure Mak had shifted after he fell, had groaned with pain, that the boy's arrow had met skin and fat, nothing vital. He prayed his memories were true.

He moved to Bert's saddlebag and retrieved some hard sausage, bread and cheese, handing some to Raif before looking at the nearby treeline. "Would you like to go there now? To Little Haven? To see what's …"

"Left?" Raif chewed on the bread, turning his back on the forest. "No," he said curtly. "No, I don't think so."

"Alright. Come on, let's walk. Stretch our legs. Though I don't much like the look of those clouds ahead."

"Okay," Raif said, casting a final gaze towards Haven Forest. "Hector?"

"Yes, lad?" Hector clicked Bert on, gently leading him by the reins.

"We'll find Rose, won't we?"

"I promised you, Raif. We'll find her."

If it's the last thing I do.

"Now let's see if we can find somewhere to shelter before that storm reaches us."

They drudged onwards as the rain began to fall, snacking as they went on over-ripe berries picked from bushes along the roadside. Before long, they could scarce see ahead. The road was streamed with mud and they were soaked to the bone. Overhead, the sky was dark as the storm raged around them. Peering around, Hector noticed an abandoned farmhouse and indicated it to Raif.

"Let's get some shelter," he called, shouting over the near-deafening rain.

Raif opened his mouth to protest.

"Now, lad." Hector shook his head. "I see how much you're shaking. Won't do you any good to freeze yourself to death before you can save your sister."

Raif's frown deepened, though he followed Hector into the farmhouse nonetheless.

Still no sign, Cara noted, darting back to his side from where she'd been scouting ahead.

Hector glanced down at her, blinking back the streaming raindrops. *Which means it's more and more likely I can't avoid the place.*

I'll be with you, his companion reminded him. *We'll be together.* He gave her an appreciative smile, though they both knew it would not be so simple in Nook Town.

Inside the farmhouse, the floor was littered with dried leaves, twigs, and debris. Hector brushed aside space for them in front of the hearth, leaving great wet puddles wherever he went.

"Stack of wood over in that corner, lad. Fetch it to the fireplace."

Raif moved about his task without complaint while Hector saw to the horse outside. There was an overhang from the house that would keep Bert dry enough for the night. The animal had a gentleness that Hector was growing fond of, regardless of his personal misgivings about horses. Despite the length of their journey, Bert's mood had remained content. He was strong and reliable, just what they needed. Hector touched the animal's brown nose, an image of Evelyn flickering into his mind as he did so.

"She was kind to you, eh?" He smiled, studying the emerging stars overhead. "Strong-headed she was. Strong-headed, but there was good in her. I hope she's safe."

"You hope who's safe?" Raif asked from inside the doorway.

"Evelyn," he said, wiping the water from his dripping moustache as he moved back into the farmhouse. "I hope Evelyn's safe."

"Ah," Raif said. "I've been wondering about that." He squatted before the fireplace and began arranging the wood. "Avanna told us she ran away—freed the soldier and fled the camp. But what if she was lying? Why should we believe her now after what she's done? I never really believed Evelyn would leave us, even after ..." His gaze dropped. "Well, it just didn't feel right."

Hector leant down to help with the fire. "I hadn't thought of that," he admitted. "Mayhap you're right, lad. Though the lass had a stubbornness about her, didn't she? Might be she thought she was helping in her own way by leaving." He struck his flint and the fire sputtered into life, helped by some leftover kindling from the last occupants of the ruined shelter. As the flames grew, Hector rubbed his hands over it, glad for the heat in his cold and tired limbs.

"I don't know. I wish we could be sure. I wish I knew where she was—knew she was safe." Raif sat back on the wooden floor, jamming a piece of broken wood into the fire. "Everything is such a mess."

Hector had no words to offer; instead, he reached a hand to rest on Raif's shoulder, his powers flowing forth to provide some small comfort. To his surprise, the lad shook his head.

"No, Hector," he said. "I appreciate what you're doing. It's just ... It's those *powers*. Shit." He threw the piece of wood in the fire. "Everything—all the terrible things that've happened—they come down to those powers; my home gone, my father dead, my mother taken and I'm not sure I'll ever see her again … whether she's even still alive. Rose, Evelyn, Avanna, the Commune—all of it." He let out a weary sigh. "I know you're trying to be kind, but … no. I'd rather feel, even the terrible things."

Hector withdrew his hand, running it through his soaking hair. "Very wise of you. You're right. I'm sorry, lad."

"Thank you," Raif said.

Avanna had hurt them both, betrayed their trust. Hector knew he couldn't compare his injured pride to what Raif had lost. He had to see this through to the end no matter the cost. He fetched his lavender tea supplies from Bert's saddlebags and prepared some in a pot over the fire.

"Here, lad. This'll help you sleep."

Raif took the steaming cup, clasping it between his hands as he stared into the fire. After a time, he cleared his throat and turned to Hector. "What can you tell me about Nook Town?" he asked. "You said they hate those with powers—that they'll have laid a trap for Avanna. What if we don't find them before they get there?"

Hector had been dreading the question, knowing where the conversation might lead, but he also knew he couldn't lie. "To tell the truth, I haven't been back in some years. I can't say for sure what they might wish to do with Rose. They despise powers, yes, but they fear those with them, too." He leant his head back, exhaling a long breath. "If they reach Nook Town before us, I will do all I can to free Rose. You have my word on that. We'll get her back, lad. We'll get her back."

Raif studied his face, eyes flickering with reflected firelight. "Okay," he said, running his hands across his face. "I know I've been … bad company. But I can't imagine being alone. Thank you for being with me, Hector."

"Think nothing of it," Hector croaked, swallowing back the hard lump in his throat.

Raif gave a fleeting smile. "Now, do you have any more of that far-too-chewy bread?"

Hector chuckled. "Of course," he said. "Nice bit of jaw ache before bed, what could be better?"

Raif laughed. "Exactly," he said. That moment of joy, as bright and fleeting as the sparks drifting from the fire, lit Hector's determination more fiercely than ever.

They finished their meals and Hector rolled his fur cloak out on the floor. "Get some sleep, lad," he said. "I'll wake you when the rain's stopped."

"But what about you?" Raif asked, barely able to stifle a yawn.

"I'll be fine. I promised to keep you safe and that's what I'll do. Don't you worry about me."

Raif wrapped himself up, falling asleep soon after his head touched the ground.

You can rest, too. Cara rubbed her head against his leg. *I can keep watch.*

"It's alright, my love," he whispered, running a hand along her back. "I want to watch over the lad."

You don't have to punish yourself.

"Don't I?" He stretched, cracking his neck. "Don't worry. I'll be fine."

As he sat beside the fire waiting for the hours to tick by, he recalled a prayer from his childhood.

By Perisma's light we are blessed,

By Perisma's light we are shown the way.

Bless me with your light, Perisma. Help me find the lass.

He almost scoffed at his own ridiculous desperation. He knew the hate that awaited him in Nook Town—the disdain he would meet in the eyes of the townsfolk. Praying to their god had never gotten him anywhere, even as a child.

Still, he had no choice. As he fought sleep, he thought of his last day with Evelyn—of her request that he watch over Raif and Rose if she couldn't.

Perhaps the girl knew then she would leave. Cara, as always, his blessed voice of reason. But this time he felt his companion may be looking at the wrong signs.

Hector shook his head. *The lad may be angry, may be young, but he's clever, too. There's only one reason I can imagine Evelyn leaving the children for.*

Cara's thought was barely a whisper, *She was forced.*

Hector nodded. *Avanna doesn't know what she's gotten herself into. What she's gotten all of us into.*

Do you think the girl is safe?

I'll tell you as I told Raif—we will find his sister.

Not that girl.

Hector watched the flames devour the largest log at the centre of the pile. *We'll find them both.* He glanced at Raif, who lay motionless in a deep sleep. *I don't think the lad will survive if we don't.*

A few minutes went by, and Hector felt Cara drift to sleep as well. When the storm passed, they'd move on—to Avanna, to Rose, and then on to Evelyn. In a few days, they'd be at the gates of Nook Town.

37

Evelyn

Her mind was focused only on escape.

She'd been here once before. Desperate, alone, afraid. She could do it again.

When Evelyn burst out of the door of that awful basement, Clim was there. He lunged at her, bony fingers clasping for her arm, but she managed to shoulder past the old bastard, darting down the hall and out of his reach.

"Stop her!" he cried, yet none of the black clad servants she passed obeyed him, blindly focused as they were on whatever tasks they were completing.

The Commune's loyal servants, ha! The bitter triumph spurred her on. She ran without pause to the front door of the mansion, out towards the fields she and the Commander had passed the day before. Her braid flew behind her, her lungs burned, heart pounded, and still her legs kept going.

There was no time to think, no time to piece together what had happened in that basement. *The Commander helped you. He saved you.* She shook the thought away—far too confusing to dwell on now. She concentrated simply on moving, on getting back to the Veritas camp—to Raif and Rose. She had to tell them the truth about Avanna. They'd find somewhere safe of their own—they had to.

Once she'd reached Raif, Rose and Dog, Hector and Cara, perhaps there would be time to process what had happened at Lord Torrant's home, with Commander Sulemon, what that *voice* in her head meant. Had it been her own—so desperate and scared she didn't even recognise it? But she remembered the light. That dim glow ... Had she truly connected to that poor man? Reached his fragile mind? Did her powers remain after all, buried so deep inside she could hardly feel them?

Evelyn stumbled—*focus, idiot, just run*. She missed her treasured green cloak as the air whipped around her. Her teeth chattered, her whole body shook, yet the day was mild—a delayed reaction to what she'd seen, she knew, even as she tried desperately to push away images of the tortured man from her mind, of Lord Torrant's bulging eyes, of the Commander's screams.

The black-bricked mansion grew distant behind her and she allowed herself to slow, though knew she must keep moving until it was out of sight. She'd have to stop at some point—to gain her bearings, make a plan.

Not yet, she told herself. *Not yet*. She pushed on, the sun drifting across the sky as her feet pounded into the ground and her legs spurred her on.

She didn't know how long she'd been on the road before she heard her name called from behind. A jolt of fear ran through her, for she knew the voice and knew what it meant. Commander Sulemon had come for her. Letting her escape was a test. She'd be punished for fleeing—something worse, more gruesome still than that basement.

I won't go back.

Beside the road was a copse of thorny bushes. She leapt towards it, hoping the thicket would provide enough shelter. She dragged herself under it, ignoring the sharp scratches across her arms. With bated breath, she waited for the approaching hooves to trot past. She closed her eyes and wished with all her might she would be invisible, somehow. Maybe he hadn't seen where she had gone.

Bloody idiot, of course he did. Still, she couldn't stop herself hoping that just this once, she would have some good fortune. *Is that too much to ask?*

Her answer came when the horse slowed to a stop beside her hiding place.

"Evelyn," Commander Sulemon called again. "I know you are there."

She stayed huddled within the prickly safety of the bush, knowing it was useless yet willing the imposing figure of the Commander to move along.

"Evelyn." This time she noted the strain in his voice, the lack of conviction. "Please."

There's no use. She dragged herself out of the thicket and stood in the midst of the thorns and bare branches, doing her best to look indignant despite the mess of bloody lines scoring her pale, freckled skin.

Then she met the Commander's gaze, and her breath caught in her throat. As he climbed from his horse and stood in front of her, he was barely recognisable— eyes bloodshot, lips cracked and smeared with blood. He clasped a hand to the gold-handled sword at his waist, but the gesture wasn't threatening—it was awkward and unsure. Without his red cloak, he didn't appear to know how to hold himself.

Wait, his cloak—

"Commander," she muttered, carefully pushing through the huddle of bushes, feeling ridiculously foolish for having dived into it in the first place. "Why are you here?" Her heart beat sporadically, still waiting for some master trap to reveal itself. They stared at each other.

"I want to help you," he blurted.

Evelyn stumbled, almost falling back into the bushes. "What kind of idiot do you–"

"I want to *help*," he said again. "Please."

She crossed her arms. "Prove it."

"I …" He bowed his head, seemed to steady his breath.

He did help me escape, after all. Maybe he finally saw Lord Torrant for the bastard he is? She glared at him. *Does he see what the Commune does now? This could still be a trick—*

Is he crying?

The thoughts in her head spun so wildly, she felt nauseous and dizzy. These last days, the camp, Avanna, the estate, and now the Commander actually making *her* feel pity for *him*? Anger, betrayal, confusion, hope, all cycled round and round.

She slapped her hands at her sides. "If everyone could just- just, pick a side and *stay* on it, that would be *fantastic*! I mean what, by the damned powers, am I supposed to do with—" she motioned at him, "with *this*? You raided villages, nearly killed Hector, blindly followed those monsters for- for how long? You *kidnapped* me and now- I mean- you- we … What do you expect me to say?"

The Commander nodded. "I understand. And I am sorry about all that has happened. I hunted you; I hunted so many, without mercy, all for ..." Commander Sulemon tilted his head back, gazing towards the sky. "I don't expect you to forgive me but please believe me when I say that I realise now how wrong I have been. How I have been lied to, led by a man who ..." He screwed his eyes shut, bowing his head so she could no longer see his face. "I'm sorry for what has been done to you—for what *I* have done to you and your friends. I *was* blind. I have let myself down and my own people. I have ignored what was in front of my eyes. I *am* sorry."

Sympathy intermingled with hatred, and Evelyn remained cautious. *Sorrow doesn't bring back the dead.* She stayed silent, waiting for him to continue.

At the sound of hooves, they both turned. Evelyn watched helplessly as a lone rider approached. She recognised the wiry form of Lord Torrant's manservant, Clim.

It is a trap! Evelyn cursed herself for even listening. She scrambled for a weapon, a branch, a rock, anything that might fight him off.

As the sunken-faced man neared, the Commander drew his weapon.

They're going to corner me.

"Traitor!" Clim's voice was a strangled scream as he jumped from his horse. At first, Evelyn believed the word was for her until she saw that the man's furious gaze was directed at Commander Sulemon. He drew a long knife, pointing it at the Commander's chest. "Always thought you were something special, didn't you?"

Commander Sulemon scoffed, positioning himself in front of Evelyn. "You are an ignorant servant," he said. "We both are." Before Clim had a chance to respond, the Commander raised his sword high, spun on his heels, and cracked the flat side across Clim's face. The smaller man crumpled immediately, mouth still open, face screwed up in unconscious rage. Evelyn and the Commander stood side by side, staring at the man on the ground.

The Commander sheathed his sword. "He was looking for me."

Evelyn raised her eyebrows. "He called you a traitor ... ?"

He shrugged.

She pointed at the gash on Clim's head, now bleeding steadily. "Suppose that's proof enough."

"Thank you," the Commander croaked.

"If Clim found us already, there will be more coming."

Commander Sulemon shook his head. "Lord To- He'll bide his time. Clim," his mouth twisted in disgust, "is little better than a rabid watch dog. He'll likely be punished for coming after us without orders."

Evelyn tapped Clim with the toe of her boot. He was still breathing.

"So you didn't kill Lord Torrant?"

Commander Sulemon looked away. "No."

"Did you try?"

A moment of silence, then, "For a moment, I ... Yes."

"You know," Evelyn said slowly, "there's still almost no reason I should trust you. This could still be the beginning of a dozen traps. And yet ..." She closed her eyes, uneasy with the truth of what she was about to say. "My options seem to be starving, getting lost in these woods, or *trying* to believe you until you turn on me again."

"I won't," he said finally. "Let me help you."

"Okay," she said, turning towards him. "You have a horse—that'll help me."

The Commander peered back over his shoulder. "Yes," he said. "I brought supplies, too."

"I'm going to the Veritas camp. I need to find my friends—"

"No."

"No? If you want to help me, that's what I—"

"No," he said again, stepping forward. For a moment, she tensed in preparation for an attack. "That's not a good idea."

She glowered up at him. "Why not?"

"Lord Torrant knows about that place. I told him where it is." He actually looked guilty at the words, lips pinching tight. "He will lead soldiers to it, of that you can be sure."

"Just another reason we need to go—to warn them!"

"No. We have other work to do."

"Other work?" Evelyn raised an eyebrow. "I have to help Raif and Rose. If Lord Torrant goes there, he'll find them. He'll take them. Rose, she—"

"What if there's a way we can render him powerless? Render *all* of them powerless?" The Commander's eyes blazed with a feverish passion.

"What? What do you mean?"

"In my homeland, there was a flower. When we were attacked by those with the powers, we used it to disarm them. It helped in the Seven-Year War in Septima. It can be dried into a powder, used on the tip of an arrow or the edge of a sword, consumed in a drink. It makes anything it touches a weapon against powers. I had some, but that woman at your camp took it."

"Avanna?" Evelyn glanced up, finally understanding what it was that had bought Commander Sulemon's release. *What use does Avanna have for … Rose.*

"Yes. What she took from me was a handful—a token to remind us of who we are. But if we are able to get enough, we might be able to stop them. All of them."

"Stop all of them," Evelyn repeated. "Stop Lord Torrant, stop the Grand Magister." The Commander nodded. She studied his face.

If she went to the camp, she could find Raif and Rose. But if what the Commander said was true … *We could rip the Commune out from its roots.*

"There's still a war marching straight to Veritas—to my friends."

The Commander held her gaze. "What if when the war started, the Commune's most dangerous weapons were little more than foot soldiers?"

Evelyn's pulse raced. "You'll have to swear one thing first."

He waited for her to continue.

"If we- we get these flowers—this weapon—we *only* use them on Commune soldiers and abusers. Anyone free—any of the children already found or still in hiding—can choose what they want."

"Veritarra's Gift is not to be used lightly," the Commander said sternly. "It can be dangerous to all, even those without powers. I promise you that I will not force it on those who don't pose a threat."

"Yes, well," Evelyn mumbled, "your past judgements do you no favours."

"I will prove to you that is in my past."

Evelyn nodded. "How … Where do we start?" Raif and Rose would be safe with Hector for now; she had to believe it. She would find them again, just not yet. Maybe she'd have more than apologies to offer them when she did.

"There are supplies of the flower all across the Noman Islands. Though we will need the permission of the holy women there to take it."

She nodded. "Okay, well, one problem at a time, Commander. Seems we're going to your home."

He let out a sigh, his shoulders slumping. "Thank you," he said. From the back of the horse, he retrieved a black cloak and sheathed sword, handing both to her. "I thought you would need these. And … it's Jonah."

"Sorry?"

"I'm not a commander anymore. My name's Jonah."

"Jonah," she said.

He gave a curt nod, allowing himself a brief smile.

Evelyn secured the black cloak at her neck, pulling it round her bare arms, and belted the sword to her waist. It felt good to have a weapon again, no matter how little she knew how to use it. "Lead on then, Jonah."

Together, they set off southward. The road to the Noman Islands lay ahead, and their journey would be long.

Acknowledgments

Ross, thank you for giving me unconditional support and love, always—through the evenings when my mind was in a far away kingdom with characters I'd dreamed up, through the self-doubt and ramblings and excited chatter, even when you had no idea what I was talking about. I wouldn't be where I am without you.

Cindy, a dear friend who has been behind this book from the very first (incredibly unpolished) draft. Your belief in this story and these characters pushed me to keep seeking publication; thank you.

Natalie, for inviting me to that first D&D session wherein Evelyn was born ... and so it began.

Evie, my dog, but more importantly, my companion through many hours of drafting and editing. Rest in peace, my darling girl.

To all of my amazing beta readers who read part or all of this manuscript from the very early stages through to later drafts, thank you so much for your invaluable feedback, insights, and honesty.

And last but certainly not least, thank you to all at SFWP for making my dream of publication come true. Special thanks to Andrew, for seeing the potential and taking a chance on my story, and to Nicole, for your inspiration, undying enthusiasm, and support in helping me make the manuscript the best it could be.

About the author

Born and raised in Essex, England, McLaren has spent many years since childhood delving into fantasy worlds through reading, gaming, and films. She lives in the UK with her husband, who is better than her at Mario Kart (but don't tell him she said that). Find her on Twitter @lucyamclaren and at lucyamclarenauthor.wordpress.com